Table of Contents

VIGGO

Preface

VIGGO

Viggo, is a character that probably has ventured into the imaginary mind of your partner...? If you don't believe it, you should ask the person to whom you're in love with...? — Well: besides the answers you must have, this saga is a romantic story of love and friendship...

Luís J Marolo = Él'Pertu

Prologue

VIGGO BRONSON
FBI Special Agent

LUIS MAROLO

A MYSTERY, ADVENTURE, AND PASSIONATE STORY OF
LOVE.

We can't deny, that in our planet exists a constant renovation of life.
The dynamics of creating what doesn't exist, it is a phenomenon that
displays itself, a great veil of mystery, which continue in this history....

Dedication

This story is dedicated to my dear wife Leona, for her immense patience, and my children, Luis, Andrea, & Che'sare.

Copyright & Disclaimer

LOVE AT FIRST SIGHT

Most of us have the ability to control our emotions, that's why when the occasion comes, we conclude that for one reason or another, it's not convenient to express our feelings out loud, and we let that moment of rage, regress and instead of venting our outrage right on their faces, we nest this anger deep inside our soul. As time passes, the collected resentments begin to effervescent inside us, and we can no longer contain our feelings, because we are just fed up with the bullshit people are giving us, that's when we want to shout out our emotions, which come out like, a furious storm of stones. —But, this usual concept of outburst, has another connotation, which I would like to comment about: let's say, you wish to express how you feel, but in that particular occasion, you choose not to say a word, instead you just decide to engage these incipient people, in a nasty hard fixed stare, which would manifest a very loud yelling of silence, this posture of silence, will tell you how I feel, at that instant, the intense livid gaze…would say it all, and many times it hurts more than a shouting fight. —Well, this last option, is not my case!!! —Because a…

Few years ago, I had stored in my soul so many emotions, that I wanted to scream my felling's to the whole world. In those times, I was wandering aimlessly in that immense city, with hundreds of futures projects, which got my dreams nowhere, that's when I decided to get out of that life of indolence, then seriously I began to consider what I was going to do with my life, and from all those options that I selected. I chose to join the US Navy Forces. And the time went by really fast…

Three years passed from that day, that's when I started a serious discussion with my dear conscience, which has the fucking habit, of bring to my attention those morality issues; about that decision I was ready to make, which is: *that I was not going to renew the contract with the Navy Seals*: knowing, that the drastic choice would bring mixed feelings. Certain decisions are hard to make I felt like I was between a rock and a hard place, because at the moment I joined the navy, I was putting into consideration, the warm reception I had from the recruiting personal. I was very grateful to the officers of the Navy Special Forces, acknowledging, that during the time I was under their command, the officers, had the ability and the patience, to transform that lost rebellious young man, into a straight arrow person, that's what I believe I have become today, that's the reason, why I am going to be forever grateful, for the struggle the Navy Seals Officers went through, to set me on the right path. —And...

After several months of being involved in those debates, with my dear conscience, I made my decision; I was going back to live the civilian unpredicted life; and no less, to the place I love the most, the City of New York. —Incidentally, that's where I was born and raised as a New-Yorker, what I'm trying to say, is that I know every corner of that amazing city: and at the moment I get there, I'm going to get really busy, planning to build a promising future, hopefully, the experiences I have gained in the Navy, will help me to achieve what I'm looking for. —Then...

Once in town, the days passed without being noticed, plus with the pleasure of being reunited with family and friends; my life had the meaning I wanted again, since a have the affection of my friends who hugged me, then they took me for a reunion celebration, to the old bar, The Half Pint, being with the guys I went to school with, that was the beginning of adapting myself into society.

Meanwhile: a few months went by, in that process of time, thanks to a couple of contacts, which I have from the Navy, I was able to get involved in the world of finances, in which a had no experience but, necessity made me learn that business quite rapidly.

Several weeks passed concentrating on what I was doing and, that particular day I was plagued with business phone calls, and, by the end of the day, I received a phone call from a friend, that I haven't seen since I had come to town. I was glad that she called, it was my good friend Alice, there she was on the phone, with her sweet romantic voice, that makes my heart began racing with excitement; the reason for my joy, was that I had an invitation to have dinner, in her apartment. —Needless to say, I was glad someone pulled me out of the routine, and I thought: this is going to be a very special day, because I'm going to meet a friend, who brings back memories of pleasant times. —Next day...

I stopped working early, I wanted to be on time for 'dinner', and for that occasion: I decided to dress casually, then happily I went to get the car. —As I was leaving the parking lot, the sunset was busy painting the skyscraper with strokes of gold, giving the City of New York, the appearance of an exquisite giant jewel. Just thinking of her: I began driving towards the city: for company in the passenger seat, I had two bottles of champagne, with a huge smile of pleasure: driving, curiosity invaded my senses, because I wanted to know, if the relationship I had with Alice, would continue like it was before; hot and steamy!!

When I arrived at Alice's apartment, she welcomes me with open arms, to my pleasant surprise, two red candles were lit on the dinner table, which was dressed for a gourmet dinner: so, the lucky—lucky guest, would never forget that special night. During the fabulous dinner, we caught-up with our past experiences, drinking champagne, and listening to romantic music, which invited us to dance looking into our eyes, embraced at a certain moment Alice, began to kiss me passionately, then very loving she was caressing me, while she was taking me to her bedroom. —Did I say hot and steamy? Alice did not behave like a cuddly cat; she really was a wild panther. —That amazing night was worth it, to set it up in the memory book, like one of the most incredible nights I experienced. But in this life, happiness can be cut short with a switch, in a second. What happened the following morning we should put it in the memory book like. —The day of they're their motherfucker God, fucking sons of bitches. —I'm telling you...

Waking up in the morning, looking at Alicia's face, who was still sleeping, I began to reflect the events of the night before, I was sure, that nothing in the world could ever tarnish those moments of pleasure and excitement: for my dismay, I was wrong!!! I will never say never, as long as I live: and the reason for my despair, it has to do, with what was happening in those moments in the city, that event had the ability to erases the happiness off my face. That day a tremendous incident happened, which could not have occurred in a billion years: but it happened, right in the heart of New York City. That horrible experience leaves you with an immense sadness in the heart, and a *hate* in my soul that I had never felt before. That day will remain in immortality, as one of the most cowardly acts in history of the human race, this heinous attack was conceived by religious ideological terrorists: these fuckers on the way to hell, threw to the back burner, the basic principles of humanity. These religious fuckers, decided to accomplish this terrific event, at the moment when New York City, just awakens to life. How not to remember that morning? If after having enjoyed with Alice an unforgettable night, I woke up to a terrorist attack: fuck...fuck my luck!! I couldn't react to the events, which were happening outside, the world was collapsing right in front of us, I couldn't conceive this is happening, figuring that the whole concept of the attack was senseless; the question is? Why these religious freaks are hell-bent, to destroy our society: Again, and again: because, the 'image' of those religious figures, who only exist in their fucking minds, play a huge role in this kind of event's!! I'm so pissed that I don't even want to think about it...

That infamous day: it was the *nine-eleven:* the horrible terrorist attack on the Twin Towers. And as always, life has a surprise for you, and did it to all of us, but I was at the center of that terrifying and devastating assault. In those dreadful moments, I had the urgency to see, if I could help in any way I could: with a kiss I reassured my friend Alice, to remain inside and, I ventured to find out what was going on. At the instant I stepped outside, a wave of dust hit my face, for my dismay, I saw people in a state of panic, which were wrapped in a cloud of dust, and desperately running away from the just collapsed Twin Towers; I went back inside and grabbed a towel, then without thinking twice, I covered my face and started running toward where the terrorist attack had happened, until the security forces stopped me: anxiously I told them that. "I came to see if I could help in any way possible!!" *And one of the men responded.* "If you really want to help, take a look at the older couple, who are sitting on the sidewalk, and please take them to the nearest hospital." And without speaking another word, because I could hardly breathe, that's what I did. —And...

After I left the hospital, I went back to see how Alice was feeling, she was trembled with fear, I hugged her tenderly trying to calm her down, when she managed to relax, then we begin talking for a long time, all about what had happened. I confessed to her that in these moments I felt a sense of helplessness, then I began to consider what I could do to protect the people I love. That day I left Alice in good mental health; she was relaxed but heartbroken by senseless events that occurred. Then, after couple of weeks of soul-searching, I conclude that my best option is to carry the badge. of the Federal Bureau of Investigation, meanwhile I was planning, which would be the best time to join the force. That particular morning, I was lying in bed looking at the ceiling thinking; entwined with my thoughts, I began to feel that inside my head were roaming the mice of doubts, the mere hesitations, had to do, that I was placing in the balance, my decision to join the FBI, which I made a few days ago, in a moment of anger and rage: looking at the ceiling, I said to myself, I better postpone the plan to join the Bureau, since I didn't think it through like I should. There, the lights of reasons led me to the correct conclusion; it wasn't the right time, to stop the projects I had in mind, at that time I decided to prioritize my economic security, because, I was determined to make a real estate investment, in New York City, and during that process...

Several months have passed, since the Twin Towers were brought down, by the South-Arabia terrorists. But, there's always something or someone, that takes you out of your comfortable cocoon, that somebody, happen to be: *The Destiny, which is unpredictable; Somehow, this mystical being, always arranges other plans for us, and when you least expect it, you get the call from this space of life, in which you don't have any control, that is why you are generally exposed to what the capricious destiny, has in store for your life.* As I have said previously, the destiny is unpredictable, and it shows the tremendous strength it has, and destiny it was present, at the moment I was walking down Fifth Avenue, minding my own business, when I had stopped at 79th street, I was standing waiting for the green light, when this incident happened right in front of me, in the heart of Manhattan. A matter of fact, it would be better, if I start to reveal the events, from the beginning of that particular day, because it was quite different, and started...

With an unusual twist: that day I was immersed in my third dream, when the doorbell, awoke me up with its pathetic sound. I looked at the clock: it was almost eight, in pajamas I went to open the door, I was quite certain about who it would be, but I was really surprised when I didn't see Susan, it wasn't her, it was Angie, the beautiful young blonde girl, who lives on the fourth floor. She was standing in front of me, with her curly blond hair, which was falling like a cascade over her shoulders; after the corresponding greetings, she said that came to see me, because she was feeling quite uncomfortable, that she needed one of those special treatments, then with the left-hand she opened her white satin negligée, reveling the lower part of her amazing body, then with an innocent naivety, she showed me, where her problem was, telling me that she had cramps on her legs. Then she asks me: if I can provide her with one of those special massage treatments.

I was just waking up, at that moment I wasn't very convinced to let her in, but I concluded, that Angie, since she was my neighbor, I should welcome her with open arms. I knew her from brief friendly encounters in the elevator. I remembered that on Susan's birthday we had a really good time, while enjoying a few drinks, and right now with a sweet smile Angie, is telling me that Susan, suggested to her that I had very good hands, to massaging away the pain of muscles cramps. I knew in that instant, what she really wanted, this time I did not expect her presence, she really took me by surprise. Anyway, I offered her a cup of coffee; at that moment, I could see a certain urgency in Angie's eyes, in that moment I figured out the obvious of the situation; she didn't come to talk to me. Angie, came to calm her anxieties, that's when very gently, she took me by the arm and tells me, that her whole body needs a good massage. —Warned, of her needs, I guided her to the guest room, and for a few seconds, we stood looking into each other's eyes, without saying a word, delicately I removed her negligee, in her tiny underwear she looked like a naked angel, and I told the girl to lie face down on the bed, I warmed my hands, and then in a slow motion I began applying a stimulating cream, all over her back and her perfect legs, there came a moment when she raised her head, and, looking at me with melancholic sweet eyes, she said. "This anxiety is killing me, please, do something about it." Then I had no choice but to turned her around, to reach the problem area and, as gently as possible, after twenty minutes of massages, her eyes were turned up and, she began moaning… "Please easy Viggo…please …Easy'V…please!!!" She was pleading and concerned for her well-being, I slowed down the rhythm of the treatment, and with love and care I continued giving her a lowing tending care massage, and she started to say. "Oh God…Oh my God…Oh my God!!!" if we are going to put the massages in context, what happens is that my hands are quite large, this why some women find the treatment a little bit over whelming, it's not the case of Angie, she really enjoys the procedure, taking into account that at the end of removing her anxieties, the young woman was quite relaxed and, with a big smile on her face. I'm sure her complaints were of pleasure. I'm glad, because at the moment she was ready to leave my place, Angie in an intimate way commented…

"Viggo, if I didn't hear wrong, today you have a business meeting, and you have to travel to the city?"

"That's right, today is a very special day for me." Viggo answers, not knowing the reason for the that kind of question, but Angie lets him know…

"Something is going on outside of this building, that you should know Viggo, if you are going out, I have bad news for you, early this morning a powerful storm arrived at the city, the news is predicting, that's going to rain quite heavily all day, I'm sure the streets of the city, must be a real mess with this weather. It would be much better if you came to have lunch in my apartment and, waited for the storm to pass?" *At that moment she looked at him like saying I would like to continue with the treatment and very loving she continued saying.* "Just think about it Viggo, I have in the fridge a couple New York steaks, we can have a nice lunch, and tomorrow when the sun comes out shining, you can go to the city and do your business: safe and sound?" Angie sweetly proposed, and Viggo looked at her with affection and responded…

"What I must to tell you, that your proposition is very tempting, but I'm sorry Angie, there always will be an opportunity to have lunch together, I know that it's an adventure driving in this weather in the City of New York. I'm certain that nothing is going to happen to me and, we will do this again. Okay Angie?"

"I still believe that your best option is to stay here with a friend, who can prepare a good lunch?" She asks very sweetly and Viggo tell her what can happen during stormy weather...

"Angie, you are young, but you must agree, that these stormy days have a magical energy, which provokes people to go out of their usual routine and do what you just did: having a pleasant massage, which have the magic touch to relax your mind and your body."

"Now that you say it, I was observing the rain through the window and, you are right I felt that sensation, of being pampered." Angie said making a cuddly baby face and Viggo goes on saying...

"I'm glad that you understood what I was trying to say, about this amazing power of nature, that also creates a natural phenomenon, which has the faculty of producing an aphrodisiac stimulation. —For instance: it's well- known, that the rainy days, have in itself, a very interesting melancholic feeling, these sensations take you to another succession of emotions, which make you dream of ventures, which are within your means, but is very possible, the opposite occur, that in this raining day, you relapse into a feeling of sadness..." *She listens to him attentively, but she did not really listen, what she really wants is for him to stay with her and Viggo continue saying.* "Angie, if you mix those clear emotions with craving curiosity, then you add some degree of mystery into the mixture; the stormy environment, has the tendency to invite people to get out of their safety cocoon and, do certain proclivities, that you probably don't do on a regular sunny day. This is a very well proven theory, and you are the example Angie, needless to say, it was a pleasure to help you, and you can come to visit me at any time." Viggo ends up saying, with a witty smile, then he adds a goodbye kiss. He feels good seeing Angie walk away smiling and happy and, Viggo is left alone with his thoughts:

"It's amazing that all these sweet women's, who assures that love is the most wonderful feeling, which for thousands of years lives in the hearts of humans and, I wonder, why those wonderful feelings didn't reach my heart yet. I'm really disappointed; while I was grumbling about my inability to fall in love, I was watching how Angie entered into the elevator. —And...

Once I got inside my apartment, I went straight to the window. I wanted to be sure, that indeed it was an stormy day, but the storm is not an obstacle to ignore my appointment, I was ready to turn a dream into reality, and with a smile that lit up my face, I headed for the elevator with my thoughts following me to the car, at the underground parking lot, at the moment I came out with the car the rain and the wind, violently hit the windshield: to add hurdles to our life, in this time of the year, we have in the city thousands of visitor, and these people drive cars, not only I had to deal with the storm, I had to deal with the tourists, after avoiding a couple of close encounters I arrived to my destination safe and sound, at that time, I had no other choice but to park a few blocks away from the Rockefeller Center, where it was the American Real Estate offices. —And...

After long negotiations, finally we reached an agreement: I signed the title deed, at that moment I felt very proud with the purchase I did, because from now on, I'm I going to occupy my own apartment, which offered me a great sense of security and, at the same time: freedom of action, which gives me the guarantee, that nobody is going to kick me out of my own place, because the girls are talking too loudly. Okay? And the dreams had come true. —What happened that it...

Was a glorious day of independence, that was the reason why I left the real estate office with a huge smile, and without being able to believe what just I had achieved, with my head full of illusions, I direct my steps, toward where I had parked the car. I was walking calmly with no rush, since the heavy rain turned into a mere drizzle; in those moments of joy, what really caught my attention, was the glare of the sun reflecting on the falling water, those drops were shining like diamonds, this magical show of nature, followed me until I had to stop, at the red light, in the intersection of 5th Avenue and 79th Street, I was waiting for the green light, with a smile in my mind: dreaming with all my future projects, and I 'was eager to tell the good news to my parents. Well, destiny had other plot to achieve; because all the plans that I had for that day, at that corner, will changed in an instant. You wonder what occurred? What happened, is the fucking 'destiny,' always has around the corner, a fucking surprise for you. As I said before, I was at the 5th and 79th, waiting for the green light to cross the street: at that instant I saw a car approaching at high speed, at that instant I could foresee, that an imminent collision it would occur, and it was going to happen, right there where I was standing: not knowing where the cars were going to stop; as a precaution I took a few steps back.

The powerful accident left one of the cars with both front doors open, and thanks, to the extensive training I had in the Navy, I managed to remain calm in those moments of extreme tension; until...until, I began to perceive an intense smell of gasoline, immediately figure that it was a sign of danger, which made me look inside the vehicle that basically was in front of me, at that moment I saw someone that was trapped between the seat and the steering wheel, at that instant I realized, that the person inside the car was in serious danger, and without thinking twice, I got into the disabled car, there was the woman sitting with her seat belt on, with great difficulty I unhooked the seatbelt, at that moment she was shocked, and rightly so: disoriented, she stretched her arms and took hold tightly of my neck. Since the woman couldn't stand up, I had no choice but to take the frightened woman and lifted in my arms, then with great care I pulled her out of the car, which could have ignited at any moment and exploded. Luckily it didn't happen. At that time, I recall, that I held the woman in my arms, until she calmed down. Those moments came unexpectedly, and they were quite dangerous.

As I said before, during our lives, 'destiny' plays with us, as if we were puppets, just reflecting, a few minutes ago, I was going happily to celebrate with my parents the purchase of a property and in the process, I was nearly injured in a car crash, but instead 'destiny', rewarded me, with pleasure of rescuing a woman, who is right now on my arms. The event sequences went so fast that in those moments of excitement, the time didn't count, and then my attention was only focused on the woman and her well-being. While a few seconds went by: I began to focus on the person I was holding in my arms, at that moment something distinctive aroused my curiosity, it was the exotic aroma of her perfume, which draws my attention, and began to invade my senses. The woman kept saying thank you, and in that swirl of emotions I managed to ask her, if she was okay: she answered with a pale smile, that she was fine. The circumstances that led to those moments of panic, were over. But whoever she was; she was holding tightly on to my neck, and in a grateful sigh, she said close to my lips...

"My name is Ember: Ember Maxwell, and I'm a very lucky woman, thanks to you, Mister...?" She asked in a trembling voice, and Viggo answered sweetly as the moment required...

"I believe that I'm the lucky one, since I'm holding you in my arms: you can call me Viggo...and she said, "I love your name: Viggo!" *To which I replied.* "You just can call me: will be a pleasure to answer your call!" After I said that silly phrase, I couldn't take my eyes off that woman, and I said to myself. "How can a man be so fucking lucky? She is the most gorgeous woman that I have ever seen, and this person is in my arms!!!" Then I tried to put her down gently; she looked at me as if she was pleased to be in my arms, unfortunately her wishes were denied, because at that moment, the police arrived. After answering all the questions from the officers, who completed efficiently their report, after that process, we went for a comforting cup of coffee at Hutch & Waldo. We were sitting down with two coffees in front of us; at that moment I felt a strange sensation, like we were inside of one of those spheres where it seems, that the time is suspended: meanwhile these feelings we're running in my brain, we were having coffee talking, with my mind clouded with this magic moment, that brought me sensations that I had never felt before; after a couple cups of coffee, I was able to control my feelings: then we began sharing different aspects of our life, with this woman who has a magnetic personality, which attracts all my attention.

Ember, was sitting in front of me, with those huge green eyes, which were looking at me tenderly, the sparks of her gaze was reaching deep into my soul, in that instant a torrent of blood surge like a runaway locomotive into my veins, my heart began to beat faster and faster: just crazy, and right now I found myself, with these strange feelings, running around in my body and, I really wonder..."This is love at first sight? What the fuck is going on?" I was losing control of the essence of time, since we're acting like two teenagers, having coffee and chatting for a long-time, trying to get to know each other better: in a moment of silence, we looked into each other's eyes. I can't describe what I felt at those moments, since I was discovering feelings well deep inside my soul, that is when Ember, in a very friendly manner, she rested her hand on mine. I never imagined that a caress of a hand, could cause so many emotions, at that instant I felt that a delicate white rose petal, had caressing my hand, then with a sweet voice she proposes. That we could meet the next day and continue chatting. At that moment, I felt a little bit uncomfortable by her forward approach since she took the initiative!! I guess Ember wants to be sure that the meeting was going to happen, after all, she didn't have to do any extreme effort, to convince me, since I was already caught in the silk woven web, that she wrapped all over me. How would I reject a such proposal? If this woman had already placed my heart, to a place where my feelings had never been? I was feeling that life was being generous to me. —And...

The following afternoon I was waiting for Ember, at the same location that we met before: for the special occasion. I had dressed casually, with a blue blazer and a gray pair of pants. I've never been so anxious waiting for a woman and, to top it off, she was late!! Fuck me: It would be the first time I was punishing myself, because, I was trying to remember, if through the events of the previous day; I said something wrong, that could had disturbed her, and for that reason she would not show up to the meeting: in that instant my hopes were clouding, but at the moment she arrived a smile bloomed on my face. Ember looked so gorgeous that my eyes couldn't believe it!!

At the moment Ember began walking towards me, I was overwhelmed by her amazing beauty, her golden reddish curly hair, was shining like gold dust in the sunlight, that day Ember, arrived dressing like a model, she wore on her shoulders, a ten-color cashmere blazer, and by design, her blouse was open almost to her waist, exposing her pearl white delicate skin, and speaking of skin; her short navy-blue skirt is showing her magnificent shapely leg, that were exposed in all their splendor, for my eyes enjoyment. —Then very casually...

Ember, said hello, then she gave me a soft kiss on the lips, then gently she held my arm, and then, she looked deeply into my eyes, as she was saying. How lucky I was to find you. And then as if we were a couple, we began walking around the fringe of Central Park. At one point, as if the episode passed by chance: Ember stopped at the door of the well-known Restaurant *Pure'Wow*. At that instant Ember, didn't show any ambiguity, because when she opens the door, and leads me inside the restaurant, with the intention to have lunch. Ember requested to be placed at a private table, and during the meal, showing genuine feeling, she kept thanking me, for rescuing her. Then Ember held my hand, and looked at me with those huge eyes, as if she was saying. "If I am the woman you desire, I'm all yours, just take me in your arms and love me!!" After all these wishes of mine, she said in a whisper.

"Viggo, I would like you to know, that right now, I have no relationship that alters my heartbeats. I know that I'm being too forward, since I can read in your eyes, that we could get along very well. Maybe we should have a long talk?" I couldn't believe this was happening, and she asks that inciting phrase, with those full red juicy lips, which Viggo was looking with desire, for him it was a quite difficult task, to contain himself, not to kiss her passionately. After controlling that torrent of passion that ran through his veins, he was silent for a few seconds, then Viggo answered...

"I'm sure, that we could become very good friends." *Viggo paused for a second, while they were looking into each other's eyes and Viggo who is thinking that he if falling madly in love, with this woman, continue saying* "Ember, I'm in the same situation as you, and until now, I do not have anyone to share my hours of loneliness. I'm ready to open the door to the right person, who would like to join my hours of joy and grief, if you have the desire to enter inside my life, the doors of my heart Ember, are open?" Viggo asks softly with a smile, and Ember is not going to miss the opportunity, to smiled back, because those words were caressing her ears, because since she met Viggo, she was waiting for that news: the man is freeeee...and Viggo, does the best he can, trying that the beauty of Ember, does not intimidate him. Then we talk holding hands, looking into each other's eyes, in that circle of emotions, I lost track of time, that was the moment we came to understand each other and, with my best smile I said to her. "Ember, would you like to take a pleasant walk in the park?" At that moment I could read in Ember's gorgeous eyes, that she was more than ready to follow my suggestion. —Then...

Like two lovers, looking into each other's eyes, holding arms, walking slowly as if we wanted to extend forever this special moment. In that space of time, something magical occurred, we were entering a side in the park, that was surrounded by a silence forest, full of romance, since I could hear Ember heavy breathing. I was sure that we had the same feeling, the place began to create a passionate emotion in us, I could feel inside my chest, how the heart was pounding like crazy. That's when I concluded that Ember, was controlling from the beginning the situation, with all the tricks women have at their disposal: She was trying to persuade me, that she was the women, I had always been waiting for; to ensure her purpose, for this special occasion, she brought with her, all the tools a women can purchase. I can still sense the aroma of her perfume, that invaded my senses, I must mention those plump full red lips, it was like a ripe fruit ready to devour, when I kissed her I closed my eyes; at that instant, I thought I was lost in the dreams of ecstasy, I must add the felling of her warmth body, which merged with mine, the sweetness of her demeanor, create sensations in me, that were driving me absolutely crazy. In that instant, I knew I was losing control of my feelings, and I loved it...I love it!! My heart was beating as it never did, could this be: *love at first sight?* How can it be? No other women had ever stimulated these emotions in my heart: if the intellectuals, call this type of feeling: love? I have to say, these feelings: it feels really great!!! Hold on my friends, this walk does not end here, because it continues...

Deep inside the park, and to liven up the walk, we stop at a magical place: The Garden of Eden. At that site: it was where for the first time, I began to feel that great sensation of love: these fillings were buried deep inside my heart, those sweet emotions, began to came out like lava comes out the volcano, igniting new feelings that my heart had never felt, I don't know if it was my imagination, but at that moment I could feel in my hand the beating of her heart, we were in a magic place, away from prying eyes: automatic and without saying a word, our bodies become one, her warm breath caresses my face, and those red lips were an irresistible temptation, the passion in my veins was beyond control, to the point that the passion flooded my body, then we joined in a long...long and passionate kiss, her lips had the flavor of passion. I would have kept kissing her all day, at that instant I felt, that I was falling in love with that person, we were so involved in kissing and looking into our eyes, that we were not able to speak, at that sublime instant of love, I was not thinking about having sex, I just wanted to kiss her, but Ember had on her mind other intentions: that is when she became sexually aggressive with her hands, in that instant her emotions burst out of control, she was so excited that she whispered in my ear.

"Oh: what do we have here. It's amazing: I love it...I love it!!!" She express at that magic moment, I saw all over her face, the forbidden desire, that's when her wild passion aroused my feelings, and for all those emotions that overflowed out of control, was only one witness: The Garden of Eden, right there in that unforgettable place, we entwine in a long passionate romantic kiss, and trembling with emotion we weren't able to control ourselves; with unrestrained passion of sexual desires, and without stopping kissing, we made love until ours legs where quivering. I never can forget those anxious moments when Ember enthralled with pleasure was repeating. "Ho, my God...I'm falling in love...I'm falling in loveee...!!!" If I start to wind back that moment, that scene is forever engraved in my memory. —Because...

That amazing day we fell in love, to the degree, that we would like to treasure those amazing feeling, and a short while after that memorable walk in the park, we wanted to certify our love, and there was no better way to do it, the getting married. It was a simple ceremony: Ember, happy and enthusiastic took care of the honeymoon trip. —How the journey of that memorable day started, from John F Kennedy International Airport. We landed hugging and kissing in the Airport of Oahu, which is one of the beautiful Hawaiian Islands; at those moments it seemed to me, that I was living a fairy tale, the whole environment has a delicious scent of tropical flowers. Our final destination was Waikiki City, we left the airport in a taxi, that left us right in the gardens of the fabulous Royal Hawaiian Hotel, which will be a silent witness of our honeymoon. After our arrival at the hotel, all the events that would happen, look as if they were deliberately premeditated by Cupid...

Upon entering the hotel room, a chilled bottle of champagne and a box of Godiva chocolates was waiting for us. We ordered a light dinner and celebrated our honeymoon in the room: I don't want to go into details, since next morning we had quite a bit of trouble waking up. After rejoicing the arrival to the hotel, that evening we went for dinner to a trendy Night Club. The ambience was ideal, and we began toasting with champagne for our love, drinking and dancing very much in love: in those moments, seems like *time* just banished in thin air: we continued wrapped in a cloud of illusions; until, the desires to leave the place reached our hearts, at that precise moment, we escape the Night Club, not alone; we we're carrying two bottles of champagne, that ended in the king size bed, where my gorgeous wife dedicated herself to made love to me, until the light of dawn peeked through the curtains; it was not a night like the others, Ember, was reading the Kamasutra book, there was no way to escape to her wishes. After a few hours of sleep: getting out of bed it was difficult, but not impossible, and before Ember wakes up...

I tried to get up without being noticed, and like a thief tiptoeing, I went straight to the shower, but I'm sorry to say, that the improvised maneuver didn't work Ember, woke up, and she didn't waste any time, and like a lioness looking for a prey, she followed me to the bathroom: with the ancestral costume to continue the human species: Noooooo please!!!!! Conclusion: after she finished soaping and scrubbing my whole body; twice. I came out of the bathroom sparkling-clean: with the certainty that Ember, is like those who practice wrestling, she won't leave you alone until you've on the mat, crushed and surrendered. Sure, that I hurried out of the bathroom before she soaps me again, then I threw myself on the bed thinking...If this honeymoon begins without self-control, how the hell it will continue? Who knowns? All I know is, that I'm completely deep in love with my wife!!! Who was coming out of the bathroom showing her splendorous beauty: with the towel tied around the waist. —Then...

I drew the window curtains: and in front of my eyes, appears an immense gift of nature, I was amazed by the incredible view, I could see how a rainbow full of amazing colors was decorating the ocean, the palms leave swayed calmly being caressed by the ocean breeze, at that instant we looked at each other, and without saying a word we got dressed as tourists, and we just went for a long walk, enjoying the ocean and the immense beach of blond sands. After having returned to our room...

Ember, proposed to have dinner in the hotel restaurant, the same one that is facing the blue ocean. After shopping at the local stores, where my wife made me buy several Hawaiian shirts, we returned to our room with a pile of packages; this time fortunately, we take a bath with only one soaping, and for dinner we dress casual, but elegant, then we left our room like teenagers in love, looking into each other's eyes, she was kissing me with such a passion, that for a moment I didn't know who I was, I returned to reality at the moment I entered at the restaurant, with my gorgeous wife holding my arm; I don't know if it was my imagination, but that night I had the feeling, that every eye in the place was checking us out, then once at our table, we spend our time just focus on ourselves, besides: we were enjoying the tropical ambience, which had a certain relaxation magic, by night ending, on the tale, we had for company two empty bottles of champagne; we look into each other's eyes, as if to say let's continue dancing as if we were alone in an island, that really was until the music stopped: the rays of the sun were ready to appear, that's when the waitress approached our table: the maître-d, literally was throwing us out of the place, but with a lot of class, she brought a bottle of champagne: as a present...It was time to close...Of course that...

We leave the restaurant, but walking as if we were the owners: after crossing the threshold door, we were among the shadows, of the mist of dawn, then like teenagers we began to play a silly game, of dodging the first rays of sun, of course, she ended up winning, since she took refuge under an old palm tree, the true of the matter is, that Ember, couldn't wait to get to the room, then without saying a word, she got busy with her hands, after her urgent desires were fulfilled, then holding hands we began to walk to the hotel.

We thought, the night was all ours to enjoy not really, something was going to complicate our evening. I remember, that at the time, we had been in our room for few minutes, that's when my cell phone began to ring, and I ask myself. "Who would be calling at the beginning of my honeymoon?" ...It was a big surprise...

It was my father. I never suspected that he would do that, his call took me totally off guard, I was more shocked, at the moment that I found out the reason of the call. My father was telling me, that in the middle of the night, two men kicked their house door open, asking questions, with a foreign accent, carrying lethal weapons, these fucking guys had the wrong initiative of invading my parents' home. —A matter of fact: There is no cure for human stupidity. We can start with these two pieces of shit, that raided the wrong house: these fuckers, entered in the house, and second, at the moment they saw my parents, they searched the interior of the house, that it was not enough, they also checked inside the closets!!! For their reckless actions these incompetent rats, left a crappy present for my mother, who in those moments of terror, and facing that horrible experience, she nearly died of a heart attack. Going back to my father phone call...

That event really struck a chord with my feelings, because of moments of fear, my parents had to go through, in that invasion of their house. That event for being so hideous brough out the worst of me. I was really pissed off, and fucking frustrated, I didn't know how to react, with clenched fists I asked myself. "How can this type of home invasion happen in my country: where are the Federal agents, who supposed to prevent this type of events? This reminds me of what happened on 9/11. Because days before, all the cameras at the airport, saw one of the Saudi terrorists entering the country. The Secretary of State or the CIA director, didn't know that this guy is after no good? Where were these people, at the moment the towers were attacked by passenger planes? Everyone in US, was watching, except these fucking incompetents? I don't want to think, that this government leeches knew, and didn't do nothing about it? I'm sure these inept greaseballs, were scratching their private parts, meanwhile the towers were collapsing? And what about the politicians in those critical moments? Those fuckers were quite busy enriching themselves, instead of paying attention to the work, which was entrusted to them. What we really need in the future, it is that the people who will be in command, really love this country, it is not too much to ask!!! At that moment I promised myself that I would do something about it. I know that I won't be able to do much, but I want to contribute with my grain of sand, if we would be able to gather many grains, we can put together mountains of sand.

At that moment, what frustrated me the most, was the emotional shock my parents suffered, and right now, my mother at home, is recovering from a minor heart attack, under the supervision of her doctor, and, finally my father tells me not to worry, that everything was under control, and we should just continue with our honeymoon: the last comments from my father left me less worried, about the well-being of my parents.

The authorities, in a fast and effective operation, solve in a couple of days, my parent's case which it was all over the news. The agents of the FBI, in conjunction with Interpol; captured two Chinese's foreign agents, right in time to save the life of a double agent: their mission had been to kill a Chinese agent who went rogue...? After returning from our honeymoon to New York, I began to contemplate the event that occurred at my parent's house. that was the final push I needed to join the Training Academy of the Federal Bureau of Investigation, at Langley City in the State of Virginia; a matter of fact, my wife Ember, was pleased to follow my steps, and after several months of physical and psychological training we graduate with honors.

I thought that I was prepared to face the obstacles life throws at you, on the road of our existence; but the events that I had to confront, led me to the conclusion, that I wasn't ready to face the reality of living with constant conflicts, with the person I married and love. If I have to analyze what happened, let's say, that the first year of marriage, was a cushion of roses. I thought I had the great fortune, to found the earthly paradise, but at certain moment of the coexistence, I came to the conclusion that my marriage was slowly deteriorating, and slowly the cushion of roses turned into a cushion of thorns; not only it was a great disappointment to me, but the worst of the letdown, it was that it took me so long to fall in love, and that love only brought me, sorrow in the soul and in the heart. After that emotional blow, I came to think that love was a big lie, then I fell into a slight depression, at one point, that I let the beard grow, just to hide my controversial emotions. Well, this is my situation: after being happily married for almost two years, in the last period of time, my lovely wife Ember, was consumed by an obsessive feeling of jealousy: unfortunately, our marriage slowly diluted, like the ocean water disappear into the sands. I still paying the price for her capricious decision: Ember, is the love of my life. I'm sure, I can never love any other woman like I love her. There is no other choice, than continue living. And not a day goes by, that I don't ask myself...

"What the fuck I did wrong?" And why I didn't put more attention, since in the last months of my marriage, I was noticing that my wife was behaving in a very strange way, she didn't stop asking questions: where I had been and, what I had done; I couldn't understand the origin of her behavior: she was always acting as if something was wrong. But I would never have expected that Ember to go that far!! Because my loving wife, without having any consideration for me or the love I profess for her, in one those jealous rages: *invited-me* to leave our lovely nest, and that I should go to dwell with *all those women,* which only exist on her prolific mind, it's very clear that her judgment, was blinded by jealousy, or maybe any other psychological trauma, that makes her behave that way: as much as I tried, I could not understand the reasons of her behavior. I know that she knew that I'm madly in love with her. For that reason, her decision has no foundation or basis for her claim. For months Ember, started a sequence of disturbing emotions, which complicate the way I was acting in life and, the way I exercise my duties. I'm still disappointed, and fucking pissed off, as the months went by, I concluded, that life doesn't stop here: goes on with all its evils and goodness's, and I decided to concentrate all my energies into performing my duties, as a Federal Agent.

Since I joined the force, I had the chance to intervene in several risky missions, throughout the world: A matter of fact, Afghanistan was one of the most dangerous places I have been, in that garbage dump, were men under those robes, which disguised them as a woman, I'm telling you, it makes your job a nightmare, because between those weirdo's skirts, I almost lost my fucking life, this event happened when I led few men, in a fierce battle against a famous terrorist. If I can rescue something good about that encounter: is that successfully I ended up killing the terrorist Abadu Malaky. For that successful assignment, I was promoted to Special-Agent of the FBI International Division. This position creates great new responsibilities, which I'm trying to implement with all my possibilities. What else can I disclose about this guardian of the law. For who wants to know. I am...

Viggo Bronson, well known by my colleagues, and also by those who hide in the shadows of the underworld, as Easy'V...If you ask me, where the nickname comes from? I would guess that it comes from the way I applied my two hundred-forty pounds of muscles, usually against those who break the law: there is no other cause, for me to brag about my nickname. —I have been telling you all about myself: Now let's change that subject and let me warn you. "Don't mess around, with the laws of my country." —Because...

I'm Special-Agent Viggo Bronson, and my mission is to enforce the law in my country the US. Now you know my name and what I do for a living. For your information, this occupation is not what you would call a safe living, there is always someone who for one reason or another, tries to erase you from the face of the Earth, and to confirm this theory: I would take you on a virtual trip, in one of our new investigations, which began in New York, about two weeks ago: but first I'm going to start by telling you, that in these times, I still suffer the emotional consequences, of what happened with my wife Ember, about two years ago. —I was melancholic, and to top it all...

The day was ending, with one of those New York City hazy winter nights: and I felt like I was traveling in a gray cloud aimlessly, the reality is that I was walking down the street, struggling with my resentments: I was alone, sad, and disgusted with the world, trying to drown my sorrows, I headed to the well-known *The Veil Nightclub*, which once in a while, for merely professional reasons, I drop by that place; usually I show up to see if I can obtain some underground information, but that particular night, I decided to go to *The Veil*, for vital causes: *I was really in need of warm hug from a friend...*The owner of the *Veil* Tania La'Port, a dear friend of mine. Like always Tania, was happy to see me, but this time, she can sense that something was not right, and she detect the sadness on my face, and without saying a word, she places her arms under my blazer, and gently dug her nails in my back, and began to kiss me passionately, that was the beginning of her welcome to *The Veil*. Tania and her exuberant personality, excel in sexuality, she was breathing right into my lips and, very suggestively she said to me...

"Hello..." *And she began to caress my hair while she kissed me tenderly.* "Hello, Special-Agent Bronson, it's been a while since you didn't come to ask for info. I hope you are taking good care of yourself, and your famous anaconda tattoo, that I never saw it, maybe this time you give me the pleasure?" Well, after that defined insinuation...

It was obvious, that she was in a romantic mood, and Tania didn't waste any time, and she suggested that we should continue 'talking' in her private lounge. At that time, it wasn't me who was getting carried away by Tania...I close my mind, and I can see her walking in front of me, with high heels and those long, beautiful legs. I kept looking at her going swiftly through the bar, where she pickups a couple of bottles of Blue Label Scotch, and without saying a word, looking into my eyes, as if she was saying. "We are going to get really drunk, and in the meantime; gladly, I'm going to fuck your brain off." Then placing the two scotch bottles in my arms, getting close to me, she kisses me biting my lips, then with a sexual gesture held my waist, at that moment, I began to predict what was going to happen to me, but I really didn't care, and, I guide my *lonely heart* into the world of her erotic dreams: I could have tried, not-to-be a such easy prey, but then like an eagle who lost his way, I let myself go:

I surrendered to her arms, which were waiting patiently for me, that's when my blasé attitude, opens the floodgates of Tania's desires; then my senses increased by the felling of her exuberance sexuality, Tania, who also has the sensibilities of a hummingbird, that's when she became aware that I was like a mature fruit, ready to fall into her lap; then with the patience of a Geisha, she started undressing me slowly, between hugs and kisses, she was peeling me like an apple—ready to be eaten. Then, she began to take advantage of this man anguish tender heart; until...I lost the spheres of time, I began to react when Tania, anxiously kept repeating... "Please Easy'V...Oh my God...Easy Viggo...please...please..." It was in that instant I noticed that Tania's heart, wanted to escape from her chest, she was struggling not to faint, in that magical time: She looks at me, rolls her eyes, and, fainted in my arms...While, my dear friend that was resting on the couch enveloped in a symbolic swoon of pleasure, with a smile on her lips...At those moments, I was feeling so good and relaxed that I continued...

Indulging with the Blue Label Scotch; looking at life, through the bottom of the glass, and I keep pouring down slowly the *second* bottle of scotch, until...until: I woke up, and began to wonder...What the fuck happened? Since I didn't remember how did I get home? Fuck me!!!...What the hell is going on? I was feeling that a bunch of city workers, ware inside my head: working? These mother fuckers didn't have no mercy, relentlessly they were banging and hammering inside my head, it was that terrible headache, which wake me up, and like an automaton, I found myself looking at the clock, I was gazing at the time machine, and for sure, the fucking clock, was watching me sleep, feeling pity for my soul. —I was sure, that my head will explode at any minute, appalled by the pain, I sat in bed like a broken robot, I was trying to figure out, what happened to me, I concluded, that I should face reality, and stop suffering about that fucking woman; but deep down there is another reality, I still love her. —Then, when my senses began to clear...

I promise for the person I love the most: that this kind of debauchery, will never happen again. Hey...it's fucking scary: I'm waking up not knowing what the hell happened during the weekend, I just can't fuck recall!! But at that moment someone deep inside me, was remembering me, about all the events that I don't want to recall about it: and I replied!!! Stop bugging me, with all the same kind of crap!! —For sure that it's my conscious: this dumb bitch, had nothing else to do, but telling me about all my failures, and I could hear in my brain. *"Special-Agent Bronson, you know the consequences you will endure, for the endless days and nights of partying, a matter of fact, for behaving irresponsible, you'll have to pay a price tag that's quite high. Isn't that right, Mr. Sexy Pants?"* And I replied. "Shut the fuck-up, you stupid conceited conscience, since I already know, the penalties my action's will endure!! It's well-known, that in my career as an old foxy fox of the FBI, I was and I'm tirelessly roaming the dangerous dens of the cities, searching for those who are breaking the law, if I collected something, in those hazardous endeavors, is plenty of experiences. —I'm asking: the assistance of that fucking conscious, where is it, when you must need it? The conscience is obviously conspicuous by its absence. At that time, I was lying in bed looking at the ceiling, meditating, just traying to recollect the events, of that night of anguish and loneliness, I concluded, that my actions had no justification, but nevertheless, I was trying to look for an excuse: then I closed my eyes, and I found the excuse for my action's, that's when...

Come to my mind, the figure of my sister Molly, because she is an explicit example, of what should not occur to us: it happens that Molly, was ready to give birth, and at the time of the delivery, she rejected the doctor's help, and my sister Molly, assures me, that at the moment of bringing the baby into the world, *she suffered like a fucking dog*: those were her precise words. And I only ask given the anguish that my sister had gone through, to deliver her child. I was amazed when I found out, that my sister was pregnant again. Therefore, I was puzzled by Molly's decision to have another child, and had to asked her the corresponding question...

"Hi Molly, I'm confused about your decisions, since I found out from mom, that you are pregnant?" I asked worried about her well-being, to which she replied...

"My dear brother, you ask me, as if it was something out of the ordinary to be pregnant. Now I ask you a question: do you feel older, for having another nephew?"

"Don't be silly: Molly, I love having nephews, but what concerns me, it is what can happen to you in the previous childbirth, if I remember correctly, you were complaining about how much you suffered at that time, doesn't bring you awful memories?" *To which she replies.* "My dear brother, that moment was awful, but in this situation, that past experiences didn't come to my aid, look brother, usually the brain does not always have control over our emotions, because when I am making love and I have James on top of me, I forgot about all the pain..." *Then Molly posed for a few seconds as if she was thinking what to say next.* "My dear brother, things happen in situations of extreme excitement. This is life, and no one tells you otherwise, it will happen again, and again, and by the way, your nephew is a boy, and will be handsome like you; this why, I'll name him Vigo, with one g." Molly said with a witty smile, and I was wondering if she only said it, to make me happy.

Well, if I placed as an example, my sister struggles, it's because it has a direct connection, with my situation right now!! —What I'm trying to expose in this case, is that nobody is exempted for neglecting experiences of the past; as my sister, I find myself in the same awkward situation, it's a self-inflicted torture; because, with no mercy I did have an automatic hammer punishing my brain: but on second thought, *I can't take all the blame*, I need a scapegoat in this conflict, for sure, that my wife is to blame for what happens to me, she is the cause that my heart and *soul* is wounded by love. What a nightmare, at that moment I was feeling like shit: struggling I made a fucking Bloody Mary, with that fucking drink, I took four aspirin and several sleeping pills, then I threw myself head first, between the pillows, I was sound asleep, that's when I began to hear those annoying bells inside my head, I was sure it was the wailing of an ambulance: it was not, in fact, it was my cell phone, that sounded like church bells inside my brain, and I asked out loud, "Who the fuck is calling me at this time? Well, the person who interrupted my nightmare with a phone call was...

My faithful partner, and a very good friend, Rachel Dansby, who is the proud daughter of a brave FBI Special-Agent Travis Dansby, who paid the ultimate price in the treacherous terrorist attack, at the Twin Towers on nine-eleven, that terrible family casualty's, does not discourage her to follow her father's footsteps: Rachel Dansby become an FBI Agent. If she is calling me, must have a very good reason, because something important is happening or is about to occur. I'm sure she would like to know, what the hell is going on with her Chief, who currently, he is not showing up at the Bureau? —Well, here is her profile...

FBI Agent Rachel Dansby, weights one hundred-sixty pounds, she is a compound of graceful energy and efficiency, her exotic beauty, would captivates any man. At the bureau: Rachel, is well known as Rocky: her nickname is very-well earned: for her resilience, in enforcing the law...Rachel, right now is trying to find out, if I got lost in the dim lights of one of the night clubs of Manhattan. I knew that I was flat on the fucking canvas, really lost in the hazy grief of oblivion, to top it all, I had to deal with the consequences, which await me when I wake up of this nightmare: and about the phone-call, I couldn't answer it, my tongue was stuck in my mouth, and was stuttering, and finally I was able to say...

"What the fuck Rocky...you better have a good reason to wake me up...what the hell is going on...that is so important?" Viggo asked in a very raspy voice and Rachel responded in a sarcastic way...

"Chief, it was not my intention, to wake up at Special-Agent Bronson, but the sun is quite high, and the life in the Bureau is in full swing!"

"What do you mean the Bureau is in full swing? And the sun is quite high...what are you trying to say?" Viggo asked trying to clear his mind all hazy and his hoarse throat. Rachel suspecting that her partner is in trouble she pointed out...

"I'm trying to say, good afternoon, Chief, it's two o'clock, then if you are interested to know, in which day you are living in, today is Tuesday, and I'm calling to inform you that in the Bureau, there is an important person who is missing you. Okay?"

"Don't tell me, that today is Tuesday? And you said that is two o'clock in the afternoon? Fuck...fuck me!!! Rocky, why didn't you call me earlier?" Viggo asked trying to wake up, and Rachel frustrated added...

"Chief, I called you yesterday and, today I called you several times, and you didn't answer, I'm sure that between those toasts, with your friend Johnnie Walker, sent you where there is almost no way to return. Really Chief?"

"Don't you even fucking remember about las night? Because I'm going back to get some more..." *There was a moment of silence and Viggo continued saying.* "Rocky, I had a great time, but who did this job to me...it wasn't Johnnie...Okay?"

"Of course, I know that story: if it wasn't Johnnie, it was some other friendly scotch. Please Chief, you better clear your head, because this morning when Officer Franklin, arrived at the Bureau, and then he realized that you were not in the office, he got quite pissed off, the case is, that he has a specific assignment for you, and Franklin, is waiting for you to show up. Okay?"

"Please Rocky, I'm not in the state of mind to understand clearly what is going on, I'm going to take a shower and I'll call you back. Okay?" Viggo with great difficulty entered the bathroom, and he took a long hot and cold shower, then with the towel tied on his waist, he dropped into the bed, and he was falling asleep when the phone rang, with sleepy voice he answered...

"I was about to call you Rocky."

"Are you okay Chief?" Rachel, asks interested in the answer and Viggo like all the drunkards, who do not like to be asked how they feel, he responded...

"Don't you worry about me and worry about yourself. Rocky, why don't you wait for me at the coffee shop, in front of the Bureau, I'd be there in an hour. Okay?"

"Okay Chief, I'll wait for you with hot coffee, and don't let the coffee get cold. Okay?"

"Please, have a little patience Rocky, I'll see you there."

Rachel was waiting for him with butter toasts, and a cup of hot coffee, at the moment Viggo arrived, he kisses her and sits down, and being a little more alert, he starts the conversation as if nothing had happened...

"Thanks for the coffee, Rocky."

"Sure Chief, I must tell you, that it shows in your face, that you were walked along some very winding road, and it is not very appealing. Okay?

"Hey, Rocky, the winding road...I can feel it, and what I'm going to tell you is very personal." Viggo said confidently wagging his index finger, how drunkards do, and she asked...

"Okay Chief, what has happened?

"Rocky, it was very curious what happened, Sunday I ended up at The Veil, and without trying, I lost myself in a cloud of pleasure, looking to chase the ghosts, which disturb my mind, but didn't help; the remedy was worse than the disease, and today I feel worse than yesterday." *Then he takes a sip of coffee and asks.* "Rocky, no matter how much I try, I can't forget Ember?" Viggo said looking at Rachel who ignore the question and answered...

"Chief is nothing I can tell you, that you don't know. When you go out with this guy Jack Daniels, always you arrive to the Bureau, showing the highlights of the night before, you must change friends Chief?"

"Don't get smart with me Agent Dansby, and tell me what's going on, that is so important?

"Chief, what I'm trying to tell you, is that we have a mission that has no turning back, if the sky doesn't collapse between now, and our departure, which is already scheduled: we are going to California Chief!!" Rachel said really happy and Viggo who still can't get out of his binge asks...

"What are you trying to say Rocky?"

"I am trying to inform you Chief, that we are going to California, but not anywhere in the state, we are going on a mission at the Santa Monica Resort, according to Franklin, the place is riddled with foreign agents, these rats are hanging around seeing what kind of secrets they can steal, and..."

"Please, slow down Rocky, I just get up all fucked up, just slow down...please."

"Okay Chief: I was saying that Officer Franklin, just appointed Special-Agent Bronson, with the mission to dismantle an espionage network, which seems to have local and international roots. Chief this mission, for you, will be like feathers of peacock!" Rachel said with a smile and Viggo looks at her with a sad face, as if saying you don't know what is happening to me, then he answered...

"I'm just coming out of a nightmare, and look like I'm going to get in another, thanks to Franklin. Then to add fuel to the fire...Rocky, it seems to me; this mission it's not the feathers of a peacock. Rocky, do you have any idea, how many countries are involved in this case?"

"Chief, there are several countries implicated in this espionage, what it is new in this case, these foreign agents, brought with them the bodyguards, just to ensure that the mission would be a success. I'm sure, this mission could turn really dangerous?"

"Well, after I learn all the details about this mission, we'll discuss how dangerous it is, Rocky, please relax, because I have a headache. Okay?"

"Chief, please listen to me, yesterday, Franklin was quite pissed off; at one point he gets up from his chair, and starts looking around the office, then he asks. "Where the hell is Special-Agent Brooks, this guy believes he's the boss in this Bureau...He shows up, whatever the hell he wants?"

"Finally...finally, Franklin said something smart. Rocky, you know, that I'm the boss of my own shortcomings, I have a lot of respect for the *Handling Officer*, in the office, but in the field, I can't trust him!!"

"Chief, it seems to me that you don't want to understand what's going on, or you are still drunk and half asleep?" Rachel said frustrated, and Viggo drinking coffee looks at her with wide eyes trying to get the news through his eyes, and then he responded...

"Don't worry about me Rocky: and tell me some other details, that really makes me wake up, because my brain it's still in sleep mode!!!" Viggo said holding his head and Rachel went to get another cup of coffee then she said...

"Come on Chief, have another cup of coffee, like I said before: the mission that you are going to undertake Chief, it's a priority: do you hear? A priority, in all the programs of Homeland Security, and this assignment should put you on high alert Chief. Okay?"

"Rocky, why you didn't say that from the beginning? If the Homeland Security Director, wants to solve this case as soon as possible, it means this mission, is of the upmost importance, for the safety of this country?"

"Chief, I'm sure, that's the reason, this why Franklin is acting like he was bitten by a giant mosquito; it's kind of annoying, because he is making the environment in the office very tense!" She said with the coffee cup in front of her face and Viggo with a sleepy face responded...

"Rocky, I don't understand why Franklin is sending us to California, I'm sure that in Los Angeles, we have capable agents that already began with the investigation? It can't be that inept, maybe there is something we don't know?" Viggo points out, and Rachel is all wound up with the prospect of going to California, and she added...

"Chief, I sure, that all the outbursts of Franklin, have to do with the events that are happening in California, and to make the situation worse, you didn't show up at the Bureau, and he's really pissed off."

"I don't know what's going on with Franklin, lately he's acting very proud of himself, ever since he found out he is a direct descendent of Benjamin Franklin!!"

"Chief, at least he's sending us to California and not at the Middle East, come on, give him a break; the man is ready to retire, he must be quite fed-up, dealing with characters like yours."

"What are you trying to say, that I'm a pain in the ass?"

"No Chief, you... you are not a pain...It happens that you...you have strong character. Okay?

"Talking about character's Rocky, I assume that must be at Franklin disposal other agents in the FBI force, I can't quite understand, why send us to La-La-Land?

"It would be so much better Chief, if you stop complaining, since you are not going to get away from this mission. Okay?"

"Rocky, you know that I hate leaving New York, do you remember, last time we left the city, we ended up in Afghanistan, we were really lucky, to get out alive from that septic hole. By the way, there is something else that I should know?"

"Chief, according to Franklin, the Bureau of Los Angeles has well-founded information, that connects the well-known gangster Santino Pascucci, with this case. Supposedly, in this intermingle, he has his tentacles all over the place, then according to the Homeland Security records, the gangster disappeared ten years ago, from New York, and..."

"Please, tell me something I don't know Rocky?"

"Today, you are impossible to please Chief, just give me a break!"

"Okay...okay, I'm sorry, Rocky, what were you saying?"

"Chief, it is confirmed, that the gangster Santino Pascucci, resides in California, and the news are, that he was recently spotted by a journalist, in the City of Santa Monica, walking casually holding hands with a woman."

"Rocky, if we are going to go back in time, this guy Pascucci has been out of circulation for several years, it means, this human trash, will never stop committing crimes!!" Viggo said placing the cup of coffee on the table and raising his hands and Rachel added...

"This's a strange causality Chief, this guy reappears now, right in the place where is happening, this espionage case, you don't think, it's too much of a coincidence, that Pascucci, was seen in Santa Monica?"

"I don't get it Rocky, what the hell this gangster is doing in Santa Monica, end somehow this guy has become a double agent, it doesn't make any sense, you're correct Rocky, the coincidence is very suspicious." Viggo said advancing his head toward Rocky like it was a secret and Rachel answers...

"I don't get it Chief, how can it be, that Pascucci was living in that beach town, and for years have been undetected by the authorities, until the moment that he decided to expose himself, just to engage in criminal acts, like in the old times!"

"I'm telling you Rocky, this old fox loses their hair, but not their behavior, let's follow the traces of his hair, and I'm sure that we are going to find him, and let's start at the Los Angeles Bureau!" Viggo proposed and Rachel who was all excited and ready to go responded...

"Chief, I did find out, that the Federal Building, is on Main Street, right in the Civic Center of Santa Monica. Don't you think that's great? We can go shopping at the Santa Monica Mall, then we could go to dinner in front the beach!"

"That's great for you Rocky, but the Bureau, is in the heart of the Mambo Jumbo: that's what I don't need right now, what I need is a little bit of peace and quiet, before my head falls off, and some asshole uses my head as a soccer ball, like in the time of the Aztecs!!"

"Don't get dramatic Chief, you know, the city is just a beach town: for that reason alone, it should be a very nice peaceful place, on the other hand, maybe it can be dynamic during the night...I guess?"

"What do you mean, peaceful and dynamic? You're rambling nonsense, Rocky!"

"Being drunk Chief, doesn't give you the right to dismiss what I'm informing you!"

"Don't pay attention to me today: Please Rocky, what you were saying?

Chief, I was saying, that the city has plenty of restaurants, and also a couple of nice night clubs, in which you can get really fucked-up, then when you are really wasted, you can go to the beach, and fall asleep on the sand, beside the water. Chief, there is always another way to look at this mission: let's say, as if we were on vacation. Okay?" Rachal said with smile and Viggo trying to compose himself responded...

"Rocky, please; if we are going to California, it has an explicit purpose: for sure we are not going on vacation..."

"Come on Chief, you know, I didn't mean it that way: it's my free spirit that always reached beyond reality. Chief, the day I stop dreaming, it must be that I'm dead." Rachal said taking his hand trying to pacify Viggo who still has some running mice inside his head added...

"Thanks, Rocky, for trying to cheer me up, your understanding, makes me see at the bright side in life, this why in that beach town, I'm going to start practicing a new way of life: while focusing on solving this fucking case. I'm going to appease my mind, trying to leave in the past, what belongs to the past!" Viggo said with energy and Rachel responded...

"That is the spirit Chief, just think, we are going to snoop around, in one of the most famous resorts in the world. I'm really excited. But you have to remember, that right now you must go to the Bureau, please wake up Chief!" She said energetically and Viggo responded...

"Okay...okay, just lower your voice please: consider that I went to hell, and I'm having a hard time coming back. Rocky, thanks for being here, you're a great friend." Viggo said lifting up the empty coffee cup and Rachel is planning in her mind, the trip to California with a sparkle in her eyes, then she proposed...

"I'm just trying to wake you up Chief, and we don't have much time to lose, because according to Franklin, we must depart the soon as possible!" Rachal said in an urgent manner and Viggo still half lost asks...

"What are you trying to propose...Agent Dansby?"

"Chief, it is almost certainly that in a couple of days we're going to Los Angeles: I propose that we should renew our wardrobe, the people in L.A, wear casual clothes, and we must dress like they do, casual! Okay?" Rachal pointed out all excited, and Viggo who still had some city workers hammering in his brain responded...

"The wardrobe? That's your dilemma." *Viggo ignores her concerns and begins to talk about his worries.* "Rocky, look at me, look at my face, there is where the quandary begins: I should start shaving off the beard, with a lawn mower, and continue with a good haircut with pruning shears, that's, if I want to be presentable, to people who don't know me!"

"That makes sense Chief, is an excellent idea. Finally, I'm going to find the Chief I lost some time ago!"

"You're right; but sometimes life is a fucking bitch, does not discriminate to who is going to hurt. Rocky, you know that disheartened with my marriage, I let my beard grow, to hide the feeling of anger that still reflect on my face!!"

"Chief, I'm sorry but you have to return to reality, and now you have the opportunity for a new beginning, please Chief, don't let sadness fill your heart with anguish, don't dwell on the past, this assignment in California, will get you out of New York and, the proximity of your wife. Chief, time erases everything?"

"'Thanks', I appreciate your support. Rocky, when I had a few extra drinks, my heart gets full of anger, and it starts to beat like crazy, and what bothers me the most, is that I can't contain those emotions!!"

"Chief, how can you be in love with Ember, with all the horrible times, she put you through?"

"Rocky, just forget about Ember: and tell me if you remember haw I looked without the beard? I know it's a stupid question, but I want to know." Viggo said stroking his beard and Rachel responded...

"Chief, with beard or without it, you always will look pretty good to me, but if you want to impress, some of the people in L.A, what you really need, is a different kind of clothing. Chief, we already talked enough about this mission, and please let's go shopping. Okay?"

"Rocky, are you proposing that a beast like me, I have to wear a Hawaiian shirt in Santa Monica, I'm sure that I will look like a ridiculous New-Yorker, I can see myself running between the palm trees, chasing after Pascucci?" Viggo said moving his arms like a windmill and Rachel rolling her eyes replied…

"That is a ridiculous version of my proposition Chief, what I'm suggesting, it is that you buy a couple of blazers and matching pants, then, you will be looking so manly and handsome, that I don't know, how I'm going to control myself, and not-to, jump all over that handsome beast." She said in a sexy voice, and Viggo who knows Rachel well responded…

"Don't you start with that sweet talk Rocky. I know what that means. Today I can't help you. Okay?" Viggo said having the fourth cup of coffee, and Rachel calmly answered…

"Well, don't take my suggestion literally, I'm just trying to help like always."

"Rocky, I'm not in the mood right now. Okay?

"Chief, sorry if I continue with this topic, if we will be working in a beach resort, since in L.A every day is like Spring, you will look out of place, are you grasping what I'm saying?" *Rachel stood up as if she was ready to leave and spoke.* "That's all I will say. Okay?"

"Okay…Ok. We'll talk about it later, because, the city workers, still have banging in my head."

"I'm sorry Chief, but we have been here for a long time, we should continue the conversation in the office, there we could discuss the details." She said sweetly, and Viggo responded knowing what Rachel had in mind and he responded…

"Sure…sure, you want to talk; like I don't know what kind of conversation you want to have; please Rocky, stop talking and get me a ton of aspirin, if you'll be so kind, please?"

"Chief, you need same aspirin; but you also need a good meal. Okay?"

Without controversy the two Federal agents got to the Bureau. Viggo, did not arrived in very good condition at the meeting, with the *Handling Officer*, who wasn't very happy with Special-Agent Viggo Bronson. —Officer Franklin, is trying to control his mood, looking at Viggo, he began giving the instructions related to the international espionage network: Franklin was acting like he didn't know much about the case, he wasn't very precise, in the delivery of the guidelines, there came a moment that Viggo asks. "What-about the Federal Agencies, they have some info?" Franklin responded, so far, the agencies don't know how many countries are involved in this espionage case; Russia and China, for sure they are after information, regarding what the NGA = *National Geospatial Agency*, is creating in their lab, seems that it is an interspace defense project, and what is very possible, the gangster Santino Pascucci, may be involved in this conspiracy. —After the meeting with Officer Franklin. Viggo left the office, as he had entered, without much information, then, he took Rachel for a late lunch, and as soon they sat down, she asks...

"First of all, Chief, what Franklin revealed about the case?"

"You just asked me the wrong question Rocky, since it is impossible to deal with this guy."

"Come on Chief, just tell me, what the hell happened in the office?"

"Rocky, Mr. Franklin, had the fucking audacity to say almost nothing, I'm disappointed, he just mentioned to me, that the NGA, was creating a space project, and the rest of the info, that's what you already reported to me, that's it. Okay?"

"Chief, don't worry about it the info, let's eat lunch, then we are going shopping. I don't want to look out of place in Santa Monica. I want to wear summer outfits. Okay Chief?"

"Rocky, please, don't force the issue, and let me eat my lunch in peace, because since I left home, the fucking headache is following me, be aware Rocky, because right now, I'm flying with a single engine!"

"I'm sorry about your headache Chief, but the point is that we don't have the time, to debate about what we should do: look, I'll help you to choose the spring clothes, but like I said before; a couple of blazers and matching pants will be perfect. Do you agree?"

"Okay, let's see what you can do for me. I'm telling you Rocky, I don't want to look in LA, like a guy on vacation, much less, in front of the local agents: for devil's sake!"

"Hold on Chief, talking about devil's, something is not quite right Chief, because I'm beginning thinking like you, because, since that the local agents started this investigation, why they don't finish it? I don't understand why Franklin, send us to L.A, I just ask out of curiosity?"

"You are driving me crazy Rocky, in a second you change from one subject to another; just calm down and let eat in peace. Okay?"

"Chief, this assignment has something weird, it doesn't make sense to me?" Rachel pointed out and Viggo replied...

"Rocky, you just asked me, about the instructions that I got from Franklin, who choose the strange initiative, to sending us to this assignment. But, if you don't stop debating with yourself, about the strange choice Franklin made, I will tell you what he said. Okay?"

"Sorry Chief, sometimes I say out loud, questions that I ask myself, I guess I'm getting old." She said coquettish fixing her hair and Viggo ignores her and said...

"Please Rocky, according to Franklin, the district attorney has a solid suspicion that the gangster Santino Pascucci and his associates, are deeply involved in feeding information to the international agents. The FBI agency has in their possession, wiretaps with evidence that directly incriminates Pascucci..."

"That's it, Chief?

"Please Rocky, don't stir the knife. Okay?"

"I'm sorry." She said with a mocking smile and Viggo answered...

"I really don't need your sarcasm. Okay?"

"Come on Chief, and tell me what Franklin, had to say?

"Rocky, the most interesting thing he said was about the NGA, they are creating an interspatial project, with the sole purpose of protecting the satellites; the rest you already know!" Viggo affirms upset, and Rachel points out...

"I'm not sure, but something doesn't fit in this puzzle. Chief, we already know, that the gangster Santino Pascucci is missing in action for quite a long time. Don't tell me, that he became a double agent over night?" *Rachel, became thoughtful for a few seconds, finding an answer to her own question and she spoke.* "Chief, but at least we know, how he looks like, will be easy to find this fucker." Rachel said rolling her eyes, and Viggo added...

"That's right, he wasn't but these guys are like the chameleon: change color depending on the occasion: and right now, this scum bug, turned into a double agent, and it's possible, that Mr. Pascucci, in his leisure hours, is purchasing from one or more scientists, whatever secrets he can buy, then he sells the info to the highest bidder. Pascucci, has become another politician, these scumbags for few dollars sell's their own country." Viggo said disgusted and Rachel ignores the last comment and added...

"Seems to me, that the scientists are getting very sophisticated, creating protection and destruction systems, at the same time. Chief, what sort of scientific project are we dealing with?"

"You just said it Rocky, the system it's fucking sophisticated. According to NGA, the scientists are creating a new *Inter-Stellar-Defense-System,* with the prospect to become a weapon of war, or preventing one, I'm guessing, because as much as I tried, I could not comprehend Franklin's strategies, he was informing me, as if he were surrounded by a cloud of doubts, he wasn't that clear at all, he never is, this fucking incompetent!!" Viggo said energetically and Rachel added...

"Chief, this case already got to your nerves, and, for me, it is getting too technical." *Rachel paused for a couple of seconds pondering what she was going to say.* "Well, I do not n know if what I am going to say, it's worth anything Chief, but when I was in Franklin's office, he was talking on the phone, and I overheard an interesting dialogue..."

"Rocky, please, you know that every detail helps, come on, let's hear it." Viggo said trying to really wake up and Rachel, informs...

"Chief, when I was in the office, I'm sure Franklin, was talking with the director of the MGA, that we know this project had been commissioned by the *National Geospatial Agency." She paused for a second looking down at the table, then she looked up and spoke.* "Chief, what we don't know, is which company in the U.S. has the potential to create this sophisticated system, we should grab the computer and start searching!" Rachel said energetically and Viggo responded...

"It's very possible, that the NGA director himself, warned the defense minister, about the serious probability, that our satellites are in imminent danger. Rocky, let's not forget, that the NGA, is in charge of developing those complex satellites."

"I know all about it Chief, but the question is..."

"Listen Rocky, the question is, that Franklin doesn't have the knowledge, to whom the defense minister gave the project to be develop, or for some unknown reason, doesn't pass the information to us. Rocky, maybe the minister assigned the project to the Air Force, the N.A.S.A, or to The Bremen Company. This guy Bremen is quite smart, and he has several successful engineering companies. —Do you follow?"

"Of course, I'm listening." *She answered and then she paused for a second organizing her thoughts.* "Chief, as I said before, it seems to me, this assignment on a turn of a coin could become dangerous. I'm sure there will be rummaging aggressive agents, to get their hands on the classified information. Don't you agree?" Rachel asks right in his face. Viggo feeling a little better responded...

"Relax Rocky, I'm sure, that in the Santa Monica Bureau, Officer Morris, must have the files of this case. I'm sure the HO, will provide all the information related to the investigation; I hope he knows the nationality of the foreign agents, and how deep these people are, trying to get information."

"Still, I can't guess why Franklin is sending us to L.A, Chief, we should confront him and ask him a simple question. What is the real reason, for sending as to California?"

"It's a good suggestion but is it not going to be necessarily see him: there must be a simple answer to that question. Rocky, it's possible, that the agents in charge of the investigation, are in a deadlock situation and, for some unknown reason, the agents are not able to proceed with the case, and for heaven's sake: who the fuck knows what is going in L.A?" Viggo said frustrated and Rachel responded...

"Excuse me Chief, but your reasoning simplifies a complex network of interests, in this case, you didn't specify the reason, why Franklin, made the determination to send us to L.A?"

"Okay, Agent Dansby, if you are so clever: please tell me what is your smart answer to this fucking mess, because I don't have any?"

"Please Chief, I'm only trying to open your eyes, because..."

"Because what? Rocky, I don't understand where you want to go with this, head game?"

"Please Chief, listen to me!"

"Okay, Rocky, go ahead but don't forget I have a headache!"

"Chief, listen, I did a simple observation analysis, Franklin is acting strangely, and I believe that in this decision, someone is manipulating him, it is difficult to prove but it is what I think.

Chief, who might be involved in a plot that will send Special-Agent Bronson to California, with the sole purpose of investigating a case, which it's already in progress with the local agents." *There was a moment of silence and she spoke.* "Chief, maybe it's my feminine intuition, that makes me distrust in this type of situation; but I'm sure that someone must be behind this assignment and must be a person how knows you very well!" Rachel said firmly and Viggo responded.

"Rocky, you have every right to be suspicious, but there are no sinister characters in this mission, I'm sure that the Bureau turned to us, because we are quite capable of giving a helping hand to the local agents, it's a logical reason. Okay?"

"Chief, you're trying to say, that we posses' certain abilities that the other agents don't have. I would like to hear all about these unusual skills: I'm so excited Chief, you are getting me in a dangerous sexy mood!!" Rachel said bringing her torso over the table and Viggo ignore her comment and asks...

"Rocky, do you want to know, in what we excel in our line of work? It is not that simple."

"Come on Chief, jest tell me, because listening to you, gives me an immense pleasure!" Rachel said opening her eyes really wide, but Viggo takes the dialogue to another level...

"Come down Rocky and listen it's well known that in the criminal's jargon, the FBI agents, supposed to be a superior class of hound dogs, since with our fine senses of scent, we can spot any elusive prey, from the farthest distances. Rocky, this is the reason the outlaws, when they can perceive a hint, that we are coming for them, these gangsters right the way, began to erase the evidence of their crimes, then like a bunch of fraidy-cats cowards, just turn in complete disarray: those emotions of panic, paralyzes their brains, that's when the criminal become an easy prey!" Viggo said-it in a seductive way, and she got so excited that her face turned all read and she said...

"Oh Chief! What you just said sounds so sexy, I can't resist your sex appeal, please let's go to the car and I'll give you a..."

"Don't do that Rocky, and take it easy with your hands: remember that we are in a restaurant?" Viggo said seriously and Rachel, makes a face of an annoying little girl.

For Viggo, it's not easy to control the constant sexual advances of Rachel, and her behavior sometimes is overwhelming. In silence, the two federal agents finished their meal. Viggo after having eaten he felt much better, then as if they were a couple, they went shopping for the clothing they will need, for the upcoming mission in California. —In couple of days, the agents were on their way to California, and dressed for the occasion.

Viggo, previously had arranged with his partner, that he would pick up her on the way to the airport; Rachel, was waiting in front of her apartment pacing the sidewalk, Rachel, felt very proud of herself, as if she were the owner of the whole world. The truth: she is looking gorgeous, for the special occasion: she is wearing a boutique designer outfit, which consisted, of a pink silk shirt, a navy-blue skirt and, to emphasize her amazing figure, a fitted matching blazer, what can't be missing is the Versace scarf, which decorated her slender neck, then, to emphasize her beauty, she has a new modern hairstyle, which complements her amazing look: to put it simply: She is looking like a model from Paris, waking the catwalk. —And...

Impatiently Rachel was waiting for the Chief, in front of her condo, at the moment Viggo arrived, he stopped the car in front of her. Rachel at first glance, couldn't believe what she was seeing, it was more than pleasant surprise, it was a miracle!! The Chief, was another man: She could not contain herself and, began to play a game of mistaking identity, then with a straight face she said to Viggo...

"Excuse me, mister, why are you stopping here and looking at me, with the face that says please love me, you're not the person I'm expecting, the man I'm waiting for, looks like a caveman, and you...and you look like my favorite actor, Sean Connery!! I guess that the cave dweller is late, because he has to remove, all the creatures from his beard, the caveman is very punctual and, I'm sure he will show up any minute." Rachel said seriously, and Viggo proud of his new look responded...

"That was a good performance Rocky, I almost believed it!"

"Thanks, Chief, I have to say, that I didn't try my best; since acting comes natural to me, I'm sure that in another life I was a famous glamorous sexy actress!"

"I have no doubt you were Rocky, but from now on, I'm going to start a new life, please listen and pay attention: I'll say this only once, I don't want to hear from you any complaints about how I look, that is an explicit order. Okay?" Viggo asks seriously and Rachel at the moment she gets in the car expresses her delight...

"Chief, I can't believe it, because you look so handsome and sexy, I swear to God, I don't know how I'm going to control myself, and throw myself on top of you, and kiss you from head to toe, until you beg me to stop!!" She said caressing his face, and Viggo with a grin responded...

"Thanks for the compliment, Rocky, but you will leave your anxieties for another time."

"Come on Chief!"

"Rocky, I have to say, that you look gorgeous, with this fantastic new hairstyle, and this outfit that fit you perfect, I'm sure, that when we arrive to L. A, and I walked into the Bureau, with you at my side, I'm going to see the look of envy, on these guys faces."

"Thanks, for the compliment Chief, but I can't be less, because, you look splendid, without all that hair, and from now on, I will try my best, not to fall in love with this married man!" Rachel said covering her face up with her hands, and Viggo ignoring the comment, expresses what he feels at that moment…

"Rocky, I'm telling you, right now I feel naked without my beard…I'm fuck, from now on, I will be an open book, since all the emotions will show on my face, and I hate to display the nasty feelings, that nest for a while in my soul." Viggo said caressing his freshly shaved face, thinking about his failing marriage, and Rocky of course she has something to say about it…

"That is amazing: how can it be, that this phenomenon happened? Since I don't believe in miracles, but I just witnessed one, for heaven's sake!! Who'll believed that another creature was living under all that mop of hair. Chief, you're a new man, and with this new suit you look like *Sean Connery*, the difference between both of you, it's that you are taller, handsome, and I'm sure that *Mr. Connery* doesn't have your lovely tattoo!"

"Rocky, stop right there. Okay? And don't even think about it!!"

"Please Chief, before boarding the airplane, just stop for a few minutes in a motel, we could shake the stress of the trip, then we will arrive in California relaxed like regular tourists. Okay?" Rachel's suggestion didn't come alone it came with a sweet caress, but Viggo who is already used to her sexual outbursts replies…

"Please, Rocky, it would be better if I don't make any comments. First, because you are behaving like a spoiled girl, and second, I fucking hate leaving New York!!!" Viggo said seriously and Rachel giving him a caress commented…

"Chief, I hate when you get in this oblivious mood." *There were a few seconds of silence and she continue saying.* "Once, I heard someone say. That a glass of water and, a little love you don't deny it to anyone: it's not fair Chief, you are leaving me hotter than erupting volcano!" And Rachel silently began to look out the window, and Viggo smiles and didn't respond. —Then for the long flight to…

California, the agents were sitting comfortable in business class. Rachel has no other choice but to keep her desires well under control, and without any sexual conflict's, they arrived in time at the airport of...

LOS ANGELES

Around noon the federal agents arrived at the airport, they were greeted by one of those splendid sunny days, which usually you find in the City of Los Angeles, to add a touch of camaraderie to the welcome, the Bureau *Handling Officer,* had the courtesy of sending a complimentary SUV vehicle, and Mike, will take the federal agents to the City of Santa Monica; where the FBI headquarters is located, right in the heart of the City, which is world-famous for all the year around amazing weather. And about Viggo: for him it will be the first time he can appreciate the nice climate of Los Angeles, and he pointed out to Rachel...

"that's amazing, I am looking at the people around me, and I just concluded, that in New York, the people look pissed off, and stressed out, like they lost the last train to happiness. Right here in L.A, the faces seem quite relaxed, and the people are walking with a smile on their faces, I'm sure it must be this fantastic weather, that already makes me feel really good!" Viggo pleased commented coming out of the airport, and he began to take off his tie and jacket. Rachel agrees with the comment and adds...

"Chief, you're taking off your tie and the jacket, I can't believe it!! We just arrived, and already you're getting into the L.A mood, taking off your clothes? I feel like doing the same, taking my blazer off, then we will look like a couple of tourists, who are coming to L.A for the first time: what do you say Chief?" Rachel asks glancing at Viggo, and he began to roll his sleeves up and pointed out...

"You just asked a question Rocky, that brings to mind, the vacation I took about two years ago, when I married Ember!" Viggo indicates helping her to take the blue blazer off. —Meanwhile...

The two Federal agents were talking: Mike, who will take them to the hotel: he began loading the three suitcases, and the heavy long case in the black Cadillac Escalade SUV. Who was paying attention to what Mike was doing was Viggo, who approaches the young man, and told him where he wants to place the luggage..."

"Please Mike, as a precaution, place these two bags on the back seat floor, those are our working tools. Okay?" Viggo pointed out, and Mike replied...

"Okay. Special-Agent Bronson, I'll tell you, that at the moment I was looking for a car to pick you up, thinking about your safety, the H.O suggested that I drive this bullet-proof SUV, which had previously belonged to the president's detail fleet. As you can see it is like new, it will be at your disposal, while you remain in town." The driver informs and the first to answer was Rachel, who expresses her feelings...

"Damn: that's good to know! Last time we jumped into one of these bullet-proof vehicle's was in Afghanistan, the bullets and the bombs were raining around us, and everywhere in the city, we were really lucky to get out alive; these crazy fucking guys, who didn't care if they live or die!! Remember Chief?"

"If I do remember? For sure I recall! I have these scars as a sample of those dangerous encounters, like you said Rocky, these poor people didn't care if they die, at least they die happy, since these idiots believe, they are going to the arms of seven virgin women!!" Viggo said proud to do what he does for his country. —Then...

When it was time to board the Cadillac. Viggo is not sitting with the driver; he doesn't want to leave his partner alone in the back, this consideration it has a reason. Viggo, it is aware of the social behavior rules she believes in, he doesn't want Rachel, to feel discriminated against, right now, he doesn't need any conflicts with his partner. Viggo prefers to travel the rest of the trip in peace, together in the back seat, and the two duffle bags, under their feet, full of weapons. Mike, who is ready to start the trip, he turns around and asked...

"Excuse me Special-Agent Bronson, do you want me to take you, directly to the hotel, or...?"

"Mike, it would be better if you leave me at the Bureau, then, please take Agent Dansby to the hotel." *Then Viggo looked at his partner and informs.* "Rocky, before leaving I did coordinate an appointment with Officer Morris, I will try to find out what the agents have discovered so far. Then I'll walk to the hotel. Okay Rocky?" Viggo said in a whisper, and Rachel who was getting closer to Viggo she whispers in his ear.

"Chief, look at this amazing weather, it's the perfect for making love on the beach under a blanket, then embrace like two tourists, we walk along the beach, stepping on the sun reflection on the waves that softly caress our feet. Chief, don't you agree that's a romantic way to begin this assignment?"

"Please Rocky, daydreaming is a free gift, I'm glad you can do it, but right now, I'm not in a very good mood. This is the first time in my career, that I have arrived to investigate a case of vital importance and, I'm not fully informed of what is really going on. I hope this guy, brings me up to speed, on what's happening in this town, then with some knowledge, of what is happening, we can start investigating. Rocky, I'm going to try to make this meeting short. Okay?"

"Yah: sure Chief, as if I didn't know how things work between you guys, when you start telling endless stories of investigations, one episode is more dangerous than the other. I'm sure that I'll wait for you until midnight, if you arrive after twelve, the next day I don't want to hear any complaints!!" Rachel quite doubtful answered, and Viggo seriously responded...

"Please Rocky, this mitting is not a social encounter, plus you have your own room, you don't have to wait for me: let's be clear, this meeting will take as long as necessary. I'm just going to obtain all the info I can get, and I'm pissed off, a matter of fact, with that kind of rhetoric you don't help me at all. Okay?" Viggo indicates, and Rachel with the face of a silly girl said...

"Chief, what I'm afraid of, that between story and tales Mr. Morris, takes out a bottle of whiskey, and tomorrow I can't wake you up, plus I'm very afraid when I'm alone." She said in a frightened girl's voice, pampering him and caressing his face, Viggo hugs her tenderly and kisses her, meanwhile they were already leaving the airport, and the driver suggests...

"Excuse me Special-Agent Bronson, but on the way to the Bureau I have two options, I can take Lincoln Boulevard or the 405 freeway, which way would you prefer to go?" Mike asked but who answered was Rachel...

"Please Mike, take the streets, so we can enjoy the sightseeing of Santa Monica, I would like to see if the palm trees are as tall as everyone says. Mike, if it is possible, I would like to pass by the sandy beaches of Santa Monica, I'm so excited?" She said happily and Mike who is ready to help responded...

"It was a good choice Agent Dansby, the calendar is telling us the summer is over, but here in Santa Monica that's not the case, this beautiful weather that we have, makes it possible to enjoy the beaches all year around, and the tourists take advantage of this gift of nature, I'm going to take a detour to pass in front of the beaches. Okay?" Mike commented and Rachel responded...

"Thanks Mike, I love it!" She said then getting close to Viggo's ear said. "Chief, since we are talking about the good weather, I brought two new bikinis, I'm sure that I'll find a minute to go swimming; did you bring your swimming suit Chief? If you haven't brought any, I'll buy one for you, one of those that enhances your figure." Rachel said and asked happily and Viggo replies...

"Please, Rocky, for god's sake, try to focus on what we came to do, in case you don't know, we're not on vacation, and by the way, you won't have the time to walk around in your bikini." Viggo whisper and she said in his ear...

"Don't tell me, that you are jealous? This cannot be happening, because for some time you neglected your look, for a woman that throw you out of your house, and the feelings you profess for her it is not healthy, this love is eating your soul away, and you are jealous, because other men are going to look at my beautiful body, I don't believe it!" And she started molesting Viggo, who annoyed reacted...

"Take it easy Rocky, this is not the place nor the time to do this, you are acting like a sex maniac, you better calm down, if not you'll be suffering the consequences!" Viggo indicates a little bit annoyed, and Rachel answered in his ear...

"You're threatening me, look how I'm shaking. For your information, sex is not an addiction, it's a necessity. Chief, your sex appeal confuses my senses, when I am with you, the barriers of decency doesn't exist I can't help it, if you, only you're to blame, for all my sexy at-burst, since you already know, that you're my weaknesses. Okay Chief?" Rachel said sweetly in his ear and Viggo responds in the same way...

"Rocky, stop all that nonsense, and please don't be so obvious, don't you see we have company. I'm sure that you don't care if someone sees or hears your personal desires. Right?" Said Viggo in a whisper. In that instant the driver announces...

"Special-Agent Bronson, at this moment we are going through the ecological reserve, this huge strip of land, which was donated by the legendary Howard Hughes, who..." —Mike could not finish the phrase because...

At the precise moment, that Mike was informing who donated the wet lands; that's when a directed ferocious attack against the Federal Agents began: The shooting started, when a vehicle that was occupied by three men, began spraying bullets towards the bullet-proof-Cadillac, it was an unexpected and vicious assault, it's a desperate attempt to eliminate Special-Agent Viggo Bronson, who had many doubts regarding this assignment, and right now, he has more pressing questions. Viggo, in those moments of excitement wonders. How the hell did these gangsters find out that I was coming to LA? And right there in that instant Viggo expressed his amazement when he shout...

"God damn-it what a welcome to L.A!!! Rocky, get the blow-up-gates shotgun, and load-it with the explosive's cartridges!!! And you Mike slows down and open the sunroof!!" When they started to slow down the gangster's car went a little bit ahead, and all this happened while they were getting a hail of bullets. Rachel handed the deadly shotgun to Viggo, who with both hands pulled the weapon out of the sunroof, and he waited until the cars where side by side, then fearlessly aims the gun in to the middle of the car of the gangsters, and without any hesitation or pity he pulled the trigger twice: the shots were lethal, the explosives blasted right in the center of the car, which first lost control, then tumbled and crushed against the road side rail, and at that moment Viggo could see the flames appearing inside the car, and Mike slowed the car down and said...

"Should I stop, or I keep going?"

"Stop Mike!! This is a fucking nightmare: these motherfuckers never rest; I would like to know if one of these fuckers is alive." *He paused for a second and spoke.* "Mike, call the police, and keep the traffic going." *And he turns around and spoke.* "Rocky, pick up the AR-15, and come with me, in case anyone shows up at this lovely greeting." And without thinking twice, Viggo ran toward the car in which the flames were getting larger and larger, then facing the imminent danger he got inside the vehicle, in his dismay he finds that one of the attackers was barely alive, and he pulls the man out of the flaming car, as if the man were a bag of potatoes, and Viggo's adrenaline was flooding his veins, then he grabs the gangster from the chest, and pulled his face next to his, and Viggo full of anger said...

"Listen, piece of shit: I know who sent you to do this job, I won't finish you off, if you tell me from who Pascucci buys the info...are you listening: from whom does Pascucci buys the information?" Viggo asks right into his face, and the gangster covered with blood answered...

"Damn you Easy'V, it has to be you...piece of shit, you...you killed my brother fuck you fucker, I won't tell you a fucking thing, damn you Easy'V, I won't tell you shit!!" The gangster showing repulse for Viggo tries to spit at his face. Then Viggo with no mercy takes the gun and shoves it in his mouth, and in the process, he knocks out a couple of teeth, then he asked...

"If you don't want me to splash your brains all over the street, just tell me what I want to know: or it will be my pleasure to see your brain scattered in the street!!" Viggo furiously said, and Rachel, who was right next to him saw what was going on, and got involved and she indicates...

"Chief, this son of a bitch, has your gun inside his mouth, this jerk has no chance to talk!!!"

"I'm trying to intimidate the mother fucker. Okay. If you piece of shit don't want to talk...Rocky, just pull his pants down, I'll shove the gun in his ass..." At the moment the gangster felt that his pants were coming down, he decided to say something, and he said it in a whisper...

"Please, have compassion Easy-V, please, don't do that. I'll talk...I'll talk...I'll talk..." The gangster said meanwhile he was bleeding through his nose mouth and ears, and Viggo out loud asks...

"Okay...Okay: I know who sent you; Pascucci, from who does he buy the information?" Viggo asks and reaches down to see if the gangster will really talk, in that instant the federal agent felt that the man's life was slowly fading in his arms, and, he has no time to lose, then he places his ear close to his face, and the gangster who was reluctant to leave this world, lying on the street sensing that it was time to go, already resigned, in his last breath of his life he whispers into Viggo's ear...

"The Bremen Compan..." It's all the gangster managed to say, then staring at Viggo as if he wanted to stab him, he died in Viggo's arms. In that precise moment a police car arrived at the crime scene. Viggo shows his credentials and informs the officers roughly what did occur in an unexpected attack. After the police officers finished their report, Viggo said thanks to the officers, who can't believe that they just shook hands with the famous Federal Special-Agent Viggo Bronson. Right after all that commotion, everybody jumped into the Cadillac, and continued their trip to the FBI Bureau. Viggo who is all wound up and worried over what just happened, he began to analyze the situation he said....

"Rocky, I trying to evaluate why I couldn't anticipate, that this kind of attack could happened, I came to the conclusion that something is quite wrong in our Bureau, seems to me, like these gangsters knew when we were coming to L.A, this event should not occur." *Viggo was thoughtful for few seconds.* "Rocky, the person who for seeing this attack is the H.O Mr. Morris, for that reason he sent the bulletproof SUV, to transport us to the city, he must know something Franklin don't."

"I think you are right Chief."

"What the fuck is going on, right now, seems like you can't trust no one?" Viggo said raising his arms and Rachel added...

"For God's sake, this fucking attack, really took me by surprise, luckily you reacted with that hero instinct that you have. Chief, we must celebrate this occasion?" She said it in a sexual way, Viggo did not answer and said pissed-off...

"I'm worried, because I don't know, what's going on in your head? Rocky, you have a fixed idea: we almost got killed and you are only trying to force the issue of sex?

"Chief, there is always a reason to celebrate that we are alive, and we can do it together. Don't you agree?

"We will celebrate later, but what really bothers me, is that we found ourselves in this fucking situation and, I can't grasp it, how on earth from the New York Bureau, did leak this classified information, and no less, down to these fucking gangsters. I'm going to call Franklin, let's see what he has to say about it!"

"Chief, if we look at this case from another angle, maybe there is some other explanations..."

"What are you talking about Rocky, there are no other angle or rational explanations?"

"Who knows Chief, it's possible that someone in the Bureau, spoke to the wrong person, about your mission, without realizing that it was a top-secret, or by chance these were in company Pascucci, maybe he saw us at the airport, and Pasccuci, assumed that we came to L.A, with the assignment to apprehend him, and he decided to send his bodyguard to get rid of us, but the shot backfired, since they are on their way to the grave; isn't that a pity Chief!" Rachel said it calmly trying to appease Viggo, who can't calm down and trying to evaluate the situation, Viggo traying to remove his paranoia in low voice added...

"Rocky, you know, that in ghosts I don't believe, and I don't get confused with false pretenses. Because this fucking attack was planned in detail: I'm sure that's what happened, since theses fuckers chose the most suitable place, for the ambush, this assault was noy a coincidence: believe me Rocky, I know what I'm talking about, because these kinds of coincidences are almost non-existent!!" Viggo said looking very close at Rocky's face, and she reacts like Rocky does, and, she said in a whisper...

"Chief, your voice is so sexy, it gives me goosebumps, and your eyes have so much passion when you look at me, that make my heart tremble. Chief, in this emotional state, I'm not responsible for my actions. It's that you drive me crazy Chief!" And she began to bite his ear...

"Stop it Rocky, I have to remind you again that we just almost got killed, and you insist on rocking the boat, stop the nonsense please?" Viggo said and Rachel kissing him whispered in his ear...

"It's not my fault if you act and talk like a superhero, when I see you in action so relaxed, as if nothing happened and, at the same time, the fucking bullets are flying everywhere, I don't know how to contain myself and jump all over you. Chief, let's do it right here, in the back seat, I don't care if the driver wants to glance, let him look, maybe he learns something Chief."

Well, the needs of Rachel's should wait because by this time they were reaching their destination. As planned in advance: Rachel, must continue the journey to their hotel, instead Viggo, stepped out of the SUV and headed straight to the entrance of the FBI offices. He's anxious to meet the *Officer* William Morris. After checking his credentials with security, he stepped into the reception office, and introduces himself to the young secretary, who was looking at him in a pleasant way, because she already knew who he was, then she stands, and with a cordial gesture, and with a big friendly smile welcomed him...

"Good morning, Special-Agent Bronson, it's a pleasure to meet you. It is an honor to have you among us, I must say that you are very welcome to L.A." She greets him shaking his hand and for some unknown reason she was blushing. Viggo noticed the blush on her face, and said...

"The pleasure is all mine." *He said holding her hands, and getting close to her, watching the young woman's face turn red like a ripe tomato and then he said.* "I believe Miss. O'Neil, I have an appointment with Officer Morris, please, can you confirm if I am correct?" Viggo indicated, and the young woman got so nervous that she could hardly talk, but she managed to say...

"I'm sorry Special-Agent Bronson, but...but I have to inform you, that Officer Ian Morris departed a few days ago to a classified destination, I know that you have come to seek information, you will not find any problems, since we have in charge a provisional H.O." *She paused for a second, worried about what Viggo, was going to said, because already she knows his fame and he is the husband of Officer Maxwell, then with a smirk between malicious and modesty she said.* "It happens to be, that who is in charge as HO right now is Officer Ember Maxwell." Miss Betty said it by looking into his eyes, to see his reaction, and Viggo, couldn't believe what he was hearing, and he wants to kill himself: with a fork? Confronting the woman who threw him out of his home, it's not an easy task: since the man is still very much in love with his wife.

The last thing Viggo was expected to hear, is that familiar name, his reaction was just instantaneous, he turned around and began a series of gestures with his arms. The secretary observes the man strange behavior; from her position she could see the intense disbelief on his face. Viggo turns around and faces her and anxiously inquired...

"Excuse me Ms. Betty: did I hear you right...Mrs. Ember Maxwell, is sitting behind the desk, as *Handling Officer*?" Viggo asks puzzled by the revelation, and the young secretary understood what is going on, but she is caught between these two unusual characters, in her dilemma she has no other choice but to ask...

"Excuse me, Special-Agent Bronson, did I say something wrong?"

"Not at all. Ms. Betty, I assure you that everything is alright, this is a strange situation. It happens to be that Mrs. Maxwell is my wife; and I didn't expect to find myself, in this awkward situation. I want to find a simple way to explain what is happening, it all has to do with the fact that I didn't expect to find my wife, in the Santa Monica Bureau, in the H.O position!" *Viggo turns as if he is going to leave the place and spoke.* "How it can be passible, at the minute I arrived in L.A, the first thing I was facing, were few gangsters who want to eliminate me, and now I have to meet my wife, who wants to do the same: facing the gangsters was just an inconvenience, but dealing with my wife has another connotation!!" Viggo said facing the exist and Betty trying to help the restless man and she added...

"Special-Agent Bronson, if there is any way I could help, I would be happy to do so? The truth is, that Officer Maxwell is waiting for you" Ms. Betty said it with a face that says, it's not my fault. Viggo frustrated said...

"Please, let me explain Ms...."

"You don't have to, Special-Agent Bronson, I already know that Officer Maxwell is your wife, and I also know that you are temporarily at an impasse." She said it as if she was guilty to know those details and Viggo complacent responded...

"Ms. Betty, then I guess that you know all about our failing marriage, and also you must know, that I haven't seen my wife for almost two years, and that right now I don't have any other choice but to face her, and see what happens?" Ms. Betty was listening as she was saying I have nothing to do with all of this, and *Viggo began to walk nervously in the office, then he stopped in front of the secretary and spoke.* "Ms. Betty, this is not a pleasant situation: I appreciate your discreet silence, but you don't want be in my shoes!"

"I'm sure, your shoes are going to be immensely big for my feet, Special-Agent Branson." She said with a huge smile and Viggo smiling back responded...

"Thank you, Ms. Betty, for trying to get me off this unpleasant mood, where I'm bogged down!"

"Jest I'm trying help. Special-Agent Bronson, do you want to keep the appointment with Officer Maxwell, or you prefer to...?"

"Of course, I do, Ms. Betty, I just come all the way from New York, to find my dear wife as a H.O in L.A!" Viggo frustrated answered, and Miss. Betty noticed that the man was still irritated, and she pointed out...

"Special-Agent Bronson, tell me when you feel comfortable to see Officer Maxwell, then I will inform her that you are here, a matter of fact, she did clarify to me, that when you arrive, I should inform her immediately, she is waiting for you." She sweetly said, and Viggo trying to relax answered...

"Ms. Betty, the truth: this situation does not match with my expectations: because I didn't foresee this unpleasant welcome to Los Angeles. You have no idea what happened to us." Viggo said in a mysterious way, and she curiously asks...

"Something you mentioned before, about gangsters tried to eliminate you. What a horror!! What happened Special-Agent Bronson?" She asks with expression of surprise, and Viggo under the full attention of the young woman, he tells what happened...

"Ms. Betty, a few minutes after we left the airport, we were greeted by a hail of bullets, it was a vicious attack, from three merciless gangsters, in that skirmish, we miraculously saved our lives and, eliminating all those fierce gangsters: do you see how life play tricks on you, and now I have a mitting with Officer Maxwell. Ms. Betty, can you tell me, with what kind of humor my wife is waiting for me?"

"Of course: Officer Maxwell, is in a good mood as always, I think she is waiting for you with a smile. Special-Agent Bronson." She said getting all flushed and Viggo said...

"I hope so, we know that Officer Maxwell, is an excellent professional, I'm sure that at the moment we'll meet, she would be all business. Please Ms. Betty, let her know that I'm in your office, I will see what kind of reception I will have!" Viggo said worried about how his wife was going to greet him. It's possible that she is aware of all those women who took advantage of his sexuality, after she kicked him out of her life and his home, this is why Viggo is getting mentally ready to deny any accusation. Ms. Betty made the call, then she looks at Viggo and said...

"Officer Maxwell, will see you now Special-Agent Bronson, her office for security reasons is located in a strategic site, do you mind if I show you the way?"

"Not at all Ms. Betty, it will be a pleasure to have your help." Viggo said with an expression of approval, and she began to walk happily moving her hips like a cocktail shaker.

The secretary shows Viggo the way to Officer Ember Maxwell's office, and before leaving she said with a candid smile...

"If you need anything at all Special-Agent Bronson, you can find me in the office's, it would be a pleasure to help in whatever you need." Ms. Betty offer can be interpreted in many ways, and Viggo who picks up her suggestion answered...

"Believe me Ms. Betty, I won't forget that generous offer, I'll keep it in mind your proposal while I remain in L.A." Viggo responded with a smile, as he watches her walking away, but he remains in front of the office door, after waiting for a few seconds, he knocks at the door, and a firm voice answer the call...

"Come in please." Ember's voice following him as he enters the office: what Viggo, didn't know, is that his wife was ready to please him, like an anxious queen who is waiting for her lover in one of the palaces galleries, but she is not in that place. Ember is in her office enlightened with hope's. She was standing in front of her desk waiting for her husband, who cannot believe what his eyes are seeing, his wife was looking unbelievably beautiful. Ember, who made a passionate wrong decision at certain times, then later she regrets having done it, this is why Ember, was waiting for long time for this moment, she accumulated emotions that she cannot hold back anymore and, like uncontrolled tornado she busted the gates of feelings, those sentiments were held for a long time, and without saying a word, she began kissing him passionately. Viggo, who was taken by surprise, by her aggressive behavior, did not place any resistance and, gladly he engages in the passionate kiss of love and, what continues deserves to be told. Her audacity takes her a little bit further, because in the middle of the feverish kiss, she began molesting him, and with a voice that was choked with emotion Ember, expresses herself this way...

"My love, I can't live without you: this moment brings back memories of that wonderful day, where we went for a walk in Central Park, and those fabulous crazy two weeks, which we enjoyed in Atlantic City, I'm sure you didn't forget those days?"

"How could I forget, if I still have the viper inside my pants, the one you're trying to wake up!"

"I recall, at the time we were drinking a little too much, and it was in a moment of total happiness, that's when I suggested to engrave this gorgeous tattoo on your body: if I remember correctly, when the artist was engraving your tattoo, you didn't complain?"

"Please, don't go there. Ember, what happened in the past it will remain in the past, that should be the end of the story, because nothing we can do about it: time erases everything. Unfortunately, it does!" Viggo pointed out and Ember with a sweet caress responded...

"I'm sure, that the time won't erase this gorgeous tattoo." *She said and began sucking his lips and when she stops kissing him, she whispers in his ear.* "Viggo, there are lovely memories that remain in my heart, of those happy moments when your passionate kisses began on my lips, and slowly ended under..."

"Ember, don't lose your composure, you should not be so specific with your memories, and don't..."

"My love, you must know, what I have in my hands, for two years, my life was filled with happiness and pleasure. I love you, and I can't live without you. I hope that those feelings, you used-to have for me, still remains solid on your heart?"

"Please Ember, I thought you knew me better than that: I would never have married a woman I was not deeply in love with; don't tell me that you don't know, since you have these unique qualities, which awakens the passion of love in me?"

"It's amazing: don't you ever change Viggo? I know that you are a sweet talker, but for the sake of our marriage, I have to believe that you're telling the truth. I need to know about the..." Ember is interrupted by Viggo who sincerely tells her...

"I'm telling you the truth. Ember, we could still be together, if you hadn't broken up our marriage with your unfounded jealousy. I hope those feelings no longer linger in your heart, disturbing your soul, and poison your mind, with nonsense. I hope you understand what I'm saying Ember?"

"Please Viggo, don't do that to me, please, you don't see that I am suffering from a penalty of guilt: from which I can't forgive myself, for how unfair I was with you!" She says trying to kiss him, and Viggo says seriously...

"Ember, right now, you must consider the factors, that lead us to the situation, in which right now we find ourselves, you have to understand, that after few months of our relationship, you really thought I was unfaithful, and that situation made me very uncomfortable, in all aspects of my life?" Viggo said sadly and Ember replied...

"Darling, I was so in love with you: anything that was flying around you, clouded my reason and, I could not control myself. I'm confessing my feelings with my heart in my hands, I was and I'm very much in love with you, the feelings I have for you are so special that I will never be able to replace-it with another person and, I swear to that!" She said almost crying and Viggo responded hugging her and he responded...

"Look Ember, I don't know if you know, that I was quite uncomfortable with your constant suspicions..."

"Not right now Viggo!!"

"Ember, please, I must tell you how I felt, if we are to continue this relationship?"

"Okay, if you put it that way, I'm listening."

"I told you at the time, and I'll tell you now. Ember, your suspicions were unfounded and, you must admit; you have no proof of my infidelity, it wasn't my fault, if you believed that every woman I was talking to, I ended up having sex with that person..." Ember interrupts him, and caressing his face said...

"Please Viggo, we better leave this topic for another time, I'm so happy that you are here with me, and, after that terrible ambush you've had, thanks that you are unharmed, in my arms!!!" She happily embracing Viggo tying to appease her brief and he added...

"Ember, I always thought, that to had you in my life, I was the luckiest man in the world, and I have to say, that you are looking like the day we met, gorgeous: please let me look at you." Viggo said and took a step back looking at his wife, and Ember very gracious to the praise responded...

"Thanks' my love, your words gave me the hopes I need, in this turmoil times: sometimes life seems so difficult, at the same time so simple, because, if we love each other, we should return to our nest, where it all started?" Ember asks looking straight in his eye, and Viggo agreed and pointed out...

"Ember, your conclusions are logical, it appeals to me. I also want to say, that when I found you as a handling officer, I didn't know exactly what I was going to expect from you, it was a surprise...from I must recover!" Viggo said trying to get off topic, and Emer asks...

"Don't tell me, that you are disappointed, that I'm the handling officer?"

"Quite the opposite Ember, I thought that I was going to meet a frustrated Officer Morris, who can't do his job properly, and I show up to clear his mess, and to my amazement, in his position, I found my beautiful wife?"

"Viggo, you must know, that I'm so happy to have you in my office!" She said kissing Viggo who was a little overwhelmed by the kisses and he replies...

"Officer Maxell, the reason why I came to this office is to acquire information, from Officer Ian Morris, and I'm sorry that FBI Director, left you in the middle of this mess, but right now, you must deal with this situation, and for some reason, Franklin, believe it's not working as it should be, otherwise he would not have sent me, to help solve this case, his decision puzzling me, maybe you can enlighten me, why I am here?"

"Especial-Agent Bronson, I assure you, that everything is under control, of course, with some minor issues, because your arrival in L.A, has created a great commotion between foreign agents, these guys became nervous and reckless dangers!"

"Ember, if these guys are in disarray, it's better for us, the more worried they are, it will be easy to identify these agents, you better have some info for me, because Mr. Franklin, didn't came through with anything!" Viggo said resign his harms and Ember ask...

"I know how you feel about Franklin, tell me, what has happened, that for some reason rattle your nerves?"

"It is simple Ember, Mr. Franklin, sent this guard of the law, with no info I can following to solve a priority case of espionage." *He paused for a second and spoke.* "Ember, speaking about the subject, it would be really helpful if you let me know, what's going on with this guy Santino Pascucci?"

"Viggo, I'm surprised that you include this gangster, in a moment where our relationship begins walking the path to solve our differences?" She said kissing Viggo who can't believe what he was hearing and Viggo answers...

"Please, we'll have a lot of time for future plans. Ember, give time a chance to react, since this situation is the least, I expected. Okay?"

"Okay my love, if you prefer to go straight to business: I believe that Mr. Santino Pascucci didn't feel very safe when you arrived in L.A, he was sure that you would be a compelling threat to him, that's why he sent he's three bodyguards to stop you, and thanks to your skills, to resolve dangerous cases, you were able to come out alive from that cowardly ambush, I believe, that we should celebrate this heroic act, with a self-indulgent night: what do you say?" Ember said kissing and caressing him and Viggo responded...

"What am I saying, I love it. But Ember, how in the hell do you know all these details?" Viggo asks puzzled, and Ember very affectionate responded.

"Viggo, before you arrived at the office, the authorities had the courtesy of calling, and the police chief told me all about the incident, in which the well-known Special-Agent Bronson, was involved in a fierce attack with gangsters, that's how I found out about it. So, you must be very careful when you move around this city." *She paused for a second and said with a sarcastic smile.* "Because the authorities would tell me everything you do!"

"It's good to know that, Ember. I see, in these latitudes, the news travels quite fast?"

"A matter of fact, Special-Agent Bronson, when I took over this office. Officer Morris, let me know that this Bureau, always collaborate with the local authorities, and therefore, when the police chief believes, that certain crimes must be investigated by the FBI, they call us, as in this case. I have nothing to do with these policy's, I just inherited it. Viggo, I only follow the rules." Ember said with a sexual attitude, and Viggo who can't take his eyes off his wife asks...

"Ember, seems to me, that communications between authorities are friendly and fluid, I'm sure that you can tell me, how the fuck Pascucci knew I was coming to L.A, I can't find an answer to this question? And I'm really troubled by the notion, that the info leaked by someone from the Bureau!"

"Viggo, the only procedure I can implement in this case is to follow the protocol, and see what I can find out, in the meantime we have to celebrate that you're in one piece, because I have immediate plans for you, and Mr. Pascucci can wait." Ember said kissing him with passion, and Viggo when he could catch his breath said...

"Ember, in this conglomerate of emotions, I must tell you, that I missed your kisses a lot, that continue to have the sweetness of honey, plus the passion you put in them is amassing, and you using them to drive me crazy!"

"Viggo, your sweet words bring calm in my soul, but at the same time they make me feel guilty: I hate that, since I'm very sorry for what I did to you!!"

"Ember, things are not as complicated as they seem; if in the near future, we decide to rebuild our relationship, we must leave the past where should it be in the past, and you will see, how wide and clear the horizon opens up in your life, then we can approach the future without any fear. I think it is the best way to proceed. Don't you think?"

"I agree: Viggo, I don't want to keep suffering, because of my lack of confidence, I do not want to lose you again, so you will find a different woman in me!" She said looking at him with affection and Viggo continued saying...

"Ember, there is something that puzzles me, it's very coincidental finding you here in L.A, I really thought you were the officer in charge, at the Chicago Bureau, do you have something to do with the transferred?" Viggo asks, and meanwhile Ember is busy trying to lower his pants, Viggo who is overwhelmed by the situation whispered...

"Come on Ember; don't you think your office is the wrong place?" Viggo said keeping his pants in place, Ember paused for a second, looking like she's planning something: She was! Then with a smile she proposed...

"Listen Viggo, it's two o'clock, don't you agree that it's too late to discuss this assignment that brought you to L.A, maybe...?" Viggo interrupted...

"Ember, what kind of arrangement you're traying to organize?"

"It's nothing unpleasant, quite the opposite, why don't we have an early dinner at my place, which is in walking distance from this office: A matter of fact: we can celebrate this happy reunion with a glass of champagne, or do you have any other commitments Mr. Bronson?" Ember asked kissing him, and Viggo can't refuse such an offer. Then, they walk holding hands, the short distance to her place. Once inside the apartment, Viggo is thinking that Rachel will be waiting for him to have dinner, and he pointed out...

"Ember, I have to call my partner Rachel, because when we are on an assignment, usually we have dinner together, you don't know her, but I'm sure that you know her reputation, she is well known as Rocky at the Bureau." Viggo explained the situation, and Ember who at this moment would allow him to do whatever he wishes, and she pointed out...

"I know Rachel reputation; I find out that she's really beautiful and a tough cookie and, don't forget, that you are her superior, I hope you are not taking advantage of her?" She said looking straight in Viggo's eyes, and he with a straight poker face answered...

"I don't know who I'm talking to, about this issue, if it's my jealous wife, or to my gorgeous *Handling Officer*, who doesn't have to remind me, what is ethical proper or morally correct. Okay?"

"Well, sometimes it's worth remind to the agents, the principles of ethics, this way the subordinates don't derail on the way forward in their duties!" Ember said seriously and Viggo responded...

"It all depends on the circumstances, which one is in, also it depends on the time and the place Officer Maxwell, because on this treacherous road that we are traveling, there are certain rules to follow, for instance, the legendary proverb of the Urban Literature says. "You don't shit where you eat." Okay Ember?" Viggo said raising his arms, and Ember has some doubts about his answers, and she replies...

"Mr. Cocky Pants: that's only fancy talk; what you are saying is one thing, but..." *Ember, is looking at Viggo, who it's gazing at her waiting for what she was going to say, and when she saw that expectant attitude, wisely she reverses the course of want she really want to say.* "Viggo, I only hope that you are following those rules?"

"Please Ember, hoping is a guessing games, which never will lead you to the truth of the matter, without trusting, how can you live in peace. Okay?"

"You know Viggo, what the famous Philosopher Confucius, a day that he was inspired said. —That curiosity, is one of the enemies of the human being, but then, regular people place the proverb in context and said." "That curiosity killed the cat!!" Ember said with a smile and Viggo asks...

"Where, do you want to go, with this mumbo jumbo?" Viggo said with a surprised face and Ember with a happy face replied...

"Well, it is all about curiosity; I'm guessing that many curious women wanted to see the anaconda tattoo, just tell me if I'm wrong Mr. Bronson?" Ember asks kissing him, and Viggo seriously said.

"Please Ember, this comment was out of line. I don't have to remind you, that the glorious tattoo was your clever idea, and don't let those traces of jealousy surface in your mind again, it is not healthy for our future relationships. Okay?"

"My love don't be so serious, and please call your partner, and relax I'm going to go change. Okay?" Ember looks at her husband with love and turns around and discreetly she went to her bedroom, then Viggo has the chance to call Rachel, and told her that he is stranded in a strange situation, that he will explain tomorrow all about what is going on, that he and *Handling Officer,* during dinner they will discuss matters of the case. —But, Rocky, who has very refined sixth sense: She is suspecting that something isn't right, and for a couple of minutes she got him against the ropes, asking questions, which Viggo answered the best he could. Finally, Viggo, told her that she should go ahead and have dinner, but before she hung up, Rachel was not happy at all, and started mumbling words that Viggo could not understand.

After avoiding all those inquisitive questions from his partner. Viggo, took his jacket off, and threw it on the nearest chair, then as he was waiting for his wife, he did walk to the petite bar and pick up a bottle of scotch, then poured himself a drink, already a little bit more relaxed, waiting for his unpredictable wife, he is sitting on the comfortable couch in the living room: at that moment Viggo, began to sense pleasant sensations of the past, those feelings remind him of the times he lived with his wife, and right now the scent of her fragrance is reaching his senses, it's the perfume that his wife always wore at the time she was ready to join him in bed, that scent is like a spell that he could never eradicated from his senses, and in those nostalgic moments he asked himself. "What the hell is she up to? I can sense her perfume; I know that she is getting ready for me?" Viggo, doesn't finish saying the phrase, that's when Viggo, can see the way his wife show's up in the living room: It was a marvelous royal entrance!!!

She was wearing a skimpy white see-through negligee, that leaves her marvelous body exposed: Viggo's eyes quite widen in surprise. This display of beauty, would give emotional problems to any normal man, is amazing the sex-appeal that she shows for him to admire. Ember remains the sexiest woman he ever knew; She looks absolutely gorgeous; it brings back memories of their honeymoon. Viggo with a lot of mixed emotions expressed his feelings...

"Ember, you look gorgeous, like in our honeymoon, it is amazing, because I feel the same sensations as that night, it was like a torrent of desires invaded my body. I hope you remember as I..." Viggo could not finish the sentences, because Ember sees the opportunity and like a flaming eagle she lands in his arms, in that spontaneous moment she kisses him passionately, after caching her breath she asks...

"I sure remember, it was a very special moment, now you tell me, what do you remember about that night?" Ember ask caressing Viggo who answers...

"I was hoping that you had changed, but you always want to put me to task. Ember, you're implying that I wasn't aware of what was going on, in our honeymoon? That's what it looks like to me!"

"My love, this question to you, is just to support my ego, remember, I'm a woman and when I love, I do it passionately, and my love for you, leads me to do things, that really I don't want to do!"

"Ember, you're loaded with illusions, and now you're shooting cupids arrows into my heart. I don't want you to keep doubting me. I'm tell you, I never forgot that memorable night."

"Okay, let's see I'm all ears!"

"This answer, is just to please your ego..."

"Come on, Viggo!

"Okay, Ember, I recall that we're in our honeymoon room and, that evening, decorating the night it was a huge shiny pearl, floating in the sky, it was the curious moon, who was illuminating our honeymoon room, that's when I saw through the white negligee, your marvelous body, at that instant, you look like a gorgeous nymph, which was floating in the warm tropical air..." *In that instant she grabbed his face with both hands, and she said...*"My love, you remain a box full of surprises, I can't believe it that you remember every detail of that night, I was so wrong: and I apologize to you." Then with the passion of a woman in love vehemently she kisses him.

Viggo, short of breath ignored her last comment and with a romantic voice pointed out...

"I'm amazed Ember, you're a unique woman, still you keep having in your kisses the sweetness of honey and, that volcano of passion, which alters the beat of my heart, I'm sure that one of these days, I'm going to die in your arms!"

"Not a chance my love, it's more than certain, that I'll die in the arms of this rough tough man, so get ready, because I'll try to make up for the lost time with my husband, who really surprises me, remembering every detail of our honeymoon!!"

"Hold on: being tough, doesn't mean that a man can't be sensitive and, caring about that special person you are in love with. Ember, there are certain moments in a person's life, which remain forever impressed on their memory, I guess you know all the parts of that life?"

"Please Viggo, stop saying sweet phrases, make me feel more guilty than ever. I lost two years of happiness, for not being at your side, that situation will not be repeated, I promise!"

"Hey, it's no need to punish yourself that way. I still have deep feelings in my heart because I never stopped loving you, I hope you realize that a person does not stop loving just like that: the feelings of love don't come equipped with sophisticated brakes, you can't stop loving a person just like that? I'm sure that I will carry this love all my life, even if you don't love me." Viggo was quite sincere when he expressed his feelings, he is very much in love with his wife, and he 'believes' that she has the same feelings, but he has a hard time forgetting all those episodes of jealousy, which tormented him daily. A matter of fact, if we are going to get deep into her displaying of sexy attitude in front of Viggo, with the passing of time, we'll find out, that Ember has only one purpose, that's to get her husband back, but still, she can't forgive herself: how could she? If she did chase him, out of their home over a nonsense rage of jealousy! And right now, to the love of her life, she wants to make amends; hopefully it's not too late, because Viggo, just finishes saying: that his feelings towards his wife remain intact, and, right now Ember, is extremely happy in his arms; then, with her heart in her hands, overflowing with emotion she asks...

"Viggo, if I heard you correctly, you're implying that your feelings remain like the time we were together? If this is the case, you just made me the happiest woman in the world!" Ember excitedly asks and Viggo replied...

"Yes, I did, but you must not exaggerate my comment. Ember, the feeling of love it's simple, or do you love or don't. I love you, and I always will!"

"My love, I can't describe in words your attitude, that is so candid and generous and, your behavior fills my soul with emotions, you're so sweet and kind, I don't know how I will reward you!" Ember full of expectations manifest her emotions and Viggo added...

"Ember, you can recompence me, with stopping doubting about my feelings, because deep in your heart, I'm sure you know, that my love for you still flaming and, you can feel the sensations in my body, when I put my heart and soul in a kiss of love on your lips." Viggo romantically whispered in her ear. Those words make her heart start beating desperately; it's the candid tenderness of Viggo that is driving her crazy, and she can't control herself, then desperately she got busy undressing that mountain of muscles that her husband is made of, and in that moment of intense passion, she is designing in her mind, the kind of sexual indulgences she is going to give to him. *This is the time to make amends, I'm going to pleasure him with love until one of us collapses of passion.* Well, her wishes were granted, because in this hot and steamy relationship, the rules in this love affair don't exist, during a very passionate and wild sexual ritual, which started on the couch, and then with an uncontrolled passion, continued rolling on the padded carpet in the living room, and for almost one hour only you could hear the sexy moaning of Ember: "Please... Easy'V... Easy' Viggo...Please my love..." The pleading: was not a request for clemency; occurred that in the ecstasy of enjoyment, she was ready to faint with pleasure, finally: after the couple was exhausted, they crawled up to the couch, and Viggo is holding his wife in his arms, and, between the scent of sex and perfume Viggo commented out of breath...

"Officer Maxwell, I would like to say, if at the last moment, the agenda did not change, I recall that I came here to have dinner? If the menu started with this kind of amazing meal, before dessert I would like to take a shower?"

"I'm glad that you enjoy it My love, it was not a dinner, but the meal was served piping hot!" Ember said kissing Viggo who responded...

"I must tell you, the dinner was hot and delicious, now I would like to know what you have for dessert, a volcano cake, with a cherry on top? That dessert it would complete this amazing night!" Viggo said embracing Ember, and she proposes...

"I'm sure that I have the answer for my sweet husband. If you want to indulge in a delicious dessert, I know a discreet place, where we can have dinner, and continue talking about our future projects. One thing I regret, is that you are here officially and, not on vacation!" Ember said in the arms of her husband completely naked and Viggo who added...

"Seems to me, that the destiny has conspired for us to meet again..." *Viggo, said unaware that Ember had made a plot for this event to happen, and Viggo goes on and saying.* "Ember, about going to the restaurant, it is a very good idea, and meantime, during dinner also we can talk about the mission that brought me to L.A, a matter of fact, I came to see Officer Morris, and instead, I found a beautiful woman waiting in disguise, with her honeymoon negligée and, ready to capture the attention of a naïve man..."

"If I start to reason, and I guided myself by your present attitude, what I see so far Viggo, is that you are really happy and, enjoying my company, or am I wrong?"

"For sure Ember, I'm really happy, the truth is that I had a hard time recovering from the surprise, to find you in the position of H.O in LA!" Viggo pointed out, then as if he came into this world: Naked holding his wife in his arms, he began walking towards the bathroom: and the passion began to flutter under the warm shower, as if it were a little game, she began playing with Viggo's tattoo, this alive object drives her crazy, and Viggo, who ignites at the first scrape like a match, he began kissing her and all aroused under the warm waters he turned her around, and she ends up facing the tiles...she sensed what was going to occur, and said in a whisper. "Viggo, not there...not there." It was too late. He continued pressing her against the tiles...in that instant she began to enjoy the warm hot shower...until enthralled with pleasure she was scratching the tiles. —After the hot...sweet shower, they dress comfortable, and the two federal agents *releasing steam from their bodies*; they walked a few blocks for an early dinner at Ember's favorite restaurant, at...

LA FORCHETTA

La Forchetta: is one of those upscale Italian restaurants, that's known for their well-designed private booths, which is usually frequented by lovers, who can discreetly *talk,* without being seen by inquisitive eyes. The location also has large rooms, which are reserved by a certain brand of tycoons, who between the exquisite meals and sipping expensive wines, these moguls take their time to arranged numerous shady deals. —In the other hand, there are the 'honest' corporations, which their CEO'S getting together in the private booths, to conspire which will be the best way, to screw the working people: Well, these hypocrites, concluded, that they would make billions of dollars, sending to China, and other countries, the jobs of the American workers: and they call themselves Americans? I don't have the proper insult to name these guys. —But, in this shitty mix, we should not forget the white-collar scoundrel's, laundering billions of dollars in Panama, Brazil and Uruguay. These outlaws are always ready to make those worldwide Machiavellian arrangements, smuggling weapons around the world destabilizing countries. —Inside the establishment there is a person who 'maybe' don't know about all those organizations: it could be because she is new to her job? Well, let's give her the benefit of the doubt: for sure, this place it suits her, to manipulate her situation and, there she was...

Ember, who chooses to have dinner at La Forchetta, in order to continue what she started in her place; recuperate the love of her husband, because these private booths will keep them away from the curious eyes, and they can enjoy a romantic dinner, looking into each other's eyes talking about those gloomy days, they suffered during their separation. —At the end of dinner; Viggo made a sign to the waiter, who knew it was time to bring a bottle of champagne, they ended up crossing arms toasting for a bright future. Ember wished that these romantic moments never ended, she is quite motivated and expresses her feelings this way...

"My love, I'm so happy that you don't hold any grudges in your heart, I feel deep inside my soul, that what happened tonight, is the spark that ignites a new beginning in our relationship. I hope you feel in your heart the same feelings. Those are my sincere wishes!" Ember said holding Viggo's hands as her eyes tear up, then Viggo reached over the table and kisses her tenderly and said...

"Ember, I assure you, that my feelings for you haven't changed, from the moment I fall in love with you, but if in the near future, we agree to live together, you must promise that I won't confront in our relationship the previous situation, which I suffered in silence?" Viggo expressed his feelings, and Ember was surprised by his thoughts, and with tears rolling down her cheeks she said...

"Viggo, you should know how much I regret what I did to you: I'm sorry, it was my feverish love for you, that overwhelms my tender feeling for you and, I'm sorry, if our marriage was destroyed, because I didn't have confidence in your faithfulness, if I was acting like a spoiled child, please forgive me!" Ember said as tears rolled down her cheek. Viggo who could feel her emotions is trying to give her hope...

"Ember, remember, since your attacks of jealousy began, I was trying to understand the origin of those feelings, and I was desperate because I couldn't find the reason..." *Ember, wanted to speak but he stopped her with a gesture.* "Ember, the feeling of guilty that you have right now, they won't solve the future dilemmas: the outlook of our situation should be focused on the future: remember that we have our whole lives ahead of us, and we are the ones who rule our life, nobody else, will come to your rescue, when you are sinking your life in the fog of doubts."

"I understand what you're saying Viggo, because I already learn my lesson by missing you immensely, and I felt very guilty. I'm assure you, that the flame of love for you, will never stop burning, I will try my best to change, I promise you, that..."

"Please, calm down Ember, we will have a lot of time to talk about our relationship. Remember, that I came here to solve this espionage case, which requires my full attention, and I don't have to tell you, that it's a dangerous situation. Ember, it would be better if we place our relationship on hold, until we finish with this assignment, then the future is going to look clear, without the fantasies, which will cloud our way to happiness, don't you agree?" Viggo asks seriously, and Ember with a happy face she answers...

"Please Viggo, needless to say, that I will wait for you as long as necessary, but with one condition, I would like..."

"Please, Ember, don't start with the same old head games, it's not healthy for our future relationship, I hope you can understand, that jealousy was the cause which contribute to the collapse of our marriage!!" Viggo points out, and Ember very clever changes the meaning of her request and said...

"Viggo, please, let me finish what I was trying to say."

"I'm sorry Ember?"

"A matter of fact, I wasn't referring to an act of infidelity, what I was trying to suggest, that in the future, you will be in the same loving mood you're showing today to me?" She asked as she kissed him, and Viggo raised his eyebrows as if he was saying. I have already traveled this controlling road before. —Right now, Viggo is trying to consolidate certain rules that keep the marriage happy and united, and at the same time: attempting to unload those chains of control, which had held him a prisoner of his own passionate love.

A matter of fact: If we study with detention, the word *jealousy*: we will find, that the *word jealous,* should not actually exist: the term *jealous* expresses an emotional condition of the human mind, which create imaginary situations, that is only in your imagination, the mind generates events that do not exist, this mental disorder, can lead to unleash outrageous situations, which you never thought, you could do for pure control; unfortunately the harsh reality, manifests itself when you realize: the heart of the matter, it has nothing to do with jealousy, since this unbalanced state of mine, doesn't counterpart with the real intention of the person. —Because, behind the word *jealous:* it's concealing the real purpose of word *jealous,* which-is *Control.* —*Nothing else but control, that's what this person pretends to exercise over the other; it's just control; nothing else but a pretext to control the other.* —And right now, it is what his wife Ember, is trying to do. She is trying to cover up her cynical intentions, which are: Controlling the air he breathe, his actions, the times, his moments and the man, who by this time: from childhood, his life was well trained by his mother: with the ancestral mandate, that establishes the transfer from his motherhood to the lap of another woman. *That's why the man in his candid innocence, really believes that a woman who is not the mother, can love him like the mother does. Do not confuse affection with love: a woman who is not your mother, can give you a lot of affection, but at the moment you do something wrong, those feelings disappear instantly, and don't forget. Okay?* —And here we have the example: Viggo, who is struggling with his feelings, because the man knows he is in love with his wife, but he has his doubts about her wife's love, and he expresses his concerns this way...

"I don't have to tell you, that I'm enjoying your company. Ember, I hope, you were aware that when we were together, we live pleasant moments, like the ones we are living right now, those happy times, should not be spoiled with the desire, to control me or my life, I hope that approach is well kept in the past?" Viggo asks sweetly and Ember trying to correct what she said before she said...

"Viggo, I don't have to tell you, since we met again, I love the candid attitude you're showing to me, it's amazing, makes me feel like a privileged woman!" Ember said squeezing his hands, and Viggo anxious to do his job responds...

"Please, be considered, think about what brought me here? Ember, when all this mess is resolved and, I capture Pascucci, then we'll discuss our relationship. It's essential that I have access to the files of this case, then I can proceed with the investigation according to the findings. Look, the sooner I finish with this investigation, the sooner we will try to organize our lives. Okay?" Viggo said with the seriousness that the case requires, and Ember responded appropriately...

"You have no idea, what I'm going through, in the last two days I was dealing with the director of *Homeland Security*, they want me to solve this case as soon as possible. Viggo, at this moment I don't know, which company is involved with the new space project. Maybe I should call the NSA=National Security Agency..." *She pauses for few seconds, and she grabs her head with both hands and said* "Viggo, here in California we have under surveillance three scientific laboratories, and we still don't know, which is the research company that is involved in this sophisticated defense system. I have called the director for this matter, and his response was, do your job and don't ask questions." Ember said frustrated and Viggo concerned added...

"Fuck, it doesn't make sense Ember, why the HS=*Homeland Security* doesn't give us the information. It must be a new policy, that makes espionage and intricate undertaking, but at the same time, our investigation process, becomes quite awkward, dangerous and unpredictable, this attitude of the HS, it is a contradiction against all codes." Viggo pointed out, and Ember in a confidential way she agrees and said...

"Viggo, I wonder, why the *Homeland Security,* hinted to the press, the notion, that under the government contract, there was more than one enterprise, developing this new project. Then, in the news they mentioned the companies, that I knew, because these corporations have the engineering capability, to create a defense system or any other space weapon." *She paused for a second, and looks with love to her husband, who listens in silence, and then she gets up and sits next to him and spoke.* "Viggo, we can continue this conversation in the apartment, and you can stay overnight, and tomorrow morning when you get up, your favorite breakfast will be ready on the table: it is not a lovely idea?" Ember proposes, and she begins to kiss him, and Viggo a little bit annoyed by her continues aggressive loving attitude suggests...

"Please, Ember, I suggest in this situation, that we begin with caution, to resuming our relationship. I don't want to hurt your feelings or consequently mine, and I'm sure that you can sense that I'm enjoying a lot being with you!"

"Viggo, it's not easy for me, to put into words what I'm going through, lately I had to take pill to get to sleep, my conscience would not leave me alone?"

"I'm sorry Ember, I know exactly what is going through your head, since I am in the same situation, to resolve this impasse, we must begin to trust each other and, on the road to happiness, let's get rid of, all the ghosts that haunt us."

"I couldn't have said it better. Viggo, I just want to be happy by your side my love." Ember said romantically and Viggo partially ignores the comment and changes the topic...

"Please Ember, let's put aside our private life, and let's try to focus seriously, on the investigation, remember that a few hours ago, a bunch of gangsters tried to get rid of me..."

"Wait a minute: Viggo, you are not accusing me of negligence?"

"Please, Ember, I just wanted to know, how the fuck these gangsters knew that I was coming to L.A. This situation worries me, since this event, it may happen again, these loose ends, could cost other agents lives, don't you agree?" Viggo asks with the sense of gravity and Ember responded...

"Okay, Viggo, if you want to change this romantic moment, with the figure of a gangster? Let's do it, but like you see, this is a private lounge, if you let me give you some private caresses, I will..."

"What are you trying say?"

"My love, just a sweet blow job."

"Ember, please, get in the role of H.O, and help in this case?

"You...you are impossible!! Okay Viggo, let's look at Mr. Pasccuci's actions, because under the prospectus of the mentality of this gangster, he came to the conclusion, that your presence in this town, has a potential threat to his dealing with the foreign agents, that's why he sent his best men to get rid of you, and you had the guts to eliminate those gangsters, then before you get to him, he just disappears, like he did ten years ago." *She pauses to sip a little bit of champagne, and she whispered.* "Viggo, you...you have become the terror of the delinquents..."

"Come on, Ember, praising me, is not going to make our relationship better." Viggo said seriously and Ember ignore the comment and continue saying...

"You just placed this guy out of business. Viggo, right now those foreign agents, are eager to get information, since their connection flew away the cuckoo's nest, and Pasccuci, can't be replaced, this why the foreign agents should look for other options!" Ember commented with seriously, and Viggo is trying to intrigue his wife and said...

"Ember, the bird flew out of the nest, but Pasccuci left behind a fucking mess, and now we have to deal with it, but what he doesn't know, that I know where to start the investigation."

"What are you trying to imply. What do you know that I don't...Special-Agent Bronson?"

"Ember, at the instant I saw you in your office, and you were waiting for me, more beautiful than ever: from that moment, our meetings were hot and steamy; this why I didn't tell you, the info I have in my position..."

"Hold on Viggo, what are you trying to say, that you were withholding info from me?"

"Not really, Officer Maxwell, because you were very busy trying to make up for the lost time, and you...and you didn't give me the chance to tell you what I know, and that's what you did to me Ember." Viggo tries to say it sweetly and Ember react as they do, when you find a woman in a committed act- she reacts pissed off...

"That's not a very good comment Viggo, and what are you trying to say: I didn't give you any chance? I didn't see any gag that would prevent you from speaking. Okay? And please, don't patronize me. Mr. hot pants and tell me what you know!" Ember pretends to be angry just to hide her guilt and Viggo ignores her attitude just to continue the relationship in peace and he said...

"Please, Ember. It wasn't easy for me, since first, I found you in the position of HO, and second, when I walked into your office, you didn't let me speak, after closing the door you kissed me so passionately that I almost fainted, then you did try to pull my pants down, you didn't give me the time or the place to tell you anything, then, I still have a hard time believing that you are my Superior." Viggo, didn't want to be interrupts by his wife, this why he said that whole phrase almost without breathing and Ember looking at him with sorrow and affection said...

"Don't change the subject Viggo, and tell me what you know, if not...I'll squeeze your..."

"No...please, it won't be necessary, because I'm already know, which company was chosen by the NSA, to send to orbit the space system." Viggo said it, with the face that said, I didn't do it, and Ember overreacted...

"Viggo, you were withholding life and death data, to your superior, it's not proper at all: how dare you? I can't believe you did that to me, and…and I would like to know how did you get that info, it should have been the first thing you should tell me. Viggo, at the moment you don't…"

"Please, Ember, if I didn't tell you sooner. it's because you were waiting for me, with more sex-appeal than ever, and your beauty made me forget about everything. Look Ember, I tried…"

"Come on Viggo, you're teasing me, and you know that I hate that, just tell me which company has the contract and, how did you get the information? The question is simple, which company has the…?"

"Okay: Ember, at the moment, I made the decision to get the info, it wasn't easy, the situation was very dangerous…"

"Just tell me what I want to know or I'll…"

"Okay…Okay, when I face the Pascucci goons in the shootout, one of the men before he died, in his last breath, he told me which is the name, that we needed to complete our puzzle. Ember, it is obvious, who is selling the secrets, I'm sure, is one of the engineers who're developing the defense system, in the company lab." Viggo informs with confidence, and Ember who was surprised by the revelation inquires…

"I'm amazed, that you were able to extract information from a gangster who was dying! Viggo, I hope that in the process you didn't break the law?" Ember said holding his hands and Viggo with a poker face responded…

"I would never do that Ember; I did what any good FBI agent should do, obey the rules of engagement, and I follow the sequences of the law, step by step; at that time, I was in the process to…"

"I'm sure that you know all the rules, but in this case what sequences of the law, did you follow Special-Agent Bronson?"

"Please, Ember, the simple things in life, usually don't come to light, because, they are irrelevant, but in this case, what do you think, that I was hunting butterflies? A was dealing with three gangsters that were trying really hard, to get rid of me; all this happened in a few minutes, and in heat of the battle, in those moments of anxiety, I blasted the gangster's car and, the vehicle was on fire ready to explode, inside the burning car, was laying one of these bastards, I pull him out and, I couldn't waste the opportunity to interrogate this gangster. I only had few seconds to assess the situation, and I said to myself, I must get some information from that poor sinner. I grab him from his jacket, and very gently I pulled his face against mine, and I told him: if you don't tell me what you know, I'm not calling the ambulance; I'm sure the guy didn't want to die in the street full of blood; that's when he did tell me what he knew!" Viggo put a little bit of drama in his story, he would never tell her the truth, that he was willing to shove his gun up his ass, then Ember not very pleased responded...

"Viggo that's not proper, those kinds of torture perform, are against our regulations!"

"What regulations? Ember, these gangsters have no rules, and this guy was terrified with the prospect of dying in the street?"

"And what the hell, this person said? Can you answer that simple question Viggo?

"Ember, don't be so anxious..."

"You are teasing my patience, and you know that I hate that!" Ember said making a gesture with her hands like she was ready to choke Viggo who said...

"Okay, Mother Teresa, I'm just going to say that I was very nice with this piece of crap, who tries to send me to hell, the paradox is that he died in my arms...peacefully." Viggo said it in a secretive way, and Ember responded...

"How dare you call me Mother Teresa? Viggo, it's all I need from you, and stop acting mysteriously, and tell me the name of the goddamn company."

"Okay...Okay Ember, we have to give time to the time, and I'll tell you how I got the info. Okay?"

"Come on Viggo, don't play with me this dumb game, because I'm going to use one of your techniques, and I'm going to grab your bal...?" And she was ready to do it and Viggo reacted and said...

"Stop their Ember: because squeezing balls is what I do, but only to obtain fast and accurate information and, this is how you treat me, after I went through so many struggles, jumping all those hurdles full of danger, to get info, from this guy who tried to kill me." *Ember, listened attentively, thinking that he was going to enlarge what happened to make her to be proud of him and he goes on saying.* "Ember, I was sorry for the man, because he was in very bad condition, then I open my heart and I offered him my lap, then he could die in peace in my arms, but before he got out of this world, he gave me the info I was looking for, and this man in his last breath said...*The Bremen Company*." Viggo said it in a whisper with a straight face and Ember can't control herself and added...

"I'm so proud of you Viggo, and it has to be none other than The Bremen Company? Viggo, I swear, I thought the NSA =*National Security Agency*, thrown the name of this private enterprise, as a diversion, into the different groups of companies, just to confuse the foreign agent's, what I don't understand is the purpose of misleading the federal agents, who are really the ones who risk their lives, to solve their incompetence!"

"Are you mentioning it, like it's something new! Ember, those are the leaders who send us to the front lines, as they sit very relaxed behind their desks, smoking cigars, talking about politics, if these people don't agree with the government in charge, they try to do their best to destabilize-it, sheltered under their position." Viggo said with a rebellious attitude and, Ember for a few seconds lowered her head thinking and, when she lifted, she commented...

"You are right: Viggo, I don't understand what kind of solution the NSA director, pretended to achieve in this case: because as far as I know, this course of action has no precedent in the Bureau?" Ember said frustrated and Viggo responded.

"What I really know Ember, is that I was not properly informed, about this project, which should be of extreme importance for the NGA=National Geospatial Agency, and now I'm finding out, that from the beginning, this project has been highly classified; this sequences happened, until one of those geniuses in the NGA, came to the conclusion that in the Lab, there was someone who had access to the designs and, consequently was compromising their project, and they tried to solve the dilemma, in a conventional way, but all the brains in the NGA, failed to accomplish the objective, and they find themselves how they started empty-handed, not knowing what to do next; since they were committed with the Feds: then the NGA director, become desperate and, don't have other option but to ask for our help!" Viggo commented, and Ember with a very sweet smile agree...

"I couldn't have explained better Viggo, because I'm sure that the NGA was boxed in, locked in their own messy procedures, and to get out fast of that situation, the director had no choice but to call the FBI, and asked if they could send their best agent's, with the hope, that we will solve this case of espionage." Ember said it like it was the right thing to do, but behind that phrase, she's hiding the truth; because she was the person who called the New York Bureau, asking Officer Franklin, to send Special-Agent Viggo Bronson, to investigate into a case of espionage in California. That was Ember's motivation to bring her husband to the City of Santa Monica, which would give her the opportunity, to see if she can seduce her husband, and bring him back into her life. Viggo who ignores her clever manipulations, answers to her pretended doubt...

"I agree Ember, but still I wander about this mission, because Mr. Franklin sends me to oversee an investigation, which was already in progress, and the info I got from him is so vague, that I didn't know where to start investigating..."

"Come on Viggo, you should not be so skeptical."

"Skeptical Ember? If I just woke up, from the lethargy that this moron placed me in a matter of fact, I just opened my eyes, at the moment these bunch of gangsters, welcomed me to L.A, with a barrage of bullets, that's when I realized that this assignment has another connotation, because without the appropriate information, I couldn't evaluate how dangerous the assignment was. Talking about Mr. Franklin: I remember that he was very evasive when he spoke to me about this case, as if it wasn't important enough...I wonder why? I'm so pissed off with him, that I don't know how I will react, at the moment, I'm going to face him!!" Viggo pointed out really pissed off, and Ember knows, why Franklin sent Viggo to California and she added...

"I don't understand how it's possible, that these gangsters had the information all along. Viggo, we are wasting precious time, investigating which company is developing the defense system. Meanwhile, the federal agents in the field, pay the consequences of their leaders' ineptitude and their behavior is unacceptable!" Ember said upset and Viggo in agreement responds...

"Precisely Ember, Pascucci has under his control at least one more scientists or engineer, which must be in charge of the project at The Bremen's lab. Ember, if we analyze the situation and, then we examine the few clues that we have, I'm sure that the evidence will lead us directly to that particular company, I believe, that first we should talk to Mr. Bremen, I'm sure, that this man has nothing to do with anything, since he is so famous and wealthy, this man doesn't know anything about it. What do you think Ember?"

"Just hold on a second Viggo, because for a while, I had under surveillance The Bremen Co. What I found amazing, regarding to this company, that it has an impressive conglomerate of companies and, one of the enterprises, is the NMRI=*Nuclear Molecular Research Institute*, this company, is the one we have under partial scrutiny, but until this moment, we haven't found any signs, of clandestine activities or associations of any kind, this is not to say that didn't happened. Viggo, it was the only private enterprise, and without knowing, that it was the chosen one, to engineer the space project, I become suspicious of this company, and I send two agents to see if everything was okay."

"Ember, it means, that you already suspected that in this company something was cooking, but it wasn't meatballs. Right?" Viggo asks interested in the answer, and Ember who continues to be irritated added...

"I'm really annoying about this situation, because..."

"Ember, what is the problem?

"Look Viggo, when I took over this position; I had little knowledge of this case: at the time I read the skimpy report, which only told me, that The Bremen Co. was the only private company, this simple detail aroused my suspicions, that's when I decided to research the owner's history..."

"That's thinking ahead. Ember, what have you found, other than the man is an eccentric person?"

"Look, I found out, that Mr. Victor Bremen, is the head of the company, this man is a renowned Scientific Engineer, and besides all his achievements he has a title of Astrophysics Doctorate. Mr. Bremen, is supposed to be a genius, like his grandfather Carl Bremen." Ember said it as if she was saying, you see that I am helping you and Viggo added...

"This data is quite interesting, if we consider the legendary trajectory of this family: what a coincidence Ember, a while ago I was reading about that scientist, Carl Bremen, if I remember correctly, Carl was one of the scientists who were enlisted with others, to *The Manhattan Project*, together with Van Broun, who joined the great Nuclear-Scientist, *Robert Oppenheimer;* who without analyzing in depth the consequences of his actions, could generate into the future of the world. —On July 16th, 1945, in the pale sands of New Mexico USA. —Was detonated the first *atomic bomb,* by a bunch of *genius scientists,* who created this monstrosity, they were the solo witness, to the tremendous devastating explosion of historical proportion; at that historic moment several of the scientist's, fell in a dead silent and, others the tears were rolling down their cheeks, they were feeling really...very sorry for Humanity: and they should be. That catastrophic explosion was the beginning of the events, that is coming to overshadows, all the creatures of this world?" Viggo commented quite sadly. Ember listens in silence and looks at her husband with love and she pointed out...

"Unfortunately, the desire for power of the leaders of this world has no limits." *Ember paused for a second grooming her hair and then she said.* "Viggo, coming back to Victor Bremen, I guess he has the grandfather's genes, the apples don't fall far from the tree: Mr. Bremen must be some kind of genius?"

"I hope the brilliant mind of Mr. Victor Bremen, will be at service to the well-being of humanity, at the moment he shows that he has and amazing potential."

"For sure Viggo, looking at his historical past, I was able to find out, that right now he has several important projects on the way, one of the company's is currently building rockets, which are to position satellites into space; I'm sure you know that Mr. Bremen, has a juicy contract with the Fed's, who are fattening his pockets."

"Ember, this guy is quite busy and wealthy enough to be involved in this case, and right now, my priority is to capture Pascucci, who's supposed to be, the ringleader in this international organization, once I have this guy at my disposal, I'm sure he will tell me what I want to know, about everything he knows, then we will know who the traitor is!"

"I completely agree. Viggo, but with one condition, you must not squeeze his ba…"

"Wait a minute Ember, how dare you accuse me, of having such low principles? I follow the strict rules of engagement. Officer Maxell!" Viggo said with a cynical smile and Ember ignores the comment and she replies…

"Officer Maxell, what really knows, that Santino Pascucci, is fearless enough to take second chances. Viggo, I feel like get out behind this desk, and go hunt down these criminals!"

"I don't blame you. Ember, this gangster came out from his long hibernation, and now this piece of shit is back in business, it won't be for long, I'm going to find the way, to put my hands on that traitors' crotch, and he will tell me everything he knows about this case." Viggo commented and Ember adds.

"Your hands on the crotch, Viggo?"

"Ember, I meant, my hands on his neck…What was you about to say? Viggo asks with the face who said I didn't do it, and Ember continue saying…

"Viggo, I wonder, how many countries are interested, in getting their hands on a new defense system, among those nations, may be North Korea, China, and Russia. These are the countries that would be most interested, in obtaining this kind of technology and, what is your opinion regarding what I just said?"

"Paradoxically; I came to the same conclusion Ember, the North Koreans…I don't think so, they are more interested in getting the atomic bomb, but I'm sure of the Chinese, and the Russians, are involved in this plot to grab the info, I'm sure, they are mingling around, trying to achieve their purposes. Ember, I think the foreign agents knows already that I'm here, just to interfere in their fucking plans. I'm going to use all the sources at my disposal, to find out who is behind this organization, then I'm going to squeeze their b..."

"Viggo: you just told me, how dare I accuse you of such misconduct, that you have higher principles; where did those principles go?"

"Come on, Ember, when you cut me off, I was ready to say their brain..." *She wants to answer but he stops her with a gesture.* "Look, Ember, I just want to focus all my energies to capture Pascucci, but one thing is not that clear, from the way I'm looking at this entire episode. Ember, I have a question, please just tell me, how the hell this man got away from the federal agents, if I know how it all started, I can get to the heart of the matter, with some proper info, with the one I can start the investigation, and perhaps I will be successful?" Viggo seriously asked, as his wife looks at him lovingly, while sipping a glass of champagne Ember, at that moment, is felling that the few sweet hours she is enjoying with her husband, are coming to an end, and she is trying to seize the precious moments, but the champagne bubbles, had already reached her head, and anxious she gets up and sits beside him, and in a very seductive way Ember said...

"You are absolutely correct Viggo, tomorrow in the office, I'll tell you all about it. My love, we're not in New York, we're in LA, we should take advantage of this paradise; forget all about Pascucci, and let's go back to my apartment?"

"Ember, all in good time: listen Ember, I'm going to ask you a simple question. How much lost time you want to recover, in a certain time, don't you believe that you accomplished enough in one day? We have many tomorrows in front of us, but in the meantime, as a professional we must not forget, why we are here. Okay? Viggo said kissing her and she answered...

"You are right Viggo, but you know very well that certain feelings cannot be controlled, because something special is happening to me. I feel like I'm walking on cotton clouds, it's a sensation that I have never felt before, it might be this immense love I'm feel for you, that covers my soul with happiness!" *Viggo listens to the declaration of love in silence. Ember pauses for a second and she continue saying.* "I know Viggo, I Know you would like to find out, what happened with Santino Pascucci, but our..."

"That's a correct assumption Ember, is not that hard to figure it out, the way I feel, because I don't understand, how Mr. Pascucci, in this city, could have escaped being under the noses of the federal agents? Please, could you explain what happened?" *Viggo asks and Ember is looking at her husband with affection in silence and he continue saying.* "Ember, it's not a complicated question to answer?" Then gently Viggo kissed his wife and Ember who was already affected with the bubbles of champagne, replies with tenderness...

"One thing is one thing and, another is another my love, if you ask with kisses, I can't refuse any of your requests, I don't want you to be disappointed, but there's not much to tell, this case is brand new to me: I wasn't here when this event happened. Viggo, I just replaced Morris a few days ago; that is when I learned all about Mr. Pascucci..."

"Ember, you just told me that you did read the report, that's why I was almost sure, that in this Bureau, the agents would have accomplished some advance in the investigation?"

"I understand your position, because I was surprised when I started to read the report, and I was intrigued to find a very scrawny details about the investigation. Viggo, in the files Mr. Pascucci, only was mentioned when he was spotted by two of our agents, in the shopping mall in Santa Monica. Viggo, this event is like any other, there is nothing out of the ordinary about it, the agents that were following a lead, at that moment they were going up the escalator, on the other side, Pascucci was going down, that's when Mr. Pascucci, became aware that he was spotted by the federal agents, there he knew, that trouble was following him, and he was smart enough to evade the agents, then in a hurry, Mr. Pascucci left the country."

"Ember, with all the intelligence network that we have, I don't think it's a problem to find out Pascucci whereabouts, I'm sure intelligence knows where he is?"

"Please Viggo, don't make a big deal about nothing, we know where he is and..."

"That's your good news Ember, I was hopeful that when I arrived at L.A, that I don't have to start this investigation, going into nightclubs bars asking the whereabout of Pascucci?"

"Viggo, don't you try to patronize me: otherwise, I will not have other choice but to take you home and squeeze your...?"

"No...no please; I apologize, just tell me what you know, and I promise you I will not interrupt you at all." Viggo says covering his private parts, and Ember says with a smile.

"Don't play that dramatic card with me. Okay? I accept your apology, and by pure coincidence, yesterday arrived at my office classified information, in which it says that Pascucci, is in France, that is the most accurate data I can give you, Mr. Pascucci, is in France. Okay?"

"In one-word Ember, that means that we do not know where this guy is hidden, and this situation is an upheaval problem. It is clear to me, that no one notified the French authorities, that this gangster, would enter the country to visit the Eiffel Tower. What happen Ember, all the brains in the FBI stopped working at the same time?" Viggo asks meanwhile he pays the bill to the waiter, and Ember confirms the Info...

"Please Viggo, don't be sarcastic, we are sure that Pascucci is in France!" *In that moment her cell phone started ringing, after answering the call, Ember with a look of urgency on her face said.* "*Viggo, that* was Detective Mary D'Layne, from the Homicide Division of Los Angeles, and she was telling me that in West L.A, there was a shooting with a couple of casualties." Ember reports concerned and Viggo expresses himself in this way...

"What the hell is going on: Ember, I just got here, and all the shit got loose?" Viggo asking at the same time they're leaving the restaurant, holding his hand, while walking to her place. Ember, ignores the comment and goes on to informed Viggo all about what happened in the shooting...

"Viggo, regarding the incident that just happened, the details I was able to rescue from Detective D'Layne, that the confrontation occurred right in front of the Bremen Company, in the western area of L.A, the detective said that it was a violent hostility, between Chinese and Russian agents..."

"Ember, you just confirmed, that in that shooting were casualties, there are any survivors, that I would like to know. Viggo asks interested in the answer and Ember responded...

"Viggo, it's a routine case, in the shootout, these fucking cowboys, left two Chinese dead, and a Russian agent, seriously wounded: and here comes the strange twist about it all, because when the Russians were fleeing from the crime scene, the comrades of the wounded agent, for some unknown reason, they threw this guy out of the car, but the great surprise was that the Russian agent is still alive. For your information, Detective D'Layne, is waiting at the crime scene for a coroner to arrive, that's all the Info I got from Detective D'Layne." And Ember is looking at Viggo as if to say you must go, and he replied...

"Why, are you looking at me like that? Ember, can you send somebody else?"

"Viggo, you should go this is the case you just came to investigate."

"Come on Ember, I just arrived at the city, and these guys got all nervous and, started shooting at me, then my lovely wife abused me sexually, and right now, I have to dance rock and roll with foreign agents, with a full stomach, and several glasses of champagne, Ember, don't look at me that way; you don't have any other sacrificial lamb, instead of this representative of the law. Ember, I just got here. Okay?" Viggo asks raising his arms, and Ember worried added...

"I'm sorry, Viggo, you only have to do a detective work, and I don't have anybody with your expertise. I told Detective D'Layne, that you're going to be at the site of the shooting as soon as possible. I asked her to protect the scene of the crime until you arrived." Ember said looking at her husband, and she stopped walking right in front of the Bureau, and Viggo could perceive that Ember was a little concerned about his involvement in the case, and he said...

"Please relax Ember, you don't have to worry, the hoodlums who really try to kill me, they are no longer in this world. Look, these foreign agents are only looking for information." Viggo says confident, and Ember commented...

"I'm nervous Viggo, I had in mind, that this assignment was only to bring to light, the person or persons who are selling the information, but I didn't consider that these foreign agents, were so vicious, they have no limitations, at the moment of obtaining whatever information they are after."

"You don't have to worry Ember; these cannibals usually eat each other: just tell me how to get to the crime scene. I hope the Detective D'Layne is still waiting for me. I don't want some fucking incompetent to make a mess with the crime scene." Viggo asked quite relaxed, and Ember worried responded...

"I'm telling you, that this is not a coincidence, Viggo, all this commotion occurred right in front of The Bremen Co. I guess the info you obtained, proves that Mr. Bremen, has the contracts, with the Fed's?"

"That's right Ember, if the information is accurate, the Russian agent, who is wounded in the hospital, when I get there, I hope this guy is still breathing? I'm sure, he will provide me with some information, one way or another!!" *He paused for a second and clenching his fist said.* "Ember, this guy, better not play hard ball with me, because I've already lost my patience, and my fuse is quite short..." "Wait a minute, Viggo, you are not going to..." "Okay...okay, I will squeeze his brain...slowly, and I promise that not only he will talk, but he will also sing his national anthem." Viggo indicates very energetic, and Ember right in front of the Bureau and she pointed it out...

"I know Viggo, that you're tough, but I have to remind you, that kind of behavior is not acceptable in any situation, and you: Special-Agent Viggo Bronson, must follow the code of conduct. This is not a prevention and, is not a request it is and order. Okay?"

"Hold on: I don't know what you're taking about. Ember, let's stop talking about my behavior, because you just gave me an assignment, and to continue with the task, I need the keys to the bulletproof Cadillac and, I hope Detective D'Layne is waiting for me, I have several questions in mind to ask her?" Viggo said kissing Ember, and that kiss made her happier and sad at the same time, and she went to the office and handed him the key. —And...

Ember is on the sidewalk waiting for Viggo, to come with the car, whit a seductive attitude, this why she took off her jacket, so that her shiny reddish hair would fall gently over her pink's blouse, which is showing most of her prominent pearl white breast. That is the scenario in which Viggo, is going to find himself, when he came out driven the Cadillac and, he will see his wife more beautiful than ever, at that moment he knew that she, had a very special farewell for him, because when Viggo, steps out of the car to say goodbye. Ember, grabbed him, like he was the last man to exist on Earth, and without saying a word: she put the heart and soul, in a passionate long kiss, as if his husband mouth, was a hive of honey. Viggo, has no clue how much Ember, was missing those enflamed moments of love they spend together? A-lot!! His loving kisses made Ember's body quiver with pleasure and, she surrenders into his arms. Well, Viggo has no choice, but to leave his wife standing in the sidewalk, more needy of attention than a newborn baby. —Feeling a little guilty...

Viggo, leaves the place, looking in the rearview mirror at his wife, who waves at him, that loving gesture, makes him believe that his wife wants him with her at home: what he is really concerned about, is her future behavior, he wonders if she will change her old customs? Then in a few seconds he stops seeing her, but his doubts continued to bother him. It took him fifteen minutes to reach the heart of West Los Angeles, where the shooting between the Russians and the Chinese happened: this is the site where The Bremen Co. has the *Space Technology Laboratories*, which are located on Sepulveda Blvd, between Pico and Olympic Blvd. The whole area was closed by the police investigation brigade. Upon arrival the special agent was signaled to stop by a police officer: Viggo presented his credentials, and asks for Detective Mary D'Layne, who was impatient waiting for him. The real fact is that she knows the reputation of the Special-Agent Viggo Bronson, and for her it was a great privilege to greet him, that's why she did it, with all the courtesy she could find in her collection of good manners, and nervously she said...

"Welcome to the city of Los Angeles, Special-Agent Bronson, it is such a pleasure to meet you."

"Thanks' Detective D'Layne, and thank you for waiting for me, it is nice to meet you, even if it's here in this crime scene, I can see that it's very well protected." Viggo said shaking hands and D'Layne who is impressed with Viggo's presence, she held his hand and said...

"Thanks, for the compliment Special-Agent Bronson. I'm glad that we can have this conversation, because today when I was in the office, I heard that after arriving in L.A, you had an all-out confrontation with a bunch of gangsters, I'm sorry that it happened in my city, I hope it doesn't happen again!" She said sincerely and Viggo responded...

"Thanks, Detective D'Layne, I really didn't expect that kind of welcome to the city, but I come prepared for these kinds of receptions; a matter of fact, this is a job-related hazard, as you know!"

"Yes, you're right, danger is always around the corner; fortunately, in that skirmish you came out unharmed. Special-Agent Bronson, I can assure you, that in the Intelligence Bureau, we did not have any kind of info, regarding if there was a plot to attack you, or anybody else!"

"Thanks for your concern, Detective D'Layne. I'm assuring you, if there really exists an information leak, it was in New York."

"Well, the most important of this event Special-Agent Bronson, is that after the cowardly ambush, you are here, to continue the case investigation." She said sweetly and Viggo trying to diminish importance to his actions, at the moment he was facing the enemies, and calmly said...

"The truth, Detective D'Layne, I didn't expect that fierce ambush, from these gangsters, putting it simple; they were unsuccessful, I have to thanks Officer Maxwell, who had the good sense, of sending a bulletproof vehicle, which saved our lives."

"Talking about gangsters Special-Agent Bronson, it seems to me, that in the last three weeks, the foreign agents are quite active searching for data, actually we don't know what they are looking for, I'm sure it must be important, because these people in order to achieve their objectives, they are willing to kill each other!" She said emphatically and Viggo informs...

"For your information Detective D'Layne, this investigation is under the orders of the director of the Homeland Security, this means that it is of the utmost importance and should be resolved as soon as possible."

"If this is the case, Special-Agent Bronson, I'm here to help you in any way I can." The detective said confidently and Viggo continued saying...

"Thanks, Detective D'Layne, you know, that I just arrived in town, and I can barely grasp what's going on in the city, it seems to me, that from your way of seeing the situation, I'm going to need all the help I can get, and thanks again, Detective D'Layne." Viggo said it in a passionate way and the detective who would like to be Viggo's partner, with a huge smile responded...

"It's an honor, to start an investigation with a legend, in this moment I feel privileged to be in this situation. Special-Agent Bronson, I'm completely at your disposal, for whatever you need, I'm ready to help!" She said with a huge smile and close to him, and Viggo trying to not disappoint the detective and he answered...

"First of all, I must thank you for your help, and second, I have to say that you don't have to pay attention, to all this gossip magazines, and the newspapers, which write stories about this servant of the law. The journalists usually let their imagination's flying, altering the events out of proportion, in their ambition, they are inserting false truths in people's minds." Viggo said feeling that she did not let go of his hand, and the Detective D'Layne who is impressed by Viggo's presence responded...

"It is quite possible that you are correct, but in this situation. I must say that your refusal to admit your achievement speaks louder of your integrity, and also that you're trying to minimize your accomplishments, that shows that you must have a very noble character, and you know that your fame transcends the borders of New York. Special-Agent Bronson, just by knowledge that your skills are recognized by the media, speaks louder to your increasing popularity." She indicates very sweetly and Viggo a little overwhelmed by the compliments responded...

"Detective D'Layne, there is an old saying. The fame is like a balloon, when a lot of people blow into it, the bigger the balloon gets, and there it goes, the more you blow the fame is getting bigger and bigger, without having any foundation to lean on. Very often the newspapers enlarge the story just to sell more units, that's all that is, clouds of smoke." Viggo says humbly, the detective sweetly responded...

"Your modesty should be complemented, I must tell you, that the absence of arrogance shows in every page of your book, *The Investigating Technique*..."

"Wait a minute. Don't tell me that you have my book? Viggo asks really surprised and she said...

"Yes, I have it: and I believe that your book, should be a vital guide for any detective. Congratulation Special-Agent Bronson, this book should be in every police precinct in this country!" She said with a smile exaggerating the complement and Viggo really surprised by the news said....

"Detective D'Layne, I'm impressed that you read, that's really nice of you, because in New York, I don't find many people who have read my book." Viggo asks amazed to find a person in Los Angeles who has read his book and the detective responded...

"It was a pleasure to read your book Special-Agent Bronson, and thanks for all the guidelines, that I will keep in my memory: what I found amazing, it's the investigating techniques that you applied in criminal cases, it is a perfect guide for any investigator, it seems to me, that clears the path for success." She said looking straight into his eyes and Viggo who can't reject those beautiful eyes and he responded...

"First of all: Detective D'Layne, I have to say thanks for your support, and second, that you have taken part of your time to read the book, that means a lot to me." Viggo said sincerely and the detective was incredulous listening to him, and she replies...

"I should say thanks to you, since I read your book, I learned a lot from your experiences. Especial-Agent Bronson, I can talk all day about the book, but I don't want to take your precious time, as a matter of fact; I was informed by Officer Maxwell, and you said it before, that you are investigating a very special case, concerning National Security?"

"That's correct, Detective D'Layne, and to begin we are going to evaluate what has happened here, I believe the confrontation that occurred in this location, has a lot to do with this case, that we are investigating, as you said earlier, there are many foreign agents in this city, running around looking for information."

"That's right Special-Agent Bronson, and you're confirming the report that Officer Maxwell, told our chief, who told me that I shall help you with everything you need." She said sweetly and Viggo complacent informs...

"Thanks' Detective D'Layne, I'm sure I'll need your help, but right now and at this moment, the event that concerns me, is what occurred between those two rival nations, and the reason why these agents tried to eliminate each other, for the sole purpose of obtaining information, I know that this confrontation left a balance of two Chinese dead, and a Soviet citizen badly wounded, that's what happened Detective D'Layne?"

"Officer Maxell, informed you correctly, that's what occurred here Special-Agent Bronson, I did my best to try to keep the crime scene untouched, until your arrival, but by orders from the police chief and the coroner, I had to clear the street, I had no other choice but to remove the two dead Chinese bodies, which they went to the morgue, and the wounded Russian agent was transported in an ambulance to the...

SANTA MONICA HOSPITAL

"Thanks' for the good work Detective D'Layne, and the coroner made the right decision, to take the injured man to the hospital. I hope he is still alive, because it is of the upmost importance, that I should question this person, before anything happens to him! A matter of fact, Detective D'Layne, I should talk to this person as soon as possible, please, can you show me the way to the hospital?" Viggo asks with the urgency and, Detective D'Layne full of expectation responded...

"Of course, I will take you to the hospital Special-Agent Bronson. I imagine you have a lot of pressure from your superiors to solve this case, like I said, I'm here to help, you only have to ask." She said with a friendly gesture and Viggo the same manner responded...

"I'm glad that we understand each other Detective D'Layne, because this case should be resolved as soon as possible, and right now the time is precious, could you please direct me to the Santa Monica Hospital, it is urgent that I speak with this Russian agent, before the devil, takes this guy straight to hell!!"

"I hope that doesn't happen and, we arrive on time, it is not that far, in few minutes we will be there, what happened Special-Agent Bronson, that meanwhile I was waiting for you, my partner took the official car, and he went to the precinct to write a report, to inform the Chinese and Russian Embassies, about what happened."

"Detective D'Layne, if you don't mind, we can go in my car, and the problem is solved, are you okay with that?"

"Sure, that would be perfect Special-Agent Bronson." She said with a smile, and Viggo is happy to be assisted by the authorities of L.A. Besides that, point: Detective D'Layne, looks really...very attractive, and quite sexy in her outfit and, she is almost tall as he, what most catches his attention, are her red lips thar are juicy like the pomegranate grains, and her features are graceful, with a pair of huge green eyes, which embraces when she looks at him. —Then...

Once on the way to the hospital, Detective D'Layne, will do her best to inform Special-Agent Viggo Bronson, all about the identity of the Chinese's citizens, who were killed in the skirmish: but something special and unexpected is going to happen, at the time she came to mentioned the name of the Russian agent, and Viggo was astonished: by the identity of the wounded man, it happens that he knows that person, really...really very well. Viggo, can't believe what is happening to his good friend!!! This Russian agent, took an heroic actions during a ferocious terrorist attack in the City of Damascus, at those dramatic times of war, it is not very common for a man, when bullets are coming, put your chest to save another, but there was a Russian agent, who was willing to risk his life to save Viggo's, who in those moments was in a compromised situation, he was being attacked on both fronts, and the person who is now one of his best friends, went to his rescue under a hail of bullets.—This event occurred, at the time U.S.A and Russia, where in serious negotiations, to eradicate the weapons of mass destruction in Syria. It would be convenient...

If we take the time to look at the history of the Russian agent, who is currently admitted with serious injuries at the Santa Monica Hospital. If we look deeply into his recent past, we will find out that he is really an intriguing character. A matter of fact, he is a direct descendant of the famous Russian General Nikolai Kaminsky, who was a member of the state, and military councils from 1917 to 1928. But those distant relatives are from another story. Let's go back to the present, and we were to insert our self's, right in the heart of the City of Moscow, were Agent Voris Kaminsky, is well known, by the nickname Dusty, who happens to be, the proud owner of the famous

Mansion, *The Love Palace*. His friend Viggo is well aware that in his luxurious palace.

Voris Kaminsky=Dusty, has a well-organized business, where important personalities from all walks of life, that from time to time, meet the residents of the palace, which is very well equipped, with beautiful young woman, and strong gifted men, who do indiscriminate services to certain government leaders, and senior officials of the armed forces. Viggo in his despair, drew in a few seconds, thousands of conclusions, about what happen to his friend...

Viggo, was puzzled by his involvement, in that deadly clash: he is the last person he expected to find in this situation, his friend wounded and, at the same site, he came all the way from New York, to investigate a case of espionage; for Viggo, this situation doesn't make any sense, because this particular Russian agent, doesn't risk his skin just like that: loosely; he is looking at situation coldly, and he comes to the conclusion, that the involvement of Voris Kaminsky, or Dusty, to obtain information about the new project; assures Special-Agent Bronson, that The Bremen Co. is subject to espionage. Viggo, partially know what the scientist are developing in their Lab's. but for sure, it must be vital for the security of the United States, and its Allies.

At the moment the detectives arrived at the hospital, Viggo presents his credentials at the reception desk, at the same time, he asks the doctor if the patient Voris Kaminsky, could be interrogated, to which the physician responded...

"At this moment, Mr. Kaminsky, will be able to talk, but the patient is not in physical condition to face a rough interrogation, a few hours ago he came out from the operation room Special-Agent Bronson, but you can talk to the patient for a little while, if you prefer you can come back tomorrow. Hopefully he will be recovered from the operation. Okay?" The doctor said with a hand shaking, and Viggo agreed.

"Thanks, Doctor Goldstein, these procedures are usually routine; I will not apply any pressure to the patient. Doctor, I assure you: the interrogation will start when he recovers, I will treat him with most courtesy, the coincidence is, that I know the gentlemen really well." Viggo promises. Then...

Detective D'Layne, start walking towards the room with Viggo, who could notice two police in front of the patient's door, the officers recognized Det. D'Layne, and make them pass. At the moment they entered the room, to their surprise found a very relaxed man, who was sitting in bed recovering from his wounds, the patient who belonged to the Russia FSK or the FSB Security-Agent. Voris Kaminsky, alias Dusty, this character has a certain halo of mystery that surround's his personality. Voris, earned his nickname of Dusty, from his classmates at school, because of his particular way of speaking: the explanation is simple, it has to do with the way he delivers the phrases, at the moment of speaking, Voris, makes parenthesis between the words seems like he's talking in slow motion. *As the actor Marlon's Brando, did in the Godfather saga.* That's the way he earned his nickname, but what Dusty least expected that his friend would come to see him, but when Viggo enter in his room, and at the moment he saw him, Dusty happily said in his classic smooth dusty voice...

"Easy'V...my brother...it's a real pleasure to see you my friend...I can believe you are in L.A!"

"Same here, my dear friend, and what the fuck are you doing here, it was impossible to believe that you were here, and for the worse, fucking wounded. What the fuck?"

"It's not a big deal...Everything has a simple explanation...Easy'V."

"The explanation it's simple, but the situation it's complicated: because, since the moment I found out that you were in this situation, I began to think how the fuck am I going to get you out of this mess, Dusty? Viggo indicates and at the same time he hugs his friend and Dusty answered...

"My friend...I just say...first thing's first...I just want to make clear...that at the time...you arrived at L.A....it wasn't us who tried to send you to hell...I swear it wasn't us..."

"I already know all about it, but for sure Dusty, you have to telling me, what the fuck are you doing here? I will need a lot of info from you." Viggo said standing next to the bed making hand gestures and Dusty with emotion answered...

"Easy'V, you know that I am in this mess, up to my ears, this's why I'm so happy to see you. Easy'V...I'm sorry...if I'm putting you in this situation, you know...it has to do with what we do!" Dusty extending his two arms out in a sign of welcoming, and Viggo sat on the bed an embraced his friend. And Detective D'Layne gives space to the friends to talked, and Viggo commented...

"Dusty, you know that for almost two years I was dealing, with emotional problems, and when Franklin decide to send me, to investigate this case in L.A, and I took advantage that I was leaving New York, so I seized the opportunity, to get rid of all the cobwebs that were trapping me, in that nightmare..."

"Come on...Easy'V...you look great!"

"Thanks, but you don't: because look what I find when I get to L.A, my friend is wounded, and the strange deal, is that I talked to you last week. Dusty, and you didn't tell me you were coming to see me?"

"I know you're kidding Easy'V...But you know...there are circumstances...that I can't control...and for that simple reason...I could not tell you...you know the drill? Easy'V...I thought you were in New York...this really is an awkward situation...I'm really sorry my friend...It is this shitty job...we choose to do...it makes us do things against our will."

"My friend, I'm very happy to see you, I regret that it has to be under these circumstances. I already told you, that I'm aware that it wasn't foreign agents, who attack us!"

"Easy'V... you know...that my assignment is to protect my comrades...it comes with the contract...I did not know...that you will be here in L.A...for that reason...I didn't want you to believe...that we were the ones who attacked you...Okay?"

"Hey, Dusty, after that heated fight, I was able to see the gangster's faces, I knew right there it wasn't foreign agents, who tried to get rid of me." *Then Viggo looked closely at his friend.* "Dusty, I'm puzzled to find you in this town wounded, and by the fucking Chinese agents, I guess these guys, are engaged in the same goal your comrades are?" Viggo asks and gets up from the bed and he started walking around the room and Dusty with a forced smile said...

"Take it easy Viggo...walking in this room...doesn't get you anywhere."

"That's very good Dusty: I can see that your funny side is showing up? But...what is going to take me somewhere, is that I know exactly what you guys are doing in L.A. I believe that at the time you were wounded, you were protecting your comrades, since that's your mission, this why I understand your situation. Dusty, wait until the waters calm down, and you're already recovered, then we'll talk all about the espionage topic. Okay?" Viggo asks intrigued, and Dusty is trying to avoid the question and said...

"My friend...the events that occurred...should not have happened... Easy'V...you said that we'll talk...that subject can wait...first of all...I would like to meet your new partner...because you two looks great together." Dusty said with a naughty smile, and Viggo who stands next to the detective said...

"Hold on Dusty, first I must clarify that Detective D'Layne, in these circumstances represents Los Angeles Police Department..." Viggo is trying to explain what she did for him, but Dusty interrupted...

"It's nice to know: Detective D'Layne, I have to say...that this uniform looks magnificent on you."

"Thanks Mr. Kavisky, I appreciate your compliment, that gives me the clue that you are not as sick as you seem, perhaps you should finish your recovery in jail?" She said with smile and Viggo added...

"Hold on: Mr. Kaminsky, because thanks to the quick response of Detective D'Layne: today, you have the pleasure of continuing breathing. Okay?" Viggo pointed out with a smile, and Dusty in his dusty voice replays...

"I knew...I knew that an angel...was watching over me...but I didn't know it was you...Detective D'Layne, how can I say thanks'...I hope when I get out of this hospital...I can return the favor...if first...you don't throw my bones...in jail, but you know...that I'm totally innocent...of all the charges against me...I came to Los Angeles...to visit the beaches of Santa Monica?" Dusty said and trying to get out of bed, and Detective D'Layne intervenes, and she warns him...

"Please, don't get up, you should not leave the bed, remember that you just left the operating room." *Dusty listens to the advice of Detective D'Layne and he decides to stay in bed, and she continue saying.* "Mr. Kaminsky, I don't believe, that any retribution will be necessary, in other circumstances I'll appreciate your offer, but don't you forget, that by chance I was in the right place at that moment you fell of the car, and when I realized that you weren't breading, that's when I was trying my best to save your life, I was only doing my job, and I would do it again, without looking who the person is." Detective D'Layne said getting close to Dusty, who added...

"Detective D'Layne...I'm a prisoner that's very grateful, and I'll never forget that you have saved my life...thanks!" *Then Dusty paused for few seconds looking for the right thing to say.* "Detective, I'm not sure if I'm going to get out of this mess...but my friend Special-Agent Bronson...I'm sure he could pay my debt?" Dusty asks with a warm smile; the proposal brought a smile to her face, and she responded...

"At this time, and in your condition Mr. Kaminsky, you should not be thinking about rewarding anybody, you have other more imperative problems to worry about, and now I'll leave you alone with Special-Agent Bronson, I guess you have a lot of things to explain to your friend." *Mary said, then she turns to Viggo and with an inviting look she said.* "I will wait for you in the hall Special-Agent Bronson." Det. D'Layne pointed out as she was leaving the room, with a sexy walk rocking her hips, as if she said, follow me!! —The show was enjoyed by the two agents, once alone Viggo began to ask questions...

"Dusty, in the name of our friendship!! What the fuck is going on? We have witnesses, that saw what happened: why did your comrades throw you out of the car, with no consideration that the vehicle was traveling at high speed? Dusty, if it crosses your mind to give this guy up, I promise you I will take care of those bastards!"

"You...you just said it right...bastards. I had the fucking assignment...to protect those fucking jerks...and these fakers threw me out of the car...like a piece of trash. Easy'V...right now you...you should not go out of your way...since the priority...is to get me out of this fucking situation...I promise...I will deal with these guys later." Dusty, said calmly and Viggo added...

"If these fuckers are in this country, I'll find them. But first Dusty, I have another objective, that's to find the scientist who is selling the info to Pascucci, and I'm sure, these transactions happen at the Bremen Co. Lab..." *Viggo paused for a few second and spoke.* "Dusty, regarding to your comrades: for my fucking life I can't figure this out, why these fuckers did that to you?" Viggo said lowering his voice, and Dusty added...

"Easy'V...I believe...that my colleagues...thought that I was dead... these morons...were in total disarray...after the shooting...I guess they didn't want to deal...with a dead body...to them I was a pain in the ass...and they decided to get rid of me...and without thinking...they throw me out of the car...I want to believe...those were the consequences of this event?" Dusty said vey dustily in a forgiving way, and Viggo disagreed.

"What the fuck are you talking about? You were not dead! About your comrades, just tell me, these guys didn't take the time to check out, if you were alive? And you have the good heart, to forgive those jerks!" Viggo said raising his arms, and Dusty let his friend know what happened...

"Listen Easy'V...and listen well...because what I'm going to tell you...seems like science fiction, after I woke up from the operation...the doctor came to see me...and guess...what he told me?

"At this precise moment I can't guess but I can tell you, that you are really...a very fucking lucky guy!"

"Exactly my friend...that I was really lucky...the surgeon was prone to assume...that when my comrades...throw me out of the car...I was already dead...and my heart wasn't ticking...I was dead Easy'V, I was fucking dead...that's what the surgeon said...and I still can't believe that I'm talking to you right now." Dusty pointed out placing his right hand on his chest, and Viggo with a doubting expression answered...

"My friend, if we look at your situation, from the logical version of the circumstances, the description of the surgeon about your resurrection, maybe could be true or not, it does not matter, if it has logic or it doesn't have any sense. The most important detail. is that you are alive, and you can tell the story more than once. Okay?"

"I know that very well Easy'V...Nobody can be happier than me...Plus, who are we to judge...what the doctors say...he expresses his wise opinion...with the knowledge he has... I don't have to tell you...that physicians...we are not. Okay?" Dusty said with signs of resignation, and Viggo responded.

"Dusty, what happened to you, it doesn't make any sense! Apart from your partial death Dusty, what else did the doctor have to say, about the rest of your injuries, would you have any impediment in the future?" Viggo asks interested and Dusty explains...

"What are you talking about...impediments? The doctor told me...that when I leave the hospital...I will be one hundred percent recup..." *Dusty, paused for few seconds and spoke.* "Easy'V...my concern is quite serious...I don't want to leave the hospital...and go straight to jail?" Dusty said seriously and Viggo responded...

"Don't worry about those minor details, the main thing is that you are okay, I will find a good excuse, to get you out of this mess. For instant: you will be the right person, to helping me to solve this case, since you have all the knowledge about this case, do you agree?"

"Do I have any other choice? Since the band is playing let's dance Easy'V?" Dusty, said raising his arms and Viggo asks...

"That's the friend I know! Dusty, I'm concerned about what happened to you, what the doctor told you about your injuries?"

"Easy'V, what I have to tell you is not credible either, it is not so simple..."

"Come on, I'm puzzled by what happen to you."

"Okay...in a few words...the surgeon explained to me in a simple way...so that I could understand...when he began to explain, the first thing he said...is that he didn't need to open my chest...to extract the bullet...according to him...the projectile was located right next to my heart...the doctor presumes...that my heart had stopped beating...just at the time...the bullet impacted my chest." *Dusty paused for a couple of seconds, organizing his thoughts, and Viggo was listening with attention.* "Easy'V...the doctor supposes...that at the moment my comrades...threw me out of the vehicle...and my body violently hit the pavement...this event makes the doctor presumed...that from the impact my heart began beating...those were the causes...for what my heart stopped...and then started beating...that is the doctor's theory... for that reason I'm alive today...why you look at me with that face? You must believe-it or not...I just repeating what the surgent said!" Dusty very calmly describes in detail all the doctor's explanations to his friend, who was listening attentively and Viggo, believed that his friend had a day, from which you could make an action movie out off, and he commented...

"My friend, since you got to L.A, what happened to you, it seems like a fictional saga, which could have been written by George Lucas. Dusty, what happened to you is quite clear, that you're not welcome to..."

"What the hell are you trying to say?"

"You just said it Dusty, because your turn to visit the furnaces of hell, had not come yet, I have the vision that one of these days, we will die together, fighting against those faker's who promote Wars..."

"Easy'V, are you aware of what you saying, you are proposing that we fight against our country's?

"Come on, man, don't take it literally: my comment was a way of expressing my feelings, freely with my friend!"

"Thanks, Easy'V, you know I feel the same way, and I know that you won't leave me alone in this fucking mess."

"Just assure Dusty, that I'm going to do everything under my disposal to get out of this situation, then you should write a detective story about what happened to you."

"Talking about detectives Easy'V...Detective D'Layne was looking at you...as if you were a delicious thing to eat...did you...already..?" Dusty asks with a witty smile, and Viggo responded the same way...

"How dare Dusty, do you believe that I can do such a thing during an investigation, I don't get sexually involved with members of another force, I hope you want to harm my reputation, because I send you back to Moscow?" And Viggo smiled like a Cheshire cat, and Dusty shaking his head up and down reminded him...

"I would never harm...your reputation Easy'V...but since you just mentioned...reputation and Moscow. An interesting episode comes to my mind...do you remember what happened...in that famous party...at the Presidential Palace?" Dusty paused for a second trying to sit in bed, and Viggo commented...

"Dusty, you are sitting on the bed, because it's the right time to say an important pronouncement, that's so significant, that will shift the axle of Earth, or maybe you're going to remind me, of that fucking episode that happened in Moscow?

"Well...it is the latter...If I remember correctly...in that opportunity...I had the good sense...to stop this eccentric American...at the moment you had the nerves to take...the Russian president wife...for a stroll in the gardens...every time I think about it...my ass wrinkles...if security had found out what you intended to do...I could have ended up...in fucking Siberia...with you as a company...That was not the plan...I had for my future life!" And Dusty at that moment started coughing and laughing at the same time, and Viggo remembering the awkward situation replied...

"As a matter of fact, if I'm going to find a guilty party, I don't have to look too far: it was all your fault Dusty, I still wonder where the fuck you got those two bottles of Chivas Regal. I remember very well that night, I was not drunk, I just had a few extra drinks, and that's it." Viggo said like it was nothing important and Dusty replies...

"A few drinks...you must be kidding...I don't know...how you were able to stand up...after having almost...two bottles of whiskey...that's when you began to whisper...into the president's wife ear...I always wonder what you said to her?" Dusty asks raising his arms, and Viggo reminded him...

"Don't make so much fuss about it my friend, because you were a witness, when the president's wife approached this gentleman, with a huge smile, which had the clear invitation to a romantic meeting, or could be one touch and go, just tell me Dusty, how could I deny the pleasure of my company to that aggressive lady, she, looked amazing, I just wanted to please her wishes Dusty. That so?"

"Come on Easy'V... you are exaggerating...but there is some truth...in what you are saying...a matter of fact, you never told me...what you said to her?"

"Okay, Dusty, do you want to know what I told her? Look, I said very sweetly in her ear. —Madam, I have to tell you, that the flowers that embellish the saloon, they withered by your presence, I think we should go to the garden to find some fresh flowers, I'm sure the guest will appreciate your gesture?" Viggo ends up saying with a mischievous smile, and Dusty added...

"That was pretty clever of you Easy'V...that's when you got decided to put your right hand on her shoulders...and you were ready to take her...to the garden...do you remember?"

"To tell you the truth, I just remember being there, if I have to be guided by what you're telling me, it seemed to me, that at that time, I was living a glorious moment. Dusty, thanks' for being in there for me!"

"That was really an awkward situation Easy'V, If I didn't have the good sense to intervene...at that moment...you were ready to create...a great international scandal...at that time...I really saved my ass and yours'...I can imagine the next day...in the front page of the newspapers it would appear...in large letters...THE FAMOUS AMERICAN SPECIAL-AGENT VIGGO BRONSON IN TOTAL...DISREGARD FOR DIPLOMACY...TOOK THE RUSSIAN PRESIDENT'S WIFE...INTO THE GARDENS OF

THE PRESIDENTIAL PALACE...UNTIL NOW...IT'S NOT KNOWN WHAT HIS INTENTIONS WERE? Can you imagine the tremendous mess that you had created Easy'V...right now both of us would be making igloos in Siberia...or worse!"

"Don't you remind me? I know and I also know that I owe you more than one favor!" *Viggo paused for a second thinking of what he could do for his friend.* "Dusty, I'm going to try my best to get you out of this mess. I have a lot of resources from where I can squeeze some help, and with that assistance, I'm going to get you an American citizenship, or maybe you change your mind, and decide to return home?" Viggo asks placing a hand on his shoulder, and Dusty takes his friend's arm and responded...

"Easy'V...I'm sure that right now in Moscow...the intelligence director...has the info that I'm deceased...if I return to Russia...like I just resurrected...after having been a prisoner...the American Intelligence...these guys will think...that I was spilling the beans...and rest assured, these guys don't have any mercy...when the time comes to punish traitors...my comrades...are capable of cutting your tongue out...or maybe something else...I don't want to even think about it!" Dusty said seriously, and Viggo tries to calm his friend and said...

"Relax my friend, because, if this problem can be resolved with money or diplomacy, the quandary has a solution, and, I'm sure that I have the way to solve this situation. Everything has a solution, except the owners of death, which are the motherfucker's you just escaped from. Okay?"

"Easy'V...I promise...I will help you solve this case... but it's essential that I remain in this country...it's the only way I'm going to come out...alive of this fucking mess...if you help me...in the process to request political asylum...and drop all the charges...your government will throw against me...This is the only way I will be an asset in the investigation... Easy'V...in Russia we say. —United we will succeed: scattered...what the fuck are we going to do? "Dusty said with sense of urgency, and Viggo calmly comments...

"Dusty, I told you that before, it's very possible that you will get what you ask for, and I'm sure the help, could come from the secretary of state," *Viggo began to explain seriously and when he mentions the secretary, Dusty who had lain back in bed, sits down again very interested in what his friend would say.* "Dusty, one of those nights, it happened that I was present in one of those dignitaries' special dinners, which are usually celebrated in the White House, the invitation came from the director of the FBI. The reception included a banquet, after that fantastic dinner, I was introduced to the future secretary of state: the minutes passed without us noticing, and between drinks, we started a fluent and friendly dialogue, which after several drinks, I asked her about her husband, she replied that she was alone, knowing that: like a good gentleman I invited her to a..." Viggo was interrupted by Dusty who said...

"You're amazing Easy'V!!...I'm sure you took that lovely woman...for a nice-cozy stroll...in the gardens of the white house...How can it be, that this fucking fame follows you wherever you go, just tell me if I'm wrong...that you and the secre...?"

"Please Dusty, don't be obtuse: it has nothing to do with me, if the husband wasn't around, I was just trying to entertain the lonely woman; you know, one thing leads to the other, and by midnight we become quite acquainted."

"I hope...that woman...continue to be your friends...?"

"I must say that our friendship, continues in a very good bond. Dusty, it is very possible that with her help. I will get you out of this mess, just relax, and try to help me to solve this case. Okay?"

"I can believe it Easy'V...that you are acquainted...with the secretary of state?" Dusty asks amazed and Viggo ignoring the question and keep talking...

"Rest assured Dusty, I will speak with the secretary, in you behave, and while we talk about our friendship, between words I will convince the secretary, that you, would be an indispensable asset in this investigation..."

"Excuse me...what do you mean...when you said...then between words you...you will convince her?...Excuse me: having sex...now they call it...between words?" Dusty asks curiously Viggo smiling like a cat that has just grabbed a mouse and he answered...

"Dusty, you know that's not for gentlemen, to talk about bureaucratic intimacies, if I do, I could lose all my privileges!

"Okay...okay Easy'V...please continue." Dusty said lying back in bed and Viggo explained...

"Dusty, what I was trying to tell you, that after I speak to the secretary, for sure we will not have problems, because with the secretary, it happens that couple of times a month, she to *talk* to me, about her personal safety concerns, you understand?" Viggo asks with a mischievous smile and Dusty worried about his future replies...

"I hope, Easy'V...the secretary of state is happy...with your tattoo, that so I'm interested in?"

"Dusty, if you believed, that all the women who pursued this gentleman, has something to do with the tattoo, you're discarding my personal appeal...that's what one least expects from a friend." Viggo said smiling and Dusty turns a deaf ear to what the friend said and responded...

"Hey, Easy'V...let's go back to what concerns me...when you will *talk* to the secretary...I don't expect that the following day I will end up...with my bones in jail. Okay?"

"Hey, I will visit the secretary at her office, but for your case Dusty, I will deal with the staff of the secretary, so stop worrying about her, then, to ensure that everything goes the way it should. I will take care personally, about your request for the asylum documents." *Viggo paused for a second, thinking about the next question he will ask his friend.* "Dusty, why don't we start from the beginning, and tell me why this project is so important, because the foreign agents are willing to die for this shit, and you almost did, I don't get it my friend?"

"I know you are teasing me Easy'V...you just told me, that you know what your government...is researching at the Bremen Labs...but you don't know how it works?"

"Hold on Dusty, I believe that in the Bureau, nobody knows how this thing works, except for the foreign agents, I'm guessing? Dusty, do you have any knowledge of how this system works? I know, that's to protect satellites, but I don't have the fucking vaguest idea, how this thing works!!" Viggo asks interested in the answer, and Dusty calmly responded...

"Now, you hold on a minute...give time the time...to remember...you know that a few hours ago...I was really dead..."

"Don't you remind me anymore, about your fucking death, because otherwise I'm going to put you, in the same state that you were before. Okay?

"It sounds good...when I say that I was dead Easy'V...because that reminds me that I am alive... Special-Agent Bronson. Okay?"

"I can see that you are getting better. Then, let's go back to what matters. Dusty, do you have a rough idea of how this space system works?"

"Easy'V, when the rope is tense...at one point it busted...and it is what it is, better than nothing...you know."

"Just cut the crap out Dusty!!"

"Okay, if you put it that way...Then I will try my best...just listen...I will tell you how it is supposed to work...yes...you heard correctly...it's all a guess...because...this is what I learned from my comrades...The info or the data...related to the new space program...and the purpose of the fucking new system... comes from

The Bremen Co...It seems like it was designed...to protect and defended the spying satellites which are...circulating in the outer space...and what you should be aware of is the..."

"Please Dusty, what I should know, is what you already know, that is the key, of the fucking question. Okay?"

"Easy'V... what I was trying to tell you...that the system is almost ready to be deployed into space...I'm sure that the key...about the answer of all this space mess...you will find it at The Bremen Lab's...but there is another subject...and for your knowledge...do you know...how these scientists named the project?"

"You are enjoying my anointment...are you? And who gives a fuck, how the fucking project the name is? Just stop fucking with me and tell me what the fuck I want to know!!"

"Yes...yes, I can't deny it...I never saw you so pissed off... I don't think it's because of this case, must be some other reason...I don't want to touch the subject because it's irrelevant. Okay?"

"My friend, there are many reasons to be pissed off, one of them, you know all about it. Okay? The other, we are talking about it: Please, Dusty, just try to tell me what you know?"

"Easy'V, I will help you to solve this case...I promise." Dusty, said sitting up on the bed and Viggo a little frustrated answer...

"Thanks, Dusty, there are simple things that frustrate me, for example, that I have to relying on a foreign agent to obtain information, which should have given to me by Mr. Franklin, before I leave New York. The people that have commanding position, are a bunch of incompetents, and this situation drive me crazy. Okay?"

"Easy'V...let's go back to what I was telling you...about how the scientist names the project...from what I heard...was named...*The Cyber Fusion System?* ...It's a clever name...if the fucking system works?" Dusty said dustily, and Viggo who is really pissed off, because he only knows half, of what is going on, then he responded...

"Dusty, the fucking Franklin, didn't mention a word about this *Cyber shit*; this fucking case, has frustrated my fucking testicles so bad, that I feel like grabbing someone's neck and strangling the son of a bitch...fuck me!!"

"Hey...hey don't look at me, remember...I'm your friend!!" Dusty said raising his arms, and Viggo responded...

"Dusty, since I got to L.A, everything went the wrong way: to make matters worse, I find my best friend, wounded in the hospital, that's a very annoying fucking situation, and I just found out, that the FBI leaders, wrap themselves in the banner of politics, trying to destabilize this government, what the fuck, is going on?" Viggo wonders raising his arms and walking in the room and Dusty tries to appease his friend's spirits and he said...

"My friend, forget about all this shit, and let's leave the frustrations for another time...and focus on this case...let's calm down...I will tell you...what we have found out...But, it doesn't mean, that you should base your future decision...on this information...which comes from my comrades...who are not specialists...in the subject of nuclear physics. Okay?"

"Thanks, Dusty, any info that you can contribute, will be essential for this investigation, tell me what you know, perhaps we will come to a conclusion, which will lead us, on the right path to solve this fuckin case." Viggo said trying to control his frustration, and Dusty responded like he does dustily...

"Okay, Easy'V...we know...who buys the info...he is the same person who sells it to us...the next step is to find out...which is the individual...who is selling the info...in the labs of The Bremen Co. Okay?"

"Dusty, all those details I know, let's go to the heart of the matter, if you don't mind?"

"Okay Easy'V...but first I must tell you...this data comes second hand...from the scientist...who sells the info from this interstellar project...it's quite complicated...if I say that...it is because my little knowledge...about the technology of the nuclear atomic physics...or the science of the fucking chemistry..."

"Come on Dusty: don't play dumb. I know that you spend three years at the science university, until the director kick you out, for fucking around with the girls!"

"Okay...Easy'V...but you have to put the subject...on the fucking scales of the nymph of truth...and you know...very well, that I am not...Igor Kurchatov. Okay?"

"Now you are telling me the truth, that you are not the famous Russian nuclear scientist, Igor Kurchatov...even a blind man can see that!!"

"Easy'V, this is not the time...to get wise with me...you are touching my sensitivity...remember that a few hours ago I was..."

"Don't even think about it Dusty!"

"Okay...Okay? As a matter of fact...The info that I will provide you...in this case...it's nothing more than an approximate hypothesis...of this fucking complex system...which supposedly is an atomic composition with...a fusion of protons...and neutrons of nuclear cells...once this atomic cocktail is being ensemble...Then will be insert into a large ballistic capsule...according to the technicians...this projectile it will be send into space...with laser guided precision...and once the device is in the right place...will be detonated near to the satellite...this exothermic reaction...will expand and create around that object a huge nuclear net...this compound of billions of cells...will protect the American satellites...against hostile missiles." *Viggo is listening in silence he can't believe what he is hearing,* and *Dusty paused for few seconds and arranges his hair with both hands and continues saying.* "Easy'V...according to the scientists...this inter stellar nuclear net...will protect all the satellites...and consequently will guard any other objects...which will traveling in outer space...this is the purpose of this new defense system...but I must say...that I heard this data from my comrades...and the point I'm going to introduce...has to do...that these guys...have no knowledge...how the neutrons or atoms works. Easy'V, that's all I know about this fucking case...Which almost caused my dear life. Okay?" Dusty with a smile finished informing slow and dustily. After that revelation Viggo felt that his friend came through, and he is going to do his best to help him...

"What you're saying is incredible, even if part of the information was guessing. Dusty, these sequences of events give me the certainty, that for sure, I have to pay a visit to the Bremen Co. and let's see who is the person involved in selling the project?" Viggo said walking around the bed, and Dusty adds.

"I wish I could go with you...just to see his reaction...at the moment you tell Mr. Bremen...one of his scientists...is selling secrets to foreign agents...I'm really I don't want to be in his shoes...with the prospect of being investigated...for espionage." Dusty pointed out, and Viggo added...

"I agree Dusty, since Mr. Bremen, takes great care of his image, because it's well-known that the government, has given him the opportunity to explore his genius capabilities, and for that reason alone, he will not sabotage his own project, don't you think?"

"I believe you are right Easy'V...Mr. Bremen, is to smart and quite busy...with all his new projects...I could start with the new smart rocket...which goes to outer space...and when comes back...the rocket sits in a fucking chair, and to complete the week...he's trying to build a bullet train inside a tube...no less, I think this guy doesn't have the time...to go around selling his own secrets?" Dusty ends up saying with an expression of wonder and Viggo added...

"I know, he is some kind of flamboyant individual. I'll say, that for the moment, let's leave Mr. Bremen alone, and take care of your situation. Dusty, are you sure that you would like to stay in this country?"

"I'm sure Easy'V, I love to remain here...but what I love the most...is the liberal part of your country...your fucking politicians...let into the country...any fucking bum in the world that walks...that is amazing..."

"Don't complain Dusty, because maybe you're going to be part of that crowd, then you, have to deal with different races, and their customs; for example, the guys who send you to this hospital, the Chinese's, eat everything that walks in the world, they eat ants' cockroaches, dogs, monkeys and they love vampire's meat. What that fuck?"

"Okay...okay Easy'V, we better return to your question...if I would like to remain in your country? ...I must say...that there are not many fucking options to choose from...A matter of fact...if I don't stay here...I'm sure, the boys in Moscow...will make sausages...from my private parts!" Dusty said raising his arms, and Viggo responded...

"Just relax Dusty, I already told you, that I was going to take care of your situation, I'll process your papers step by step; first I am going to apply for political asylum, once the government grant the permission, the other procedures, will be easy to acquire..."

"Sound good, but in the meantime, I'm here at the hospital!

"Dusty, I understand, that being at the hospital, produces mixed emotions, but I'm sure that in a couple of days you'll be fine."

"Maybe you're righty Easy'V... I never imagined finding myself in this situation...but, if I have to swim against the current I will...Just tell me what I have to do...and I'll do it?" Dusty said rehearsing a pale smile, and Viggo is relieved to know that with his friends help, he has half of the espionage case solved and he adds...

"Thanks, Dusty, I'm sure, we will solve this case in no time, but first I have to make sure, that all your documents will be in order, second, we must have a good grip of Pascucci, what I'm going to tell you, is a little bit hasty, but since I'm sure that you're going to stay, if you don't have any other projects in mine? I'll help you to start your own business in this country?"

"You are a fucking motherfucker Easy'V...you have this amazing ability to seduce...and persuade a fucking dead body...I hope I can help you to solve this case...And remember...that I came here with the only mission...to protect the operators...I didn't come here to steal...anybody's girlfriend, okay?" Dusty said very slowly and really dusty. Viggo interested in the response he might get, asks...

"Dusty, I love it, we are going to work together, and I'm glad, that your ass, going to remain in the US, but I'm very sorry that you won't be able to take care the girls at the Love Palace Mansion."

"That's the least of my problems...the truth Easy'V...I do not know...how to thank you enough...for everything you're doing for me...Just tell me...what else you want to know...and I'll see if I can really help?

"Dusty, first thing first, at this moment the most important scenario, is to identify the person who sells the secrets. It seems that the Bremen's Co. employ's a lot of different technicians, engineers, physicists and scientist: what I really would like to know, is which of these *geniuses,* has access to all the documents, this person with total impunity, copies the secrets and sells them to foreign agents?" Viggo asked to his just recruited allied and Dusty added...

"Well..." *Dusty pausing for a second scratching his head and looking at Viggo.* "Easy'V, all I can tell you...is what I know and what I don't know. Okay?"

"Now you're talking Dusty, first of all, tell me what your suspicions are about the person who is selling the information?" Viggo said getting close to Dusty, who was a little bit uncomfortable according to his situation and he said...

"Okay, listen." *Dusty lowered his head, because his friend is not going to be pleased with what he is going to tell him, then he looks at his friend and spoke.* "Easy-V...you know, that in the universe of the espionage...there is a very dark road...and it's quite treacherous path to travel...in that complex world of mysteries...no one knows the name...of the scientist...who is selling the secrets...inside at The Bremen Co...we really don't know who this person is...I hope you're not disappointed...with my answer." Dusty said slowly and precisely, and he was right: Viggo believes in his friend but waited for another answer and Viggo asks again...

"If this is the case Dusty, now let's see how we can reverse the situation, and tell me what you know substantially." Viggo asked raising his hands, and Dusty with apprehension responded.

"Easy-V...you won't like this info either...the person who has the answer...to all of your questions...is Mr. Santino Pascucci, he is the only one..."

"He's the only fucking scumbag!! You must be kidding Dusty, there has to be something else: you... you must squeeze your brain and come up with something, come on think?" Viggo frustrated asked, but what he just heard, left him thinking, and Dusty will try to please his friend with his answer...

"I'm not kidding Easy'V...I can't give you info that I don't have...if you were a foreign agent...and you are seeking information...about the *Inter-Stellar-Defense-System*...you have no other choice...but to pay Pascucci...dearly for the errand. Okay?"

"Dusty, that's not such bad news, if you have scheduled a future meeting with Santino Pascucci. I'm sure that you guys have a designated site, to meet with this scumbag, even if he is in France right now?" Viggo asked interested in the answer and Dusty responded...

"Easy-V...about a week ago...my comrades...made plans to meet Pascucci on Monday...In that process...you arrived in L.A...and you have the audacity...to kill his three men? ...this is why the meeting collapsed...because you came and fuck everything..."

"Dusty, are you trying to say it was all my fault. —Don't you dare, Mr. Kavisky?"

"I know...you're kidding Easy'V...but the guys who weren't fucking around...were the Chinese's...because at the moment...they learned about the incident...they thought that Pascucci bodyguards...were executed by the Russian agents...the Chinese's...were quite upset...since they lost their contact...and they knew we were the competition...the Chinese's thought...we had killed Pascucci's men...this is why these fuckers tried to give me...one-way ticket to hell...but I got lucky...and now I am here alive...and kicking...ready to enter into another mission...that will take me...again straight to the fucking hell!"

"Hey, let's not go to hell: because many guys, will be waiting for us with open arms!" Viggo said *and Dusty agreed, shaking his head up and down and Viggo continued saying.* "Dusty, if you look at the event sequences from another prospect, you'll see, that it was quite predictable that Santino Pascucci, at the moment he learned that his men were dead, didn't take much time, for the old fox, to figure it out, that he was in real trouble, and without thinking twice, he split bound to France, and he left the Chinese's and the Russians, hanging like a kite, hanging in the air and very pissed off, blaming each other for having lost the precious contact. I'm sure that's what happened?" Viggo affirms, and Dusty adds...

"That's right Easy'V...that is what happened." *Said Dusty getting up off the bed and sits in front of his friend* "After all this mess my comrade's arranged a meeting with the Chinese's, right there in front of the Bremen Labs, that meeting was a huge mistake...because right away...began with a huge argument...blaming each other...for the death of the Pascucci's man and...the fucking Chinese's started shooting...with no reason...I believe I was the only one wounded...I guess, since in that instant I passed out...then I came back to life when a person...was blowing hot air on my mouth...that's when I opened my eyes...and I saw that beautiful woman...who very sweetly was kissing my lips...in that moment...I felt that I was in heaven...an angel was welcoming me...to paradise...with kisses...until...until the moment I raised my head...and I looked around,...and I realize that I was...in this fucking world...where half of the people...don't give a fuck...about the other half!!"

"Dusty, that was a profound philosophy thought. I never imagined that you had those qualities. I must say, I'm impressed, I hope after that profound reflection, we'll continue being friends: since I am the other half?"

"My friendship, you should never doubt and ...Fuck you...and your anaconda to...and what philosophy...you're talking about? I'm just trying to get rid of this anger...that I have for being in this situation...Easy'V...Okay?

"Don't complain Dusty, consider yourself lucky, you are alive with friend and philosophizing, as a good thinker, much better that you cheer up, because from this moment Dusty, your life will change forever!"

"Changes...scare me more than marriage Easy'V...I heard you say once...There is always...a place and the time to die...between the legs...of a beautiful woman..." At that moment Dusty got out of bed without any care, and Viggo said...

"What the hell are you doing Dusty, in your condition, you shouldn't make sudden moves, you got off the bed, like nothing happened!"

"Don't worry...I'm just fine...the doctor said...that I didn't lose any blood...and the fucking bullet...that hit my chest...didn't do any harm...to my internal organs...I feel fine Easy'V...I'm preparing myself...mentally to be ready for the trip...to France." Dusty said with confidence, and Viggo frowning asks...

"Dusty, what do you mean, when you say, I'm ready to go to France?"

"Easy'V…you just said it…Pascucci is an old smart fox…and when he found out…that you killed the three goons…the next day…he took off for France." Dusty informs dustily, and Viggo asks…

"Dusty, we already know that Pascucci is in France, but what I would like to know, is where is this piece of shit is hiding, that's the million-dollar question?" Viggo firmly asks, and Dusty who does not lose his cool responded…

"If you're going to put…his whereabouts…at that price Easy'V? …Because with a million dollars…we will have a great time in France!"

"Dusty, please, it's getting late, let's see if we can get something done, do you know in which bunker this fucker is hiding?"

"Sure I know…where this guy is…Easy'V…there is something that we do very well…It happened to be…that the Russian Intelligence…has quite a few agents that specialize…in monitoring people…and before you arrive my friend called me from France…his name is Igor Verzenco…he is well known in the spy community…as *The-Shadow*…who on this precise moment…Igor is following the steps of Pascucci…closely…If he didn't move in the last twenty-four hours…from where he was…Mr. Santino Pascucci…right now is relaxing his bones…in the South of France." Dusty said very calm and Viggo added…

"What the fuck did you say Dusty? That data that you just threw carelessness, means that you know very well where Pascucci is hiding, I bet it's somewhere on the Côte Bleue: I see…no wonder you want to go after this guy…"

"Hey, hold on a second…I swear, if I want to go to France…it's only…it's only to help you Easy'V…you know me very well…I never stopped helping my friends…for that reason I will tell you… that I'm sure that Igor knows…where Pascucci is hidden!" Dusty said with an expression that said, I don't know if you understand me, and Viggo happy with what he just heard answers…

"Thanks Dusty, with this info, you just handed to me, this case on a tray, and for sure that is going to clears the path of many obstacles, if you have *The-Shadow* following Pascucci, you must know in which city he is hiding? Viggo asked impatiently and Dusty stood up and ignoring the question said.

"Easy'V...I just realized that I don't have my documents...I believe Detective D'Layne has them...Please Easy'V... please could you get my documents back? ...I really want to go with you to France...let's see if we can capture Pascucci...and the only way we can do it...if we have my documents, to obtain the American doc.."

"Relax, Dusty, I'm sure we're going to France, the difference is, that you are not going to enjoy the Côte Bleue, we won't have the time?" Viggo said shaking his head side to side and Dusty asks...

"Come on Easy'V...pleas...let's see if you can get my documents?" Dusty said seriously, and Viggo, without saying a word got up and left the room, after few minutes he came back with all Dusti's documents and handed then to him, then Viggo said...

"Okay Dusty: here are all your documents, I hope they relaxes your nerves and clears your mind, it would be beneficial if you will remember some other details, about this case?" Viggo pointed out, and handed him the documents, and Dusty happily responded.

"Give me time Easy'V...you know that without credentials...you don't exist...if you don't exist...for one reason or another...anyone can throw you in a garbage can...and, you know that very well. Easy'V... with my documents...you can start the procedures...to request political asylum?" Dusty asks, and Viggo seriously responded...

"At least one of us, is thinking about the future, and talking about the near future. Dusty, *the Shadow*, knows where Pasccuci is hiding?"

"Until the other day...we knew where he was...I'm sure we are going to find him...one way or another...Incidentally Easy'V......free working trip at the French Riviera...It is the least gift I expected...for a free vacation!" Dusty said rubbing his hands and Viggo responded...

"It's not free Dusty, you already paying for this fictional vacation, with your collaboration in this case. Okay?"

"Hey, Easy'V...these kinds of opportunities don't appear every day...since the American taxpayers...will pay for the entire trip...As you say in America...there is nothing better than a free lunch...?"

"Okay, Dusty, remember that a few hours ago, you were in heaven playing the harp with Saint Peter, and now, you would like to travel all the way to Europe and, you will feel well enough, to chase all over France, after Pasccuci, ?" Viggo asked trying to bring some sense to his friend, and Dusty is listening to him and walking around the hospital room with those ridiculous gowns, which are open in the back, and showing his backside, and Viggo looking at his friend said...

"Dusty please, stop walking around the room, showing your ugly furry ass, to the whole world!" Viggo said jokingly and Dusty covering his butt said...

"I can't trust anyone...just tell me, with what kind of intentions...you're looking at my ass? ...that's all I need right now ...is that you are going to tell me...that I must shave my ass...if I want to become an American citizen?" Dusty asked smiling: at the same time, he's checking that nothing is missing from his wallet, and Viggo, smiling ignores the comment and responded accordantly...

"Dusty, I' sure that nothing is missing in your wallet, and I don't want to talk about your ass, because it makes me realize that we are descendants of Apes!" Viggo said smiling but Dusty was worried for his future and answered.

"We better put that issue aside...Okay?" *Said Dusty and paused for few seconds and looking down he said.* "Okay, Easy'V...I will collaborate with you in whatever way I can...But from now on, I can never show my nose in Russia."

"Dusty, remember that I'm your friend, and I'm telling you, that you, just you, should consult your conscience about your situation."

"Tanks Easy'V...I know that this conflict...is only my mess to solve." *Dusty paused for a few seconds thinking what he wants to say next.* "I know...I can count on your help Easy'V...and I'm going to help you to capture Mr. Pascucci...if he didn't move his ass...I already told you that...he is on the Côte Bleue near the city of Nice."

"Great, Mr. Kavisky, you just came through: that's precisely what I wanted to know, where Mr. Pascucci was hiding, and now get ready. Dusty, because we are going to get this asshole, right there on the beautiful beaches of the blue coast, or the Côte Bleue!"

"Just...name that blue coast with any name...it sounds pretty good to me." *And Dusty started scratching his head, like something is coming to his mind.* "Easy'V...I remember something vaguely...*The Shadow*, told me that Pascucci...was under the protection...of an Italian guy named...named what the fuck was his name...?"

"Come on Dusty, think...just think of the South of France and its beaches, the girls in bikini, and the good food...!"

"Okay...Okay...don't squeeze my brain Easy'V...I know that his name is Michael...and his last name... yes...Oh, yes D'tella...Michael D'tella...!" Dusty remembers and he stays thoughtful and Viggo anxious to know said...

"Come on, Dusty, what else do you rememb...?"

"Okay Easy'V? If I remember correctly...this guy D'tella...is the owner of an Art Gallery...A matter of fact...the Gallery is located...at the medieval village...of Saint Paul de Vence...nothing less...Easy'V, I'm sure that you once walked and wandered...through all the streets of that village?"

"Dusty, I'm remember the village, for sure I did walk on those cobblestones streets, thinking in all those skill masonries who made this path thousands of years ago." Viggo said nostalgically and Dusty added...

"This ancient village...have something magical...that attracts your imagination Easy'V, when I had to leave, I felt that I will miss the place...and I said to myself...I have to return to this place."

"Dusty, it must be, the way that place was built, it's amazing, because according to the stories, in those medieval times, it was a fortress impossible to penetrate: a matter of fact, about three thousand years ago, the fucking Romans were on a campaign to conquer all the territory they could. The Roman army no matter how hard they tried; they could not take over the fortified village." Viggo indicates with certain appreciation for the past residents of the village, and Dusty added...

"You're right...Easy'V, this village was and is impregnable...but what it was then a great fortress...now this site became a famous tourist attraction...and what is remarkable is that the village...is preserved almost intact." Dusty said remembering the place and Viggo added...

"Dusty, I'm amazed: by how the mind of these gangster's works, he's choosing an unusual place to hide; I'm sure, that Mr. Pascucci must feel very secure in that Gallery, without imagining that he has a mastiff watching him?" Viggo said standing up and beginning to walk around the room, and Dusty sitting on the bed commented...

"I'm sure that Pascucci...doesn't have a clue that we know in which cave...he's hiding...what a surprise...it will be when he sees our faces...Surpriseeee...!!!" Dusty said out loud with confidence, and Viggo added...

"It would be great, if we found him in a coffee place, enjoying his freedom, watching tourist pass bay...drinking coffee and smoking a cigar, and we will approach him and spoke. Can we, join you...?"

"I'm sure, this fucker is going to shit in his pants! Easy'V...if The Shadow is following him as it should...for sure, we will know where to find him."

"Dusty, please take my phone and call him, let's see if *The Shadow* knows where the fucking prey is."

"Look Easy'V...for my safety...we are going to do things...the right way. Okay, first I want to have all my American documents in order...at the time we are sure that... we are going to that village...I will call him...?"

"Okay, Dusty, seems like a good decision; but you agree that the village is an impressive place, it would be nice to go back, and walk in those thousands of years old cobbled streets, which have certain magic charm from that mysterious past, this place transports my thoughts to the Knights, it's a really strange feeling, I imagine myself walking through those streets with a cape hanging from my shoulders and a sword tied to my waist..." Viggo said in a melancholy tone and Dusty added...

"You are not the only one...who dreams about it... because the village...brings to our imagination...living in those times...you know what this means Easy'V?"

"What are you talking about?"

"That...Mr. Pascucci...did something positive...gives us the opportunity to return to the historic site...what you don't know...is that some time ago...I visited the village with a young woman...with whom I had a love affair...and I almost got married...but..."

"Hey, hold on Dusty, you always were a lonely wolf running free in the wilderness, it's almost impossible to catch you off guard, the wolf in danger is when he is most alert. What happened to you Dusty, that episode of your life is new to me?" Viggo asks raising his eyebrows and Dusty tells his adventures to his friend and he said...

"That was a crazy moment of my life Easy'V...I had the wrong feeling...to get involved with the person that I shouldn't have..."

"Don't tell me: Dusty, the woman was married with some big wig?

"No: much worse...Claire, was a lovely twenty-year-old girl, the daughter of a Russian dignitary...and we started sneaking out...and I thought that I was in love with the girl...not only was she beautiful but she was a lot of fun...one day her father and mother had gone on a trip for couple of weeks...and we decided to escape...and go on a trip with her...I had a hard time to convince her...but the following day...we flew from Moscow to Paris...where we rented a car...then, already on our way, we stopped in Leon, Cannes Nice, and after a week of traveling...finally, we ended up in Saint Paul de Vence..."

"Dusty, that wasn't an escape, it was a sneaking out. I bet you, that was a fantastic adventure: think about it, from Moscow to Paris, then by car to Saint Paul de Vence, that getaway was great Dusty." Viggo said happy for his friend and Dusty added...

"Easy'V, to reach the summit of the rocky mountain, it was amazing...and there it was, in front of my eyes...the ancient village...like a giant Colossus remembering their ancestors...I'm ready to go back...and I guess that you too...the inconvenient is that the village...has become an tourists attraction and they...come from all over the world...with an open imagination, to enjoyed the intriguing charm of the place!" Dusty said like he's in love with the place, and in that moment Viggo's phone rang. It's his partner Rachel, who was quite upset she said...

"What's going on Chief, it's midnight and I'm in bed all alone, hugging the pillows, but the pillow has no tattoos, and don't have the overwhelming warmth that your body has, I'm missing you: where are you Chief?"

"Calm down Rocky, you know that I was at the Bureau, and I had a conference with the HO, and now for other circumstances, I'm at the hospital, because..."

"What is going on, are you okay Chief?" Rachel, asks concerned, and Viggo, who knows the temper of his partner is trying to defuse the situation and he said...

"Rocky, noting happened to me, bat I'm here in the Santa Monica Hospital, with our friend Dusty, who was injured in a shootout with the Chinese's, and I'm trying to..."

"What the hell he's doing here? Can you tell me, what the fuck this fucking Russian is doing in the US? I bet this piece of shit, is involved in the current case of espionage. Fuck him Chief and squeeze his testis until he tells you everything he knows, show no mercy Okay!!" Rachel asks quite loud over the phone, and Viggo responded.

"Please Rocky, can you relax for a minute, everything has a rational explanation? When I get to the hotel, we will talk. Okay?" Viggo after finished talking with Rachel he turned around and said...

"Dusty, that was Rocky, she said hello, and she wishes you a speedy recovery." Viggo said with a face that say it's not my fault, and Dusty commented...

"Thanks'...but last time I talked to Rocky...it seemed like she didn't care much about me...it's possible that I said or did something that she didn't appreciate...and she was offended...I really don't know what to think?" Dusty asks with a grin, and Viggo reminded him...

"Dusty, you remember that famous social gathering at the Government Palace in Moscow, you forgot to invite Rocky, she doesn't forgive this type of fuck-up, I guess you're on her shit list." Viggo point out and Dusty just frowned and said...

"I swear Easy'V...that detail never crossed my mind...I had no idea that she was offended...I swear that I had no intention of ignoring her...please, tell Rocky, that I'm so sorry...that I will make it up to her...at the moment we come back...from France?" Dusty said getting out of bed and covering his ass with the gown, and Viggo said...

"Dusty, don't worry about Rocky, because three of us are going to France, and you don't have to worry about any silly things, when you leave the hospital, it would be nice if you gave her a couple of dozen roses, I'm sure you would get on Rocky's better side."

"I hope so Easy'V...I really like Rocky...from what I've heard of her she is a wonderful person...and great agent...by the way...did you already...?"

"Please Dusty, forget about Rocky, and let's return to our subject, because I have to decide what to do first. Okay?"

"Okay...okay...Easy'V...how are we going to continue...this amazing saga...walking or running?"

"Running and running: Dusty, when we are going after Pascucci, and now we walk and think, while we are planning the next moves. Okay?"

"Very good strategy Easy'V...and you have already decided...what will be the future plans?"

"Just about: Dusty, tomorrow morning, at the moment I arrive at the Bureau, I'll go and see Ember, and the first thing I will give her all the information, you just gave me regarding this case, *then on top of the desk*, we'll arrange the details about the trip to France, this is the plan, Dusty." Viggo said with a wicked smile and ready to leave, and Dusty quite quickly responded...

"Hold-on Easy'V...are you telling me, that will you arrange the details to the trip to France...*on the top of the desk?*...You have no shame you...Son of..."

"Just think Dusty, you are a Russian agent; and I'm doing all these nasty sacrifices, only for your well-being my friend."

"Thanks' Easy'V...since you're making all these sacrifices for me...in return for your kindness...I want to help you...but first, I'm going to need my cloths...the problem is...that I can't show up at my hotel... just like that..."

"Why not?"

"Hey, Easy'V...are you forgetting a minor detail...that I'm dead...I can't go to the hotel...I'm dead...Mr. Hot Pants. Okay?" Dusty said out loud and Viggo answers...

"Dusty, don't worry, tomorrow I'll send Rocky, to pick up your belongings, just give me the keys to your room, and the address of the fucking place."

"Okay...okay!! Here are the keys and the room number...the hotel is in downtown L.A, and the address is South Broadway 829...I hope that Rocky, is not going...to lose my suitcases...just to get even!" Dusty said with smile and Viggo who is ready to go asks...

"What is the name of the fucking hotel Dusty?"

"Easy'V...I'm a guess of the world famous...nothing more nothing less. Then...*The Ace Hotel*...and I'm sure that you know about the fame of that hotel." Dusty said smiling, and Viggo shaking his head responded...

"You must be kidding Dusty, but you are right, it's world famous, in New York we have one of those brothels, these hotels are where the two thousand-dollar girls' vacation. I wonder why you selected that hotel?" Viggo asked with a witty smile, and Dusty of course he dustily answered...

"My dear friend...for your information...I'm a guest in that hotel...it happened...that some of these girls...were visitors in the mansion in Moscow...I'm sure that you were socializing with Annabel and Bobbie...because the girls were asking for Special-Agent Viggo Bronson...it doesn't surprise me, that you we're involved with these girls?" Dusty ends up asking, and Viggo curiously asked...

"Don't tell me? The girls are in the hotel?"

"They are...and with great curiosity they asked me...if I was still your friend...you fucking lucky dog!!" Dusty says in an ironic way, and Viggo adds...

"You are right. Dusty, I was lucky, but it was just a coincidence, because it all started about six months ago, when I was following a lead in the heart of Manhattan, at that time a fucking moron mobster, had the bad idea of kidnapping a senator's wife, the investigation took me to The Black Cat Night-Club, and who do you think frequented that place?"

"Easy'V, we were talking about...Annabel and Bobbie...Correct?" Dusty, ask's raising his arms as if he was implying, you're a lucky SOB and Viggo ignores the comment and said...

"The girls were there, yes, Dusty, right there in the bar counter, began our friendship, between drinks; a matter of fact, the girls became an important source of information. Sometimes these girls had to deal with devious and dangerous people, when these types of events happen, the girls didn't hesitate in calling me."

"These girls...remember you with a lot of affection...it seems that you treat them really well?" Dusty asks with a witty smile, and Viggo looking at his watch responded...

"It's the only way I do my job Dusty, you know that it's the under-world law, if you want to obtain info, you must reciprocate with assistance, and talking about assistance I need your passport, I want to be sure that you have your papers in order, and I'm going to erase your fucking crimes, and I'll start a speedy process, your American citizenship; then you will have your American passport."

"We only have a few days...are you sure I'm going to get the document in time?" Dusty asks worried, and Viggo confident responds...

"Don't worry Dusty. I have all the connections to prosses the documents; it will be handled under the law of Homeland Security, more secure than that is impossible. It even came out in rhyme!" Viggo says smiling trying to reassure his friend and Dusty responded...

"Thanks, Easy'V...I'm concerned about Detective D'Layne, it seems to me that she has all the intentions to put me behind bars...I know that she has every right to do so, why don't you talk to her?"

"Don't you worry about it, the two policemen who were guarding your room, they're no longer there, they're gone." Viggo throw that phrase carelessly and Dusty took the bait and ask...

"What does this mean?" Dusty asks with an expression of doubt and then he begins walking towards the door, to find out if it's true what his friend said, and after verifying that the guards were gone, then he turns around and said...

"It's true...Easy'V...the guards are no longer there...and now what happens...this does not mean that I'm a free man?" Dusty asks raising the arms, and walking showing his hairy ass and Viggo responded...

"Dusty, it means that right now you are my prisoner, and you have no doubt I'll keep you well guarded; in the meantime, I will get you a room in the same hotel we are staying."

"Easy'V...I hope that in the near future I can repay all the generosity that you are showing to me...this is one of the saddest days of my life...coming to my friend's country and trying...!" Dusty said embracing his friend, and after that friendly hug. Viggo on the way to the door said...

"Stop Dusty, you are talking nonsense, if nothing changes, I'll see you tomorrow afternoon, and don't walk around the hospital, creating panic among people, showing your hairy ugly ass. OK?" Viggo said as he was leaving, and Dusty gets up and starts walking towards the door, and Dusty said in his dusty voice.

"Easy'V...Detective D'Layne...is waiting for you in the hall...My friend...I hope you have a good time...because if she waited all this time for you...she must have something special prepared for you!" Dusty said and saw his friend walking away in the hallway, and Viggo turns around and makes the Okay sign with his thumb, then Dusty looks around, and he can't believe that the police are not there with their large display of weapons, and he went back to bed happy, mumbling something in a dustily way.

"Okay...okay tomorrow...for my own sake...I'm going to become a heartless American capitalist...full of debts and worries...just stuck on the freeway...with millions of fucking cars...where these people are going?...Who knows?...To hell?...I'm sure!...What can I say...about my new nationality?...Only I have to look...at the sunny side of the situation...as a matter fact...it's not so bad and...God bless America...said Lincoln, Martin Luther King, and Kennedy...and they shot them dead...But it is better than being send back to Russia!!" After that expression of wonder, Dusty, called the nurse, and spoke. "If it is possible, for dinner I would like to have, a McDonald's hamburger, with cheddar cheese, and fries. Please."

Meanwhile Viggo went down the hall to meet detective D'Layne, who is waiting for him with a big smile: if we look closely at her demeanor, it will tell us loud and clear, that she is very happy to see him, and Viggo in the same manner smiled back, after the greetings Viggo started to inform the detective, about the situation of Voris Kavisky =*Dusty*. the prisoner would be under the protection of The Federal Bureau of Investigation, and the Russian agent, for security reason will be granted political asylum. Detective D'Layne was aware of the situation, since that information had already reached the ears of detective D'Layne, through the two police officers that earlier left their post. But any way she did pay close attention to Viggo's info, and she responded...

"Special-Agent Bronson, I'm so glad that we're going to work in conjunction: if this is the case, I'll need from Officer Maxwell, the transfer documents, I'm sure his release will not cause any inconvenience?" She asks sweetly, and Viggo agreed and adds...

"Thanks, for your concern, I'm going to make sure that transfer would be done correctly. —Detective D'Layne, it's okay, if we meet at the police headquarters, about noon tomorrow, I'll be there with the proper documentation to transfer Mr. Kavisky."

"I will be waiting for you in my office special agent. —Maybe we can have lunch? There is an excellent gourmet place in Beverly Hills." D'Layne said with a smile, while they were walking towards the car and Viggo responded.

"Detective D'Layne, I can't promise anything, the best approach, is to see how the day unfolds, then we decide." Viggo said opening the car door for her to get in.

Viggo had a full day of unexpected roundabout, and after had the stamina to deal with different uncommon subjects: right now, as a gentleman, he had no choice, but ending his hectic day driving Detective D'Layne home. But she is sitting next to him very relaxed. —*Did I say relaxed?* Hummm nooo.—This is not the case, because inside that car, in the air you could perceive one of those symbolic erotic silences, which usually occurred between a man and a woman, when sex is on the mind of one of them, or both: and the person who breaks the conspicuous silence: is Detective D'Layne, and she said very sweetly...

"Special-Agent Bronson, I did tell you that your book it's quite amazing, if you have the courtesy and the time to autograph your book, I would be very grateful, a matter of fact, I live nearby, if you turn to the right in Wellesley, it's about a mile and a half." The detective already assumed that he would do it, attracted to her beauty, and Viggo had doubts about her real intention, and just played along and said...

"It's a bit late Detective D'Layne, but it will be a pleasure to autograph the book." *At that moment Mary raised her arms behind her head and with a quick move let her blond hair loose over her shoulders, and getting closer to him she whispers in his ear.* "We could celebrate the autograph of the book with a couple of glasses of champagne, I hope you have the time?" Mary said the phrase in a very sensual voice. —We already know Viggo's basic philosophy. *A glass of water and a little love should not be denied to anyone.* Viggo was not surprised by the request, and Mary suggested...

"I have something on my mind, and I would like to share it, Special-Agent Bronson."

"Sure, go ahead, every suggestion helps."

"I was thinking, if I have the opportunity to join this investigation, it would be nice to set aside the formalities, and you should call me Mary, of course, without breaking the rules."

"Okay Mary, but we are already transgressing the rules, if this is what you prefer; then you can call me Viggo." *He didn't finish saying his name, and Mary's hands began to search for the famous tattoo, and Viggo surprised by the woman's speed and the ability to get inside his pants, and Viggo said.* "Please don't do that here, it is not wise." He pleaded in vain it was already too late, the blond hair of Mary's was covering the legs of Viggo's, which begins to perceive the pleasure of the Divine Gods—under that sweet and unique spell; it wasn't easy to maintain control of the vehicle. They were very lucky to arrive at her place in one piece, then Viggo adjusts his pants, and asks himself. *Why I always have to fall into the traps of all these women?* Once inside her apartment Mary with a sexual attitude indicates...

"Viggo, my apartment is not very big, but I hope you find in the cupboard your favorite drink, and while are you enjoying a drink: I'm going to look for the book, and meanwhile I'll change this uniform for something more suitable for the occasion." Mary said walking to her bedroom, upon hearing those words Viggo knew that he could be in a lot of trouble. He began to look around, and saw that the place was quite nice, then he looks at his wristwatch, and the timepiece told him that it was after midnight.

If we would have to review Viggo's long and stressful itinerary: we would learn that early that day, he had to confront those three gangsters who wanted to send him to the nearest cemetery: if that skirmish was for him not enough struggle, then Viggo had to face his jealous wife, who started sexually abusing him at the moment he entered her office: and to top it all, he found his good friend shot in the hospital: after all these unexpected events, the man is still in a good mood. Viggo, looks around and then he takes off his jacket, and placed it on the couch that looks really comfortable, already more relaxed he pours a generous amount of scotch, then with the glass in his hand, he began to walk through the room looking at the pictures decorating the furniture, finally he sits on the couch, and leaned back comfortably, waiting for the hostess and thinking. *"Finally, I can relax: maybe she'll show up only with the book? Hopefully!!"*. Viggo was already for his second scotch, and he begun mumbling.

"Where in hell, does this woman have the book?"

At that precise moment, he got the answer to his request. Viggo can't believe what his eyes are seeing, the same scenery he had to witness before. — Is that Mary appears in the living room looking so gorgeous that his jaw just dropped, amazed by her display of beauty, instantly he sits straight up, remembering that he had seen that show before, and his time of relaxation was over. What happened?

Happens that Mary is looking like a radiant diva, she is wearing high heels with a skimpy see-through negligee, which reveals her fabulous body, in that space and moment, she was creating an unusual sexual show, she was coming slowly swinging her magnificent voluptuous body, and Viggo at that moment was saying to himself. *"I can't believe this woman, she is like a bullfighter, in the car she began the job of lowering my energies, and now she comes with serious intentions to finish me off; and for the occasion she is wearing practically nothing. This kind of event has never happened to me twice in one day: first, my wife, and now Mary, two gorgeous women with a sexy see-through negligee: and there we go, I'm going to be sexually abused again!"* And he just had enough time to put the glass down, because at that instant, the woman like a pink butterfly throws herself into Viggo's arms.

Well, if we start to analyze those moments of sexual anxiety, we will encounter that when there is extreme passion between lovers, there is no time for any romance, for this reason, Miss. Mary, has a natural instincts of a geisha-queen, she began kissing him with passion, and at the same time, with her skillful pair of hands strips him naked, once the man was at her mercy, then she began moaning of pleasure for almost an hour, thrilled rolling around in Viggo's arms, then Miss. Mary, got off of Viggo and said. "I give up...I give up; if I don't stop, I'm going to collapse of pleasure!." then she lays face up in the couch, then Viggo kisses her, and without any rush he begun dressing, finished his scotch calmly, then he places the empty glass on the table, and before leaving. Viggo glanced over Mary's naked body, she is lying on the couch, and not to disappoint Mary, he said with a voice of a dramatic novel actor...

"Miss. Mary, I must tell you, this evening was a little more than interesting. I would say it was the coronation of an unusual day, with amazing occurrences?" *He stops at the door threshold and speaks.* "Mary, I'll see you tomorrow at the office, and thanks for the drinks." Viggo pointed out, and Mary from the white couch, put her red lips together, and threw him a goodbye kiss.

Viggo arrived shuffling at the hotel, at three in the morning. and went straight to take a shower, then he drops in bed thinking about the schedule of the following day: At eight in the morning Rocky, is doing her best to wake up her Chief; the problem for Viggo was that it wasn't easy to pick up the phone, after struggling for a while to wake up, then with his overnight-fuckup voice he answered...

"Please Rocky, can you lower the tone your voice, it's rumbles in my head."

"I'm sorry Chief, but I have been trying to wake you up, for an hour..."

"Hey Rocky, since I entered the Bureau, I've been working all day, and I got to the hotel, at three in the morning, half dead.

—Listen Rocky, I'll take a shower, and I'll see you at the coffee shop. Okay?" Viggo said mumbling the words, and Rachel who is not in a very good mood replied...

"Okay, if I have no other option, I'll wait for you Chief." Rachel said not very happy, and Viggo threw the phone and pushed his head into the pillow, after a few minutes of reflection he took a long shower and wrapped in a towel he sits on the bed, and he began to deliberate what type of clothes he is going to wear, he does not want to look like a dead man, his dilemma was to bring color to his face, then he picked up a pinkish shirt, a red tie and he finish his outfit with a blue blazer; then with confidence he went to meet Rachel, who was waiting at the coffee shop; at the moment she saw Viggo, coming very well dressed, wearing a pinked shirt and flashy red tie; right away she knew, that he was playing around, and now he was trying to erase the traces of evidences from his face: and wandering about what happened last night, she mumbles. "*This son of a bitch was fucking around all night, and now he is going to tell me, that all night he was investigating the case!! Why doesn't he want to tell me the truth, if he knows that the only thing, I want from him is his fucking tattoo?*" Just at the moment that Viggo arrives, she welcomed him with a smile, then Viggo thanks' her, for removing him from Morpheus's arms. After the apologies he began to give Rocky the reports about the Bremen Co. That he was at the hospital sitting next to the bed of his injured friend, trying to get as much information as possible, and the arrangement astutely he proposed to Dusty, then he began to tell his partner all about the schedule he has in mind for the day, but in the agenda is an errand that she has to do, which Viggo must precent with a lot of diplomacy, because Rachel, has to do the dirty work, pick up the belongings of Dusty, from his room at the Ace Hotel. Needless to say, that Rachel didn't say a word, but her eyes were blazing, then...

Rachel, after leaving the café, she headed to the filthy downtown L.A, with the instruction to go to the Ace Hotel and retrieve Dusty's luggage. But Viggo, had another important assignment, after leaving Rachel, he went to the Bureau, with the purpose to obtain from Ember, the Russian prisoner transfer order, from the L.A police, to the custody of the FBI, then he must submit it, to Detective D'Layne, who during this process, she looks at Viggo with forbidden desire, and she was eager to take him to a private office to continue last night saga, but Viggo eludes the situation with diplomacy, and after that awkward moment. Viggo must go to the hospital to have Dusty discharged, and take him to his hotel, where he will be staying; Viggo hopes that by this time Rocky, with Dusty's luggage, will be at the hotel...

Well, as always in this complicated and haphazard life, everything didn't go smooth as Viggo planned. —At the time he shows up to pick up Dusty at the hospital, he came across with bad news. Dusty, last night had an internal hemorrhage, and with all the symptoms that come with it, this unforeseen inconvenience, will leave Dusty, hospitalized for a few more days. Probably, the bleeding was provoked by all the walking around he did, yesterday with his pal Easy'V. —Dusty must remain in the hospital, and Viggo, doesn't have any other choice but come back empty-handed to the hotel, at the moment he enters. Viggo, saw that Rocky was sitting in the lobby surrounded with a bunch of tourists, that's when Viggo, noticed on her face the signs of anger: at the same time, she is aware that Viggo, is coming, and Rachel that has no gray in her character: she could not contain herself and she stands up and asks...

"What's going on Chief, what the hell happens to the fucking scumbag Russian? Don't tell me, I know: all the crap went to his head, and now he is really full of shit?"

"Come on, Rocky?"

"Chief, this guy didn't show up, and I already went to that distinguishing hotel, to pick up his filthy luggage, how the hell this filthy Russian got reservations at the Ace Hotel? Where a room costs one testicle and part of the other." She asked ironically, and Viggo is trying to appease Rachel, who seems quite pissed off.

"Calm down Rocky, during the night Dusty had a relapse, it's nothing to worry about. Okay?"

"Like I care? It's your fucking friend?"

"Come on Rocky, my fucking friend was giving me information until two in the morning, I was performing my duties and you..." Rachel interrupts because she knows he is lying to her, and she responded...

"Chief...you can tell me the truth: you know that I'm an easy-going girl, I guess you know, I was trained to conduct interrogations, and monitor people's behavior, and to me your face is like a map of New York, which is telling me that you...you were fucking around all night..." *Viggo stopped her at the right time and said in a whisper.* "Rocky please, there's a bunch of tourists next to us, calm down please, and try to control your imagination."

"Okay Chief, I'm sorry if I interrupted your nonsense excuses." She smiles and Viggo answers.

"Look Rocky, the events got a little bit complicated. Remember that upon arrival into L.A we suffered this unexpected attack, and then we went directly to the Bureau, and supposedly, I had a meeting with Officer Morris. Well, Morris was sent on a special mission out of the country." *Viggo pause for a second and asks.* "Rachel, who do you think it was sitting behind Morris's desk?" Viggo asks seriously and Rachel is looking at him with a face of mistrust and said...

"You just called me Rachel Chief, that's why I believe that it must be a person that you never...never expected to be in that position, and less sitting behind that desk, it must be someone really very unusual." *And she paused for few seconds pretending that she is thinking and then she said.* "Chief, I don't have the slightest idea who that person can be!" Rachel said with a gesture of resignation and Viggo informs not knowing how she was going to react...

"Trust me Rocky, it was one of those moments that you think could never happen to you, and I wish that no man goes through that..."

"What the hell Chief, who the fuck is this person?

"Rocky, guess who was sitting behind the desk in Morris's office? It was Ember. I couldn't believe it; my wife is the Handling Officer in the L.A district!!"

"Ember? —How is that possible Chief, how come you didn't find out, before leaving New York, that she was the HO in L.A?" *She paused for a second looking at him.* "I'm sure, that she didn't say anything because, Ember was the one who had the gall to have Franklin, assigned this mission to you, remember Chief, what I said to you, that in this case. Franklin, didn't follow the protocol, that something was smelling really fishy, and now I find out, that the fish is quite rotten?"

"I don't know what you're talking about. There's no signs of conspiracy Rocky, why would Ember, for her personal problems, go through the trouble to approach Franklin, besides, Franklin will be, what he will be, but I don't believe that he is corrupted enough, to get involved in a marriage dispute?"

"Well, I guess Mrs. Ember Maxwell, having you close, she has the chance to hold you in the palm of her hand, then would be very easy, for her to recover her husband, and she would hide you under her skirts!" Rachel ends saying with a tiny smile said and Viggo replied...

"Thanks, Rocky, it doesn't occur to you, that it is a much easier way to achieve her purposes?"

"Okay, Chief, just give me a rational explanation?"

"For God's sake Rocky, the only thing Ember had to do, is call me, there is a better solution, this way she didn't have to bother to go and talk to Franklin, don't you agree?

"I believe that she is using all the resources at her disposal, to see if she can get you back in her arms. By the way Chief, how did she reacted when she saw you, she was surprised, really happy, or her face shows quite the opposite?" Rachel asks interested in the answer, then Viggo brings out his poker face and responded...

"Please Rocky, what are you trying to imply?"

"Noting Chief, I only ask out of curiosity?

"Rocky, Ember, was pleasant and strictly professional, after we discussed our assignment in L.A, then we went from the office to have dinner, and for those circumstances that life has, at the moment we were leaving the restaurant..."

"Don't tell me, she was pretending she was going to faint?

"You don't make any sense Rocky, why would she simulate that kind of fantasy?"

"Chief, fainting it's one of the tricks, women have saved up their sleeves, to take advantage of the naïveté of man, to take us to bed, with that trick Ember, gets you in her place, then pampers you, and tell you how much she misses you, and then she fucks your brains out. Okay?"

"Please Rocky, sorry to disappoint you, but none of that has happened, plus, you have an imagination that makes Nostradamus a dumb dreamer!"

"Okay Chief, if the situation was not like that, then tell me how it all happened. Okay?

"Okay Rocky, and calm down, I was telling you that when we were leaving the restaurant, Ember received a phone call from the Los Angeles police department, reporting that there was a shootout in front of the Bremen Company, this confrontation happens between Chinese and Russian agents, then..."

"I know...Chief, the fucking Russian was wounded in that shooting, then what happened?"

"Rocky, this attitude is not necessary there's no reason to show this kind of annoyance..."

"Chief, you know. This guy gets on my nerves, and I can't help it!

"Rocky, please: I'm telling you, Dusty, is a good man and a better friend." *Rachel looks at him with pity as if she is saying, how wrong you are, and Viggo continues with his information.* "Listen Rocky, you know that he saved my life and, since then we become very good friends, I asked him to tell me everything he knew, but because Dusty, was dead for several seconds, he didn't remember much of what had happened..."

"What the hell you are talking about: Dusty, was dead?"

"Rocky, when he was wounded the bullet stopped his heart, and the comrades threw him out of the car, and at the moment he hit the pavement, his heart began to beat again..."

"Come on, Chief, that is pure fantasy!!

"Rocky, the surgeon told me, what happened." Viggo said firmly and Rachel commented...

"They are hard to die, this fucking Russians!"

"You know that it took me a long time to convince Dusty, to spill the beans, and when I was ready to leave, about two o'clock in the morning, Dusty, began to remember and told me all about the new *Inter-Stellar-Defense-System*. Dusty, in his convalescent bed, gave us very good info. Rocky, there's nothing to complain about it. Okay?"

"If you believe in your friend, it's all fine to me Chief, I'm proud of what you have conquered. It's better than being lost in a thick haze, at least now we know where to begin the investigation." Rachel pointed out with a doubtful face, and Viggo ignored her sarcasm, and continued telling Rachel all the details of his meeting with his friend Dusty and he said...

"Listen, Rocky, the info I just got, it's quite relevant: because the complicated dilemma only becomes an annoyance: this revelation is telling me, that I should change the course of this investigation." *Viggo pause for a few seconds thinking and spoke.* "Rocky, to continue this investigation we are not going to France, as I had planned, and right now..."

"Wait a minute, Chief, this is an unexpected change, you must have a very good reason, to alter the original plans. What happened that suddenly you changed tactics?"

"You just mentioned it Rocky, since we know, where to begin the investigation, now we have the knowledge, which gives us the security, where should we go and knock on the proper door, when is open, then we'll continue to open other doors, that will lead us to solve this case. Okay?" Viggo whisper that phrase and that attitude unleashes a passion of love in Rachel who said...

"Oh Chief, you are killing me, your voice sets my heart on fire, why don't we go to the room for a while!!

"Please Rocky, I'm not in the mood, and you know it? Please let's get back to what we were talking about. Okay?

"Okay, Chief, I was going to ask you, if the person who has to know all these details, is aware of what is happening. I mean Ember, knows all about this new information?"

"Not yet: because I just woke up Rocky, I need a good lunch, to regain all the mental strength, that I lost last night to convince Dusty to give me all the info." *Viggo said facing his partner with stone-face and continue saying.* "I just need a ribeye steak with a spinach omelet, don't you think, that would be a very good start, to regain strength." Viggo said with a face that said I didn't do it, and Rachel agree and ask...

"Ribeye steak, sound delicious. Chief, after you recover your mental energy, the one you spend, last night trying to convince your friend. —Now tell me, what are we going to do next?" Rachel commented and asked sarcastically and Viggo replies...

"Please Rocky, don't break my balls, and listen to what I'm going to say. Okay?"

"I promise that I won't interrupt, Chief."

"I was saying that the info I got from Dusty, they are clear evidence, which will take us right inside the Bremen Co. and our next move, will be to unmask the scientists who are involved in selling the info to foreign agents. Look Rocky, once we solve this puzzle, then we are going after Pascucci, once our purpose is achieved, we already have half the battle won, we only have to catch that fucking gangster." Viggo said with conviction, and Rachel who is listening and looking and studied his face, she concludes that he was fucking around all night, but she does not know with whom, but she imagines who this person is: and Rachel is thinking. "*Why he doesn't tell me the truth, because he knows I'm not in love with him, I'm just using him, and tonight, I'm going to have my revenge, Mr. Special-Agent Bronson, I'm going to tear-you-apart until you beg me for mercy.*" After projecting in her mind, all those malevolent and wicked sexual torture she will perform to her superior, then she asked him very sweetly...

"By the way Chief, I guess that after lunch, we are going to pay a visit to...

THE BREMEN COMPANY

"That's right Rocky, after we have finish eating, let's see if we can have a meeting with Mr. Bremen, we'll see what he has to say, I'm sure he will have the good sense to collaborate with us, I don't believe this man is protecting a traitor to his country, in his own company, and in the process, tarnish his sparkly reputation." Viggo said decisively and Rachel added...

"Chief, if Mr. Bremen has the willing to cooperate with us, it will clear the way to interrogate all the crew, who works in the plant, and in the process save us a lot of time!" Rachel said taking Viggo's arm and walking towards the restaurant, and Viggo stopped walking for a second and said...

"Rocky, we should approach this interview as if we were doing a courtesy visit, a matter of fact: we don't have to raise any suspicion, since the interested party, could be there around us."

"Wait a minute Chief, pretending a courtesy visit, is not going to be easy, because at the moment we present our identifications, what are you going to say?"

"Rocky, I'm going to say that we came to pay a visit to Mr. Bremen, then with a little bit of class, we find out about what type of knowledge he has about the life of his employer's. Do you follow?"

"Of course, Chief, if you are a genius!"

The Federal agents walked a short distance to a restaurant on the second Street. During lunch Rocky was not behaving like she usually does, cheerful and sexual and Viggo asks.

"Rocky, you're okay, you don't act like you usually do, are you in...?"

"No Chief, what happens is, that since we arrived in Los Angeles, you don't pay attention to me, as you always do, I'm hoping that you're not aware of the situation, because I feel neglected. I'm not complaining, but I have the feeling that you're absent. I sense that your mind is somewhere else, in another dimension, like…"

"Stop right there: what kind of nonsense are you talking about Rocky, please, can we have this meal in peace? I don't wish to discuss a subject that does not have consequence or purpose at this point. Okay? And it's three o'clock; let's finish our lunch and let's see if we can talk to Mr. Bremen." Viggo proposed and continued to have lunch in silence, until they finished eating that's when Viggo decided it was time to go.

By the time they arrived at the Lab's. Mr. Bremen was in the process of leaving his office. —Upon entering the building Viggo present his credentials to Ms. Lillian, the Secretary, who welcomed them graciously, and he proceeded to inform her, that they were in the city on official business, and decided to pay a courtesy visit to Mr. Bremen. —Ms. Lillian made a quick phone call to Mr. Victor Bremen, who welcomed the two Federal agents, with a gentle gesture.

"This is a pleasant surprise, what can I do for the Special-Agent Bronson, and you Miss…?" Mr. Bremen said looking at Rachel, who answers…

"I'm Agent Rachel Dansby, Mr. Bremen, it's nice to meet you." Rachel responded and the businessman cordially replied…

"Agent Dansby, it's a pleasure to meet you, and I'm really intrigued by your presence in my establishment, what unusual event brought the FBI attention to West side of L.A?"

"The reason Mr. Bremen, we are in in L.A is to investigate an organization which is involved in espionage, with that mission, we just arrived from New York. I must inform you, that this case is a matter of national security, that's why we are here in the city trying to solve this case of espionage, that is quite serious, and the high authorities of the government are very concerned." Viggo informs, and Mr. Bremen fairly worried said.

"That's quite intriguing, but in meantime, what are you trying to imply Special-Agent Bronson?" Mr. Bremen asked frowning, and Viggo officially informs...

"Mr. Bremen, the details of this case of espionage are quite complex, a matter of fact, in this plot are several foreign entities interested in obtaining information regarding the new system..."

"Are you trying to say, that I have that kind of insurrection in my establishment? That suggestion is a very serious accusation Special-Agent Bronson, I hope that you have solid evidence, that prove what you are implying!" Bremen said starting to walk nervously in the office, and Viggo who sees the concern on his face replies...

"I'm sorry Mr. Bremen, if our visit has the result of creating some inconvenience, but we are sure that inside this laboratory, someone it's involved in getting their hands-on the secrets, which should not be disclosed under any circumstances." *Viggo paused for a second meanwhile the two-man stood face to face and Viggo said.* "Mr. Bremen, with your help we'll solve this case in no time, and I expect your collaboration, if it's possible?" Viggo asks looking straight in his face, and Bremen did not look away and said...

"Wait a minute: this is disturbing news, it never crossed my mind that this kind of traitors could be in my lab's, it is a situation that I cannot accept, it is inconceivable that this happening in my establishments." *Bremen said really upset and continued on saying.* "I'm sorry about this outburst. Special-Agent Bronson, and now I ask you the million-dollar question. How worried should I be?"

"For what I know about all this situation. Mr. Bremen, you personally, are not involved in this case, and consequently, they are out of suspicion, the Houston Co. and the ISS=International Space

Station, except this lab complex." Viggo comments trying to gain the trust of Mr. Bremen who comments...

"That's amazing Special-Agent Bronson, how the authorities concluded, that this unpleasant situation it happens in this lab. Because it's well known that we supply the ISS, with rockets that don't get lost in the ocean, you know that our rocket after being launching into space, they come back safely to earth, landing smoothly on a platform, this innovation is saving billions of dollars to the government, the same people that right now are investigating me." Bremen mentioned disappointed and Viggo pointed out...

"I believe, Mr. Bremen, that the recovery of the rockets, which return intact to Earth, and land on a stage, it is one of the greatest achievements of this century, and I'm sorry for the invasive questions, I just following procedures, and thanks for your patience, we appreciate your precious time." Viggo ends up saying and Bremen added...

"Special-Agent Bronson, regarding the Houston plant, I should inform you, that in that location not only we design and assemble rockets, also we started a human brain development, that technology, will protect us from diseases, and will increase the human's lifespan."

"That's amazing Mr. Bremen, and how did you get to the assumption that the human brain can be improve? Would be an incredible achievement!" Rachel asks very interested in the answer and Bremen was not going to disappoint her...

"Agent Dansby, this project started by having long talks, with NASA technology engineers; just think, right now we have a technological brain, which guides the scalpel of a surgeon, to a computer brain that also guides with precision a spaceship to Mars. In one-word, Agent Dansby, our brain is one of the most complex computers ever created, which direct our actions at all times, under any circumstances, at this moment, we are studying and researching how to increase our brain potential, to protect us from disease and, to be able to live a longer and healthy life." *He pauses for a few seconds, and looked at the federal agents who are listening very attentively and he continues saying.* "*And* that is not all Agent Dansby, I just started another revolutionary project: about two years ago, we began building the future cities, currently we are developing the highways and streets, in which the vehicles of the future will be traveling with a visionary technology, these futuristic cars should not have any problems finding the places, where do they want to go, and this is just the beginning."

"That comment you just made Mr. Bremen, means that you have other projects in mind. Viggo asks and Bremen pauses for a second and said...

"Special-Agent Bronson, I'm going to talk about what we are doing, only because you're not a journalist. As a matter of fact: right now, we are developing the vehicles of the future: in 1950's the kids used to read in the cartoon's, about the flying cars of the future, and dreamed of seeing flying cars one day. —Well, we are going to make that dream come true. I will call this new vehicle, the *Versatile-Aircraft*. Versatile: because it has the capacity to land in water and navigate; for this flying vehicle we are creating a brand-new Aircraft-Technology, with this biotechnic system advances, you can safely guide the *Versatile-Aircraft* along the path of airspace routes. For this new development, we are ready to launch in orbit an internet Beaming-Satellite, which would cover the Earth in high-high-speed, which will provide billions of users with an internet system, extremely fast and trustworthy; at the same time, we will be feeding specific safety's information codes, to the computers of the vehicles. With this system would be no impediment for everyone to arrive without any difficulty to their destination. All these advances are what is coming. Special-Agent Bronson, the future is in front of us, and don't be surprised, if one of these days you hear me say. "Beam me up Scotty!!" Bremen finished with a joke his generous information, to Rachel and Viggo, who were listening with a face of disbelief, about what that just heard and Viggo said...

"Mr. Bremen, first of all, thanks' for sharing your future project, I wonder about the future cities, seems to me that's quite complex?"

"Special-Agent Bronson, the project seems complicated, but if you have the chance to take advantage, of the brilliant minds of others people, who dedicated themselves to developing an advanced technology, which is currently available, and I must say, that in this particular case, I took all the advantages that were at my disposal, then for this task, I higher technician and architects, who would be in charge of creating the new city, applying the new, but old technology in the project."

"Mr. Bremen, you explain the project as if the task, were a simple thing to do, but you need the wisdom to applying available technology in an amazing project!" Viggo commented and Bremen proceeded to remove out a credit card from his wallet, and he began to give a simple class of advanced technology to the agents...

"Special-Agent Bronson, it's not a great secret what I'm going to expose, is well-known that there are other corporations, which are experimenting with this type of technology, that we are applying in our project." *Bremen, paused for a few seconds looking at the federal agents and spoke.* "I'm sure that you know, that on the back of your credit cards, they have a *magnetic stripe,* which carries all your personal information, and when is time to use it, you just swipe the card, and the main computer will read the magnetic stripe, and in a split of a second and, will processes the info. —A matter of fact, in this particular project, we are going to follow a similar concept, but the concept would be applied in another manner: instead of being behind a credit card, the magnetic stripe, would be applied, basically on the faces of the streets, then like the credit card system, the collected info from the future cities residents, will be transferred to the main computer brain, this innovation going to guide the car to the right place in the Future City, consequently to this technology, in the streets of the Future City, car accidents will be events of the past." Bremen ends up reporting, and Rachal asks...

"That's amazing Mr. Bremen, it means that the computer of the smart car reads what is applied on the street, that's how eventually work?

"Agent Dansby, the use of this technology, it's quite simple, when you are inside the Smart-car, you have to tell the computer where you want to go, then the vehicle will take the info, which was previously entered in the main computer, then the vehicle will take you where you wish to go, and by the way, the, future city is being built on the outskirts of Las Vegas, and the advantage is that the whole city will be energized with solar panels, and will included parking lots, sidewalks, and every roof in the city. What do you think?" Mr. Bremen ask placing back the card in his wallet, and the Federal agents were listening with attention and Viggo commented...

"Mr. Bremen, this project is amazing, I'm sure it will change how people mobilized and will have a different way of life, all over the world." Viggo commented and Bremen added.

"Well, Special-Agent Bronson, many times you have to dare to lose your balance, looking to achieve success. I don't know, if the new city will change the world, but I'm sure, it will make a lot of difference. I'm very excited with this project, it will take some adjusting, but it's coming along very well." Bremen informs and Rachel interested asks...

"It's fabulous Mr. Bremen. I would really like to see the Future City, for me it would be how to jump into the future, I'm so excited, when you think it would be ready to visit?"

"Agent Dunsby, we are currently under construction, right now we are building houses and shopping centers, if we continue at this pace, you can visit the city in about two and a half years, and when the project becomes a flourishing city, then: only then we'll show it to the U.S Government." Bremen said it proudly, and Viggo commented...

"I'm looking forward to becoming resident of the Future City Mr. Bremen."

"Special-Agent Bronson, if you got rid of this dirty-rat that I have in the lab, I will name you an honorary citizen of the Future City, and if you are willing, I'll take you with me to Mars?"

"Thanks for the invitation, Mr. Bremen, now that you touch the subject, I hear in the news that you are planning to send a spaceship to Mars, and to give the project the credit it deserves, you will be the crew leader?"

"That's true, reaching the red planet it's one of my dreams, set foot on the lands of Mars, the mission is very possible, but first; we have to solve a little minor technical problem; how to return to Earth? The project is difficult, yes, but not impossible. At the Houston plant, we have already begun the assignment to prevent future obstacles, and meanwhile for this purpose, we will put in orbit an immense space fuel station, which will have several functions, the main object would be supplying fuel to the spaceships, which will travel around the world or to Mars, and also will fulfill the function of a transition hotel, if the scientists and engineers continue at this pace, in about 5 years the fuel station will begin to be assembled in outer space, and it will be open for travelers in 2030, and I don't want to brag any more about me, and my future projects." *Bremen after answering the question, he paused for a few seconds, and then he asks.* "Well, Special-Agent Bronson, what can I do for you?"

"Mr. Bremen. I don't know if you are aware of the shooting, which occurred two days ago in front of this establishment, you were here that day?"

"Sure, but when I heard those loud popping, I wasn't sure it was gunfire, until the police arrived at the crime scene, by then everything was calm and I went out to check what happened, that's when Detective D'Layne told me, that all the commotion was between two rival gangs." *Bremen paused thinking for a few seconds.* "Special-Agent Bronson, your questions and your presence in my office, is suggesting that this shooting between the two gangs, have something to do with the system we are developing?" *Viggo looks at him as saying you are correct, and Bremen said.* "Thanks, you don't have to answer me, your face says it all!"

"Mr. Bremen, the shooting that happened in front of your place, didn't happened by chance, I must tell you, that I'm absolutely sure; this event has direct consequences with the type of research that's going on in your scientific laboratory, I'm sorry, but that's the situation you are in right now."

"Special-Agent Bronson, it is in the interest of all Americans, that you solve this case as soon as possible, and to speed the action, I will help you in everything that is necessary, this means that you have to start asking questions. Okay?"

"Thanks' Mr. Bremen, I have a vague idea of what you are doing in this place, since I don't like to walk blindly, I would like to be aware of what you are creating in this lab. I would appreciate it, if you would let me know what is going on, because there are a few countries involved in getting hold of this project?" Viggo asked seriously, and Bremen responded in the same manner.

"Special-Agent Bronson, as you know, we are doing this project in absolute secrecy. The nuclear scientists' engineers and technicians, did not have it easy, quite the opposite, they had a very difficult task to complete the defense system, and I never thought I would find myself in this awkward situation, where my company should be investigated!" Bremen said raising his arms and Viggo keeps asking...

"For sure, because it's not easy to be prepared for the unexpected, and your mission is quite challenging Mr. Bremen, that is exactly what is happening to me, I'm the head of this investigation, and I don't know even if you have a name, for what are you doing in the lab?

"Special-Agent Bronson, I will try to give you the info that would be relevant to this case, and about the name, it was the first thing we did with the scientists, and we came up with the name, CLASU = *Cyber Logistic Autonomous System Unit*. And let's be clear: in this lab we only do sciences research." *Bremen paused for a few seconds.* "I'm sorry but I don't know what else to tell you, because, it is a matter of National Security, and I hope you understand my position?" Bremen said in a serious manner. Meanwhile Rocky is listening quietly, and Viggo who is not very happy with that negative answer responded.

"Mr. Bremen, I understand your situation, but this is a state of urgency, this espionage case should be resolved as soon as possible..."

"I agree with that assumption." Bremen affirms and Viggo continued saying...

"I'm glad that we agree that it's very positive for solving this case. Mr. Bremen, in this particular time, we are representing the Federal Government, and I'm not going to beat around the bushes. I don't pretend that you will give up any extra details about the project, but I want to be assured that the project is not in any jeopardy."

"I understand your concern Special-Agent Bronson, just tell me what you need and what do you want to know?"

"Well, the information we need right now Mr. Bremen, involves the scientists, engineers and technicians, who are working in the lab, and to complete this puzzle, I would like to have all the data that you have in their files, therefore, our investigation will be simplified and, we can move on quickly!" Viggo asked firmly and seriously and Mr. Bremen grasp Viggo's serious mood and with a worried face he responded.

"Special-Agent Bronson, you are completely sure, that among my scientist, there are involved one person or maybe more, who are selling secrets, for the benefit of other countries."

"I Couldn't have said better, Mr. Bremen, that is what is happening in your laboratory!" Viggo affirms, and Bremen worried responded.

"I can't believe that in my lab, this insidious event is happening." *Bremen said and began walking around the office, and he stopped in front of Viggo.* "I guess tonight I won't be able to sleep Especial-Agent Bronson, as soon as possible this traitor must be put behind bars, then hopefully I be able to relax!" Bremen points out raising his arms in a sign of frustration, and Viggo happy to hear his reaction added...

"That's our goal Mr. Bremen, and to proceed with this investigation, we need to study the archives of the nuclear scientists and the rest of the crew who are involved in the CLASU project, it's the only way to identify the person or persons, who are selling the secrets to foreign agents?"

"No wonder, those goons the other day were killing each other. Special-Agent Bronson, the confrontation was only to obtain information, is that right?" Bremen asks with an astonished face and Viggo agreed...

"That's right Mr. Bremen, these people are willing to kill each other, for this information that must be vital to them."

"These foreign agents are not very smart, to say the least, these guys come to shoot each other in front of this building, where is what they are looking for."

"You are right Mr. Bremen; in that foolish act the mentality of our enemies is demonstrated, without going any further, the Russians threw one of their comrades out of the car thinking he was dead!"

"It's amazing what a human being can do. What really worries me, is this type of affairs should not happen in my organization,

I'm really disappointed!" *Bremen paused for a second thinking then said.* "I agree Special-Agent Bronson, you should have everything you need at your disposal." Bremen said quite disturbed, and Viggo is hinting that he is going to get what he needs and said...

"Thanks. Mr. Bremen, we need all the available information about those scientists and engineers; only those who are involved in the research of the CLASU project, I don't want to waste time with any other information. Mr. Bremen." Viggo asked, and in that moment, Mr. Bremen went to the office door and called the secretary...

"Ms. Lillian." *And the beautiful young lady appears in the office dressed very elegantly, with four-inch heels shoes and walking very short strides* and she answered...

"Yesss Mrrr. Bremennn?" Lillian said stretching the words but very sweetly.

"Ms. Lillian, Special-Agent Bronson, is conducting a national security investigation, and he will need your collaboration, please help the federal agents in everything they need." And *Bremen turns around and facing Viggo he asked.* "You need the scientist's and the engineer's files, it's right?"

"It's exactly what we need, Mr. Bremen."

"Okay Ms. Lillian, please give the files that Special-Agent Bronson asks for, and any other he needs. I hope this investigation will be conducted with strict privacy; it is a very delicate situation!" Bremen says frowning and walking around the office, and Viggo said.

"Mr. Bremen, from now on you don't have to worry, after I read the files, we will know where the tumors are, so we are going to operate efficiently and swiftly, and we will solve this case in no time. We already know who is the mastermind of this operation, and he has already left the country, his name is Santino Pascucci, this is the person who was buying the information, from the scientists, and right now he is in the South of France!"

"I'm very grateful for your commitment to protect our country Special-Agent Bronson, and I don't forget about you, Agent Dansby, thanks' for your cooperation, considering that this is an unexpected event!" *Bremen began walking toward the office door and before leaving said.* "This unexpected event, it's an incredible paradoxical situation, because, in about half an hour, I have a meeting with the minister of defense…just wish me luck, I'm going to need it." *And touching his forehead with his fingers in the form of greeting he said.* "I'll see you after this case is solved. Okay?" Bremen said from the office threshold door.

Meanwhile, when the agents were alone with Lillian. Viggo did not want to waste any time, and with a big smile he tries to dazzle Ms. Lillian, who swiftly went to the archive and with a big smile she brought the photocopies of the files, and handled them to Viggo, who looked at the five copies with surprise, he expected there might be several more, and he thinks: this venture must be fucking important, only five people work on the project. After thanking Ms. Lillian for her help, they left the place with the documents he requested, but before getting into the Cadillac Viggo asked Rachel.

"Rocky, give me a favor, why don't you drive, and in the meantime, I'm going to brush through these files, let's see if I can find out, who these people are, and where they come from. Okay?" Viggo requested and Rachel already in the driving seat asks…

"Chief: you didn't tell me where we are going, or maybe you want to be sitting here?" She asks starting the car, and Viggo answers.

"Don't get smart with your superior. Okay? Viggo said seriously and Rachel cuddly kisses him, and Viggo said…

"Rocky, just take Santa Monica Blvd. toward the ocean, after I finish reviewing these files. I'll tell you where we are going. Okay?"

For a few minutes Viggo, was flipping through the files, and the only positive information he could find, where names and nationalities: in the records were two foreign scientists, one of them was from Israel Dr. Simon Goldstein, and the other scientist was Dr. Ian Haltom, a Belgium citizen. The other files belong to three American-born logistics cyber system engineers. Dr. Jimmy Macbeth, Dr. John Hirohito and Dr. Christian Volt. Viggo finished reading the last name when he noticed that the folders that are in his lap, began to move: *no...it's not the spirit of a person in the files, just trying to get out of there*: not at all; it's the right hand of Rocky, that is busy trying to reach inside Viggo's pants, when he notices her intensions, he places the files at his side, as he pulls her hand out of his pants, and Viggo in those instant points out...

"Please: Rocky, at this time all you have to do, is to pay attention to the traffic, and leave your urgent needs, until later tonight. I don't think that's a lot to ask?" Viggo proposed, and Rachel that always has an excuse to be naughty complain...

"Chief, since we arrived in California, you have become strictly professional, and I feel neglected. Okaaaay?" Rachel gets cuddly trying to kiss him, and Viggo kisses her and replies.

"Please: Rocky, in these files, I'm trying to find some connection between these people, who are supposed to be involved in espionage, and there's nothing here—Fuck this shit!!" Viggo exclaims frustrated and Rachel not so happy asks.

"Why don't we stop at a coffee shop Chief, and with a little more patience, we can look through the files?

"Rocky, I was thinking about it: but now, I'm sure that..."

"What are you talking about Chief?

"Rocky, I know the person who can help us, let's stop at the hospital, I would like to have a good talk with Dusty, maybe he knows some details, about the lives of these guys in the files, with a little help he can clear the way for us." Viggo said looking at Rocky; she looks at him with pity, seems that she has in her mind a plan, which has to do with the Chief. *When we get to the hospital parking lot, I'm going to fuck your until you beg me to stop what is funny is that you don't know that yet.* She is all excited just thinking about what she is going to do to her superior. When they arrived at the hospital, she did not stop at the valet parking. She continues driving straight up to the top floor, and Viggo intrigued asks...

"Rocky, what the hell are you doing?" She didn't bother to answer, and she kept driving all the way to the 4th floor: no one was parked in that area, and with the eyes flaming of desire she said...

"Right now, I have to find the man from New York; because you're forgetting about me. Chief, you have to put out the flames that consumes my entire body, first take care of me, then you can go to see your friend." She said very sweetly caressing his face, and then with a feline grace she jumped in the backseat of the car: it took her only a second to take off her underwear and she stick it in her boot. Viggo, who was still in the front seat, looked at her and spoke. "Fuck; you will never change!" At that moment Viggo slips in the back were Rachel, was ready waiting for him, exposed like a flag unfurled in the wind; with one of her legs well above the backrest seat, and the other resting on the seat, with that sexual position, she grabbed him firmly from his tie, and with evident experience she lowers his pants: then after a few seconds the car started shaking, and after long...long minutes of passionate encounter, she said. "Oh my God...Oh my God...I feel so good...so good!!!" And she keeps pulling from his tie so tight that it almost choked Viggo to death, and he said...

"Fuck Rocky, you are getting fucking crazy, try to control yourself." *Viggo grabs her face and spoke.* "Now that you have what you wanted, be a nice girl and let's go to work. Okay?"

"I promise it won't happen again. Chief, you were amazing, I almost fainted in your arms, and I love it! I feel renewed without that anxiety, now I have the energy to concentrate on the investigation!!" Rachel says as she kisses him passionately, and Viggo trying to protect his physical integrity and said...

"That's enough." *Viggo gets the files getting out of the car in case she decided to grab him again by the tie and he spoke.* "Rocky, I'm going to see Dusty; if you want to join me fine, if not wait for me in the lobby. OK?" And he walks to the elevator, and she answers...

"Okay Chief, I will wait for you in the lobby." Rachel said, throwing him a kiss.

At the moment Viggo entered Dusty's room, he was comfortable sitting in bed, reading a magazine. When he saw his friend, in his dusty voice he said...

"My friend...I'm glad to see you." *Then Dusty got out of bed and hugged his friend and spoke.* "Easy'V...I hope you came...to take me out of this place?

"Dusty, I'm glad that you're in such good shape, and ready to go?

"Easy'V...you must take me out of here...these people...practice mental and bodily torture...the earlier I leave the hospital...the sooner we can go hunting...for Santino Pascucci?" Dusty asks walking in the room, and Viggo tries to stop him and responded...

"Please calm down Dusty, and do me a favor, sit down, we have to talk."

"What's going on Easy'V...all of a the sudden...you got so serious?"

"Dusty, it's not a big deal, but right now, have changed the priorities in this case, and I must alter the course of my plans."

"What do you mean? Don't tell me...the decision you have made ...has to do...with my physical condition?"

"Dusty, it's only a strategic decision, now I know the sources from where this conspiracy begins, and the right thing to do, is to find out who is the scientist who sells information to Pascucci, and for that purpose I paid a visit to the labs of The Bremen's Co..."

"Fantastic Easy'V...I hope you find out who is working in this project?" Dusty asks interested in the answer and Viggo responded...

"Yes, I did Dusty, but I need your help, I'm sure that you can help me to search for the missing link, because at the moment we find the person involved in espionage, we have the case solved, then we leave for France, searching for Pascucci." Viggo asks firmly, and Dusty who is willing to assist, answered...

"About the missing link Easy'V...from where we are going to begin the search...have you already began the process?

"Don't get smart with me, remember that you are my prisoner?

"Okay...okay...I see that you brought some files...let's see if I can help you. Easy'V...I hope we solve this case as soon as possible...before they throw my bones in a dungeon?"

"Stop worrying about that, and put your mind on what we need right now: in these files there are five scientists, if you can give me a clue, which one of these five guys, is the scumbag who sells information to Pascucci?" Viggo asks and handed the files to his friend. Dusty, sitting on the bed, begins to dig into the pages, and Viggo is watching in silence. After a few minutes of reviewing the files, Dusty said in his dusty voice.

"I'm sorry...my friend...but the images in my brain are all confused...in these files only the guy with an Asian name...come to my mind." Dusty said raising his hands, in a sign of frustration, and Viggo insists.

"Think...think." *Viggo said and placed one of his hands on his shoulder and encouraged his friend.* "Dusty, it is possible that you, or one of your colleagues, saw or heard something weird, abnormal, or maybe these guys were doing unusual trips: for instance, going places that you don't usual go to; some things that were not quite right...Think, I'm sure that you will recall; some of the things your colleagues commented?"

"Hold-it Easy-V...just hold-it...for a second!" *Said Dusty looking down and holding his head with his hands.* "You...you just mentioned trips...I remember...yes...I recall that...*The-Shadow*...was in charge of following this weird-guy...I don't recall if he was Chinese or Japanese...I think by his name...it must be Japanese?" *Dusty asked-himself and paused for a second and Viggo impatient asked.*

"Come on Dusty think, remember at what place...*The-Shadow,* was following this person to?" Then *Dusty raises his head and looked at Viggo and said...*

"Look...I vaguely remember...that *The-Shadow*...did follow this guy to a casino...I believe it was the...the...God dammit...dammit...I have a lake in my brain..."

"Take your time Dusty, there is no rush, we are not going anywhere right now." Viggo said trying to calm him down, and Dusty reacted and said...

"Yes...yes...I remember...it was the Comemeness no...was the Commerce Casino...yes the Commerce Casino!" Dusty said hitting his forehead with the palm of the hand, as if he had lifted a heavy weight from his shoulders, and Viggo anxious asked...

"Dusty, if *The-Shadow,* followed him into the casino, maybe, he saw this guy gambling, if not, what the hell was he doing there?"

"Okay, calm down Easy'V...If I recall correctly...*The-Shadow,* was cursing...the sun of a bitch...because he couldn't open a bottle of vodka...while he was commenting...that when this weird-guy entered the casino...he went straight to the cashier." *Dusty got up and started walking in the room looking down and holding his forehead.* "Easy'V...I believed that *The-Shadow* said...that he was looking at the guy from the side...but he thought...that saw the man signing a check...because the cashier gave him two trays...full of one hundred-dollar chips."

"Dusty, two hundred chips of one hundred dollars: equal—twenty thousand dollars, that is not a spare change, this fucker was gambling loosely, like the money wasn't a problem?" Pointed Viggo, and Dusty stops in front of his friend and said...

"Wait...wait a second...Easy'V...If I remember correctly *The-Shadow,* also was talking...about a night that...he said that was quite stormy...it seemed to him...that it was strange...that in this weather...the guy went out...to play poker...then he sat at a table with several people...and gambled for hours...until...until all the chips disappeared in front of him...and *The-Shadow* commented...That this guy got up, and went back to the cashier...and withdrew...another twenty thousand dollars...then he went back to the table...and kept playing until the tray was empty...finally after losing all that money...really pissed off...he got up...and left insulting the poker God's...and all the holy gospels!" Dusty informed trying not to laugh, and Viggo said. "It's not funny Dusty!" And both started laughing; and the friends continued talking for a while about the trip to France, then...

Viggo hugs his friend while thanking him; then he left the hospital with the promise, that when Dusty is discharged, Viggo will be taking him to the hotel, but in the lobby, Rachel, was waiting for the Chief, and quite delighted, about the exercise she did with the Chief previously, that left her very relaxed, and when Rachel saw that her superior was arriving with a great smile on his face, then Viggo sits next to her and she commented...

"Chief, that sexy smile that you have on your face, drives me crazy, and I would..."

"You better calm down, or I'm going to call a taxi! Okay?"

"Okay Chief, but that smile of confidence is telling me, that we have good news, could you tell me all about it, so I can smile too, please?"

"That's right Rocky: Dusty came through, at first, he had trouble to remember, but then he managed to recall the identity of the scientist, who is selling the secrets to Pascucci." And Viggo open the files and it shows to Rachel who the person was, and she said...

"Now we know who that piece shit is; and to make thing worse, he had to be an American citizen, a Nuclear Scientist John Hirohito.

—We better get out of here; I want to breathe some pure air." Rachel said standing up and Viggo said...

"Rocky, now we have to prove, that Hirohito is the person who sells the secrets, it means, let's get busy, Rocky!"

"I can't believe-it, this dirty Russian, is giving us information that is worthwhile, for sure, I would like to see if that information, has any truth?" Rachel said it in a distrusting way, and Viggo tries to calm her down...

"Believe-it Rocky, remember: that he's fully cooperating with us and, without any restrictions, and don't forget, Dusty, is trying to help us, and in the meantime, he helps his own situation, you're going to blame him for being useful?" Viggo asks while walking her to the car, then she asks...

"Okay, I understand that Dusty is your friend, but I can't forget that I had to stay in the hotel alone, while you were with Dusty having fun with the Russian President, and bunch of who...!"

"Hold on: Rocky, actually, it's my fault, because with invitation or not, that night I should have taken you with me, I was really the one who didn't think of you, if there is a culprit, it is this man in front of you!"

"You're very sweet Chief, but let's forget about my personal cases, because it seems that things are settling into place, and now that we know, who sells the secrets, how our mission will continue, Chief?"

"Well, first thing first: tomorrow, I'll call the H.O at the Bureau, and talk about the..." Viggo couldn't finish the sentence, because Rachel interrupts him a little jealous and said...

"Seems to me, that the phone call, is not only for the HO; it is also intended for your wife. Chief, I'm sure she will welcome you with open leg..."

"Hey: that comment is unnecessary."

"I'm sorry Chief, but I still think, that Ember was the person who brought us from New York to Santa Monica, and somehow

I'm going to prove it!" Rachel said seriously and Viggo ignored the comment and kept saying...

"Rocky, let's focus on what we're going to do next. Please?

"Okay; it seems to me, that lately I can't talk to you!"

"Listen Rocky, I must inform the HO all about Mr. Hirohito, and reporting his dealing with the mafia, because Ember, urgently she has to find a judge, for sure, a judge who is willing to issue a search warrant, this is the only way, we can continue with the investigation, this way we will find out, if the scientist, has and open account at the Commerce Casino, I'm sure that he does, because I believe that the info Dusty gave us, is good. Okay?" Viggo said with confidence, and Rachel not so sure questioned...

"Well, I can't forget that this guy came with his colleges to steal our secrets, and I don't know, how can you put all your trust in his info, when he is our enemy. Chief?"

"I'm going to tell you just one thing, and I don't want to talk about it anymore: Dusty is my friend and that's it. Okay? And now back to our mission. Rocky, let's focus on Mr. Hirohito who withdrew from the cashier forty thousand dollars, and it took to this fucker a few hours to squander all that money. What does this mean? It means that he is cashing out, selling secrets." Viggo said opening his arms, and Rachel responded.

"Chief, I know that in a casino, it's unusual to have an account, but this action does not prove that this man is guilty under the law. I hope we don't get in trouble poking into this guy's life."

"Rocky, the only person who can get in trouble is the judge, he is the one who will provide the search warrant, and the sooner he does it, the sooner we will solve this case."

"Chief, this kind of search, we had never done this before. Right?" Rachel asks as if she was worried about what might happen and Viggo responded...

"Would you stop worrying about nothing Rocky!"

"The point is Chief, that I don't want you to get into trouble."

'Rocky, I'm telling you what I'm going to do. Tomorrow after we get the fucking subpoena, we are going straight to the casino, and see if we can find out, about what kind of money Mr. Hirohito has in the account, if he has quite a bit of money, then we are going to pay a visit to the people at The Bremen Co. —Meanwhile I will prepare a few questions for him, I'm sure that Dr. Hirohito in this case, would give me the answers that I'm looking for." Viggo explains his plan to Rachel who concerned asked...

"I don't know Chief, but if this guy, has deposited in the casino a large amount of money, so far I know, it's not a crime having money in the casino coffers?"

"Rocky, for what purpose the spiders weave a web?"

"That is a very strange question Chief? It is to catch insects."

"That's right: Rocky, but instead of weaving a web, we are going to weave a braid, then when we began braiding, we are going to entrap in the braid, all the participants in this case." Viggo says it in a whisper and Rachel can't deal with her passions said...

"Oh my God, you are so sexy, when you whisper, you drive me crazy, and you know it and you do it on purpose!" She said trying to kiss him, Viggo ignores the comment and continues asking...

"Rocky, have you heard the phrase. Follow the money?"

"First you ask me a strange question and, now a beginner's question, what are you trying to say?"

"What I'm trying to say is simple, what we are going to do is follow the path of the money, because everything has to do with the amount of money, that Hirohito accumulate in his account, if he has a large amount of money and, he can't prove how he earned it, then we can charge Hirohito, with the illicit enrichment." Viggo says it in a low voice so as to remain a secret between them and Rachel go's crazy...

"Oh, Chief, don't do that, I'm getting all wet..."

"Please, don't be silly Rocky, you make me lose track of my thoughts, please concentrate on what we are doing!"

"Come on Chief, you never lose control of anything, just tell me what we're going to do tomorrow?" Rachel said arriving at their hotel and Viggo said...

"Rocky, tomorrow we'll see, if we find enough proof to prosecute Hirohito, then the judge will be decided what the hell he will do with Hirohito, usually traitors are punished with very harsh penalties." Viggo finished explaining while they were walking to their hotel rooms. Rachel, before entering her room, she kisses Viggo goodnight, and she said...

"Come on Chief, stay with me tonight, after all that you made me suffer, now you are going to leave me hotter than the Sun?"

"Please Rocky, your proposal is very tempting, but I'm very tired, goodnight, Rocky. See you tomorrow."

Viggo, once alone in his room, he decided to call Ember, the first thing she does is invite him to spend the night with her, Viggo told her that he was really tired, and would see her the next day, then he began to inform her of the evidence he had obtain regarding the case, after Ember was made aware of what happening. Viggo asks for the documents he needs to continue the investigation. The next morning: Ember, began to process to work on the documents, she will need to be sure that when Viggo arrives at her office, the search warrant, will be ready to present to the casino authorities.

The following day, Rachel and Viggo went to the Urth Caffe for breakfast, to a trendy place on main street. Then Viggo drove to the Bureau, and parked the car right in front of the building, and said to...

"Rocky, I'll be back in few minutes." Viggo upon entering the reception office, he meets with Ms. Betty, who welcomed him with a sweet smile.

"Good morning, Special-Agent Bronson, I will inform that you have arrived at Officer Maxwell."

"Good morning to you too, Ms. Betty." *Viggo paused for a second and looking into her eyes he said.* "Your hair has something different; I don't know what it is, but your eyes are like two stars shining?" Viggo asked, and her whole face turned crimson, and she nervous and happy responded...

"Thanks for the compliment Special-Agent Bronson, I'm really surprised that you noticed that I change my hair style, I thought men didn't notice when women change their appearance." She commented arranging her curly blonde hair. In that moment the phone rang, it was Mrs. Maxwell asking if Viggo arrived, and Betty informs...

"Special-Agent Bronson, in her office Officer Maxwell, is waiting for you."

Viggo thanks Betty and he heads to Ember's office, at the moment he arrived, the office door was partially open, he knocked gently twice at the door; nobody answers the call; that it's odd: then with some proven suspicious, that his wife maybe was plotting something unusual...*then he slowly begins to open the door. —For Viggo, this scene belong to one of those mystery movies, that's when the mystery music takes the clever detective, to the site where the crime was committed, and the detective reaches the door of the crime scene, and that door is partially open. At that moment the mystery music began playing louder and louder, that's when the detective, opens the door.* —At that crucial moment of excitement, it's when Viggo got there, and with great curiosity he opens the door, which was partially open: He was correct to be cautious, because his gorgeous wife sitting on the front of the desk, right on the edge of the countertop, then Viggo talking to himself trying not to lose control, and he babbles a few words. — "Not again: this cannot continue like this, because one of these days I'll disappear between the legs of this woman?"

For this special occasion Ember, was expecting her husband, with the best sexual clothing can be purchased. Mrs. Bronson Maxwell is welcoming him, with a loose see-through silk blouse, and by design, the delicate garment was opened all the way to her waist, letting show her firm white breasts: that's not all; the short skirt had an open slit that revealed those long, beautiful marble white legs. Viggo was amazed by her sexual attitude, and he remains at the threshold of the door, looking at her in disbelief, and she could not wait, and went to meet him at the door, she locked it, then she didn't waste any time, she took her husband to her beloved desk. *That's when Ember begun to kiss him all over,* after being abused for quite a few minutes: Viggo commented...

"Officer Maxwell, I only came to your office, to pick up a warrant. I'm sure that in your intense training sessions, you have been taught that you should not abused your subordinates?" Viggo asks out of breath and pulling his pants up, and she is fixing her skirt replies.

"My love, this moment was incredible Viggo, you have no idea how much I was missing you, and now that I'm enjoying your love, this investigation takes you to France, it's not fair!!" Ember commented kissing him, and then she turned directly to business: From her desk Ember picked up an envelope, and said in a very professional way...

"Special-Agent Bronson, here is your search warrant to be presented at the Commerce Casino, and I must warn you, it won't be easy to enforce this warrant, if the manager in charge, gives you any trouble, don't hesitate to call judge O'Connor, I guarantee you that this judge will make the warrant be enforced." *Then Ember hugs him and started kissing him and she whispered in his ear.* "My love, I feel so lonely and lost in that huge bed of mine, why don't you come tonight and cuddle with me, I don't think it's a great sacrifice?" Ember said like a little girl, and Viggo responds to that suggestion...

"Ember do not mix our personal life with this case; I don't want to sidetrack this investigation. Please, Ember, you must bear with me, until I finish with this..."

"I understand, it's that I'm very anxious because I don't want to lose your love again!"

"Please Ember, with melodramas we are not going anywhere, and for now let's put that issue aside. Okay?

"Okay, but with reservation!" Ember said kissing him and Viggo continued saying...

"Ember, to continue this investigation, first I have to go to The Bremen Co. let's see if I can unmask that scientist, Hirohito, and after I apprehend this guy, then I'm going to chase Pascucci, through the streets of Paris." *Viggo paused for a second organizing his thoughts and spoke.* "Ember, going back to business: you should contact the secretary of state, and start the arrangements of extradition of gangster Santino Pascucci, to the –US."

"Special-Agent Bronson, is there anything else that I can help you with?" Ember, said sarcastically, and Viggo seriously replied...

"Of course, Officer Maxwell, and what I'm going to ask it is quite serious, if you want to bring this investigation to conclusion. I'll need as soon as possible an American Passport, with the picture of Voris Kavinsky, it must have a French name, since Dusty speaks French, and it also happens that he is cooperating with our investigation. Please Ember, really, I need that passport. Okay?"

"Do you have any suggestions, about the name, Special-Agent Bronson?" Ember asks smiling, and Viggo suggested.

"Well, I was choosing a few names, and finally I selected this: René De'Baron, what do you think, Ember?"

"Okay...okay, the name has really a French essence, I'm sure that after a couple of days, I'll have the passport in the office. Viggo, do not send Rocky to pick up the document, I rather prefer that you come to see me. Ember said frowning, and Viggo responded.

"Officer Maxwell, are you forgetting something; you are the H.O of this Bureau?"

"What do you mean, Special-Agent Bronson?'

"I must come to see you Ember because you're the *Handling Officer*. You are in charge of suppling the airline tickets, hotels, and money for expenses, I'll come to collect all those goodies for the trip to France..." *Ember wanted to talk but he wouldn't let her.* "Ember, I'll see you in a couple of days: thanks for the search warrant, and if you don't have any objections, Officer Maxwell; I must continue with the investigation."

"Viggo, you can't do that to me, you know that there are urgent decisions to be made, we must talk about the arrangements with the French authorities, and you leave me here, like a flagpole without a flag!!"

"Like a flagpole Ember? Please, I'm sorry, but you can do those procedures with your eyes closed, it means that you don't need me for those errands, plus I'm going straight to the casino, and I'm going to repeat this again, the sooner I..."

"I know Viggo, the sooner you finish the investigation the sooner we will be together!"

"I'm glad that we agree." Said Viggo and kisses her and he spoke. "Ember, I must go, because Rocky is waiting in the car, and she must wonder what's happened to me!"

"Come on, Viggo, I hope you tell Her the truth, or there is a motive why I must be suspicious?" Ember said seriously and Viggo didn't pay attention to her comment and said...

"Thanks for the amazing job of getting the warrant. Ember, one way or another, we are going to enforce the search warrant, at the Commerce Casino, and I'll see you in a couple of days." Viggo says firmly, and Ember grabbed him under the threshold of the door and kissed him, Viggo kisses her back and before being attacked sexually again he is leaving, but Ember managed to accomplish her wishes and said...

"Special-Agent Bronson, here are the keys to my apartment, in case you wish to surprise me, and you decide to sleep with your wife." And *Ember throws the keys at him and Viggo cleverly grabs the keys and Ember said.* "I will wait for you tonight." And Viggo went to meet Rachel, and at the moment he arrived. Well, she was walking up and down really upset, and she said pissed off...

"Chief, this was the longest fifteen minutes of my life, I was ready to go and see what the hell happened to you, I was wondering if your own wife was able to kidnap you!" She said getting in the car with Viggo and started driving, then Viggo very calmly apologized...

"I'm sorry Rocky, but at the moment I entered her office, Ember was in a phone conference, then when she finished talking, she apologized, because she was talking with the secretary of state, and the authorities of France, she was coordinating Santino Pascucci, extradition!"

"What did she say Chief when she finished talking. That everything was in order?"

"Don't be sarcastic Rocky, she said that everything follows its course, then she proceeded to hand the search warrant to me, and to end the meeting. She proposed that we should start organizing our mission to France." Viggo said it with a straight face and Rachel who wants to believe what he said, but for her it's not easy to swallow all the bullshit, then she asked with no emotion in her voice.

"Chief, when you say we: I wonder who is going to France?"

"Rocky, I did tell Ember, that I would need three airplane tickets; one for you, and another for Dusty."

"Chief, I thought you were sending me back to New York, when I heard that you were going to France, with your friend Dusty." Rachel said seriously, and Viggo responded...

"That's not so Rocky, because you are the only agent in the bureau I can trust with my life, this is the reason you're coming with me to France. —Only except if you don't want to come, with us?"

"Chief, you must be kidding, you know that I'm going with you to the end of the world, even to explore an erupting volcano. Chief, you are so sweet, I can't wait until tonight..."

"You must wait because I'm anxious to get to the casino. Rocky, I'm sure we will find what we are looking for."

"Don't be so cruel Chief, you know that I love your company, and always enjoy that magnificent tattoo of yours's, that drives me completely insane!" Rachel says fixing her hair, and Viggo uncomfortable with the situation answers.

"Rocky, can you stop acting silly, this is a serious procedure, keep in mind, that we are going to enforce a search warrant, no less then at the Commerce Casino, one of the most important gaming houses in California, if we have the opportunity to find out, that Dr. Hirohito, has large amounts of money in an open account: then only then, we'll have the chance to obtain enough proof to arrest this guy." Viggo pointed out with certainty, and Rachel kept quiet, but she looks sideways at her companion, and her beautiful face became serious, and Viggo was thinking "I wonder why she is so serious?" Rachel is unhappy, because she began to figure out, about the recent events, that she believed Viggo had distorted the truth: this is why she's thinking. "Like an idiot, I was waiting for him, forever and ever, and I'm sure, that this son of a bitch was in that office with his wife, for forty-five minutes: in that period of time, the Chief is capable of making love to me twice, and in between, he can smoke two cigars, and now, that we are alone in the car, he doesn't pay any attention to..." At that moment Viggo interrupts her thoughts.

"Rocky, why are you so quiet, what kind of thoughts are running in your head, that are bothering you? Don't tell me, I know you are sure that in the time I was with Ember: we can't control ourselves, and crazy with passion, we throw on the floor all papers and documents that were on the desk: and like in the porno movies, I was fucking my wife on top of the desk, while the secretary was watching masturbating. That was the bizarre intrigue you were weaving in your head. Isn't that right, Rocky?" Viggo asks with a small wee of laughter that sneaked out between his lips, and Rachel was surprised that her Chief, could read her murky thoughts, then she replies...

"Well Chief, it's a little bite suspicious, that you went to see the H.O of the Bureau, but the fucking consequence remains, since she is your wife, the same person who kicked you out of your house, and now she has the audacity to want to win back your heart, and I'm sure that she was missing the tattoo!!"

"Don't do that Rocky, this scene of jealousy has no place in our relationship, beside; I put my life in your hands, in any dangerous missions, and right now you, are doubting about my integrity? I can't believe that Rocky?" Viggo asks seriously, hoping to appease her doubts and Rocky didn't answer, they had already arrived at the casino.

Upon arrival at the casino, Viggo parks right in front of the door, getting out of the vehicle, told the parking attendant who he was, and leave the car where he parked. Once inside the casino the federal agents went straight to the cashier, Viggo shows his IDs to the teller, and he asked to speak with the person in charge. The teller escorts the federal agents through a long corridor that goes to the administration office. Viggo shows his credentials to the accountant, Mr. Travis, and Viggo without any formalities, informs the man that he is investigating a case of national security; then looking straight in his face, he present the search warrant to Mr. Travis, who got really nervous, and began to read the document, and after learning about the contents of the warrant, he tells the agents that he does not have the authority, to disclose any of the accounts of the players, the only person who can authorize the sensitive information is the general manager of the casino, then Mr. Travis took the Federal Agents to the office of the General Manager Mr. Redford, who after reading the search warrant very cordially said...

"First of all, Special-Agent Bronson, first of all, I must tell you, that I admire the dedication of the Federal Bureau, that has been keeping our Country and us safe. I admire the integrity of people in the force, thanks for your service." Mr. Redford ends up saying with a smile and Viggo replies seriously...

"Thanks' for your support Mr. Redford, as you know it's our duty to enforce the law, that is what we are doing at this moment, trying to keep everybody safe and sound, and complying with the laws of this country." Viggo says seriously, and Redford responded...

"That's very noble of you Special-Agent Bronson, but in this particular occasion it's impossible for me to help you. I can't disclose the accounts of any of the players, if I reveal this information, it would be a compelling proof, that we are untrustworthy, and we cannot allow that to happened, without a doubt it would be the downfall of this casino. Special-Agent Bronson!" Mr. Redford said with his chin up and showing a remarkable arrogant attitude. The Agent Rachel Dansby, was listening in silence at this guy excuses, and she was getting really pissed-off, then she looks at Viggo, who said, "Excuse me." and calmly turn around and picked up his cell phone, and calls Judge O'Connor, who issued the search warrant, and Viggo said...

"Good afternoon your Honor, this is Special-Agent Viggo Bronson, and..."

"What can I do for you Mr. Bronson?"

"Your Honor, right now I'm in the Commerce Casino, and..."

"Now I remember, you are Special-Agent Bronson, Officer Maxwell, asked me to issue a search warrant to execute at the Commerce Casino, don't tell me—is about the search warrant, and these people are giving you trouble?"

"Well, your Honor, the general manager of the casino refuses to comply with the warrant, he claims that looking into the accounts of the players will establish a negative precedent for the casino."

"Special-Agent Bronson, let me talk to the person in charge, I'm going to take care all his casino entitlements, at the moment I finish talking to him, this man is going to have such cerebral pain that he will open that safe, and hand over all the books, for you to see inside and out. Please give the phone to this unwilling person."

"Sure, your Honor, you're going to talk with Mr. Redford, and thanks for your collaboration." Viggo turns around and says...

"Mr. Redford, Judge O'Connor, would like to talk to you." Viggo said and handed the phone to Mr. Redford. After listening to the judge for few minutes, Mr. Redford began repeating. "Yes, your Honor...yes your Honor...yes your Honor." Finally, Mr. Redford returned the phone to Viggo, and with regretful attitude said...

"I'm apologizing Special-Agent Bronson, you would like to see Dr. Hirohito account. The files are at your disposal, you can take as long as necessary."

After Viggo reviewed Mr. Hirohito account, the suspicions he had turned into solid evidence, it was clear that the scientists were depositing large amounts of money at the Commerce Casino account. To be precise: the amount of the deposit in his account adds up to, almost 10 million dollars. These revelations are so conclusive that Special-Agent Bronson decides to arrest the Nuclear Scientists Dr. Hirohito.

Once the search warrant was enforced with success, the federal agents were leaving behind the hostile attitude of Mr. Redford, and came out of the casino, walking embraced towards the car, and Viggo's features were illuminated with a huge smile, and he commented...

"Rocky: get ready because this is the beginning of the road to France. And let's clear the way and begin to unmask...

THE TRAITORS

Viggo, fervently said, and Rachel, who was walking with Viggo embracing him tight from the waist, his body heat began to revolutionize Rachel hormones, because the manly attitude of Viggo's, takes her to the extreme of the desires, and there she was; melting like a piece of butter, next to this man who drives her hormones out of control, and trembling with emotion she said with a smile...

"You since so cool Chief, when you called the judge, I swear, that scene it was a masterpiece, I love the way you handled that hostile awkward situation, because you put this conceited asshole in his place!" *She paused for a second thinking, I would like to make love to this man right here right now, then she very casual asks.* "Chief, I wonder what the judge said to Mr. Redford? Seems to me, that after he finished talking with the judge, this guy was paler than a fucking corpse."

"It's not that hard to guess what he said Rocky, I'm sure that Judge O'Connor informed to Mr. Redford, the search warrant clearly says, that this situation is a case of national security. I promise you, if you don't comply with the warrant, I'm going to show up at the casino, with ten federal agents and, close up that fucking casino, also I will bring with me the I.R.S agents, and they will go through every fucking account, that you ever opened!!! Okay? That's when his fucking face turned so white, that I thought Redford, in that instant was going to faint!"

"I could see it; this proud bastard was really shook-up. Chief, what are we going to-do with Mr. Hirohito?"

"That question has a simple answer Rocky, right now, we have in our possession the evidence we were looking for, and they are conclusive, now all we have to do, is to go straight and arrest this fucking traitor. Okay?"

"We better do it right now, Chief, before that fucker Mr. Redford lets him know, that we are going to arrest him!!"

"You are right Rocky, come on, let's get the sirens wailing, I hope we get there in time, to prevent this guy from escaping!!" Viggo said it excited.

And so, they did leaving the parking lot with the sirens wailing and the red-light's flashing, at the wheel of the bulletproof Cadillac was Viggo, and Rachel is sitting next to him, trying her best to contain her impulses. Instead Viggo has only one thing on his mind, just to arrest this piece of garbage traitor; and a mile before reaching his destination...

Viggo, turned off the siren and slowly approached the door of The Bremen Co. —As if Rachel, had guessed the future events: at that precise moment, a man was leaving the building, that's when they managed to see that the man was of Asian descent, and the guy was in a big hurry, to get into a waiting car. —Rachel and Viggo looked at each other as if they were asking: "that's him?" Because the man fits the profile of Hirohito, and he was inside of that car that took off like a rocket. And Rachel out loud said...

"Chief, Mr. Redford, took the time to alert Hirohito, that we were coming to arrest him, come on, Chief, let's chase these guys, they are leaving in a hurry!!!" Viggo immediately reacted, and began the pursue, the fleeing driver, who was warned by the rearview mirror, that an SUV Cadillac was following him, that's when the pursue driver, decided to lose his pursuers, and he speed away, for sure that he was eager to escape, and he didn't think about the consequences could bring his reckless driving, just thinking that Special-Agent Bronson was after him, the driver crossed Venice Blvd. at high speed, and without slowing down he was trying to turn into the freeway entrance: that's when the fatal maneuver occurred and, condemns the fate the passengers of the car, that is when the driver lost control of the vehicle, which hit the defense barrier with such force, that the car turned over in the air twice, and car began to tumbling like a tumbleweed. After that spectacular show of acrobatics, finally, the vehicle ends up, standing on all four wheels.

At that moment, the Federal Agents, saw the car turning twice in the air, and twice on the street pavement, Viggo and Rachel, waited patiently inside the Cadillac for a few minutes, to see if anyone moves inside the car, which remains in place, standing on the four wheels. The agents wanted to be sure that there were no signs of life, then Viggo proposed...

"Rocky, let's see if there is any body lying around, and we must be sure that these guys are injured or are all dead."

They got out of the car with their guns drawn, then with caution begin walking toward the disabled car: not knowing if some of the passengers in the car were still alive, that expectation creates instants of great tension in the federal agents, who only could hear the moans of the car, which had been quite smashed, then inside that circle of tension, all of a sudden, that's when the ghost of betrayal appears!! One of the foreign agents traveling in the car was quite alive, and with a fucking bad intentions, the man was inside the smashed car crouched, waiting for them to come out of the Cadillac, when one of the Chinese's believed the federal agents were at the appropriate distance, he began firing his gun: what are the odds that a guy who turned inside a car five times, then he can aim a gun with such precision that wounds one of the agents; unfortunately it happened; that's when Rachel was hit by one of the bullets: Viggo, worried about what might have happened to his partner, right away came to find out Rachel condition: she was wounded but alive, then with the courage that his fame represents, Viggo, grabs Rachel's gun, retraces his steps, and through a curtain of bullets, he started walking toward the disable vehicle, but he was quite pissed off, because this fucker's wounded Rocky, he continued walking towards the vehicle, with a feverish of revenge and with two guns in his hands, he began shooting until the Chines, hiding in the car shell, fell dead, them Viggo had a consoling thought "I'm going to really finished off these pieces of shit!!!" And he aimed the guns to the car gas tank, and he continued firing until the car exploded, covering the fucking vehicle in flames. Then immediately went to assist Rachel and he shouts...

"Rocky...where the hell are you wounded; I'm not seeing any blood?" *At that same time, he opens her jacket, and he finds that Rachel is wearing a bulletproof vest.* "Rocky, I don't know what is wrong with you, but I'm calling the paramedics." And Rachel responded. "Please Chief, sit next to me and place my head on your lap: I would like to die kissing my favorite pet."

"You...you will never change, Rocky." Viggo said and took his jacket off and placed it under her head. At that moment a police car stopped, one of the officers called the fire department and let the traffic flow, the other officer approach Viggo who promptly showed his credentials, and explained in broad outline what did happen. At that moment the Ambulance arrived, immediately began to check what was wrong with Rachel, one of the paramedics noticed that she had no bleeding wounds, but she was suffering a lot of pain in the left shoulder, the paramedics provided Rachel with a painkiller, then gently picked her up and then placed her in the ambulance, and Viggo anxiously asked...

"Please, at which hospital are you taking my partner?"

"Special-Agent Bronson, we're taking Agent Dansby, to Santa Monica Hospital." And Viggo is thinking. *"Oddly enough that's where Dusty is being hospitalized."* In that moment Detective D'Layne, arrives at the scene of the crash site, and she seemed very happy to see Viggo, who greets her cordially and he commented...

"Detective D'Layne, you just came in time: I was chasing this bunch of traitor's and unfortunately it ended in this incident. I really wish I had captured these people alive!!" Viggo said right in front of the face of the detective and she with a face full of pleasure responded...

"What a surprise Special-Agent Bronson, I'm very happy to see you. I don't have to tell you that this place looks like a war zone, I imagine these people were desperate trying to escape, I must say, that in the way the car has finished, only remain ashes Special-Agent Bronson, what happened?"

"What happened? Shouldn't have occurred, because how indicate earlier, I would have preferred to catch those spies Chinese's alive, but I have to accept that ending knowing, that the career of spying, for these guys are over." Viggo said firmly looking at Det. D'Layne who responded...

"It's a pity Special-Agent Bronson, that you could not have captured these people alive, to be able to interrogate them, we could use them to trade."

"You are right, but when we saw what had happened to the car, we thought that these guys were all dead, then at the moment we got out of the car, one of these guys got the chance to started shooting, and I was quite lucky, but agent Dansby wasn't, she suffered a shoulder injury, but the good news is, it doesn't seem so serious." Viggo pointed out, and Detective D'Layne worried asked.

"Special-Agent Branson, have the paramedics reached any conclusion, regarding her injuries?"

"I guess they did, because one of the paramedics, believes that she has shattered the clavicle bone, that is why she was suffering so much pain, but knowing Rachel, I'm sure that she will be fine." And Viggo gave Detective D'Layne, all the details of the chase and the final shooting: —She would love to keep talking to Viggo, but he has another urgent need to attend to. Viggo thanks Detective D'Layne, for her efficient collaboration, and then he jumps in the Cadillac, and takes off after his partner Rachel, who is in the ambulance on her way to the hospital. At the time Viggo entered in the emergency room, Rachel was quite sedated; but Viggo did not move from her side, until Rachel entered the operation room, then he was at her side when she woke up in the recuperation room, Viggo, spoke to her for about ten minutes until she fell asleep. Then he went to the third floor, to find out, how Dusty was doing. When Viggo entered the room, Dusty was sitting on the bed, and he said out loud.

"Finally, you show up." *Dusty right away gets up from the bed, and begins walking around Viggo, and talking.* "Easy'V, I can't be in this hospital anymore...the nurses refuse to bath me...the only thing they can do, is complain...and I can do nothing with my inner soul...when I see a nurse my spirit's gets alive...I'm going nuts. Please Easy'V... get me out of here!!" Dusty said and stopped walking in front of Viggo, who responded...

"My friend, those are very good signs, pay attention to your own body, which is giving to you the right signals, and..."

"What are you talking about signal...what fucking signal? I can't stand anymore looking...at those beautiful nurses...Just please, take me out of here...Easy'V?"

"Dusty, I just finished talking to the head nurse; I'll pick you up tomorrow morning, and please Dusty, don't keep harassing the nurses. Okay?" Viggo pointed out, Dusty ignored the comment, and he asks curiously...

"Easy'V...if you haven't come...to get me out of here ...what the hell are you doing here?" Dusty asked and sat on the bed, and Viggo sits on a chair facing him, and tells him what had happened...

"Dusty: I have good news, which it's a huge breakthrough in the investigation, thanks to you my friend..."

"What the hell happened?

"Dusty, today we found out that Dr. Hirohito, was the fucking parasite, who was selling to Pascucci the Space System, and..." And Dusty all exited asks.

"What happened...finally...did you catch Hirohito?" Dusty asks anxious to know, and Viggo does not lose the opportunity to inject into the history a little bit of mystery and began talking like Dusty.

"Well...this was a complicated...and a dangerous investigation...first we had to acquire a search warrant...from a Federal Judge...then with the search order...we went straight to the Commerce Casino...and the manager did not want to give any records...but after I told him I was going to close the casino...he gave me the accounts records...then after saying goodbye with a smile... we left the place with the most needed proof...that Dr. Hirohito...had a large amount of money in his private account...in those moments of darkness...a light of hope came on the horizon...and the suspicions became clear evidence...just then...we tried to detain this miserable traitor...when the shadows of the night were falling on the city...only...only then did we appear at The Bremen Co. and..." Dusty was listening as Viggo was imitating him and he reacted...

"Come on Easy'V...stop acting like me...and no matter how hard you're trying...never will you be able...to have my personality...and please...leave the mysteries to the film producers...and tell me...what the hell happened? If it's not too much to ask? Dusty asked eager to know, and Viggo moved closer to him and whispered.

"Okay...it happened that Dr. Hirohito leaves The Bremen Co. in a big hurry, then he gets into a car that was waiting for him, with several foreign agents inside, then desperately they tried to escape; that is when the pursuit began, and I'm telling you, the chase became really dangerous, we were crossing avenues without stopping, and the speed reached over one hundred miles..."

"Come on man...Easy'V...how did the chase end-up...I'm sure that you hunted these assholes...until the end of hell?"

"Dusty, you should have been there, it was a scene directed by Scorsese, in a gangster movie, and the chase ended when their car turned over in the air two times and, three times on the pavement, we waited several minutes to see if anyone was alive; one of them was quite alive, that's when this guy began shooting at us, and of course we responded with a burst of bullets, and the car with all the Chinese's inside, blow-up in the air, as if it were fireworks." Viggo said it raising his arms, and Dusty reacted happily.

"I don't believe it...Easy'V, did you really get those bastards? I must say it just feels good...just to listen to you...I guess...they got what they deserved...that's what they get for...messing with the wrong person!!" Dusty said very dustily, and Viggo with sparkles in his eyes, responded...

"Dusty, the guys who put you in this bed are all very dead, but in the fucking process, unfortunately Rocky, was wounded, and by chance she ends up in this Hospital."

"Rocky, is wounded...how is she...I guess she is okay...if you have taken the time to come see me? Dusty asked frowning and Viggo pointed out...

"It is nothing to worry about it: Rocky, is very cautious, she was wearing a bulletproof vest, that's why she only has a broken shoulder!"

"What the fuck...Easy'V...you didn't take precautions... how come she was clipped...it doesn't make sense...what the hell happened?" Dusty asked concerned, and Viggo told in detail what happened in the shooting to Dusty, who said...

"Easy'V...now the whole trip is upside down...the fact is that Rocky...won't be able to go...to France with us?"

"Well, I guess you are right, I'm afraid that Rocky won't be able to travel; she just came out of the operation room, and the doctor diagnosis, indicates that her recovery is going to require about two months. I have to call the Bureau and inform the HO of the bad news." *Viggo takes his phone and makes a call, then he gets up and starts walking around the room, while he starts talking.* "Hi honey, I called to…" *Viggo started by saying, and Dusty who is listening and wondering who the hell this man called at the Bureau, that Easy'V mentions the person by "Hi honey?" Viggo is unaware that Dusty was paying close attention to his conversation and continued saying…*

"Hi honey, I'm calling to let you know, that we had an important setback, we had a confrontation with the Chinese's and Rocky…" But Ember interrupts him and said…

"Viggo, I'm aware what's happened to Rocky. Detective D'Layne just called, and she told me all the details about what happened, and I'm sorry that Rocky, was wounded. I hope that she's alright?"

"Detective D'Layne, was unusually quick to communicate to you what occurred in that incident. Ember, did she make any other comments? Viggo asks concerned in case the woman had said something about him an Ember asks…

"Why do you ask?"

"I think, she didn't like the fact that the car has caught fire and the people inside, where turned into ashes."

"No Viggo, no, the way she talks about you, I would think that she believes that you did a very good job."

"I thought just the opposite, but forget about the Chinese's, and you ask me about Rocky, right now is recovering from the operation, her situation complicates the trip to France, because the surgeon instructed, that Rocky should be inactive for forty days, otherwise, she's fine."

"I'm sorry Viggo, that for this mission you lost your partner, now you're stuck with Mr. Dusty. —This Russian agent worries me a little. I've been thinking about what you told me, that we can't select the nationality of our friends, I know that he saved your life and, don't blame you if you help him in any way, you can."

"Ember, you don't question a sincere friendship, and Dusty, is my friend and I know about his intentions at the moment he came here, but right now, he is an asset to the success of this mission: please relax Ember, I have full confidence in my friend."

"Viggo, he is your friend, and he is your responsibility. Okay?"

"Ember, the unfortunate person in this case is Rocky, since she will miss the trip to France, she will be really disappointed." Viggo said with sincerely and Ember said pretending to be dishearten...

"Silly me twice, Viggo!!"

"Why do you say that?"

"My love, I thought you called me, to tell me that you love me, and you only called to talk about Rocky, your partner, not your dear wife!!"

"Please Ember, I can't talk to you now, because..." Dusty gets involved in the conversation and he said...

"Hey, Easy'V...I don't know who you're talking to...but if you give her roses and diamonds, she'll love you forever."

"Please, shut the fuck up." Viggo exclaimed and Ember with disbelief asked...

"You're not talking to me, are you?"

"No...no. I'm dealing with Dusty, who has the nerve to tease me, right now I'm seriously thinking, of leaving him in the hospital, for a couple of months!"

"My love, what is Dusty saying to you, that has the ability to unnerve my tough husband? Because you're not easy to disturb!"

"We would have to talk about that, and regarding about Dusty, he wants me to tell you something, that you already know." Viggo answered, and Dusty who is comfortably sitting in bed responded...

"Come on Easy'V...tell her how much you love her...and she will wait for you with open...arms...or she will open a bottle of French champagne...who knows what could she open...Women always surprise you...in one way or another" Dusty said with mischievous smiling, and Ember who is listens partially asks.

"What is Dusty saying?" Ember asks and Viggo pointed out...

"Dusty does not know, who I'm talking to, and he insists that I tell you how much I love you."

"Please Viggo, tell Dusty that I already know, that I have your unconditional love: do I?" Ember asked, and Viggo responded.

"I'm sure I can answer that question tonight over dinner, and..." *Dusty interrupted.* "Very good Easy'V...that was a fantastic answer...I'm sure you stole that phrase...from the Gigolo's manual."

"Shut the fuck up Dusty, I'm talking with my wife Ember, she is the H.O in Los Angeles Bureau. —I'm sorry darling, but right now I'm dealing with Mr. Dusty, he is a real pain in the ass. Ember, I'll see you in a few hours, if I don't kill this guy first." Viggo finished talking with his wife, and Dusty paused for a second and scratches his head and asks...

"Easy'V, when you entered the office...and you found your wife...Ember Maxwell Bronson...as *Handling Officer*... sitting behind the desk...what was your reaction?"

"This is a long story Dusty but doesn't mean that this situation is breaking my ball, and I have to accept, that she is the Bureau H.O, and I have to deal with her, trying to be as professional as possible." Said Viggo sitting back in the chair in front of his friend, who grabbed Viggo from the lapel and expresses his frustrations.

"You son of a gun...you are so fucking lucky...tonight...for dinner, you're going out...with your gorgeous wife...then...then...you can finish the sentence...for me."

"Don't you fucking feel sorry for yourself, you're very lucky to be alive. —And with the possibility of living in this great country, and don't forget, a trip to France with your friend, who has a surprise prepared for you." *Viggo paused for a second, and Dusty is listening with interest about what his friend is going to say.* "Dusty, for your own security I'm making changes that it is designed for your own protection. Okay?"

"Okay...I'm listening."

"Dusty, tomorrow, instead of going to my lousy hotel, you will be a guest, of the famous Beverly Hills Hotel, which is known for the lovers, as the Pink Palace." *Dusty didn't say anything, but opened his eyes really big, and raised his eyebrows, then with a dubious smile he looked in silence at Viggo, who says.* "Dusty, I'm not joking, you will be a guest of the Beverly Hills Hotel, and everything is already confirmed. Okay?"

"You're serious...I'm in danger...because something happened...in these couple of days...that you...that you...make these sudden changes?" Dusty asked wondering, and Viggo pointed out.

"Look, I'm going to confront this situation, with nothing less than a simple prevention. —Dusty, yesterday, a car was parked in front of my hotel, and two men where inside the vehicle, these guys arouse my suspicious, and my instinct told me, these guys were Russian agents, and I believe they were following me, to get to you, and my instincts tell me that I'm not wrong!!" Viggo says with confidence of a hunting dog, and Dusty with curiosity asked...

"Easy'V...you must be kidding...how could you know...these guys we're Russians?" *Dusty looks down and spoke.* "My friend...I'm sure...the car didn't have our flag in the window fluttering...right...Special-Agent Bronson?"

"Don't you get smart with me Mr. Kavisky, and for your peace of mind, your comrades we're not so obvious in showing their identity, but what they didn't know; that I have a good sense of smell, and when I passed by these drunkards, the smell of *vodka* stunk so bad, that I could smell them from my hotel room."

"Easy'V, are you trying to say...that the Russian Intelligence, really believe...that I'm alive, and for that reason...they are following you...looking for me?" Dusty asked getting a little nervous...

"Well, a matter of fact. I don't know what they are looking for Dusty, but what I know for sure, that as long as you are under my protection, I'm going to do everything possible to keep you alive, and really far away from your comrades, for that reason, I'm going to keep you in that hotel where the Russian Intelligence, won't go looking for you. Okay?" Viggo said padding his friend's shoulder, and Dusty who does not understand why his friend wants to set him up in a luxury hotel, he dustily asks.

"This change of plans...it's not a conventional move...Easy-V, I'm sure my comrades...believe that I'm dead...why do you think...they would be looking for me?"

"That's what I also thought Dusty...but I have reliable Info from Ember, that the Russian Bureau of Intelligence for some unknown reason, they believe that you are alive...That's why you're going to be far away from me, until we will go to France, his is the motive to hide you...in that place...nobody would look for you...in luxurious hotel." Viggo said dustily imitating Dusty who said...

"I can see, that acting...is not your forte...Special-Agent Bronson...but for sure...you're the best...at the moment of captivating anybody...Easy'V...thanks for what you're doing for me."

"Dusty, don't you be confused: help someone, most of the time has a personal gain behind it. —For instance, in this case, I'm taking advantage of your knowledge, just to help me to capture Mr. Pascucci —If it wasn't, for this huge, little detail, —you would be sleeping with the cockroaches at my hotel." Viggo said smiling and Dusty pointed out...

"Come on Easy'V...put aside the cheap philosophy, and get me out of here please?" Dusty says frustrated raising his arms.

"Calm down Dusty, have patience because tonight will be the last night, in this lodging. Just think that tomorrow you are going to be in one of the most famous hotels in the world!"

"I hope you're right...Easy'V...by the way...who will be paying...for all these luxuries...at the Beverly Hills Hotel?... that was a stupid question...since I know who pay the bills...the taxpayers...Isn't that right?" Dusty asks rubbing his hands and Viggo informs...

"Don't worry about small things Mr. Kavisky, the case is that tomorrow, you will have an American passport, because I understand that you speak some French, and from now on, I'm going to call you Mr. René D'Varón, I believe that this name, fits really well your personality!" Viggo said padding his shoulder, and Dusty replies.

"Very good Easy'V...it's not bad at all...Mr. René D'Varón...I think it will not be difficult...to get used to this name...from now on...it will be helpful...if you called me Mr. D'Varón...sounds really good Easy'V... Mr. René D'Varónnn!!"

"Okay, Mr. D'Varón, like I promise I have already brought your suitcases, they are in the reception office, and for security reasons, tomorrow, I'm not taking you to the Beverly Hills Hotel, because..."

"Wait a minute! ...Then, who will be taking me to the hotel?" Dusty asked worried and Viggo explains...

"Relax Dusty, these are the precautions I'm taking, I'm sure that I've been discreetly followed by your comrades, that's why you are going to take a limousine to the hotel, and I already instructed the bellman, to take your luggage and you, to the right limo, everything is coordinated. Okay?"

"Thanks' Easy'V...I don't know what to say?" Dusty said embracing his friend.

"Mr. D'Varón, I want you to listen carefully to what I am going to tell you, once you check in at the hotel: from your room call the front desk, and ask for Madam Divine, she is the person that in the hotel, will pretend to be your companion, and I don't want any discussion about it. Okay?"

"Okay, but...who is this Madam Divine...Easy'V...are you sure...that she can be trusted, in this assignment? Dusty asks worried and Viggo tries to put his mind at ease.

"Don't worry, Mr. D'Varón, she is my confident, and Madam Divine, is really a good friend of mine, just like you Dusty, she is very trustworthy, all this métier that I started, has to do with not raising any suspicions, I was considering Mr. D'Varón, if you have a partner, you will go unnoticed at the hotel, these are normal procedures in these cases, and you know it?"

"Okay Easy'V...I have total confidence in you, but just tell me...how you met this Madam Divine?"

"Okay, if you are ready to listen to my depressed fucking story, but don't interrupt me. Okay?"

"Okay, how you met her?"

"Mr. D'Varón, I remember as if it were today..." *At that moment Viggo becomes very serious, lowers his head and begins to tell his story.* "Dusty, it was on one of those nights in New York, where the drizzle kept falling, and I was walking in the rain, hugging my sadness arm in arm with my grief: I was not well, the demons of not knowing what happened to my marriage, were hovering in my brain, I was really pissed off, upset with me and the world, and I was afraid that in some point I was going to lose control, in that turmoil of feelings, I was trying to find someone to talk to: this why I was walking downcast and when I raised my head, I could see in the distance the lights of Tania's Night Club, when I get to the door, like a dog I shook off the water on top off me, and I entered the Club, Tania was busy talking to several customer, and she didn't see me: in that occasion, Madan Divine, approached me, like a guardian angel, that came to save a lost soul, who was ready to be wasted in hell, I'm sure, she could sense that inside my brain, were running the devious demons of doubts..." *Dusty finally broke the silence* "Come on man...what the hell happened?" — "Well, I guess she felt sorry for my soul, and she invited me to sit at the bar, and we talked for several hours, while we finished a bottle of *Chivas Regal*, that night we became good friends, and the good aspect about our friendship, is that she became my informant, but in return I helped her in many other ways, this why we..."

"Fuck me: Mr. Hot Pants!! There are guys...who are born...with built-in luck...they flick an eyelash, and the women drop dead of love; that is a mystery that I would like to reveal?" Dusty pointed out, and Viggo answered.

"Dusty, everything has logic, all the accomplishment you get in life, it doesn't fall into our lap just by chance, what the fuck: why I'm wasting my time, telling you what you already know. Mr. D'Varón. Okay?"

"Okay, Easy'V...but how could it be...that all your informants are women and beautiful...but meanwhile it would be nice...if you told me...where Madam Divine is from?" Dusty asks with curiosity, and Viggo informs.

"Mr. D'Varón, that question is out of context, the nationality of the person, has nothing to do with what we are talking about..."

"Hold down, Easy'V...I wonder if that woman is from Russia, if she is from my mother country, I don't want to know anything about that person at all. Okay?

"Look, Mr. D'Varón, she is not from Russia; she is from France and Madan Divine, was in your country for a while. Okay?" Viggo dropped the last sentence just to intrigue his friend, and Dusty thought for a few seconds, and asked...

"Easy'V...what is the real name of...Madam Divine? I'm sure you must know...her name? It would be helpful for me to communicate better."

"That is a very good question? You know that I never thought to ask her, but if the situation comes to be, that it happens that she breaks the law, then I will ask her name, do you follow?"

"What the fuck are you talking about?...I'm sure that you know her name...and for some reason...you don't want to reveal it!" Dusty said seriously. Viggo knows her name, but he wants Dusty to be surprised when he meets Madam Divine, and he responded...

"Mr. D'Varón, don't worry about her name, I'm placing you in really very good hands, and rest assured that the whole situation is under my control, everything will go as I planned, if you handle yourself like the gentleman that you are Mr. D'Varón, and remember; that in the hotel, Madam Divine will take care of you. Okay?"

"I hope so...Easy'V...there it is a point I would like to clarify...when you said...She would take care of me...she will take care of me...really? Or just you threw a phrase, which sounds promising?" Dusty asked with a big smile, but Viggo answered seriously...

"First of all, Mr. D'Varón, I did tell you that Madam Divine is a very good friend of mine, that's why she is willing to perform this silly parody as a favor to..." Viggo was trying to explain but Dusty interrupted and said very dusty...

"Hey...Easy'V...I know...I know the drill...don't tell me...hands off...Dusty...hands off...I know the rules of engagement...when I'm in your territory....and when becomes about to woman...first You...Then you...After you ...Always you...Fuck you...and fuck you...again!!"

"Calm down champ, and I didn't say that you can't seduce Madam Divine, Mr. D'Varón, your relation with her, it's a private matter, between you and her, and you must consider, that she will be your escort; she will keep you company for breakfast, lunch and dinner, and during your stay Dusty, you should keep a low profile, until you become an American citizen, that's when your comrades won't be able to touch you. Okay?"

"Don't worry...so much about me, my friend...I will try my best...to get out alive...from this assignment...Easy'V, everything will be smooth...it seems to me...that my reputation...is at stake in this situation...and that is not going to occur...because...I'm not going to lose my dignity...in this case...Okay?"

"I could not have said it better Mr. D'Varón, I'm sorry Dusty, but I have to check how Rocky is doing, and remember, I'm coming to pick you up tomorrow at noon Mr. D'Varón, you should be ready to go like this time in Jakarta, when we escape through the hotel windows, because you fuck the governor daughter, and the old man came with half regiment looking for you." Viggo pointed out from the door threshold, and Dusty replies...

"Those were the good times...Easy-V...please let Rocky know...that I hope she gets well...and I guess I would not see you tomorrow...I hope everything goes well!" Dusty said walking in the room covering his ass. —And...

Viggo, at the moment he leaves the room of his friend, he begins to wonder about his wife Ember: she is waiting for him for dinner, and he is thinking of buying a couple bottles of champagne; keeping that thought in mind, he goes to see his wounded partner; at the moment he entered the room, Viggo, found Rachel seated in bed having dinner, she was a little bit uncomfortable, because her left arm was strapped to her chest. —At the instant Rachel, is aware that Viggo was coming to visit her, Rachel, eyes began to shine like two stars, and a smile blossomed on her face, then Viggo, gently sits beside her and affectionately kisses her and he commented...

"I'm looking at you, and this beautiful smile gives me the clue, that you feel much better Rocky, you always look gorgeous, no matter what; you're an amazing girl, this mission that we are going to carry out in France, without you, will be like swimming in an empty pool!" Viggo said and kisses her affectionately, but Rocky is not that happy with the tender loving kiss, then she grabs Viggo from the back of the neck, and with the right arm, pulls him towards her, and kissed him with passion, and Viggo surprised by her attitude commented...

"I must say that you're showing a very healthy attitude, Rocky, I'm sure that by the time I come back from France, I will find my partner Rachel Dansby, ready to go." Viggo said holding her hands, then he goes ahead and informs Rachel, all about the procedures to be taken to capture Pascucci in the south of France: —while Viggo, is talking sitting on the bed next to Rachel, who can't contain her desires, and like a puppy looking for warmth, she get very cozy next to him, but her right hand got quite adventures looking for her favorite pet, making Viggo very uncomfortable, because at that moment one the nurses showed up, the woman did her best to ignore what was going on, then the nurse with poker-face inform...

"Special-Agent Bronson, it is time to give the patient a bath, I'm sorry but..." She said and Viggo responded...

"Don't be sorry Ms. Webb, I was ready to leave."

"If you wish, you can come back later." The nurse said sweetly, and Viggo responded...

"I'm afraid at this time I can't do that Miss. Webb, and I would appreciate if you took good care of Rachel, she is my partner, and I need her by my side as soon as possible, and I thank you in advance for your collaboration." Viggo said and Viggo gave Rocky a sweet kiss and he said...

"Rocky, tomorrow I'm coming to pick up Dusty, and I'm going to take the time to come and say goodbye." Viggo gets off the bed and walks to the door and blowing her a kiss and he spoke. "Rocky, I'll see you in the morning."

But in the other end of the city: Ember, anxiously is waiting for her husband; she has everything ready for the special occasion, she has arranged that from La Forchetta, to bring Viggo's favorite meal, and with all the love, she can displayed, she began to prepare the event, to welcome her husband, then Ember, with that special touch woman have, she began dressing the table with a beautiful embroidered tablecloth, and with great care she began placing the *Limoges dishware,* which was given to the couple as a gift at their wedding, then to continue with the display, right on the center of the table, she place a silver candlestick with four candles, that will give the ambience a romantic flavor, tower above the entire table it's a bottle of *Ménage á Trois* wine, Viggo's favorite, it was placed uncorked on the table: that way it will be ready to serve when he arrives: to complete the welcoming, in a romantic décor, she sprinkled her bedroom with petals of roses, and on the bed, the scent of lavender can be felt on the silk sheets; to compliment her husband, she placed on the nightstand a silver lighter and box of Havana cigars. —Ember really wishes to impress her husband, and she is paying special attention to every tiny detail, that's when it comes to her mind his favorite music, because at the moment Viggo, will enter her place, he will be listening to Shirley Bassey, singing his favorite song: *C'mon baby light my fire*. She wants to make sure, that Viggo would encounter a scena of pure romance. —At her place, everything is more than ready, to welcome the love of her life: the man who once she chased out of her life, for pure jealousy. —Then she begins babbling. "I'm promise I'll never creating another of those manic scenes." Ember said while a tear fell on her cheek.

Viggo after leaving the hospital went straight to the hotel, took a shower and dresses casually, on the way to see his wife he stopped at a local store and bought a couple of bottles of French champagne, in case Ember is preparing a traditional home dinner, or she decided to ordered dinner from her favorite restaurant. He can't discount that, or maybe she is waiting for him with a see-through negligee, escorted with her irresistible essence of her body, which is driving him crazy: in case this happens, it will be better if he gets ready, maybe, Ember proceeded to buy all the perfumes end creams that money can buy, if this is the case: it will be better to be ready. But Viggo, deep in his heart, he has the feeling that this night, will be loaded with mixed emotions. —The time has come and Viggo, is in front of the door, of his lovely wife, with two bottles of champagne in his arms, and he is wondering: what is going to happen when he crosses the threshold door...his thought was cut off at that moment: because...

At that instant his wife opens the door, the magnificent outlook of Ember took Viggo by surprise, then instead of entering: he took two steps back, to admire her, is that his wife is looking amazing, Ember's reddish hair fell like a waterfall over her silky white shoulders, she was wearing the pearl necklace and the earrings, which he gave her on their first wedding anniversary, Viggo, was speechless, then Ember, advanced towards him, then she kissed her husband like the first time they met: —But...

What they didn't know: That one of those God's from the Greek mythology, was waiting behind the scenes; and who was that celestial being? None other than Cupid, who is intruding in their lives, and he is ready to shoot a gold-tipped arrow right into their hearts, in order to light again the flame of love. —While Cupid, was trying his best to unify those two loving hearts. —The harsh reality is present, in this case, Ember, was the one who extinguished the flame of love, but now she is doing everything possible to light the flame of passion and love: that's why she was quite busy preparing for this special occasion, but her effort was not in vain, because now she has her husband in her arms, and her heart was racing like crazy, after a long appassionato welcome kiss. Ember was sure that in her place, she had already spread the net, to grab the man that she loves. And Viggo, is feeling that he is walking like a mouse toward the trap, resigned is thinking, that he has been caught again, by the woman he loves, but he fears that he will suffer again, the scenes of jealousy, with those feeling running through his head, cross the threshold of the door and when he entered the place hugged with his wife, he was admiring the pleasant ambiance Ember, prepared for the occasion. —Then...

During the delicious dinner, they tried not to touch on the subject that distanced them, in those moments they were heart to heart, trying to certify the bonds of love, in that process, with a lot of cordiality in part of both, they sip away the bottle of *Ménage à Trois* and also one of the bottles of champagne, the other bottle had another intimate destiny, would be consumed in her decorated bedroom: were this married couple put a parenthesis in their coexistence, these two souls will be trying to find the way to happiness. —After dinner: that night could not began in any other way, hot and steamy, and with a lot of sweltered between sheets with lavender scent, that is when the couple began the path to bind their relationship. Then, in one of those moments of tender love. Viggo, after a grueling section of love, he promised Ember, that when he returns from France, he was going to take her for a second honeymoon to Hawaii, at the beautiful island of Oahu, where the lovers will reinforce the marriage commitment. —After that tantalizing promise, Ember fell asleep thinking of a new promising beginning. —Then...

The next day, after taking a wakeup hot bath, Ember and Viggo, went out for breakfast at the Urth Caffe, a trendy place on Main Street. They left the place hugging each-other and walked a few blocks to the Bureau. Upon entering at the reception office, in front of the desk was Miss. Betty, who handed Ember a 'bundle' of mail, and Viggo very attentive address the secretary...

"Good morning Ms. Betty, it's nice to see you, when you're here, this office light up, must be your personality that beautify the office." Viggo says and a wise smile escape between his lips, and the young woman, just looking at Viggo, and her cheeks blushed. Ember who walked ahead managed to overhear what Viggo said, she continues walking and prevents him...

"Please, Viggo, don't do that to Betty, she admires you, I want to believe, that you are not trying to seduce her?" Ember said walking away and Viggo responded.

"Ember, I don't know what's going on with Betty, when I say hello, she blushes, that's unusual, don't you think?"

"Right now, Viggo, I don't want to get involved in silly discussion, and less, about your infamous fame, because this issue has nothing to do, with the case we have in hand. Okay?" Ember said and took him by the arm, and she began to walk to her office, and Viggo added...

"Infamous fame Ember? You're suggesting I'm famous only for the tattoo? And not for my performance as an astute officer of the law, and my personal attraction that led you to marry me. —I'm only asks?"

"Don't be so pompous: and about your fame, I don't want to talk about, it's not funny, and please Viggo, stop teasing and provoking that sweet girl, since she thinks you're a superhero. Okay?"

"What do you expect me to do Ember, it is that I should greet her, when I enter the reception, plus I love the situation, at the moment I began talking to her, she turns all red?"

"Look Viggo, I'm working very hard trying to coordinate your assignment, and you play head games with the receptionist?" Ember said as she sat behind her desk, then in all seriousness she went straight to business, and began to inform Viggo, that she had already contacted the French Intelligence, and for this assignment, they will provide with two agents, who will be waiting for Viggo at the Nice Airport. —When Ember finished reporting all the details of the trip to France, then Ember changes her demeanor, and sweetly she pointed out...

"I must tell you my love: Last night I had an amazing evening, it would be delightful, if before you leave in this assignment, you should make some time for a similar meeting? It would be magnificent if we said goodbye with a big hug of love!!" Ember, proposed, and Viggo gave her a kiss and trying to get out of the office, and he said...

"Ember, you know, I would love to be with you—but also you know, that you're sending me, to carry out a dangerous assignment, and I have the duty to comply with it." *Viggo said looking at Ember who is shaking her head side to side as if to saying, finish it please, and he continued saying.* "Honey, I have many details to solved, since I'm in charge of the security of Dusty, who is the one who is going to help me to solve this case. Okay?" Viggo said it with a witty smile, and Ember replies...

"Please, don't play the victim, because I know your weakness: now you are playing hard-to-get, but when you've been taken care of then you—you really love it, and like an aphrodisiac, you come back for more and more abuse!" Ember said throwing him a kiss, and Viggo from the threshold of the door replied...

"I'm glad Ember, that you recognize, that you have an insatiable desire of love, and to fulfill your wishes: when I come back from France, remember, for our second honeymoon, you're in charge of booking the trip to Hawaii. Okay?" Viggo indicates and closed the office door behind him, and Ember remained smiling full of hope. —And...

Viggo, happy with the prospect to solve his marital problems, went to the hospital to supervise that his friend, Dusty, will check in at the Beverly Hills Hotel, safely. —What Viggo doesn't know, is that after he left Ember's office, on top of her desk, it was a 'bundle' of mail, in which is hidden two airplane tickets to Nice France, with departure date? —Without having that news. Viggo, on the way to the hospital, had the courtesy of stopping to buy flowers for Rachel, who was happily surprised seeing the Chief with a bouquet of flowers in his arms, that is when Rachel, instantly placed the book she was reading at her side, and began kissing the man she fervidly desire, then she was full of enthusiasm and gratefully said...

"Oh my God!! Thanks for the flowers, Chief, they are gorgeous!" And she kisses him, but in that moment, what drew the attention to Viggo was the kind of book Rachel was reading, and he reacts...

"Rocky, what a nice surprise: you are reading my book? I'm really impressed." Viggo commented and Rachel happy with the bouquet of flowers in her arms answers...

"Of all the pleasures of life, being confined to bed, is really not my way of spending the day, and now I have the time to read, and I have to say congrats Chief, for your book, how come you didn't sign one and gave it to me?"

"You knew that I had written the book. Rocky, really, I didn't want to force the issue. Okay?"

"I am in the last chapter Chief. —Thanks to your book, now I have a different outlook, how to handle an investigation. I am already learning a lot about your philosophy, and how to deal with different scenarios, in which I could find myself entangled." Rachel points out and Viggo happy because his partner is reading his book responded...

"Thanks' Rocky, I'm glad you are enjoying it, and you have some other books here, what is this book all about? *The Mystery of the Petrified Heart.*"

"It is very entertaining Chief, this novel is an adventure, that captures the sweet moments of passion, seduction and friendship, as four curious young people venture into an unknown world, to prove a romantic theory. Chief, on the way to France, you should read this book." And she handed the book to Viggo who said...

"Thanks'!" *Viggo said looking with interest at the flaming heart in the book cover and continued saying with loving care.* "Rocky, I'm glad that you keep yourself busy, I'm going to miss you in France, Rocky, I'm sure that when I come back you will be ready to join me!"

"I hope so Chief; but I just wish, this injury doesn't leave me, with some trait of disability?" Rachel said trying to hold back her tears, and Viggo responds trying not to show weakness...

"This is not the case Rocky; I spoke to the doctor about your injury, and he assured me, that you would be able to use your arm without any inconvenience and stop worrying about it. Okay?" Viggo said kissing her as she were a child and she trying to hold back tears looks at him lovingly without saying a word, and Viggo showing desire not to go said...

"Rocky, I'm sorry, but the time has come to say goodbye, since I have to visit my next patient; Dusty, I'm going to see if he is in good shape, ready to leave the hospital." *Viggo kisses her sweetly and continue saying.* "Rocky, please take care yourself, I'll need you in your best physical condition when I get back." Viggo didn't finish saying the phrase and, she unleashes her passion in a farewell kiss; at that moment Rocky felt like she never imagined she could be...She felt like an unprotected little girl, but she didn't cry, and overwhelm by the moment she throws him a goodbye kiss, and Viggo went to see his friend, and...

When Viggo enters the patient room, Dusty, was waiting with open arms for him. —At the instant that he finishes greeting his American friend, Dusty like a man who has to fulfill a mission, he began dressing. —Viggo, seeing his friend busy, he went to the nurse's station, to pick up the discharge papers. To his surprise, when he came back to the room, his friend was properly dressed, with a white shirt and a red tie, and on his lapel jacket, you could see an American flag. Viggo was happy to see his friend very well groomed, and he commented...

"Let me see Mr. D'Varón, I'm really impressed—My friend I'm sure, that you will go unnoticed at the Beverly Hills Hotel, you look really sharp, and that perfume reminds me, of a certain person, that I know!"

"Come on Easy'V...you are the one who is wearing this perfume, because...you smuggled furtively...a bottle of *Givenchy Cologne*...in my suitcase...It was 'not' a very subtle suggestion...my friend!!"

"Come on, Dusty, you know, it was 'not' my true intentions. I want to give you a little advantage, listen Mr. D'Varón, in one of these encounters with Madam Divine, I was wearing this cologne and she told me that she loved. —Look Dusty, I just trying to provide you, with some of the advantages you should have, but won't be easy, I have some advice for you, at the moment to meet this fabulous person, you have to be ready, to dribble the issues of feeling: that's all I have to say my friend." Viggo said seriously and Dusty responded...

"Only one thing...I have to tell you Easy'V...After everything I've been through...and having dealt with Miss Death for a few moments...I certainly need a few moments of joy...and hoping that this fuckin cologne of yours...it does the job...it is supposed to do!!" Dusty pointed out meantime he was dusting his jacket lapel, and Viggo ignored the comment and asks...

"Are you ready to go, Mr. D'Varón —It's time to confront the outside world?"

"The world does not concern me...who worries me...is Madan Divan...May friend...And I'm ready...and let's go to France, to solve this fucking case!!" Dusty said very enthusiastic, at that moment Viggo's phone rang. Ember is calling from the Bureau, and she said...

"Hello, my love, I have news, but I don't know if your friend Dusty, will be pleased with this news?"

"If you are trying to say something unpleasant, don't beat around the bush, just say it, since you know, that we are fucking vaccinated against bad news: what is going on Ember?"

"Viggo, the news is not so terrible, I'm calling you, to let you know, that I have in my possession, the airplane tickets to France, and tell Dusty that I have his American passport; you see the news are not so bad?"

"That's a really good news. Ember, and when is the day of departure...?" Viggo asks knowing that there was the bad news and Ember with a certain wickedness informs...

"That's the million-dollar question Mr. Bronson. —Well, here comes the bad news. My love, to my dismay, you guys are leaving on Air France, tomorrow afternoon." Ember's revelations created a few seconds of silence and Viggo responded...

"That it's not a very good news Ember, after all the trouble you had to secure Dusty in the Beverly Hills Hotel. —Well, at least one day it's better than nothing." Viggo said feeling sorry for his friend and Ember has a proposal...

"I have a suggestion Special-Agent Bronson. —To entertain the Mr. Kaminsky: your friend, why don't you buy lollipops, and during the flight suck on the lollipops all the way to France!!" Ember ironically proposed, and Viggo said seriously...

"Please: Ember, I'm not in the mood to celebrate silly jokes. I'm in the hospital coordinating with the limousine driver, who will take Dusty to the hotel, then I have to go and pack my fucking suitcases, and..."

"Calm down Viggo, I have the solution: after you've done with your suitcases, would you like to spend this last night cuddling with me in bed, I don't think it's such a bad suggestion?"

"Come on Ember, you can't save some of that fervor of love, until I get back; my love, I'll come to say goodbye. Okay?"

"Viggo, I promise, that for a farewell, I'll give you a full special Ember treatment, the one you never forget. I'm going to start: bringing down your zipper with my teeth, really slowly, then after you see the lights of the heavens like the old days, you—you'll fall asleep in my arms, what do you say?"

"Honey, I say that tomorrow I have a long day, I'm sure I'll miss you, but I promise, we'll continue with this tête-à-tête about seeing the lights of heavens, when I return from France." Viggo said, and Dusty who was listening commented...

"Come on man...cut off that loving...French talk, and let's, go to the hotel...I'm very curious to know who the hell Madam Divine is?" Dusty suggested, and Viggo doesn't have any other option but to end the phone call with his wife and he said...

"Ember, I'll see you in a couple of hours. Okay?" Then Viggo turns around and facing his friend said...

"Dusty, I have bad news…

"Don't tell me, what the hell happened now, Ember, wants to send me back to Russia?" Dusty worried interrupted and Viggo informs…

"Don't be silly Dusty, it is not that bad, because tomorrow we are going to eat dinner on the plane, — heading to France."

"You must be kidding Easy'V?" Dusty said facing his friend and Viggo, who just finishes dealing with his wife doesn't have much patience and responded…

"This is not a joke Dusty, and that's the way it is. Mr. D'Varón, you just try to enjoy these twenty-four hours." *For a few seconds the friends looked at each other in silence and Viggo said.* "Dusty, you must make the most of the time. Okay?" Viggo confirms the bad news for Dusty who answers disappointed…

"How can this happen to me?…I'm almost an American citizen… Easy'V…this is a paradox…because at the time I arrive at the hotel…I will say…Hello Madam Divine…I'm René D'Varón…Goodbye Madam Divine…I have to leave the fucking hotel…fuck…fuck my luck!!"

"Don't complain, you have almost a full day to get acquainted with Madam Divine…just enjoy it…Listens Dusty, because we change your name, you are going to change your personality, where is that guy who was dealing with twenty women in Moscow?" Viggo pointed out, and Dusty responded pretending not to be happy…

"Thanks, Easy'V…but this news brought down…my fucking plans!" Dusty said seriously, and Viggo answered the same way.

"A matter-of-fact Mr. D'Varón, I'm assuming that you will have two jobs in front of you, the first one, after you are leaving this hospital, trying to be unnoticed, and the second one, it is really good news: you can spend all you want in the hotel, everything you buy will be free, just charge to the room. Okay?" Viggo said raising his arms and Dusty with a happy face responded…

"This latest news...is giving me confidence that capitalism is the way to live Easy'V...you are making a very good American Citizen...from this Russian...May friend...I promise...that If nothing is changing...we are going to solve this case...with no problems...I promise!"

"This is my friend, full of confidence, with that attitude you will not have any problem, to meet Madam Divine, just relax and enjoy her company!"

"I was sure...Easy'V...that you don't believe...in miracles?" Dusty said with a spare smile and Viggo responded...

"Mr. Kaminsky, if we are going to review what has happened to you in recent days, I really believe, that you are the one, who represents the real miracle..."

"I guess that you are right."

"Hey, Dusty, how many people can say, that he was dead and resurrected? Mr. D'Varón, come on let's go, I'm sure you will enjoy the hotel and company of Madan Divine." –Viggo is trying to encourage his friend, and Dusty looks at Viggo as if he was his older brother, then he looks at his luggage picks it up and started walking towards the door.

Viggo, had to make sure that Agent Voris Kaminsky, alias Dusty, or René D'Varón, would arrive at the hotel safe and sound, because the next day, Dusty and Viggo, must be ready to jump on in airplane, and endure the long journey to the International Airport in Nice...

FRANCE

Special-Agent Bronson has plenty of experience, when he going to intervene in a mission, in any part of the world, because in less than one hour, he packs two large suitcases and, he is ready to go. That night, Viggo takes a taxi and arrived at his wife's, with the suitcases. —When Ember opens the door, she only has eyes for her husband, and without saying hello she greeted him with a long sexy kiss, she was trembling with emotion, trapped in the spell of this passionate kiss full of sexuality, and when she come out of that amazing moment of tender love, Ember, saw the suitcases, and with a little poison of jealousy she asks...

"My love, what is the reason for these two suitcases, and this long case? Viggo, are you planning to stay and live in Paris?" Ember asks smiling but with hint of control, and Viggo who knows his wife responded...

"Come on, Ember, this is not the first time you see me going on a mission, have you forgot already how I travel? Remember; in one of the suitcases, I have the clothes, and in the other, I'm mixing some of my clothes with the guns, and in the long case, I'm taking my favorite..."

"Just a minute: Viggo, your favorite weapon, you know that in the arsenal of the FBI this weapon is not available?" Ember said holding her husband by the arm and taking him into the living room. Meanwhile Viggo reminds his wife...

"Darling, I'm guessing that you forgot, but this weapon saved my life in Afghanistan, and I did use it a couple days ago, when I got to Los Angeles, you remember, those gangsters, who tried to shorten my life; well, I blew their car with this weapon, which works just fine." Viggo said, and Ember raising her eyebrow asks...

"Come on Viggo, you are not going to tell me, that you are taking this powerful weapon to France? If you do, I hope you don't have to use it!"

"Ember, if I'm going to engage in any skirmish, I wish to have the advantage of having this weapon with me, and I'm expecting that the French authorities, should not give me any problems; for sure, these people are hard to please."

"For your info, I already called the intelligence Bureau, and I warned the director about Special-Agent Bronson style: I told the director, that you will bring your own weapons and, he didn't appreciate it—but they have to swallow their pride, since I told him that they knew, that Santino Pascucci was a well-known gangster, and they let him into their country."

"It's amazing Ember, how can you be so smart and efficient, and at the same time so beautiful, usually these two attributes go together on very rare occasions." Viggo said kissing her, and Ember didn't waste any time and begins fondling him while she said...

"Thanks, for the compliment, besides you are very lucky, because I have all night to bring you to my world of dreams, and together we'll travel, the fantasy of the eternal dream of happiness." Ember whispered in his ear, and Viggo knows when he's in trouble and he said...

"I did tell you Ember, that I preferred to arrive in France in one-piece and, you begin the evening, with those romantic words. I wonder, what do you have, in that Machiavellian mind of yours?"

"Don't worry my love, nothing's going to happen to you, that didn't happen before, just relax and..."

"That answer worries me, and it's not very comforting to say!"

"Don't be silly, it would be wise that before starting to drink Champagne, we should go over a few details, regarding your departure tomorrow." *Viggo is listening meanwhile he opens a bottle of Champagne and she continue saying.* "Listen Viggo, for Dusty's safety,

I have delegated Mike, to pick him up at the hotel, then he'll take Dusty to the Los Angeles Airport; at the International Terminal, where he should wait at the VIP lounge of the French Airlines. Okay?"

"I couldn't expect less from you Officer Maxwell, that's really thinking ahead: your proficiency, assures me that I am in good hands."

"Thanks, for the compliment Special-Agent Bronson, and I must inform you, that you are going to have two French agents, who will be waiting for you at the airport, the agents going be your guide, in the search of Pascucci."

"Thanks' Ember, but since I remember I have my own compass, and I don't think Pascucci, represent a great danger!"

"I'm really frustrated Viggo, because there's nothing, I can do about those Russian agents who are following you, and..."

"Honey, I was never in any danger: these guys are just looking for Dusty, and you told me that the Russian Intel, believes that he is alive, so, if these fuckers ever find Dusty, I'm going to be there to protect him."

"Viggo, I'm trying to prevent, that nothing happens to you. 'Prevention is the mother of safety.' Okay?" Then Ember started kissing him passionately, and when Viggo was able to breathe he pointed out...

"Ember, if the night starts this way—what kind of surprises is waiting for me?" Then, Ember grabs a bottle of Champagne and very smoothly took her husband to the bedroom: once in bed she began to play with her favorite tattoo, she should know better: you don't tease a viper to amuse yourself: that is not wise, because then you pay the consequences, and after a couple of hours of passionate love, she was begging for a little bit of compassion. "Please...Easy'V...stop...please!! —And for sure that...

Ember was happy: Because she was able to recover her marriage, and she joyfully fell asleep embracing her husband, but in the morning, she wakes up feeling worried, because she knows that she is sending her husband on a dangers mission. They started walking carrying the suitcases the short distance to the Bureau; Ember was thinking that she should control her emotions and remain calm. That's why when she walked through the office door, she became all business, as she is trying to hide her real feelings; then with the seriousness that the occasion requires, she handed to Special-Agent Bronson an envelope with official documents regarding his assignment. Until that moment, Ember remained quiet calm; she is trying to project a sense of security. —But...

What is going on in the head of Viggo, at the moment he has to embark on this dangerous mission; There could not exist a more painful action then to leave behind the person you really love; and the feeling gets worse when you know, that you have the possibility of not returning, but special-agent of the Federal Bureau of Investigation, knows how to hide her or his true emotions. Ember is kissing her husband goodbye, and her eyes got a little bit damp, and Viggo kissing her back said...

"Ember, when I come back from France, and finish with all the reports, I'm promising you, that our next investigation is going to be, at the Royal Hawaiian Hotel, on the beaches of Hawaii, there we will go in search of our second honeymoon, just get ready. Okay?"

"I would love that Viggo, and rest assured, that I'll organize the trip by the time you return, and I'm also sure, that in the first week, you're going to grab Mr. Pascucci: and by the way, don't forget that I'm waiting for you. Okay, my darling?" Ember said with emotion, and Viggo under the office threshold door, kisses his wife goodbye. And when Viggo had taken a couple of steps, Ember calls him and said...

"Viggo remember, that Dusty is waiting for you, in the VIP lounge of the French Airlines." Then Ember doesn't want to see her husband leave and enters the office closes the door in tears.

Meanwhile this romantic moment was happening in Santa Monica. —The previous day: Dusty, was checking into the Beverly Hotel, and very proudly was showing his temporary US citizen identification as René D'Varón. Once he was settled in his luxury room, feeling fine safe and cheerful, Dusty, sits in the comfortable couch, after reviewing in his mind, everything he experience in the last days and, wandering how the hell did he get to that luxurious place, with those thoughts in mind finally he relaxes, then he looks at the phone, sitting on the side table, and he remembered his friend suggestion: to call Madam Divine, and he did, and she answers...

"Hello: who is calling?"

"I am René D'Varón...Madam Divine."

"Mr. D'Varón, I was waiting for your call?" She said very sweetly, but that hello with a French accent, it was one of the sweetest hellos that Dusty, heard in a long time, and all excited he responded...

"Our mutual friend...spoke highly of you...I'm anxious to meet you...Madam Divine!"

"Mr. D'Varón, welcome to the hotel: I would like to let you know—that a lot of water went under the Seine River bridges, but it's possible, that my voice reminds you of a person that you met a while ago?" She asked sweetly, and Dusty was puzzled by the question, and he curiously replied...

"Madam Divine, are you trying to say, that we had already met before? If this is the case, I'm confuse, I guess I'm a little stunned...since I just got out of the hospital...I hope this is the reason...for not recognizing your voice." Dusty said encourage and Madam Divine inserted some mystery to the answered...

"Sure, Mr. D'Varón, we met before, I was associated with you some time ago, if you would like to come to the penthouse, you'll see, that at the instant I open the door, you will remember that sometime ago we—we were acquaintances?" Madam Divine said very inviting, and Dusty that was intrigued by her comment, and a little confused he commented...

"Madam...in this situation... the only thing I have to say...is that I hope I didn't lose my memory...in those couple of minutes...when the chinses sent me to the eternal peace ...but right now I'm here...talking to you...and that itself is a greater miracle!" Dusty said happy to be alive and Madam responded...

"Mr. René D'Varón, that's an amazing story, I would like to know what happened and, for any discomfort that you are feeling, I will take care of those aches, and be sure, that when you leave this hotel, your health will be in perfect shape. —Can I call you René?"

"For sure...you...you can call me...René...Madam Divine, and please...you have to excuse me...if mentally I'm not in my right potential."

"Please René: take your time and relax, I'll be waiting for you with some appetizers, I hope they are to your liking?" She says that phrase with such a romantic French accent that Dusty, began to dream that he already was in her arms, and he answered...

"Thanks'...Madam...I just got here...and I'm dressing like a mannequin...I will wear something more comfortable, and...I'll be there...in a little while...I'm quite intrigued...to know who you are? I will see you in a little while."

"Okay, René, I'll wait for you." She said sweetly, and Dusty is full of joy, because he is sure that he will become a good friend of that French voice: of course he is sure of himself, the man is alive and free; besides he will carry an American passport, with his new name, then with Viggo, his friend, they will go to hunt gangsters in France: to complete his joy, is waiting for him an amazing gorgeous woman: nothing less than, at the penthouse of the Beverly Hotel.—For sure this lucky Russian agent is thrilled, because right now, he is singing in the shower and, thinking in the moment he will caress her silky skin, and, kiss her all over: The time has come, to came out of his dream full of desires, and Dusty dresses elegant but comfortable: then with a blind date in mind, he went to the hotel lobby and bought French champagne, and he said to the cashier with a mischievous smile. "Please, charge to my room." Then with two champagne bottles very confident he is heading to the elevator, on the way to the penthouse. Dusty, still wonders who is that woman, who speaks with a sweet French accent, and she claims to have dealt with him, sometime ago? —And...

This is the moment when he is going to reveal the mystery. —Dusty is in front of her door, of the person who has all his attention, the curiosity increases when it was time to act at the moment to knock on the door, he tries to do it very gently: when then the door opens, right in front of him, as he imagined-it, appears the person who was in his fertile imaginary mind. —She was not only gorgeous, but she was also looking like a sensual diva, with the couture pink silk translucent pajamas, that is showing her marvelous and perfect body, she looks more like a sophisticated doll, than a real person. She's right there in front of him, and, that gorgeous face can't ever be forgotten: instantly he recognizes Madam Divine...Who is this marvelous person? —She is no less than...

Brigitte De'Gaún. The young French woman who worked a few months at the *Palace of Love* in Moscow, until one of the generals of the Russian Army, became so obsessed with her, that the general considered, that she, should be his own sex slave and, he decided to take Brigitte to his home, as his own property, the situation was quite untenable. That's when Dusty, became aware of the unbearable circumstances, and the difficulties Brigitte should deal with. As an owner of the place, he decides to handle the matter, and without any fear of retaliation, which could come from the general, upon learning that he is trying to protect Brigitte, that's when Dusty, is going to intervene in her liberation, Dusty must appeal to the powerful influence of some of his clientele, who were visiting the *Mansion of Love*, at that time he was risking his future, or more than that, to save the beautiful young woman, from the claws of the controlling general. Dusty had organized the escape in one of those ice-cold Moscow nights, it was a very risky maneuver, but he managed to get Brigitte out of Russia. —A matter of fact, from what he is seeing in front of him right now, his involvement in her dangerous escaping mission; it was a total success, since right now she looks just stunning. —And...

Brigitte, who is feeling emotional, and, anxious to see the man who rescued her from that despotic general. —With open arms she was waiting for him. After the welcome kisses and hugs, like good old friends they started talking about the struggle she went through, and after several glasses of Champagne, they started talking enthusiastically about their future business associations, it was in that subject were they lost the measure of time. Brigitte, as if everything had been coordinated beforehand, she looks at her watch and, decided to ordered dinner, Dusty that can't be happier, was thinking that it was the right time to opened the second bottle of Champagne, and in a sign of solidarity looking straight into each other's eyes, crossing their arms with a bubbly glass of champagne in each hand, Brigitte and Dusty toasted for a promising future, until the bottle of champagne end up in her bedroom. And what happened? After that exquisite meal, what happened? The events of that night, only have it clear the people of high spirits, since these two souls, who were looking for each other in the spheres of eternity, finally, they consummated their dream between silk sheets. A matter of fact, the rumor spread in the hotel employees, that night Morpheus, did not pass by Brigitte bedroom...

Well, what we know for sure, is that Dusty really enjoyed all the dinner's with his old friend: next day over breakfast, he has a promise from Brigitte, of a lasting relationship. —Unfortunately, that day Dusty, has to meet with his friend Special-Agent Bronson, to embark on an assignment, that will take him out of her friend's arms, and when the time came to say goodbye; it was a delight for Dusty to kiss Brigitte De'Gaún, and he did it gently, and with emotion he says in his dusty voice. "My dear Brigitte...for sure...we will continue this friendship...when...I return from France." Dusty said feeling sorry that he has to leave, and she responded. "René, when you come back, we will continue talking about the businesses we have planned." And Brigitte sees how Dusty disappears in the elevator.

Waiting for Dusty in the lobby of the hotel was Mike, who handed him his American passport, then he took Dusty to the airport, and Dusty was happier than a dog with two tails.

Once Dusty arrived at the French Airlines VIP lounge, he decided to have a cup of coffee; meanwhile he is waiting for his friend, he began to review his brand-new American passport, with utter curiosity: right at that moment Viggo came into the lounge area: seeing that his friend was busy reading and sipping coffee; he decided to take that space of time, to call Rachel at the hospital.

"Hello Chief."

"Hi Rocky, how are you?"

"What a surprise Chief, are you at the airport, with Dusty?"

"Yes, I should be with you, but I have to settle with Dusty, and we are ready to climb the Eiffel Tower, perhaps — perhaps from the top of that magnificent sculpture, we can see where Pascucci is hiding!" Viggo said says it to get a smile from Rachel who responded...

"That's a brilliant idea Chief, I'm jealous, because I would love to be with you guys, and no less that in the south of France, dipping my feet in the waters of the Côte Bleue!"

"I'm sure there will be another opportunity for you Rocky, now tell me, how are things going?"

"I'm feeling much better Chief, in a few days Doctor James Anderson wants me to recoup outside of the hospital: I can't wait." Rachel said very cheerful, and Viggo happy to hear that said.

"Rocky, you're sure that you want to return to New York, and not wait for us? On second thought, this is good news: you are going home."

"Well, it is not so simple Chief, certain circumstances occurred, because Doctor Anderson, is trying to…"

"What are you trying to say Rocky?"

"Chief, it all started, when Doctor Anderson, began to pay frequent visits, and things…"

"Wait a minute; what do you mean frequent visits? Rocky, seems to me, Doctor Anderson, has other intention, or am I wrong?"

"Like I said Chief, he came to see me quite a few times every day, he is trying to prevent that my shoulder, ending up with some kind of disability, which will inhibit any movement of my arm, and James…"

"Excuse meee…James? You already call this guy by his first name. What the hell is going on in that hospital? Rocky, this guy knows, that you are in a vulnerable state, and he's taking advantage of your disability."

"Please, Chief, James, shows a lot of interest in this disabled federal agent, and he looks pretty good, in that white doctor outfit. — Plus, he also just made me a serious offer." Rachel says it calmly as if it were normal, and Viggo responded…

"This doctor is quite fast, doesn't wasted no time eating appetizers, he goes straight to the main course—did I hear right —you and this doctor —don't you tell me that!!"

"Relax Chief, James, only suggested that I should finalize my recovering at his house in Malibu, that is what he proposed, I don't see anything strange in that?"

"Hold on Rocky, you are telling me to relax, this guy appeared in your life a couple days ago. —Well, I'm sure you'll make the right decision Rocky, but to be sure, why don't you send his ID to the PIB" = *People Investigation Bureau.*

"I'm ahead of you Chief, I already spoke with the director of the PIB. The only feature that appeared in his record, has to do with his medical diploma, he has a clean spotless record—Doctor James Anderson, is a decent good man." Rachel said with confidence, and Viggo has no other choice but to say...

"Hey, I wish all the luck in the world to you. Rocky, I'll see you when I come back, and take care of yourself."

"Chief, you have no idea how much I miss you and, your tattoo. Please, come home in one-piece Chief. Okay?" Rachel said with deep feeling, and Viggo responded...

"I'll miss you in France. Rocky, and don't do anything stupid, which will prevent your full recuperation, keep your wild side really deep inside your heart. Okay?"

"Chief, I'm going to miss you a lot, please come back as soon as possible Chief?" Rachel asks with tears in her eyes.

Meanwhile, Dusty, had finished with his breakfast, and also, he went through the entire brand-new American passport, then he stood up to see if he could spot his friend, and when he saw Viggo, he was coming to meet him, and with a friendly hug greeted Viggo and Dusty full of gratitude said...

"Easy'V...is nice to see you...and thanks for all you've done for me...that experience was fabulous...but let say that you lied to me...since you knew who that woman was, and you left me hanging...like a t-shirt on the clothesline...drying with expectation!"

"I want to know only one thing: when you saw Brigitte, you were surprised?"

"It was a spectacular surprise, thanks Easy'V, I have an unforgettable day!"

"I'm glad that you have a good time. Dusty, in the meantime, we avoid that your comrades, throwing you out of the car again, we really pulled this thing off, Dusty!"

"Easy'V...I just hope that the *Shadow*...still doing his job, and hope he hasn't lost his prey?"

"I hope so too, it would be very helpful, to know where he is hidden, it will make our job much easier!"

"You're right; it would save us a lot of work and, I'll call him when we arrive in France." Dusty, said with a smile and Viggo asks curious.

"Dusty, you are acting in a very youthful way: you know what that means? It reveals that last night, you had a very good time with Madam Divine, your face is an open book, Dusty!"

"A matter of fact, I have no words to described Brigitte...Easy'V, she is a dream come true...and you...you already knew...who she was...Isn't that right, Special-Agent Bronson?" Dusty said euphoric raising his arms and Viggo responded...

"My friend, I just wanted you to have a good time, that's all. Okay?"

"And what a moment it was. Easy'V...I must tell you, that at the instant she opened the door...that's when that incredibly...gorgeous woman appeared before my eyes...and I couldn't believe she was Brigitte...the same French girl...that drove all the men out of their minds...in the Mansion!" Dusty said excited, and Viggo added...

"Dusty: I want to clarify something, because I see that you like her a lot, I don't want false interpretations that break our friendship. Okay?"

"Okay, Easy'V...but first I want to say...that no matter what happens...nothing can ever break...our friendship. Okay?

"We agree on that concept. Dusty, I want to clarify something with you, and I told you this before, I was very depressed, at the time I met Brigitte, that night after talking for several hours, and in between we drank a bottle of Chivas Regal, we became friends, then over time, she decided to help with info, which she believed could help me; because the informant relationship continued, I had no choice but to have her investigated by the PIB, my concern was, that I couldn't put my trust in this person, since I didn't know if she was a foreign agent, and consequently, she will provide me with false info, and from the PIB info, I found out, that she wasn't a foreign agent, and she had been a guest in *The Mansion of Love*, few years ago." Viggo ends up saying and Dusty agree...

"Sure...Brigitte was in Moscow...for a couple of months...at the Mansion, and she was one of my guests."

"Brigitte, is a very sweet and lovely person, and looking at your outlook Dusty, I'm sure that the last night was steamy and quite long night; that during dinner, and, between one glass and, another glass of champagne, you were planning future business together, and the night ended—ended—remembering past times?"

"It seems...like you've been...dining with us. It's just amazing Easy'V...and far as I know, you don't have a crystal ball...and how can it be...that you are predicting...the past and future events. It must be because...you're reading the happiness...that shows all over my face!"

"You're right, your features told me all about last night, other than that my friend, for my own predictions, I just use the legendary art, of guessing!!" Viggo said as not giving importance to his predictions and Dusty grateful he answers...

"Anyway Easy'V...I can't thank you enough...and you know why? At the end of our meeting...Brigitte, promised me...that when I come back from France...we will meet again!" Dusty said with glitter in the eyes of happiness, and Viggo added...

"That's great news Dusty, I guess that you're falling in love, I'm really happy for you, I'm sure that you would make a really good couple." *At that moment the loudspeakers called to board the airplane and Viggo said out loud.* "Come on Dusty, it's showtime." Viggo announced walking to board the airplane. What Viggo didn't know: is that the captain had informed to the crew that Special-Agent Viggo Bronson would be one of the passengers. —Then...

During the beginning of the flight, Dusty could not stop talking about the pleasant moments he enjoyed with Brigitte, and Viggo, had no choice, but to listen to his friends rambling tails, until the lights in the cockpit went out, it didn't take long for Dusty to fell asleep, with a pleasant smile on his face, instead Viggo, couldn't do the same, thinking about the promise he made to Ember, he was extremely concerned regarding his wife mental well-being, because her extreme way of handling her feelings of control towards him, that situation worries him. This is the reason that kept Viggo moving side to side in his seat, that's when one of the female stewardesses, noticed the Special-Agent Viggo Bronson was not comfortable in his seat: it happened to be: that the crew already know about the presence of the special passenger, and the kind of fame he carries with him: the stewardess aware of the situation, she invites Viggo to their station at the rear of the airplane: since their jobs were over, and all the flight attendant are gathering at the food station. —Then she said in a pleasant way...

"Hello, Special-Agent Bronson, I noticed that you're not too comfortable in your seat, near to the food station are quite a few seats empty, there you will feel more comfortable?" She asked very sweetly and Viggo asks...

"Thanks' Miss...?"

"Margaret, my friends call me Margie." She says smiling and delicately rests a hand on his shoulder, looking straight at Viggo's eyes.

"Okay Margie, if you have better seats where I can rest, I would appreciate it—but I hope I don't disturb anybody?

"Just quite the opposite, the captain informed us that you would be on board, and that we should take care of you, and the girls are eager to meet you, why don't you come to our station and have a couple drinks with us?"

"I love that Margie, you were reading my thought, because I was thinking, with a couple of drinks, I could fall asleep with no problem."

For reasons unrelated to rationality Viggo, has among women certain kind of *unnoticed immense charm,* which is really difficult to explain in basic words, since very few men have this gift: it is not the physical appearance, I guess is the mystery of nature, that reward few men with the luxury of being pursued and pampered by women, and in this case, it's not going to be any different; and for a couple of hours between drinks. Viggo, was entertaining the crew, with his experiences as a special-agent: this why the stewardess close to him were listening attentively, —at one point there was a moment of silence, and one of the girls had the guts to asks, where the anaconda tattoo was engraved on his body? —To which Viggo replied, that everything was a myth, and he did not have any sign in his body to identify him. The girls didn't believe him, they know exactly where the tattoo was hidden. As if to say the party is over, at that moment the lights of the food-station was diluted, it's time to rest. —And...

Margie already had the bed ready for Viggo, she took him by the arm, and in the darkness guided him to a seat she already had prepared with blankets: then, under those blankets she is trying her best to give Special-Agent Bronson a V I P relaxing treatment, to see if her feminine touch can put Viggo to sleep. Margie really did a good job, because next morning it was difficult for him to wake up for breakfast, and Viggo half asleep decided to go back to where his seating was: and when he arrives, he found his friend, the way he left it: sleeping with a smile on his face, just as Viggo is going to seat down, Dusty wakes up. And Viggo said to his friend...

"My friend, I guess, you were smiling all night, dreaming about Brigitte, isn't that, right?"

"That's right…Easy'V…and since you know very well this topic…My grandmother…used to say…about this subject…That wealth and love…it's impossible to conceal…because…somehow somewhere always shows up…and I can't hide these feelings…I'm in love…and I'm in big trouble." Dusty said dustily and with a subdued smile, and Viggo responded seriously…

"I'm sorry my friend, I must tell you something that you will not be happy about. Dusty, if you have pneumonia, I will take you to the nearest hospital and save your life. —But in this situation noting I can do, the vires you just contracted, is going to give you a sickness that has no cure; you are really fucked up. Dusty, you are in love…loveeee!!"

"Please, tell me something I don't know Easy'V?

During the flight, the two agents were debating what kind of procedures they going to follow, to capture the American gangster. With those thoughts in mind, they arrived at the Nice Airport in France. Viggo was inside the gate like a racehorse, ready to go into action, and he said to his friend…

"Dusty, I'm grateful that you are helping me on this mission, but in pursuit of this gangster, I'm really don't want to put your life in danger, I just want you to take care of the logistics. Okay?" Viggo said seriously and Dusty replied…

"Don't worry Easy'V…you will get all the bullets…because in this mission…I will always be behind you…besides I'm just a guide…you must do the pursuit…of Pasccuci, Easy'V…and I'm going to see…what kind of method you're going to apply…in this chase. Okay?"

"Dusty, I assure you, that traitors are the people who annoy me the most, and this fucker I will bring to US in handcuffs, if that is not the case, a wooden crate is not going to be so fucking bad." Viggo said it, imitating a carpenter hammering nails.

Finally, the American agents are touching French soil, they were carrying out a specific mission: one of the agents is American citizen;

the other is a Russian born, with American citizenship. These two friends of different culture and backgrounds, have the same goal; joining forces to capture the gangster Santino Pascucci, and the pursuit would be no less, than in one of the most famous ancient cities in France. *Saint Paul the Vence.*

Upon leaving the airport, waiting for them were two agents from the French Intelligence. —Rosél Du'Pont, was one of the agents, who stands out for her beauty: her partner, Agent André Duvalier: looks like he escaped from a French movie. —Rosél and André, from the moment they were introduced, they were all over Viggo, she was asking one question after another, and by the time André, has the chance to say a word: he is trying to find out, how Special-Agent Viggo Bronson, wants to proceed with the mission that brings him to France. — What the fuck? Nobody pays attention to agent René D'Varón=Dusty, is like a lonely tourist, who comes to visit the Eiffel tower, he is walking behind the two French agents, who are attacking his friend with questions, and in that moment, he asks in a whisper. *"What the fuck am I doing over here—well, everything is for the sake of a friend?"* Finally, the French agents took the American agents to a V I P exit, where they met with their luggage.

Leaving behind the Nice Cõte D'Azur Airport; Rosél and André, drove the American agents to the Radisson Bleu Hotel, with the promise: they would return in the morning after breakfast, to take Viggo and Dusty, to the medieval village of Saint Paul de Vence, where supposedly, Santino Pascucci took shelter in the Atelier Galerie d'Art, which belongs to Michael D'Tella, supposedly a very good friend of Mr. Santino Pascucci.

After the two agents checked into the hotel and putting their belongings in their own rooms. Dusty, went to see friend, and when he enters the room Viggo, saw his friend with a tired face and proposed...

"Dusty, I know you are tired, but we have to find out what's going on, in the village. could you please call *The Shadow,* I need to know if Pascucci still hiding in that village?" Viggo asks, and Dusty picked up the phone, and called a couple of times without success, and he said...

"*The Shadow* does not answer Easy'V...but...I don't think it's...something to worry about it?"

"Dusty, we have to be sure that this piece shit of Pascucci, is in that fucking village, don't you agree?"

"Relax Easy'V, the only thing I can say...is that before leaving Los Angeles...I spoke with *The Shadow*...and he told me that Pascucci was there...it's all I can say my friend...I'm sure he is there." Dusty said with certainty and Viggo who is tired responded...

"Okay, Dusty, you're right, let's relax, and tomorrow on the way to Saint Paul de Vence, let's see if you can contact *The Shadow,* if he is not in the village, we have to do the fucking work of intel ourselves!" Viggo said seriously, and Dusty tries to put a little humor to the problem and said...

"I'm sure *The Shadow*...is in Saint Paul de Vence Easy'V...This guy ...enjoys being with woman...he is a frequent client of the *Mansion of Love*...It's very possible that he's engaged in a heated conversation, with a French girl...and I bet you...that between words...he is fucking her brain out." Dusty said dustily with a guessing face, then dead tired, he drops on the couch; meanwhile Viggo, proceeded to order dinner with two bottles of wine; during dinner they toasted for their friendship and, the success of the mission: they were almost done with dinner, when someone knocked on the door, the two agents were tired, but that surprise visit, put them on guard, and the fatigue just disappeared, Dusty draws his gun and stands behind a piece of furniture, and Viggo with his service weapon in hand, went to answer the call, in firing position he stands to one side of the door, and Viggo asks...

"Who is it?"

"It's the service: Sir." A female voice with a French accent sweetly answers.

If the surprises began like this, since they just arrived, what will happen the next day? —Because, when Viggo opens the door, standing right in front of him, was Agent Rosél Du'Pont: without her uniform. Rosél, came fully dressed to attract a lot of attention, and She enters the living-room walking very sexual, with high heels shoes; her mini skirt, could not be shorter, which reveals her gorgeous long legs: to overflow the men's fantasy; she is wearing a pink blouse that opens generously showing a lot of skin. Dusty, who saw that was no danger, returned to seat on the couch, and Viggo, surprised by the unexpected visitor, watches with interest at the entrance of that beautiful woman, who in one of her hands she carries a book, it happened to be, Viggo's book, *The investigation Technique*. That amazing show of sexual beauty, it has all the intentions, to get Viggo's attention: she was unlucky because she come across a situation, that she had not foreseen on her plans, to conquer the favors of the anaconda, the inconvenience is that Viggo was having dinner with his partner, and the 'Snake-Hunter', was very disappointed: to hide her frustration. Rosél, is trying to display her best smile, and with a very cute French accent she said...

"Hello gentlemen: I'm sorry if I interrupted your dinner, it was not my intention to disturb your evening, a matter of fact, I'm intrigue, and I would like to satisfy my curiosity, if I can steal a few minutes off your evening." Rosél said and enter the room walking very sexy and flashing Viggo's book, and he looks at her with a pleasant surprise, and with a smile Viggo responded...

"Welcome Agent Du'Pont, this is a pleasant surprise; we have just finished dinner, and we are chasing it down with a glass of cabernet sauvignon, would you like to have a glass of wine with us?"

Viggo invites her to sit, and he has no choice but to sit next to her and she answered...

"Sure, you are so sweet: I would love to." Then with great emphasis she places the Viggo's book on her lap, and sweetly said...

"Special-Agent Bronson, your book is fascinating, I'm amazed about the different techniques that you show solving crimes, I have to tell you that during the course of some of my investigations, your method has guided me in the right direction, it would make so happy if you would autographing the book?"

"It's a pleasant surprise, that you purchased my book Agent Du'Pont, it will be my pleasure to autograph the book." Viggo signed book and handed to her, then very sweetly she said...

"Thanks', it's very nice of you, I have to say that your book is very clever, I could not stop reading it, and what I love the most, is the way you approach your investigations, it seems that you inserted yourself, directly into the heart and mind of the criminal. —I guess the concept is to anticipate the next move of the person, who is trying to break the law, this way you are one step ahead of the outlaw: that is a very smart strategy Special-Agent Bronson—after we finish with this investigation, I would like to continue talking with you, about one of the cases in the book, that fascinates me. *The Widow's Night Mystery*, that you resolve the case successfully, but I believed that you, left out some important details out of the story, and I would like to know why you did it?" Rosél, asked very sweetly, and Viggo looks at Dusty and said...

"There is no specific reason: but in this case I owe you the explanation Agent Du'Pont, I promise that when we finish with this investigation, it would be a pleasure to talk with you all about the book." Viggo said with a smile, while serving Rosél a glass of wine, and then he proposed a toast for the success of their mission. —After a while the Rosél got frustrated because she could not get her hands on Viggo's pants, then, with the same glamour in which she entered the room. Rosél, said goodbye with the promise, that her partner and her, would arrive at the hotel, at nine in the morning to pick them up.

The next morning Viggo and Dusty came down for breakfast; during the meal Dusty called *The Shadow* with the same result, no answer, and Dusty commented...

"That's strange...he doesn't answer...I wonder Easy'V...if Intelligence returned him...back to Moscow...or Mr. *Shadow*...still he's fucking around?"

"Don't worry Mr. D'Varón, in a few hours we'll be in the village of Saint Paul de Vence, and we'll find out, if *The Shadow* still is following this fucker, if they sent him back to Russia, we already know where this traitor is hiding." Viggo said firmly. —And...

Agent Du'Pont, and Agent Duvalier, arrived on time at the Radisson Bleu Hotel, and Viggo and Dusty we're ready to go, the same as their weapons stashed in two cases. At the moment they got in to the transporting prisoners extra-long SUV, Agent Du'Pont didn't say a word about what happened last night, but she noticed the two cases, and she asks...

"Special-Agent Bronson, excuse my curiosity, but I don't believe that you are carrying fishing rods, in these cases?"

"Agent Du'Pont, in these specials cases, we carry our most important working tools, and I hope we don't have to use any of these weapons." Viggo said very smooth, and she answers in the same smooth way...

"I just hope that this man that we're chasing, he gives up without resistance Special-Agent Bronson, since already I did shoot a man, and that's not a very good feeling, you know?"

"Agent Du'Pont, you know that I was recently involved in a case with international repercussions, in which several people perished, this why I understand how you have felt." Viggo said with his thoughts put on his partner Rocky. —Well...

Special-Agent Bronson must carry out this mission without the help of his partner Federal Agent Rachel Dansby, she was wounded during a shootout with Chinese agents. There is the reason that Viggo must place his trust, in the professional skills of his French colleagues, to carry out this investigation, which is going to begin at the medieval village of Saint Paul de Vence, and the agents left to...

CAPTURE SANTINO PASCUCCI

In charge of driving the SUV, is Agent André Duvalier, that was explaining to the visitors the historical sites they were passing, it took him almost half an hour to cross the beautiful City of Nice; once out of town, André decided to took *Via Route Napoléon*: this road is the shorter one that brings the agents closer to their destination, as they advanced towards their destination, the panorama was changing, with the passing of the minutes, they are reaching the higher elevations, right now the agents are traveling on a natural ancient road, which cuts throughout an amazing hills of solid white rock, of immense proportion, this incredible scenery, and the huge dimensions of the landscape are imagines that could be confused from sceneries from another world, this is the feeling they have at the moment to reach the mountain top; from that higher elevation, the views of the Vence green valley is amazing: with this spectacular view, slowly they are approaching their destination, which will be in front of their eyes, with all the medieval village of Saint Paul de Vence, ancestry. —And...

For the security and safety of the habitants, the tourists have to park their cars about three blocks from the village, entrance. There is where Agent Duvalier, parks the car like any other tourists, the agents have to walk up the hill, to reach the entrance of the small town, in the village winding streets, you can encounter all types of business, most of them dedicated to tourism. —One of those well-established businesses is the Atelier Galerie d'Art, which belongs to Michael D'Tella, friend of Mr. Pascucci, who supposedly, he was closely followed by *The-Shadow, a Russian agent*. —Then, at the moment the agents...

Entering the village, Viggo and Dusty, walked side-by-side with the French agents' who stopped about ten yards before they saw what they were looking for: in the business façade of the store, you can read, Michelle D'Tella Atelier Galerie d'Art. —The first thing that caught the attention of the agents, is that in front of the Galerie d'Art doors, it was guarded by two stereotypes of CERBERUS: Cerberus is a mythological guard dog: this creature had three heads, and replacing the tail, has a quite long snake; the Greek legend tells, that this dog was the guardians of the great gates, which leads you to the *Gloomy Underworld*. —That figure or symbol: tells Viggo that he is in the right place, and with confidence of knowing what he is going to do next said he said...

"I wonder if this guy knows what this dog represents. Agent Duvalier, let's see what Mr. D'Tella, is hiding in his place?" Viggo said to André, who informs...

"I'm sure that he knows, and you know why he is aware? Because it's exactly what Mr. D'Tella is doing in his Atelier; like Cerberus, Mr. D'Tella, is the guardian of an individual who's living as a criminal in the underworld!" André said as if he knows what is going on, and Viggo added...

"Agent Duvalier, I'm ready to enter into Mr. D'Tella's underworld, it's the place where I find myself very comfortable, let's see what we can find out?" Viggo asks ready to march right inside the place, and Agent Duvalier said...

"Special-Agent Bronson, you must be prepared, since you will be doing it literally, because behind that store, really is an underworld..."

"What you just said is very interesting, can you be more specific?" Viggo asks interested in the answer and Duvalier informed...

"Sure, as you can see, Special-Agent Bronson, half of the place is almost carved inside the mountain rocks, it is well known that in the rear of the Atelier Galerie d'Art, is the entrance to a tunnel that was built in the medieval times, this tunnel, it was an escape route for the leaders of Vence, in case the village was overtaken by warriors who wanted to take their land."

"Agent Duvalier, if I understood right, the village was never invaded by anyone, that's true?" Viggo asked, and Special-Agent Du'Pont with a big smile gets involved in the conversation...

"That's a correct assumption:" *And Du'Pont to confirm the theory gets close to Viggo and said almost in a whisper.* "Special-Agent Bronson, a matter of fact, during the early eighteenth century, the pirates Jean Lafitte, and Estede Bonnet, had roamed European and American seas, and they were plundering and robbing cities, and then they brought..."

"Agent Du'Pont, don't tell me, these people came all the way to this remote place, just to hide the stolen goods? That is amazing!!" Viggo said thinking that he doesn't believe a damn thing she just said, and she continued saying...

"That's right, in those times, the pirates arrived to the Village with enormous treasure chests, filled with gold coins, jewelry and precious stones, the leaders of Vence, charged a high percentage to the pirates to conceal in the tunnels the loot, which benefited those who lived in the village, on many occasions these pirates did not return to recover their loot, because maybe they were killed in some battle, and those fortunes, naturally, engrossed the coffers of the leaders of Vence." Rosél informs and Viggo with a wee of laughter that sneaked out between his lips responded...

"Agent Du'Pont, since I was a child and I read the pirates adventure in the cartoons magazines, and I always believe that the pirates, when being chased by the authorities, made a hole in the Earth and buried their treasures, but your story doesn't confirm that theory, that is amazing Agent Du'Pont."

"What's amazing to me Special-Agent Bronson, is the legend that is following you, it would be great if after you solve this case, maybe we could talk about your book and the fame that following your career?" Then in a friendly gesture, she grabs Viggo's arm: and the forgotten Dusty, who just finished making a phone call gets Viggo's attention...

"Special-Agent Bronson, I just got in touch with *The Shadow*' and..."

"Where the hell is this guy? Finally, he shows up!!" Viggo asks approaching Dusty who responded...

"He is right here in the area, attentive to the movements of Pascucci." Dusty responded, and Viggo losing his patience said...

"I only hope Agent René D'Varón, that *The Shadow,* known's the whereabouts of Pascucci!!" Viggo said raising his arms in a sign of relieve, and Dusty informs...

"According to *The Shadow*, Pascucci is inside the Atelier Galerie d'Art, the last time he saw him, he was walking inside the place: *The Shadow* assures, that he has not left the gallery." Dusty responded, and Agent Duvalier who is listening with attention asks...

"Excuse me, who is *The-Shadow*? He is another agent involved in this case?" Agent Duvalier intrigued asked, and Viggo naturally, he was not going to involve himself in a problem by saying that *The-Shadow* is a Russian agent, and with a poker face he said...

"*The Shadow:* Agent Duvalier, is a French private eye who was hired by the FBI, and he has been following, Pascucci's movements, with very good results, because we know where he is right now!"

"Excuse me, Special-Agent Bronson, but I wasn't informed by my superiors, that your people had hired a private detective to follow this person."

"Agent Duvalier, this is not an excuse, but we sent all the information to the French Intelligence Bureau, as you know, we have all the extradition documents in order, with the procedure of getting Mr. Pascucci out of France. I thought you were informed about the French detective?"

"I was not briefed on any detective. Special-Agent Bronson, but this is beside the point, because it's like you say in America, *forget about it,* because, I do have a warrant to search the place, let's go and get this guy. Okay?" Agent Duvalier proposed. —Then...

Agent Duvalier, with his badge in hand and the warrant, he walks toward the entrance of the Galerie d'Art, to get to the door, the agents must pass through the two mythological guard dogs: at the moment he opened the door, some small bells announces that a person has entered the Atelier; upon entering the first thing they saw, was a middle-aged man facing the wall, trying to straighten a picture, it was Mr. D'Tella who turned around and said...

"Hello gentlemen, welcome to the Atelier, we have an extensive exhibition of local portraitists and contemporary artists." Mr. D'Tella said gently with a smile and Duvalier responded...

"Good day sir. I'm Agent Duvalier, from the French Bureau of Investigation, I would like to talk to Mr. Michael D'Tella?"

• "I'm the person you want to talk to Agent Duvalier, what can I do for you?" Mr. D'Tella, answered gently showing no worries, but a pronounced tick of the left eye gave him away, and agent Duvalier proceeded to show his credential, and said...

"We come to inform you Mr. D'Tella, that we are looking for Mr. Santino Pascucci, a well-known gangster, and this man has and international search by Interpol." *He paused and said,* "We have witnesses that this person entered in this Atelier, and for some unknown reason you are giving him shelter in this place." Duvalier said firmly and the left eye of Mr. D'Tella began flicking like crazy and said...

• "Excuse me Agent Duvalier how dare you accused me of giving sheltered to a gangster, I'm living all alone, and I don't give shelter to any person, and less to a gangster, how dare you accuse me of such a thing!!!" He expresses with a shaking determination, then Viggo who was watching impatiently intervenes in the dialogue, and out loud he said...

. . .

"Please Agent Duvalier, show Mr. D'Tella the warrant, and don't give this person further explanations. Okay?" Viggo said firmly, and Duvalier handed to Mr. D'Tella the warrant, after reading the permit, the man was speechless; and Viggo seeing that Mr. D'Tella does not react, he took the lead and said…

"Come on Agent Duvalier, let's not lose any more time, and start searching this place!!" —And then…

Methodically they did the search, Pascucci was nowhere to be found. Then Viggo took charge, and he placed his face right in front of Mr. D'Tella's, and he read the pages of his future…

"Mr. D'Tella, I came all the way from United States, to arrest this criminal, and we are being very considerate to you, if not by now you would be hanging, like that picture you were fixing, I'll give you one opportunity, to tell me from where your friend took off and escaped, because he didn't go out from the front door. I think you know what I'm talking about, and don't give me the runaround, because right now, my fuses are getting very…very short, start talking or thing are going to change in a second!!! Okay?" Viggo said it loud and clear, and D'Tella responded…

"You're not intimidating me, and leave my place right now, get out…get out!!" D'Tella says raising his voice, and Viggo who does not want to waste any more time, he's sure that Pascucci escaped through the tunnel, and Viggo knows how to deal with this kind of jerk, and he responded…

"René, give me the duct tape, and all of you, please wait outside for me, I'm sure he will tell me whereabouts of Pascucci."

Dusty gave him the *duct tape*, and walked out, so did the French agents, then he locked the door behind him, when Viggo turned around, Mr. D'Tella was trying to escape, from the rear of the store; it didn't take much effort for Viggo to catch up with old man, then with no consideration, he slammed the fragile man against the wall, and he said in a not friendly tone…

"Mr. —I did tell you, that you had the opportunity to walk out of this mess free: now I will give you two options: first, just tell me where he is, and the second choice, this is really an option you should want avoid it at all costs, because I'm going to duct tape your hands; that is the beginning." *Viggo took the duct tape and started to tie his hands behind his back, and he said in his ear.* "Also, I'm going to tape your mouth, then I will squeeze your testis so hard, that the pain will be so unbearable, that you won't be able to scream—your mouth will be sealed, you won't be able to release the pain, at that instant you will wish you were dead." *Viggo paused for a second, squeezing his neck.* "And now, you only have the first option, it's the easy one, tell me where Pascucci is, and I will let you go free." Viggo ended up saying, and Mr. D'Tella with the promise that he will face a terrible torture, gives him no other option but to betray his friend, and babbling he said...

"When he saw you arrive—he was hidden in the tunnel, waiting for you to leave, and..."

"I'm sure he's escaping through the tunnel, from which exit will he come out?" Viggo asks shouting, and Mr. D'Tella could hardly speak because Viggo was squeezing his neck.

"From the tourists...parking lot."

"What car is he driving?"

"Rolls Royce." D'Tella answers trembling, and Viggo asks out loud...

"He has company?"

"Yes...yes two bodyguards." Mr. D'Tella answers and then rolls his eyes up and faints. Viggo, surprised by the unexpected reaction of the man placed him on the floor, unties his hands, then he runs out of the Atelier and said out loud...

"Come-on let's go!! This piece of crap, is coming out of the tunnel, from where we left the SUV, Pascucci has two bodyguard's, and he is getting away in a Rolls Royce!!" Viggo alerts the rest of the agents and began to run toward the exit of the ancient city, and everybody is running behind him, asking questions. At the moment they reach the vehicle, Viggo could see the Rolls going downhill, and Viggo said out loud...

"Come on Agent Duvalier, follow that black Rolls Royce: the one that's speeding down the hill!! —Then, like if they were playing who gets into the car faster...

In a matter of seconds everybody was inside the vehicle. Behind the wheel Agent Duvalier, who with great skills maneuvers the car towards the parking lot exit, in that instant, two man who were crouched on their knees, started shooting at the windshield of the armored S.U.V, which was splattered with bullets. Without hesitation Agent Du'Pont, pulls out her pistol, and Viggo does the same, and at the moment they approached the two gangsters, both of then lowered the windows, and simultaneously pulled their gun's trigger once, with great precision brought down the two goons that were shooting at them. —Agent Duvalier is trying to stop the car, and Viggo said out loud...

"Don't lose the Rolls!!" Without responding, Agent Duvalier continues with the chase. —Agent Du'Pont puts her gun in the holster, then she picked up the phone, and reported the incident to the city authorities. Viggo was a witness to the amazing performance by Agent Rosél Du'Pont, under those sudden and dangerous situations, and Viggo looking at her expressed his feelings...

"That was amazing, Agent Du'Pont, your reaction under fire is to be admired, it showed courage and readiness at the time of facing the enemy. I'm very impressed; congratulation Agent Du'Pont!" Viggo said sincerely, and she was a little bit shocked about the events that just occurred, and she replied...

"Thanks' for the compliment Special-Agent Bronson, coming from you, the praise has double value. I must mention that my reaction in this case, has a lot to do, with all of those days of training, that were very demanding, but now are paying off: although the price is very high!" She said with sadness since she just had taken a life. —At that moment something unexpected occurred...

Agent Duvalier made a sharp maneuver trying to get through another vehicle, because Pascucci, just find out, that he was being followed, and he sped-up the car, trying to get away from his pursuers. Viggo assessed the situation, and suggested...

"Please, Agent Duvalier, don't get too close to him, because he is getting nervous, if Pascucci, gets involved in an accident, he can be killed; I preferred to take this traitor alive to the US!!" Viggo said with emphasis and Duvalier agree...

"Okay...okay I'm going to keep a prudent distance." He said a little bit nervous, and Dusty, who is sitting next to Agent Rosél Du'Pont. He is all relaxed enjoying the ride, because for him, this kind of skirmish is an everyday occurrence: like a cool-cat, Dusty calmly observes everything and doesn't say a word. —And...

For almost an hour, they were chasing the Rolls Royce; already they left behind the Rocky Mountains, which protect the ancient village of Vence, and right now they are driving through the city of Grasse, also a medieval village. —At that moment Viggo commented to Agent Du'Pont...

"I wonder, if Pascucci, will keep going in this direction, in a few minutes we will be at the Blue Coast, after passing the city of Cannes we will be right in the frontier of Spain?" Viggo asks, and Agent Du'Pont agreed and said...

"I'm watching his behavior, and I'm sure, that's his true intentions." Rosél said and Viggo added...

"You are right, this dirty-rat, wants to reach Spain: the old fox knows, if he is in Spain, I couldn't extradite this piece of crap, but I can guarantee you is one thing, that Pascucci never will cross the border—alive, I'm sure of that." Viggo promised seriously.

Meanwhile Agent Duvalier, continues safeguarding the distance with the Rolls Royce, following Viggo's instructions. By now the chase become just another routine pursued, and Agent-Rosél Du'Pont, become quite bored, and she decided to be a tourist guide, and began to entertain the crew...

"Well, I think this pursued is getting quite boring, if you don't mind, I'm going to tell you, that we just passed through a place that holds a lot of glamour, the City of Cannes, is world famous for celebrating every year, the International Film Festival, and in a few minutes, we are passing through St. Tropez, one of the favorite beaches for tourists, who arrive from all over the world." And she continues naming the cities they pass through, like Toulon and Marseille...

By this time, they have been pursuing the Rolls-Royce for three hours, and right now Pascucci is entering the ancient city of Arles, and the first thing that came in front of their eyes, was the magnificent Coliseum that was built over two thousand years ago, by the Romans in Arles France, after ten years in the city of Rome, they built a similar Coliseum.

While all of them, were admiring the architectural relic, they also were seeing as the Rolls Royce, was slowing down, and down until—until the car stops, and who gets out in a hurry? —Mr. Santino Pascucci, who like an old rabbit, begins running towards the Coliseum, as if he were chased by the devil himself. —At that moment Viggo saw that he was trying to escape, he reacted immediately and said...

"Let's go and get this guy alive please!!" Viggo said out loud, and everybody got out of the vehicle, and ran towards the Coliseum chasing after Pascucci. —Every day in the...

Arles Coliseum, there are diverse events scheduled, and today was not going to be different, that night the main performer will be, a famous opera singer. —Earlier in the afternoon, the soprano was testing the sound for her presentation, she was on the stage: at the precise moment that Mr. Santino Pascucci was desperately trying to escape from Viggo's claws...

The gangster, almost blind with fear rushes into the Coliseum, then in a matter of seconds he climbs on top of the stage, and began running desperate looking back at his pursuers, but what he didn't see, that on the stage floor was laying down electric cables, that's where he tripped, Pascucci, lost his footing and he was stumbling desperate tries to prevent his fall and, who was within arm's reach? No less than the huge body of the opera singer: like a wounded bird who is trying to land, Pascucci, desperate grabbed the woman from the waist: The opera singer, surprised by the actions of the man, she thought that the man was cowardly attacking her, the frightened woman, trying to protect herself, with a quick reaction pushes the men to the floor. Then as a man of action...

Special-Agent Viggo Bronson, on the run and in a single jump he was on the stage and, at that instant, he saw what was happening in front of him, and he said to himself, the chase ended here: but the gangster was not going to give up without a fight: with the paradox, that he's luck was going from bad to worse, since the gangster was laying on the floor down face up: there is when he just felt, that there was no way out, because one of the most feared hound dogs in the FBI, was approaching him with a huge gun in his hand, in those moments of despair, Pascucci is trying to pull-out his weapon, but it was too late: Viggo positioned his left foot on the gangster chest, preventing him from drawing the gun, and Viggo with a smirk but seriously said...

"I'm sorry, but today you are not going to make my day. I'm taking you alive to the USA, you are going to rot in jail, you understand—you will rot in jail. I have no empathy with traitors!!" Viggo said very calm, and lifted Pascucci like a sack of potatoes, and handcuffed him, then Agent Rosél Du'Pont approaches and takes Viggo by the arm and she commented...

"That action was fantastic, Special-Agent Bronson, it looks like a scene from an American action movie, I was waiting for the bullets to start flying, I'm glad it didn't happen, because with what happened earlier, I had enough." Rosél said with a smile very close to Viggo, who thanks her and handed the prisoner to Agent Duvalier, who seated Mr. Pascucci in the back seat of the SUV, which is customized to carry prisoners: but in the meantime: Agent René D'Varón=Dusty, who is relaxed and enjoying the side scenes of the ancient City of Arles, like a good tourist, he began to observing the place, from the Coliseum across the street, he spotted the famous *Van Gogh Café*, and Dusty proposes...

"I don't know about you guys, but I'm hungry, come on let's go and have something to eat." And Dusty begins to cross the street, and Agent Rosél Du'Pont, gently takes Viggo by the arm and followed Dusty.

After having enjoy some of the great French delicatessen: Viggo, place an order for Mr. Pascucci, of a mortadella sandwich. —Then before returning to the City of Nice, Agent Duvalier got quite busy, and called the local authorities to impound the Rolls Royce, Dusty-seeking privacy goes to the bathroom, to call *The-Shadow,* and told him that his job was over, and he has to options, one is going home, and the other is to go to Los Angeles, and ask for political asylum, and *The-Shadow* answered. "Dusty, I'll see you in Santa Monica." —Meanwhile Viggo is calling his wife Ember at the Bureau and telling her that in a couple of days he will arrive in Los Angeles with the prisoner in handcuffs.

That night: the four agents in charge of the prisoner took a flight to Paris. At the moment they arrived, the F B I Handling Officer of the Bureau of Paris, was waiting to take hold of Pascucci. Viggo and Dusty have a reservation at Le Bristol Paris Hotel, that is located near by the Arc de Triumphe. The Bureau sent a driver to take the agents from the airport to downtown Paris. During the trip Agent Du'Pont was busy planning how to entertain the American special-agent, and before reaching the Bristol hotel she said...

"Special-Agent Bronson, it was a real treat working with you, I never imagined having an experience like that, it was amazing!"

"Thanks Agent Du'Pont, in the investigation process, I have to admit that I was feeling secure working with both of you, it is a pleasure to deal with professionals, thanks, to both of you, it was a great experience, work with people who know what they are doing!" Viggo commented, and Rosél with very forward intentions said...

"Special-Agent Bronson, luckily everything went well, and the mission is over, it would be nice if you call me Rosél, this way we can leave the formalities aside during dinner, if you don't mind, to throw the regulations out the window?" Rosél proposed sweetly and Viggo said...

"That would be fine with me, and you can do the same; if I heard correctly Rosél, you just mentioned dinner, what did you have in mind?" Viggo asks, and Rosél was thrilled that she could call him by his first name she said...

"It's nice, that I can call by your first name. Viggo, we solved this case by working together as a good team. I'm sure, that we can become very good friends?"

"For sure Rosél, there is no better relative, than a real good friend."

"You're right Viggo, and to start the friendship: we would like to invite you, and Agent D'Varón for dinner, at one of the most famous restaurants in Paris: at Maxim's." Rosél said it, with a very pleasant gesture, and at the moment Viggo looks at Dusty, and he agreed with a head signal and Viggo commented...

"That's a very tempting proposition Rosél, I have eaten at many restaurants in Paris, but I never had the opportunity to eat at

Maxim's, Rosél you just said it, that it's one of the most famous, there must be a reason for the fame, which distinguish Maxim's from others?" Viggo asked, and Rosél gladly satisfies his curiosity.

"Well, gentleman, where we are going to have dinner is a legendary restaurant, which was founded as a bistro in 1893, and it is currently located in the original location: at No. 3 rue Royale. Maxim's is not only famous for their food, but also is well-recognized for the Art Nouveau Décor, the restaurant happens to be, for your convenience, in walking distance from the Bristol hotel." Rosél informs happily and Viggo was thoughtful for a second, and he commented...

"I know that restaurant: yes, I remember it's featured in the movie Midnight in Paris, and the scene's that were filmed at Maxim's, gave me the feeling, that when I'll enter the restaurant, I will be living in the twenty's, in those days there was no television to distract you, at that time, the love scenes began at sundown, finished at dinner time, and continued at dawn. —Those was the times!" Viggo says seriously without thinking about the consequences, and Rosél took the compliment as it was directed to her, and she answers...

"J'aimerais baiser ce mec!" She thought in French. "I'm going to fuck this guy." Then, she said. — "Viggo, with that romantic expression, it means that you will accept our invitation?"

"For sure Ms. Rosél, it will be a pleasure." *He said looking at Dusty.* "What do you say René?" Viggo asked, and Dusty answered like he always does, in a dusty voice...

"That is a great idea...I know the place has legendary fame...but I never had dinner at Maxim's...I'm sure it will be unforgettable...Thanks' for the invitation...Agent Du'Pont." Dusty graciously said as he and Viggo, got out of the car and he said goodbye with a smile: "I'll see you tonight." Once at the hotel Viggo made a few important phone calls, and then they got ready for a special night out at Maxim's.

VIGGO

About eight o'clock the French agents show up at Le Bristol Hotel, waiting in the lobby was Viggo and Dusty, they looked really sharp with their dark suits, and ties? Miss. Rosél Du'Pont, who is wearing a sexy navy-blue dress, which highlights her figure, and the light brown long hair is falling loose over her bare shoulders, her green eyes shine like two suns. Rosél looks absolutely stunning. Viggo and Dusty like two perfect gentlemen, and they complimented her beauty: after the respective greetings, the four agents walk the short distance to Maxim's Restaurant, and Rosél is walking holding Viggo's arm, she was happier than a two-tailed dog.

At the moment Viggo and Dusty entered the restaurant, they had the feeling they were going back in time, to the Roaring Twenty's: observing the luxurious place, they saw the cute petite stage, in that instant the imagination began to fly, imagining that in any moment maybe they could see Édith Piaf, singing her favorite song; *Non, Je ne Regretted Rien*. Then with interest they stopped to observe the Maxim's luxurious Art Nouveau décor. At that moment, the well-mannered Maitre-d' leads them to a reserved table, that was set up in a discreet area for four, on the other side of the room, where a pianist playing *Gricel*, a famous Argentine tango.

At the moment Rosél enters at Maxim's, she can feel that the romance is in every wall and, in every adornment in that place, this ambience took over her young heart; she couldn't control herself, and Rosél prompts Viggo, to sit next to her: during the four course dinner, her behavior was courteous but possessive, most of the time she ignored André and Dusty, and she spends her time talking to Viggo, while she is telling him about her professional career, and stories related to her private life, then she overwhelms Viggo, with questions, then in a moment that Viggo, engage in conversation with Dusty or André.—Rosél, hopping no one noticed her indiscretion, elusively she placed her hand under the table, touching Viggo's lap, that friendly gesture made him feel quite uneasy, knowing there were two witnesses that are aware of her indiscretion; looking at her Viggo said. "Rosél, you need both hands to eat the escargots, it would be a shame if you stain your beautiful dress, which looks splendid on you."

Fortunately, that imprudence was the only embarrassing situation of the night: at the end of dinner, having dessert, they were happily toasting with champagne, for their lasting friendship, and for the job well done. —Then...

Walking back to the hotel, with an extra few glasses of champagne, life could not be better for the beautiful Miss. Rosél Du'Pont, besides: she's holding arms with the famous Special-Agent Viggo Bronson, to whom she desires and wishing to know him more intimately: the American end French agents, are almost reaching the hotel, and for sure, Ms. Rosél is not going to miss the opportunity to take Viggo to task, and in that special moment she cut off all the formalities, and with the desire to have a sexual adventure, she would express her feelings this way...

"Viggo, I must tell you, that it had been a long time since I was so happy, and right now, I feel like I'm walking in clouds of joy." *Ten Rosél who is feeling that she's walking in thin air said. "Viggo, these moments should remain in the memories of the eternity." Then Rosél whispers in his ear.* "I'm wishing to finish this very special night in your room: I would like to enjoy your company." Ms. Du'Pont said with a look that can hypnotize the most cunning of men. But there is a hidden fucking problem: Mr. Viggo Bronson, promised faithfulness to his wife; right now, he is in very deep shambles: *because his motto has been*: A glass of water and a little bit of love you don't deny it to anybody. —What the fuck? Ms. Rosél proposition really is knocking on the door of his conviction's, right now he has to answer the call, and he comes to the conclusion that he is madly in love with his wife, and when he comes back home, he doesn't want to face Ember, with a deceiving face, and he has no other choice but to disappoint Ms. Rosél Du'Pont, he will try to do it without hurting her feelings, then, Viggo very polite, with a dismayed face he replies to her sweet offer...

"I really don't know how to respond to that proposition Rosél, it was a great pleasure working with you, but it's unethical on my part if I get..."

"Viggo, you forgot that we have agreed to put the formalities aside?" She whispers and Viggo, who doesn't know how to say NO to this class of propositions, now he has hart time to say it, and he replied...

"Rosél, I know that you mentioned that I was fallow by a great fame, it's just a legend created by my colleagues at the Bureau, I assure you, that the whole thing about the tattoo is only a myth, and I would love to have you as a guest, but in this moment, the circumstances are telling me, that we should cancel our meeting for another occasion..."

"What are you trying to say?" She asked very disappointed, and Viggo answered the best he could...

"It has nothing to do with your lovely suggestion, Ms. Rosél, it's..."

"I don't understand your attitude, what is it all about, that kind of nothing answered?"

"Ms. Rosél, you deserve the best time a man can give to a woman, of your beauty, the circumstances and the time don't coordinate for this meeting, I'm very sorry, if I..."

"Tu es désolé? Je m'excuse!!" "You are sorry? You are sorry? I'm sorry!! I never imagined that a gentleman would reject such a direct proposition, I'm very disappointed Special-Agent Bronson, I was hoping that we would get acquainted, and you are playing hard to get? How could you do that to me?" Rosél said out loud, she was shocked by Viggo's attitude and, immediately she releases his arm. — Dusty and Agent Duvalier, were right behind them; Dusty in that instant realized that something was wrong, he sensed what was going on, and right the away came to Viggo's rescue, then Dusty with a tone of urgency said...

"Please excuse me, if I interrupt Agent Du'Pont, but I have to remind Special-Agent Bronson, that unfortunately we don't have much time, Viggo, we have to pick up our prisoner, because our flight to the U.S, is leaving very early in the morning." Dusty updated, and Viggo turns around and said...

"Ms. Rosél, that's what I was trying to tell you, that I'm sorry that I don't have the necessary time, to engage in a long 'conversation', I hope you understand?"

"*Je comprends, mais je suis trés décu*!" — "I understand, but I'm very disappointed!"

"Please Rosél, you are a very special woman, and I'm treasure very deep in my heart, those special moments, we enjoyed together, that never will be lost: a matter of fact, when the right time come, I will relive these marvelous times, we have spent together, in future occasion's..."

"When I found out you were coming, I moved heaven and earth to be able to be in this investigation, next to you Special-Agent Bronson..."

"Thanks, Rosél, I wanted to tell you is that nothing is lost between us, our story is going to be like the pirate Jean Roberval, who wants to conquer the princess, for that purpose, he wants to give her a proof of his love, and he bring to the surface the treasure that he hides deep into the earth, a long time ago, and very loving Jean, offered her..."

"Ce mot avait l'air trés romantique." "Viggo, those words sounded very romantic." Rosél said feeling she is making love to this guy and Viggo answered...

"Rosél, I hope that in the near future, we'll have an unforgettable evening, and that night, we will be intimately toasting with champagne, I'm sure that moment will be remembered as the Reckoning Day." Viggo said that phrase in a romantic manner very close to her sexy crimson lips, and Rosél almost melts down when she hears it, —in that intimate instant, she felt that *unique* sensation of *pleasure* that human can have, that's when a big smile of satisfaction appeared I her face, she can hardly talk, after few seconds she said...

"Oh my; you are so romantic: I was so sure that tonight, we could be romantically acquainted, just a few minutes ago, I was walking on clouds of hope, and now, I don't know what to do with myself!" Then Rosél takes him by the neck and kisses him, after the sweet kiss Viggo said...

"Unfortunately, Rosél, we have to end this magnificent evening, and I know that it's my loss; but pretty soon, we will continue this encounter in the U.S." Viggo said romantically. —Then...

At the Bristol Hotel door: Viggo and Dusty said farewell to the congenial and helpful French agents, with hugs and with the promise of meeting again in the USA.

Once in their rooms the American agents, the first thing they did, was to get rid of their formal suits. Then Dusty dresses comfortable and went to see Viggo, who is placing a phone call to the FBI Bureau in Paris, informing them that they will go to get the extradition documents, and retrieve the prisoner, to take Mr. Pascucci, to the International Airport of Paris.

During the flight to L.A: Special-Agent Viggo Bronson, has to deal with stewardess's curiosity, that was all the inconvenience they had during the flight. Viggo and Dusty bringing the famous gangster Santino Pascucci in handcuffs, arrived at the International Los Angeles Airport, a bunch of media was waiting with their cameras ready to report the news. In front of everybody was the FBI Officer Ember Maxwell Bronson, who was anxiously waiting for her husband: the first thing he did, is handed the prisoner to Ember, in charge of supervising the operation of handling the prisoner, at the moment Pascucci, was secure inside of the bulletproof SUV, then Ember, wants to welcome her husband as he deserves it, and she proceeded to hugging and kissing him passionately, then looking at him she said.

"I'm so happy that you're home. I felt very guilty for sending you to a such dangerous assignment, Viggo, now I have you here safe and sound, and I have to tell you, that the French Intelligence were very courteous, considering I was bothering them every day, because I was checking for news about investigation, and they told me that everything was going according to plan, and that was good news, because I was worried that you might find yourself in a dangerous encounter!" Ember commented, and Viggo showing signs of relieve to be at home answered...

"Ember, at the beginning of the investigation, we had a hostility with two of Pascucci's bodyguards, but we solved the problem swiftly, then the mission went smoothly, thanks to Dusty, who knew where this gangster was hiding." Viggo informed and called his friend Dusty, who very courteous shook hands with Ember. Well, the Russian agent, who became a collaborator of the American intelligence; Agent Voris Kavisky=Dusty, at this precise moment is an American citizen, under the name of René D'Varón, and right now he is going with Viggo, and Officer Ember Maxwell to her office at the FBI Bureau, where Viggo and Dusty, will present officially their respective reports, of the assignment that was carried out in France.

Once they completed the procedures. Dusty, understood that the couple wished to be alone, and he wanted to see Brigitte, and Ember, picks up the phone and calls Mike, who took Dusty to the Beverly Hills Hotel, where Madam Divine or Brigitte De'Gaun, was waiting for him, with very good news: as a matter of fact; Brigitte had the opportunity to purchase a lingerie store, and no less...than at the prime location of the famous Rodeo Drive in Beverly Hills. This legit business is the main reason that Madam Divine or Dusty, will be able to collaborate in the future with their sponsor and good friend: Special-Agent Viggo Bronson. —And...

Of course, the woman wanted to be alone with her husband, and she was waiting patiently for Dusty to leave her office, and it was not a question of wasting time, because Ember, at the moment they were alone, and she can have the pleasure to grab the man she loves; that's when Viggo noticed that Ember's eyes took on an unusual glow, he knows the meaning of those bright sparks, and he is getting ready for a battle, the eyes of his wife are telling him that she is ready to make up for the lost time. But something occurred at that moment, and the repressed feelings has to wait: since someone is knocking at the door, it's Ms. Betty, who came with a little crisis on her hands, she can't get rid of the Santa Monica chief of police, who insists on seeing Officer Maxwell, who will have to set aside her husband that was ready to be loved, she has no other choice but to release Viggo, from her sexy embrace, and Ember looking at him said...

"My love don't think for a minute, that you are going to escape from my arms. I was dreaming of this moment, and look what happened to me, your arrival made me forget all my obligations. I forgot that I had an appointment with the chief of police. I'll be back in a few minutes, don't even move!! Okay?" Ember kisses him on the way out, and Viggo sees the opportunity to call his partner, Rachel Dansby =Rocky.

Viggo, who talking to her, he doesn't understand what was going on with her? Because I left Rocky alone for a couple of days, then what happens, she is getting involved in a speedy romantic situation? —Rachel, at the beginning of the conversation with Viggo, she is telling him, that, she is no longer a patient at the Santa Monica hospital. Doctor Anderson, who released her from the hospital, since he considered, that it would be better for her condition, to finish her recovery at the doctor's residence, in Malibu, a famous neighborhood. This news was not the only one, there were more surprises: Viggo wants to know, what had happened in this short time, for her to make that drastic decision: to which she responds. —Sounds corny, but that's what it is; Albert is madly in love with me, he promised to marry me as soon as I could reach the altar. *Viggo could not believe what he was hearing, and that was not all.* Because Rachel, said to Viggo: that she would miss him, because she would be no longer his partner, because yesterday she called Officer Ember Maxwell, and asked to be discharged from the force. The news really surprised Viggo, since he, would miss Rachel, and Viggo had to say goodbye, because Ember is returning, and when she enters in the office, she locks the door, at that moment, Viggo knew what that move meant, she didn't want to be disturbed, then she began to walk slowly towards him with semi-closed eyes like a panther in heat, ready to tear apart her lover, and Viggo, has no other option but to remain calm, waiting for what is coming, and when she arrived, with her feline attitude, Viggo very calm asks...

"Ember, what was the appointment with the chief about?" Viggo asked partially sitting at the desk trying to defuse the moment. Ember didn't answer, because this is the man, she was anxious waiting to arrive, and when the passion explodes through her skin, she can't control herself; and like a female Siamese cat, she gets between his legs and started kissing him passionately, then she gets intimate; when Viggo could catch some air, he reacted and said...

"Please Officer Maxwell, you are abusing your authority, remember; I'm your immediate subordinate, this act is a sexual harassment of the worst kind, I will not report it! This time. —Don't you worry. Okay?" Viggo pointed out, and in that instant the phone rang, it's Miss. Betty, and Ember reacted...

"I told her not to pass any calls." And *Ember picks up the phone.* "What is the urgency Ms. Betty? Ember asked looking at Viggo, and he looks at her, and Viggo started to walk towards the door, and Ms. Betty informs...

"I'm sorry but the FBI Director would like to talk to you."

"Are you sure, that the person on the phone is the FBI Director?"

"I'm sure, the phone call came from his office, right from the Washington Bureau."

"Okay Ms. Betty, please let the call through, let's see what the director wants.

Well, the phone call from the FBI Director, it's all about good news: It happened that at the New York FBI Handling Officer, Victor Franklin, after being in the force for forty years, he decided to leave the Bureau, and present his resignation. —The directors phone call was short and precise, at the end of the call. Ember, turns around and with an expression of happiness she said...

"My love, the director just told me, to convey congratulations to Special-Agent Bronson, for the swift and safe captured of Santino Pascucci."

"That was nice: this sort of courtesy, on the part of the powerful FBI Director, it makes one feel recognized, in this profession of meager affections."

"I hope that last sentence is not addressed to me?" She said kissing him and Viggo responded...

"Of course not! Ember, the director just called to congratulate me, or does he want to send me somewhere else?" Viggo asks interested in the answer, and Ember with a big smile said...

"This is not the case: and that's not all Viggo, listen and listen well. —Officer Victor Franklin submitted his resignation; he is retiring how do you like that. Viggo?"

"Finally, he quit!! And Franklin, can take his pride with him and shove it; Ember, the director gave you a hint to who is going to replace Franklin?" Viggo asked from the office door, and Ember started walking slowly towards him, and she whisper in his ear...

"My dear—I'm the person who will replace Franklin." She said kissing him, and Viggo happy for the news reacted...

"Congratulation Ember, I'm very proud of you, this designation came right in time to solve all our logistics problems; this is a fantastic news, a matter of fact: I don't have to ask the transfer to L.A." And *Viggo starts kissing her and said* "Ember, we are going back to New York, I'm so happy I don't know what to say!!"

"Viggo, you can start by saying, that you're missing our home." Ember insinuates, and Viggo replies.

"Sure, it would be really nice to return to our nest."

"I'm glad we feel the same way Viggo, but by this transfer to New York, create a dilemma!"

"What are you trying to say Ember?"

"Well, Viggo, while I was talking with the director, he suggested that I should find a competent replacement for my post." Ember, said with a witty smile, and Viggo frowning ask...

"This smile that sneaked out between your lips, is telling me, that you have someone in mind, a person that you know?"

"You haven't lost any insight: I do." Ember said it as if she wanted to keep a secret, and Viggo had no choice but to ask...

"That is a very short answer, it means that you can't reveal his or her identity, it's a secret that you can't even tell your own husband?" Viggo asks happily, because he is going back to New York, and Ember replayed...

"Don't be silly, there is no conspiracy against you, as a matter of fact, I chose a person that you know very well."

"Are you kidding me Ember, how could this be possible, because I don't know anyone in this city, who can qualify to fill your position?" Viggo sked seriously, and Ember with a smile said...

"I'm sure, that you know the person very well: would you like to guess?"

"Come on, Ember, I'm not in the mood for a riddle!"

"Okay, my love, the parson who will occupy my position is, your partner, Agent Rachel Dansby." Ember says hoping to see her husband's surprised face, and Viggo was really surprised by her choice responded...

"I just talked to her: Ember, she told me that she had presented her resignation to you?"

"That is true, she did, and that's where I started thinking, that before to process the papers through, I proceeded to check her record, that was flawless, and wanted to consult with you, my decision. Viggo, I'm going to call her right now, to offer her the position, don't you believe that she deserves the promotion?"

"She's very qualified, and she will love it, right now she is dating a doctor, who does not want her to continue in the force, I'm sure Rocky, is going to drive this guy crazy, until she gets what she wants!" Viggo said and Ember sat at the desk then...

Ember picks up the phone and calls Rachel, and offered her the position of *Handling Officer,* at the Santa Monica Bureau. —Rachel at that moment was speechless. When she realized the importance of the proposal, she reacted like Rocky does, and very excited she said...

"I never thought that you would consider me for this position, what a surprise Ember, I cannot believe it, this is great, I don't know if I want to scream, laugh or cry. Ember, I'm sure that in less than ten days I'll be there, and thanks and thanks,' again and again Ember!!!" Needless to say, that Rachel kept Ember's position, against the wishes of her future husband, and all his efforts were in vain to prevent that outcome. The discrepancy between the couple, was not serious enough, to break Doctor Anderson promise, the one, he made to take Rachel to the *altar.*

There are certain situations or events, which produce miracles for some people. *This is one of those cases of a fast healing.* That's what happened to Agent Rachel Dansby, after the great news, the recovery of her wound, it was a healing wonder of the human body.

—She didn't lose any time, after two days of receiving the news of her promotion, there she was at the Bureau, signing papers. —As a matter of fact: within a week Rachel Dansby, is taking over the Santa Monica Bureau, and she will be in Ember's office, sitting on her own comfortable chair; as a very proudly *Handling Officer Rachel Dansby*

The amazing recovery of Rachel—has in itself: the blessing that gives Ember and Viggo the opportunity to take a well-deserved vacation. Ember, was not going to miss that opportunity, to have some leisure time with her husband, then Ember informs...

"My love, I don't know if you are aware of what is going on. Ember whispers as if she is keeping a secret and Viggo happy to have returned from the mission in France asks...

"Why don't you enlighten me, please?

"Viggo, as a matter of fact, Rachel, will take over my position at the Bureau, within a week. —And what do you know? —We will be free..."

"What are you trying to say Ember?"

"It is a simple deduction my love; I'm saying that we will have some free time for us, and we must use every minute of it; because I want to recover all that time in which I was not with you." *And she begins kissing him and at the moment she stops, she looks at Viggo and spoke.* "It would be marvelous if we renew our marriage vows at The Royal Hawaiian? —That was your promise, what I know, is that you remember really well our first honeymoon, and we are going to repeat it, and we're going to do it!!" Ember said it convinced of what he was proposing and Viggo responded...

"Ember, your suggestion could not have come at a better time, I need a vacation, but first let's go home, while I take a shower you can make the reservations."

"No way you're going to shower alone, my love, you need someone to soap your back, and I'm the geisha who will do it, with love included!" She said kissing him, and Viggo rolls his eyes and reply's...

"You can do that, with one condition..."

"No way Viggo! The way I feel at this moment, conditions are out of the question, tonight—tonight, you are all mine!!" Ember said with emphasis trying to grab him, and Viggo turned around, and took her by the waist, and they began walking to her apartment, on the way home she was planning one of the most sophisticated sexual encounters, that a woman can do to a man. —And He knew very well who he has to deal with, and that evening Viggo didn't reach the shower for a long time. —For Ember, it was not enough that short encounter of love in the Bureau; she wishes to continue what she started in her office, she was full of desires, waiting for this opportunity, and those needs drove her crazy, and desperate she begins to take her clothes off, and at the same time, she undress her husband, at the moment she has all those muscles naked in front of her; then she laid him down gently on the couch; he could see the burning desire in her eyes, and right now, she has a defenseless man at her disposal. After being skillfully sexually used for quiet long time, Viggo, after having satisfied his wife's sexual desires, he still has enough strength to lift his wife in his arms, then as if carrying a treasure, he heads to the bathroom kissing her with love, wishing he'd already put out the fire that consumes her body. —Well...

Next morning? To get up from the bed, it was not an easy task, but Ember who was more than happy: did it, and she made a delicious breakfast, at the time Viggo, came out of the bedroom: he can sense the aroma of fried eggs and bacon. After that nutritious breakfast, full of energy they arrived at the Bureau. — In time to find out that Special-Agent Viggo Bronson, has to testify in front of a judge, in the Federal court of New York. Viggo must respond about his intervention in the death of American citizen's, Scientist Mr. John Hirohito: and two Chinese spies, who ended dead in the same incident. And the judge would like to know, in what circumstances did Viggo capture Mr. Santino Pascucci, and if the FBI procedures were properly followed?

Ember was quite disappointed: Her husband must travel to New York. Consequently: She has to cancel the honeymoon trip she had scheduled. Ember is not a person who expects that others to solve her problems, once she was alone, she didn't waste any time, and called the FBI director, who assured her that it's just a bureaucratic process, that in less than a week he will be at home.

Meanwhile Viggo, arrives in New York, and began visiting his friends, and one of those night, that he was alone and thirsty, his steps took him by chance to one of his underworld contacts: Tania Barecci, owner of the well-known *The Veil Nightclub*. At the moment Tania saw Viggo entered the club she was very happy to see him and welcomes him...

"Hello —hello, my dear friend, and, congratulations, you were all over the news a few days ago, when you brought home that fucking traitor, from France, no less!! It's a great pleasure seeing you again Easy'V." She said kissing him, and Viggo responded...

"Great seeing you Tania, like always you look amazing, you know that I love to come to *The Veil,* I was missing you, as a matter of fact, I come to say thanks, for all the help you have given me, during all these years of friendship, you are an amazing woman, and you can always count on me for whatever you need."

"Thanks, for your sweet words, but they are not necessary Easy'V, you know that you are always welcome at this refuge, and what are we waiting for? —Let's celebrate your return to the streets of New York, with one of your favorite drinks."

"That proposition sounds really good Tania, because since I have arrived, I haven't had a drink, and when you drink in good company, the liquor tastes better!"

"I can feel that you were missing New York?" Tania said and took him by the arm and began walking and Viggo responded...

"I miss this city, a lot! Tania."

"Easy'V, let's go to my private lounge." *Walking to the lounge she picked up a bottle of Johnnie Walker black label, she knows Viggo's taste, then she asks carelessly.* "Easy-V, your wife or ex-wife, is she okay, because I don't see Ember around Manhattan anymore?" She asked seriously and Viggo responded...

"Tania, I have news for you, Ember, will take Franklin's place, you know what that means, it will be a new boss in town."

"I hope that Ember's promotion won't prevent you from coming here to get info.

Talking about Ember, and her compelling character, plus other greater quality's she possesses, it's not difficult for her to make her wishes come true, and another of her virtues: is to be persistent, that's why during the five days Viggo was in New York, she calls her husband a few times a day, and in the last one, she has the pleasure of informing him, that the following day Rachel Dansby, will be taking over her position of HO, at the Santa Monica Bureau. What that means? It signifies that she is free of responsibilities. Ember, being fed-up with the situation, she called the FBI Director, to confirm the return of the Special-Agent Viggo Bronson, as soon as possible to Los Angeles: concerning private matters.

The day Ember becomes aware of the arrival of her husband from New York. —Then she like a hamster gets really busy making all the necessary reservations for the honeymoon trip. Full of impatience, that day she couldn't wait at home; because they would not return L.A, Ember, went to the husband's hotel and took all his clothes, once in her apartment, she packed three suitcases, it was all their clothes, then she went straight to the Los Angeles airport, to wait for Viggo's arrival from New York. —What's all this rush about? It was a matter of time, because the flight that will take them to the Hawaiian

Islands, will depart in the next three hours; and when that time came, she would be eagerly waiting at the airport for her husband, who arrived just in time to board the other plane, which would take the lovers to the islands of paradise, for a second honeymoon. —Well...when Viggo, arrived surprised by his wife actions, he didn't have time to react, he was already getting on another plane. —And...

During the flight Ember felt a little bit annoyed, it is the coincidence that the crew recognized Special-Agent Bronson; and his presence created a parade of stewardesses who complimented the couple with drinks and all kinds of goodies. After a six-hour flight, they landed at the Honolulu airport. Waiting for the two federal agents was a driver from the Bureau, who took Ember and Viggo to their destination.

The Royal Hawaiian hotel, it's a Waikiki landmark beach resort, one of the charming symbols of grandeur; the legendary *Pink Palace of the Pacific,* has remained an icon of luxury and romance, the perfect resort for selective honeymooners: the remarkable distinction about this specific hotel is that countless couples arrived to Waikiki from all over the world, to get married in the hotel's tropical gardens, in which the newlyweds find themselves surrounded with essences of plumeria and the sweet perfume of jasmine. This magnificent garden is the ideal place to renew their marriage vows; in addition to all this beauty, you can enjoy the fabulous sunsets, and for this special occasion, the Phoebus, borrowed the immense talent of Van Gogh, and painted crest of the forest gardens, with a touch of many yellow shades of ocher and brushes of gold, this magnificent site was witnessed at the simple but emotional marriage ceremony. —Life couldn't be more beautiful for the couple, since...

For the occasion, Ember, was wearing a white linen dress that in the warm breeze fluttered like a butterfly, and Viggo who was full of emotion, placed a necklace of jasmines blossom around Ember's slender neck, and trembling with happiness she did the same, and placed in her beloved husband a wreath of aromatic leaves: which represent a symbol of loyalty and eternal love. After the ceremony Ember and Viggo, holding hands they went for a walk to the pristine beaches of Waikiki, and in the meantime, they are enjoying the magical splendor of the sunset, which decorated the clouds that covered the immense blue sea with watercolor nuances.

Ember: who was in charge of all the details of the whole honeymoon affair, she is trying to follow the same sort of events they enjoy on their previous honeymoon, for that simple reason, before the ceremony began, she books reservation at the beach hotel restaurant; that's a gourmet place that has live music and a dance floor: a matter of fact, thanks to the bride, the newly married couple were dining and dancing like lovers and sipping champagne, past midnight, until the naughty bubbles got to Ember's brain, she was in a state of complete happiness, and right now she's feeling like reliving those exciting moments of unbridled passion, that came when they were dancing to a romantic song, and she felt her husband's tattoo on her body, which drives her crazy, and, makes her blood boil; that's when she propose to her husband to go to their room: how can Viggo deny, the wishes of his wife in such a special night? —Then Viggo, picked a bottle of champagne from the table on the way out; hugging and kissing they left the place, and for their enjoyment, the newlywed was rewarded with a spectacular night; the amazing sky was studded with stars, which shone in their entire splendor, and between all these grandiose displays of beauty, the full moon was shining in the firmament like a giant white pearl. This fantastic scenery of nature touched Viggo's romantic side, and he commented...

"Honey, look at this display of stars, why don't we sit for a while in the lounge chairs, I would like to possess this splendid night, and as the owner of the galaxies, I would like to take the time to enjoy the view of the stars, which are decorating the whole firmament and, the sound of the ocean waves brings to me those unforgettable memories of our first honeymoon: do you remember Ember?" Viggo asks hugging his wife tenderly. *Viggo's proposal is spoiling her premeditated plans, she doesn't want to see the moon or the stars, right now she doesn't care about the stupid ocean waves, right now she only wants to feel the immense sensation of pleasure when her husband is making love to her.* —It happens, that her husband is in a very romantic mood, and, Ember, has no other option but to go along with her husband wishes. The newlyweds were sitting in silent for a few minutes; but the environment creates a quite romantic setting, which gets Ember, wrapped in a sexy romantic mood, and she could not contain her desires, and her hands became busy molesting her husband, in that moment Viggo said...

"Please honey, let's enjoy the stars, they are sparkling like gleaming jewels in the sky." *Viggo at that moment points to the infinity with his arm.* "Ember, look at that galaxy, it's the Milky Way, that magnificent vastness it's absolutely amazing and overwhelming, the scenario of this magnitude is amazing, I would like to stay here all-night staring at the galaxies." Viggo says as if the night had won his soul, and Ember replied...

"My love, the scenario is very romantic, but we can look at the stars from the window in our comfortable bed —making love. Come on Viggo, let's go and see the stars from our room." And she gets up and tries to pull him up from the lounge chair, and Viggo responded...

"Honey, from our bed: you will not only going to see the stars, but you will also have the pleasure to see the entire universe!!" Viggo promised, and Ember added...

"My love, your offer, sounds promising, I hope I'll be able to see all the galaxies, and the other worlds that surround it!"

The happy couple embraced were walking to their room, when Viggo opened the door, a pleasant scent invaded his senses, their bed was sprinkled with petals of plumeria and jasmine; on the coffee table: an ice-cold bottle of champagne is waiting for them: and as always, the naughty moon, would not miss the opportunity of spying on the honeymooners. Well, as a matter of fact, the curious moon will have quite a few hours of entertainment. —How it happens in many cases, his wife misleads the husband, that's what happened this time. Ember didn't give him any chance to look at anything and, quite less at the stars: but for sure she saw the *galaxies and the surroundings areas*, at the moment she was moaning and moaning of pleasure and began begging. "Please...Easy'V ...please Easy Viggo...I'm going to faint...—But..."

One thing is for sure: Viggo would never forget this Hawaii honeymoon: because on this occasion *Ember,* really had the opportunity to honor her name, because during the honeymoon she really was a scorching *ember*: Viggo suffered the consequences of her feverish passion, until; they were tired but ready to fly back to New York. —At the Hawaiian airport, you could see on Ember's features, the immense pleasure of having recovered the love of her husband. Once on board Viggo, told the flight attendants not to disturb them, that they were going to sleep.

They woke up when the captain announced that they were arriving in New York. —Well, the couple that just renewed their vows, went directly where their first marriage began. Viggo who was absent from his home, for almost two years, he was standing in front of the door with two suitcases in his hands, he placed the luggage on the floor, then takes the keys out of his pocket: That was the moment when all the memory's come to his mind, when he opened the door, in the ambience, he can perceive the fragrance of Ember's perfume, which invades his senses, in that instant he said to himself. "I'm finally home." But Ember didn't waste any time, she wants to welcome her husband home, she must take advantage of her husband while he is under her spell: She placed her purse on the table, then she hugged him tightly, and breathing right in his mouth Ember, expressed her feelings…

"My love, your presence in our home makes me extremely happy: this nest was the beginning of our love, and would be the witness of a happy family, with a couple of kids, running in the living room." Ember said full of happiness, and Viggo added.

"Ember, you are just expressing my feelings: when entering in our home I felt like I never left this place; I can sense your fragrance in all the rooms, I always had the feeling that your perfume was following me at all times, it's infused in my skin, like you are in…" Viggo, didn't finish to say those words, because her cell phone rang with a distinctive sound, and right away Ember, looks at Viggo and said…

"Viggo, it's the FBI director." Ember, who didn't expect this call, answered with curiosity…

"Hello, this is Ember Maxell…Yes sir…yes sir…yes sir tomorrow early in the morning I will be at the Bureau." At the end of the phone call, she looks at Viggo and announced…

"Our vacation is officially over, and…"

"What is going on, Ember?"

"The director's call implies: that tomorrow morning we have to present ourselves at the Bureau, I'm going to fulfil the position of Franklin, and you have to organize the protection and safety of the president of the United States…

"Don't tell me, the president is coming to New York?"

"Yes Viggo, he is coming, and that is not all, the director just told me, that there is a serious warning of a terrorist attack, everybody is in high alert. My love, the president is coming to talk at the United Nations."

"What the hell: this event does not make any sense? What are they thinking off? —Look, they know, there may be a terrorist attack, why put the life of the president in danger, the FBI should cancel the trip. —By the way, this guy has nothing else to do, but come to New York? What a pain in the ass... fuck...fuck!!" Viggo said raising his arms, and she reminds him.

"Please Viggo, remember that I will be in charge of the Bureau, and now more than aver, everything has to go perfectly!!" She said it: kissing and fondling him as she led him to the bedroom, in that moment you can hear Viggo saying." "Please honey, have a little bit of compassion, remember that tomorrow I have to take care of the life of the presidents: listens, if something goes wrong it will be all your fault!!" The reasons Viggo, bring to light, there's not enough to calm down the sexual craving of his wife: as usually Ember's, moans bounce like an echo off the walls of the bedroom...Please...Easy'V...please...easy Vigo...

The following day, Viggo and his wife head to New York City, Ember Maxwell will take the position of Handling Officer, at the Federal Bureau of Investigation. —Special-Agent Viggo Bronson will do all the duties the agents belong to the F.B.I have to do; they are dedicated to protecting the United States and their citizens. These brave men risk their lives every day, for the well-being of the American people, and many times for our allies. In these moments Viggo is in charge of a vital assignment, he must coordinate the protection of the president of the United States, against an alleged terrorist attack. I don't doubt that he's going to be successful carrying out his mission. —But one thing is for sure, the enemies that Viggo, gained during his time in the FBI force, these gangsters will never forgive the terrible harm Viggo, caused to them.

That's the cause, that when Viggo, and his new partner Agent Mali Lagos, were leaving the Bureau, in a bulletproof SUV, on the way to the United Nation, they hadn't traveled even a couple of miles, when did they start to feel, loud explosions in the rear of the SUV, Viggo looks in the rear-view mirror and sees a car with two men shooting at them, the rain of bullets were bouncing in the SUV, and Viggo, is thinking. "There it goes again." And Viggo tells his partner. "Mali, gets ready, pick up the blow-up-gates shotgun, and load it with the explosive's cartridges!!" Then, Viggo, pressed a button and all the seats went flat: at the same time in the rear door, shows up a small opening, from where Mali, aims the loaded shotgun to the car, which they were being shot, and she, without thinking twice pulled both triggers, and Viggo who was looking in the rear-view mirror, saw how the car blow up and covered in flames flew through the air. Viggo stops the SUV, and the two agents get out to see if anyone had survived, next to the burning car, one of gangsters was hardly breathing, Viggo, picked it up from the lapels and asks. "Which criminal organization do you working for?" The answer was.

"They all want to see you fucking dead Easy'V...fuck youuu..." The gangster said in his last breath, and he dies in his arms. The agents called the local police, at the moment they arrived they made their report and continued their journey to their destination, that's when Viggo comments...

"I'm impressed Mali. Thanks', that was an amazing job, and you did it calmly as if nothing was happening, this act of pure professionalism deserves an award, how should I reward you, Mali?"

"Chief, I was a very good friend of Rocky, and a talked a lot with her...and I like the same things she enjoys, you know Chief?" Mali said getting close to him...—And looks like Mali, is going to replace Rocky, and life goes on with all its contradictions—if you don't live life now...then—when...!!!!! —And...

Special-Agent Viggo Bronson, with Agent Mali Lagos, will travel all over the world in search of the criminal organizations that want to get rid of him and his fame.

Epilogue

Post data. —The American gangster "Santino Pascucci" was killed by the jail inmates: in the state of Virginia, on October 29 -2018. —Who really was killed that day? Search! —And...

The character of *Viggo Bronson* really exists: 'Oscar', is his name.

Thanks for your support: Luis Jose Marolo = Él'Pertu.

Look for more of my work on my Facebook page Él'Pertu.

About the Author

Luis J Marolo is originally from Carreras Santa Fe, Argentina and now resides near the beach in southern California. When he is not writing, his other artistic interests are painting and rock sculptures. One of his other many loves is playing poker for which he enjoys the competitiveness and the camaraderie, somewhat like Viggo.

Keep an eye out for his next book, which is a work in progress and might be entitled, The great Adventure.

www.ingramcontent.com/pod-product-compliance
Lightning Source LLC
Chambersburg PA
CBHW021941120726
47992CB00001B/83